PRAISE FOR THE NOVELS OF
BRENDA JOYCE

"Romance veteran Joyce brings her keen sense of humor and storytelling prowess to bear on her witty, fully formed characters."
—*Publishers Weekly* on *A Lady at Last*

"[A] classic Pygmalion tale with an extra soupçon of eroticism."
—*Booklist* on *A Lady at Last*

"Joyce's characters carry considerable emotional weight, which keeps this hefty entry absorbing, and her fast-paced story keeps the pages turning."
—*Publishers Weekly* on *The Stolen Bride*

"There are no limits to the passion and power of a Brenda Joyce novel. With her full-blooded characters, her page-turning prose and her remarkable creativity, Brenda Joyce is a force of nature. Her books are so intensely satisfying, you never want them to end."
—*New York Times* bestselling author Lisa Kleypas

"[*The Masquerade*] dances on slippered feet, belying its heft with spellbinding dips, spins and twists. Jane Austen aficionados will delve happily into heroine Elizabeth "Lizzie" Fitzgerald's family.... Joyce's tale of the dangers and delights of passion fulfilled will enchant those who like their reads long and rich."
—*Publishers Weekly*

BRENDA JOYCE

The PERFECT Bride

HQN™

ISBN-13: 978-0-373-77244-5
ISBN-10:   0-373-77244-0

THE PERFECT BRIDE

Also by

BRENDA JOYCE

Brenda Joyce and HQN Books
are also excited to introduce
Dark Rival
The second book in the exciting
Masters of Time series
Coming in October

For all of you who asked for
Rex and Blanche's story—enjoy!

The
PERFECT
Bride

CHAPTER ONE

March, 1822

TWO HUNDRED and twenty-eight suitors, she thought. Dear God, how would she ever manage, much less choose?

Blanche Harrington stood alone by one of the oversized windows in a small salon, outside the vast room where soon, the invasion of callers would begin. Just that morning, the black draperies that indicated she remained in mourning had come down. She had avoided marriage for eight years, but even she knew that with her father's death, she needed a husband to help her manage his considerable and complicated fortune.

But she dreaded the deluge—just as she dreaded the future.

Her best friend swept dramatically into the salon. "Blanche, darling, there you are! We are about to open the front doors!" she cried enthusiastically.

Blanche stared out of the window at the circular front drive. Her father had been awarded his title as viscount many years ago, having made an impossible fortune in manufacturing. It was so long ago that no one considered them nouveau riche. Blanche had never known any other life than one of wealth, privilege and splendor. She was one of the empire's greatest heiresses, but her father had allowed her to break off an engagement eight years ago, and although he had never stopped introducing her to suitors, he had wanted her to marry for love. It was an absurd notion, of course.

Not because no one married for love. It was absurd because Blanche knew she was incapable of falling in love.

But she would marry, because although Harrington had passed too swiftly to have verbalized a dying wish—he had been suddenly stricken with pneumonia—Blanche knew he wanted nothing more than to see her securely wed to an honorable gentleman.

Three dozen carriages littered her beautiful drive. There had been five hundred condolence calls six months ago. Of the cards left, 228 had belonged to eligible bachelors. Blanche was dismayed but resolved. How many of them were not fortune-hunting rogues? As she had long ago given up on ever loving any man, her intention now was to find one sensible, decent, noble man in the lot.

"Oh dear." Bess Waverly came up beside her. "You are brooding—I know you better than you know yourself—we have been friends since we were nine years old! Please do not tell me you wish to send everyone away when I have announced your period of mourning to be over. Is there a point in mourning for another six months? You will only delay the inevitable."

Blanche looked at her best friend. They were as different as night and day, and that was one of the reasons she loved her so—and vice versa. Bess was dramatic, vivacious and sultry—she was on her second husband and her twentieth lover, at least—and she made no pretense of the fact that she enjoyed every aspect of life, and that included as much passion as possible. Blanche was almost twenty-eight years old, she had chosen not to marry until now, and she remained a virgin. She found life pleasing enough—she enjoyed walks in the park, shopping and teas, the opera and balls. But she had not a clue as to what passion was, or how it felt, not in any shape or form.

Her heart was entirely defective. It beat, but refused to entertain any extremes of emotion.

The sun was yellow, never gold. A comedy was amusing, never hilarious. Chocolate was sweet, but easily passed up. A buck might be handsome, but no one could take her breath away. She had never, not once in her entire life, wanted to be kissed.

Long ago she had realized she would never have the passion for life that a woman was supposed to have. But other women hadn't lost their mother in a riot at the tender age of six. She had been with her mother that Election Day, but she couldn't recall it—and she couldn't recall her life before it, either. What was worse was that she didn't remember anything about her mother, and when she looked at her portrait hanging above the stairs, she saw a beautiful lady, but it was like looking at a stranger.

And vague, violent shadowy images of the past lived somewhere far back in her mind. They always had. She knew it the way some people claimed to know that they lived with a ghost, or the way a child knew that imaginary playmates lived in her bedroom. But it didn't matter, because she didn't want to ever identify those monsters. Besides, how many adults could recall their lives before the age of six?

However, she hadn't shed a tear in grief since the riot. Grief was beyond her heart's capabilities, too. Blanche was very aware of being different from other women, and it was her secret. Her father had known the entire truth and the reason for it. Her two best friends assumed she would one day become as passionate and insensible as they were. Her two best friends were waiting for her to fall wildly in love.

Blanche had always been sensible. She turned to Bess. "No, I do not see a point in delaying the inevitable. Father was sixty-four, and he had a wonderful life. He would want me to go forward now, as we have planned."

Bess put her arm around her. She had medium brown hair, spectacular green eyes, a lush figure and full lips which she claimed men adored—in more ways than one. As Bess loved to gossip about her lovers, Blanche knew exactly what she meant and could not imagine a woman doing such a thing.

Once, Blanche had wished she could be like Bess—or even a watered-down version of her. Recently, she had realized that she was not going to change. No matter what life offered, she would sensibly and serenely navigate her course. There would be no drama, no torment, and certainly, no passion.

"Yes, he would. You have spent your entire life hiding from life," Bess said pointedly. Blanche began to object, but Bess went determinedly on. "As tragic as it is, Harrington is dead. You have no excuses left, Blanche. He certainly is not here for you to dote on. If you continue to hide, you will be entirely alone."

It was incredible, but she felt almost nothing at the mention of her father's name. She was numb when she should have wept and sobbed—she had been numb since his death. The sorrow was a gentle wave, and it was very nearly painless. She missed him—how could she not? He had been the anchor of her life ever since that terrible day when her mother had died.

If only she could weep in grief and outrage. But only a few drops of moisture ever gathered in her eyes.

Blanche smiled grimly, leaving the window. "I am not hiding, Bess. No one entertains as much as I do."

"You have been hiding from passion and pleasure," Bess cried.

Blanche had to smile. They had argued over this too many times to count. "I am not passionate by nature," she said softly. "And Father is gone, but thank God I have you and Felicia," she said with a small smile. "I dote upon you both. I do not know what I would do without you."

Bess rolled her eyes. "We are going to find you a handsome young buck to dote on, Blanche, so you can finally live your life! Just think of it! Over two hundred suitors—and you have your *choice!*"

Blanche felt a frisson of uncertainty at the thought. "I dread the onslaught," she said truthfully. "How will I ever choose? We both know they are all fortune hunters and Father wished for more for me than that."

"Hmm, I can think of nothing better than a fortune-hunting twenty-five-year-old rake! As long as he is obscenely handsome—" she grinned "—and even more virile."

Blanche gave her a look and, accustomed to such outrageous remarks, did not blush. "Bess."

"You will be happy when you have a virile husband, dear, you may trust me on that. Who knows? Your blasé indifference to all of life's offerings may suddenly vanish."

Blanche had to smile, but she shook her head. "That would be a miracle."

"A good dose of passion can be quite miraculous!" Bess sobered. "I am trying to cheer you up. Felicia and I will help you choose, unless, of course, there is a *real* miracle and you fall in love."

"We both know that isn't going to happen. Bess, do not look so glum! I have had a nearly perfect life. I have been blessed with so much."

Bess shook her head, as anguished now as she had been happy a scant instant ago. "Never say never! Even though you have never been in love, I will continue to hope. Oh, Blanche. You have no idea what you are missing. I know you believe your life to have been perfect until Harrington passed, but I know better. You are an island unto yourself and the loneliest person I know."

Blanche stiffened. "Bess, this day is difficult enough, with all those suitors queued up at my front door."

"You were lonely before Harrington passed and you are even lonelier now. I hate seeing you alone and I believe marriage and children will change that." Bess was firm.

Blanche tensed. She wanted to deny it, but Bess was right.

No matter how many calls she made, how many callers she had, how many parties she gave, how many balls she attended, she was different and she knew it acutely. In fact, she always felt separate and detached from those around her.

"Bess, I don't mind being alone." That was the truth. "I know you cannot understand it. I will be terribly honest now. I feel certain that when I marry, I will still be alone, in spirit, anyway."

"You will not be alone in spirit when you have children."

Blanche smiled. "A child would be nice." Bess had two children she adored—in spite of her affairs, she was a wonderful mother. "However, even though you have this fantastical notion of matching me to some very young buck, I want someone older, someone middle-aged. He must be kind, strong in character. He must be a true gentleman."

"Of course you want someone older who will spoil you terribly—you wish to replace your father." Bess sighed. "We are not replacing your father, Blanche. Your husband must be young and attractive! Now, that solved, may I have the choice of your leftovers?"

Blanche laughed softly at the idea and knew Bess really wished to find a new lover from amongst her two-hundred-odd suitors.

"Of course." Blanche walked away. She couldn't help it, but now, at this eleventh hour, when she thought about her suitors, a dark, brooding image came to mind. One eligible bachelor had not called. Not only hadn't he called, he hadn't even offered his condolences six months ago.

Blanche did not want to continue her line of thought. And very fortunately, her second best friend hurried into the room. Felicia had recently married her third husband, her previous husband having been a young, handsome and very reckless equestrian who had died jumping a terribly risky fence. "Jamieson is opening up the front door, my dears!" she cried with a smile. "Oh, Blanche, I am so happy to see you out of that drab black. The dove gray suits you so much better."

And Blanche heard the sound of dozens of male voices and footsteps. Her stomach dropped. The hordes had arrived.

BLANCHE SMILED POLITELY at Felicia's jest, not having really heard it. At once six young men surrounded her and fifty-one other gentlemen filled the salon—there was no seat left untaken. She was already acquainted with almost everyone who had called—she had been Harrington's hostess for many years now. But she was exhausted in a way she had never been before. For she was the center of attention in a far different way. She wasn't sure she could withstand another admiring glance or respond to another flirtatious remark.

She must have been told that she looked well a hundred times in the past few hours. A few rogues had dared to tell her she was a beauty. As she was ancient compared to other marriageable women, she was tired of pretending she believed the flattery. And how many gallants had asked her to drive in the park? Fortunately, Bess had privately whispered that she would arrange all of her engagements. Her dear friend hovered by her elbow and Blanche was certain her calendar was now thoroughly booked for the next year, at least.

It was so stuffy inside. She smiled politely at Ralph Witte, a baron's dashing son, fanning herself with her hand. She wondered when the afternoon would end, or if she should dare to make her own escape.

But more callers were arriving. And Blanche saw her dear friend, the countess of Adare, entering the salon with her daughter-in-law, the future countess, Lizzie de Warenne. Then a tall, dark man strode in behind the women. For one instant, Blanche went still, surprised.

Rex de Warenne so rarely appeared in society, and she had wondered about him, who hadn't? But it was Tyrell de

Warenne, not his brother, who was entering her salon. Of course the future earl of Adare would be accompanying his wife.

"Blanche?" Bess asked. "What is wrong?"

Blanche turned, aware of a slight and absurd disappointment. It was nonsensical to feel let down that Sir Rex of Land's End had not called with his family, as she hardly knew him. She had once been briefly engaged to his brother Tyrell, and because of that, she remained close friends with his mother and Tyrell's wife. Yet she doubted she had exchanged words with Sir Rex more than a half a dozen times in the eight years since that betrothal. Society knew he was a recluse—he preferred his estate in Cornwall to the ton and was rarely present at gatherings. Still, every now and then they would encounter one another at a ball or a tea. He was always quiet and polite; so was she.

And she decided that it was for the best that he hadn't offered his condolences or called; his dark, intense gaze had always made her uncomfortable.

"I am going to greet Lady Adare and Lady de Warenne," she said swiftly, now pleased by their presence.

"I will start hinting that you are very weary," Bess said. "It shouldn't take too long to clear everyone out."

"I am weary," Blanche returned, moving through the crowd. To do so required some determination in order not to be waylaid. And her smile became genuine. "Mary, I am so pleased you have called!"

Mary de Warenne, the countess of Adare, was a handsome blond woman, strikingly dressed and bejeweled. The women clasped hands and hugged. As Blanche had broken off her betrothal with Tyrell all those years ago so he could marry the woman he loved, it had been easy to develop a deep friendship. "My dear, how are you managing?" Mary asked with concern.

"I am fine, considering," Blanche assured her. "Lizzie, you are looking so well." Tyrell's titian-haired wife was radiant. She had a year-old toddler now—her fourth child—and Blanche wondered at her secret.

"Ty and I have been enjoying the afternoon," Lizzie said, squeezing her hands. "I so rarely have him all to myself! My, Blanche, this turnout is stunning."

Blanche somehow smiled. "And they are all suitors." She faced Tyrell, no longer mistaking him for his brother. Rex was a war hero and the more handsome of the two, even if he rarely smiled. Besides, Tyrell's eyes were gentle and dark blue—Rex's hazel stare was very dark and at times, unnerving. "My lord, thank you for calling," she said, deferring to his rank.

He bowed. "It is a pleasure to have you back with us, Blanche. If there is anything I can do to help in any way, you must let me know."

She was aware that he still harbored a deep gratitude for her having left him so he could marry Lizzie. Then she turned back to the women. "Will you be in town long?" As Adare's seat was in Ireland, she never knew if the family was coming or going.

"We have been in town since the New Year," Mary smiled. "So we are about to depart."

"Oh, I am sorry to hear that." And she merely intended polite discourse, didn't she? "Are Captain de Warenne and Amanda in town, too? How are they?"

"It is just the three of us," Lizzie said, "and my four children, of course. Cliff and Amanda are in the islands, but they are coming up to town later in the spring. They are doing very well—they remain madly in love."

Blanche hesitated, now thinking about Sir Rex. "How are the O'Neills?"

"Sean and Eleanor are at Sinclair Hall, and Devlin and Virginia are celebrating their ninth anniversary in Paris, *without* the children."

She smiled, aware of some tension now. It would be rude not to ask about the remaining de Warenne. "And Sir Rex? Is he well?"

Lizzie's smile remained. "He is at Land's End."

Mary said, "Only Cliff has seen him lately, and that is because he stopped at Land's End on his way back to the islands last fall. Rex claims he has been renovating his estate and cannot leave. I haven't seen him since Cliff returned to London with Amanda as his bride."

That was a year and a half ago. Blanche became somewhat concerned. "Surely, you believe Sir Rex? You don't think something is wrong?"

Mary sighed. "I believe him, of course I do. You know he avoids society at all costs. But how will he find a wife if he closets himself in the south of Cornwall? There are hardly any eligible young ladies there!"

Her heart lurched oddly. That in itself was a stunning sensation, as she was never taken aback. "Does he now wish to marry?" He was two years her senior and should have taken a wife long ago; still, this was entirely unexpected.

Mary hesitated. "It is hard to say."

Lizzie took her arm. "Put it this way, the de Warenne women are determined for him to have a family of his own. And that requires a wife."

So the de Warenne women would plot to see him wed. Blanche had to smile. His days as a bachelor were undoubtedly numbered. They were right. He should marry—it was wrong for him to live alone as he did.

"And it requires his leaving Land's End," Mary said emphatically. "However, in May, Edward and I are sharing our twenty-third anniversary here in town. Rex will attend—the entire family will gather for a celebration."

Blanche smiled. "That sounds wonderful. Congratulations, Mary."

"I have so many grandchildren, I have lost count," Mary said softly, her eyes shining. Then she took her hand. "Blanche, I have considered you a daughter ever since your betrothal to Tyrell. I am hoping, very much, that you will one day find the joy and happiness that I have."

The countess was one of the kindest and most generous women Blanche knew. She was also adored by her husband, her children and grandchildren. She meant her every word, but Blanche was somewhat saddened. She would never find the joy and happiness Mary de Warenne had. Had she the ability to fall in love, she certainly would have done so by now. Gentlemen were always sniffing about Harrington Hall. She could only wonder what it must be like, to be so loved, to love so much, and to be surrounded by such a family.

"I will no longer avoid matrimony," she said slowly. "There is no point. I simply cannot manage these estates by myself."

Mary and Lizzie exchanged pleased glances. "Do you have anyone in mind?" Lizzie asked with open excitement.

"No, I don't." Blanche realized that half the room had cleared—and it was much easier to breathe now. She fanned herself. "That was a long afternoon!"

"And it is only the beginning." Lizzie laughed while Blanche felt a moment of dismay. "Well, I have seen a number of interesting prospects. If you wish to gossip, let me know." Lizzie laughed again, now holding out her hand for Tyrell. He instantly left his group and came to her side, clasping her palm, their gazes meeting briefly in an intimate communication.

"We should go, as you seem very tired, dear," Mary remarked. The women exchanged hugs and goodbyes.

Blanche then spent the next half hour smiling at the departing gentlemen, doing her best to seem gracious and truly interested in each and every one. The moment her last caller was gone, she went to the nearest chair and collapsed, her smile gone. Her cheeks actually hurt. "How can I do this?" she gasped.

Bess grinned, settling on the sofa. "I thought it went quite well."

Felicia asked a servant to bring sherry for three. "That went very well," the voluptuous brunette smiled. "My God, I had forgotten how many dashing men remain eligible!"

"That went well? I have a raging migraine!" Blanche exclaimed. "And by the by, the Earl and Countess Adare will be celebrating their twenty-third anniversary in May."

Felicia looked surprised; Bess did not. "And Rex de Warenne will attend," she said.

Blanche looked at her and their gazes held. What did her friend mean?

"Are you certain you want an elderly husband, Blanche?" Bess smiled.

Blanche was uncomfortable. "Yes, I am very certain. Why did you just mention Sir Rex?"

"Oh, hmm, let me see. I was standing behind you while you were discussing Sir Rex with his family," Bess said pointedly.

Blanche failed to understand. "I am bewildered. I asked after the entire family, Bess. Are you implying I am somehow interested in Sir Rex?"

"I hardly said such a thing," Bess gasped in mock denial. Then, "Come, Blanche. This isn't the first time his name has come up."

"He is a family friend. I have known him for years." Blanche remained confused. She shrugged. "I have merely wondered why Sir Rex never called. It was a lapse. It was somewhat insulting. That is all."

Bess sat up straighter. "Do you wish for him to court you?"

Blanche could only stare. Then she started to smile—and briefly, she laughed. "Of course not! I wish for a peaceful future. Sir Rex is a very dark man. Everyone knows he broods—and that he is a recluse. We would never suit. My life is here, in London, his is in Cornwall."

Bess smiled sweetly. "Really. I have always found him disturbingly sexual."

Blanche paled. She did not want to know what that meant! And only her friend could get away with such an inappropriate remark. She decided to ignore it. "If anything, I want my old life back," she said sharply.

"Yes, of course you do. Your old life was just so perfect—doting on your father, and living vicariously through me and Felicia."

Felicia pulled up an ottoman as they were finally served the sherry. "Bess, I tried to seduce him after Hal died. He is truly a boor. In fact, he was so lacking in charm, he was almost rude. He would be the worst possible candidate for Blanche's hand."

Blanche didn't hesitate to defend him, for she hated malice of any kind. "You mistook an introversion of character, Felicia," she said gently. "Sir Rex is a gentleman. He has always been the perfect gentleman around me—and perhaps, just perhaps, he did not wish to dally with you."

Felicia flushed. "The de Warenne men are notorious for their affairs—until they marry. Perhaps he simply isn't virile."

"That is a terrible thing to say!" Blanche cried, aghast.

Bess cut in. "He has a reputation for preferring housemaids to noblewomen, Felicia. He also has a reputation for great stamina and skill, never mind his war injury."

Blanche stared at her friend, aware of heat rising in her cheeks. "That is gossip." Then, "I do not think it appropriate to discuss Sir Rex this way."

"Why not? We talk about my lovers all the time—in far more detail."

"That is different," Blanche said, but even she realized how lacking her rationale was. She had never thought about Sir Rex in any way except as a family friend, albeit a distant one.

"It is unbelievable that he would bed servants," Felicia said with condescension. "How crude!"

Blanche felt the heat in her cheeks increase. "It cannot be true."

"I overheard two maids discussing his prowess very frankly—one of the maids having been the recipient of that prowess," Bess grinned.

Blanche stared at her, more uneasy now than before. "I really prefer we not discuss Sir Rex."

"Why are you becoming the prude now?" Bess asked.

"It is *reprehensible* for a nobleman to dally with the servants," Felicia said swiftly, obviously determined to be catty.

"Well, I enjoyed my gardener very much," Bess shot, referring to an old affair.

Blanche didn't know what to think. She would never judge Sir Rex; it wasn't her nature to judge and condemn anyone. Still, it wasn't really acceptable for noblemen to dally with the servants, but now and then, they did. A mistress was acceptable, as long as vast discretion was used. Sir Rex probably kept a mistress. And now she was thinking about Sir Rex in a way she had no wish to continue. How had this conversation begun? Did he really have a reputation for stamina and skill? She truly did not wish to know!

"When was the last time you spoke with Rex de Warenne?" Bess now asked.

This was far safer ground. And Blanche didn't have to think about it. "At Amanda de Warenne's comeout—before she married Captain de Warenne."

Bess gaped. "Are you telling me you have pined for a man you haven't seen in two years?"

Blanche sighed and smiled. "Bess, I am *not* pining for him. And that was a year and a half ago. And frankly, I have had enough discussion for one day." She stood abruptly, her feet hurting, too, forgetting all about the most enigmatic de Warenne.

Bess also rose, but like a terrier with a bone, plunged on. "Darling, do you realize that Sir Rex has not presented himself as a suitor?"

"Of course I do." She hesitated. "I know what you are thinking—he needs a fortune and a wife, so that lapse is odd. Obviously he is not yet inclined toward matrimony."

"How old is he?" Bess asked.

"I think he is thirty, but I am not sure. Please, Bess, stop. I can see where you lead. Do not think to match me with Sir Rex!"

"I have distressed you," Bess finally said. "And you are never dismayed. I am sorry, Blanche. It must be the strain of your comeout. I would never match you against your will—you know that."

Blanche was relieved. "Yes, I know. But you did begin to worry me—we both know how tenacious you can be. Bess, I cannot bear the strain of these suitors—and it is only the first day. If you do not mind, I am going to retire for the evening."

Bess hugged her. "Go and have a hot bath. I'll leave instructions for supper to be sent to your room, and I will see you tomorrow."

"Thank you." Blanche smiled at her friend, embraced Felicia and left the two of them alone together, and as they started whispering, she knew they were discussing her. It didn't matter. They had her best interests at heart and she was truly exhausted. Besides, she had to escape the conversation about Sir Rex. It had been oddly disturbing.

"I SEE YOU ARE SCHEMING," Felicia declared.

Bess seized her hand. "I think Blanche is finally interested in a man—even if she doesn't know it. My God—and for how long? I believe she has known him for eight years!"

Felicia gaped. "Surely you do not think she likes Rex de

Warenne? He truly is a rude, boorish man with a highly defective character!"

"I was eavesdropping when she spoke to the countess of Adare. I am not sure she even realizes her interest. Her expression changed completely when she began asking about Sir Rex and her color heightened. And Felicia, when is she ever distressed? Or embarrassed by our chats? And she is insulted by his failure to send condolences! No one can insult Blanche."

Felicia was aghast. "She can do better! How can she prefer him? He is so *black*."

"He is very dark—some women prefer brooding men. You are piqued because he turned you down. If Blanche has any interest in Sir Rex, we must do something about it."

Felicia sighed. "If you are right, if Blanche has any interest in him, then we should do something about it. But, God, I hope you are wrong." Then, "What *are* you planning?"

Bess hushed her. "Let me think." She began to pace.

"He will be in town in May," Felicia offered.

"May is too far away."

Silently, Felicia agreed with that.

Bess turned. "You do know the saying—if one can't lead the pony to the cart, one brings the cart to the pony."

"They also say one cannot force the horse to drink, even if he is led to the trough."

"We are going to Cornwall," Bess said flatly.

Felicia could think of nothing worse. Cornwall was the end of the world—and at this time of year, freezing cold. "Please, no. I have just remarried and I happen to like my new husband."

Bess waved at her dismissively. "Oh, we will plan a little ladies' holiday—but when it is time to depart, you will be ill and my daughter will have suffered a riding accident."

Felicia's eyes widened.

Bess continued, smiling, "I do think in a week's time, Blanche will need to escape this crush—in fact, I am certain she will wish to do nothing more. And we, her dearest friends, will convince her to take a holiday at Harrington's estate in the south."

"I didn't know Harrington had an estate in Cornwall."

"He doesn't. At least, not that I know of. But I have been helping Blanche sort through the vast fortune she has been left, and I will make a few interesting adjustments to her papers. So you see, there really is a small estate in Cornwall—just kilometers from Land's End. Imagine what she will have to do when she arrives and realizes there has been a mistake. Surely, surely, Sir Rex will not turn her away."

Felicia slowly smiled. "You are so bloody brilliant," she said.

"I am, aren't I?"

CHAPTER TWO

HE SWUNG HIS HAMMER as hard as he could, driving the nail so deeply into the beam that the head became level with the wood. Sweat blinded his vision and poured down his naked torso. He swung again, and the head of the nail vanished. But Rex knew that the savage physical exertion would not change anything.

Although almost ten years had passed, he saw the Spanish Peninsula as if he was there still. Canons fired from the ridge above, sabers rang, men screamed. Smoke filled the air, blocking out the midday sun. And he ran, horseless, to rescue his friend Tom Mowbray. Suddenly a burning pain exploded in his knee....

Fury and frustration mingled. He didn't want to recall the war now, or ever again. He flung the hammer aside and it skipped across the hard ground, hitting a supportive column. The men who were helping him build the barn carefully kept at their tasks, ignoring him.

But the letter always rekindled his damned memories and with them, the bloody pain, which he was adept at burying. Rex leaned on his crutch, breathing hard. The worst part was, he desperately needed the letter, and in the light of day he couldn't regret saving Tom Mowbray's life, nor could he regret his brief liaison with the woman he had once, foolishly, loved.

He wiped sweat from his brow, some of the fury receding.

The past was just that, the past, and it needed to stay buried. But what he could not avoid was the letter about his son.

For even as he dreaded its contents, he was as desperate to read it, too. There would be so much joy—and there would be even more torment.

Rex gave in. The letter had arrived earlier that day and it had been sitting in his study ever since. As he only received one such missive every year, he could no longer delay. He rapidly traversed the structure that would be his breeding barn. Outside, a number of stone buildings faced him, the four-teenth-century chapel behind them. It was a typical Cornish day—the skies above were brilliantly blue and dotted with clouds that might have been spun with cotton, while the moors seemed to stretch away into an eternity, stark, treeless and mostly barren. But even from where he passed, he could glimpse his sheep and cattle in the distance. The sight gave him a moment of hard satisfaction. Closer to where he stood, stone hedges he had laid with his own hands bisected the nearby hills. A prize crop of yearlings raced in one of the pastures, brood-mares grazed in another, fat and close to foaling. And always, he could hear the roar of the ocean crashing on the rocks behind him, a staccato reminder of where and who he was.

Bodenick Castle was his home. It had been built in the late sixteenth century upon sheer black cliffs that fell into the ocean below, and was a stark, square structure, with only one tower remaining. He had spent four years renovating it upon first being awarded the manor for his valor in the war, but he had not tried to reconstruct the second tower, where only a few original stones had remained. Local legend held that pirates had taken it down, stone by stone, looking for their buried treasure. Some folk claimed a treasure remained buried there.

A single oak tree graced the castle, while ancient ivy and wild rose bushes crept up its walls. Rex quickly entered the timbered hall.

It was even colder within than outside. He shivered, having forgotten his shirt in the rising barn. Rex hurried into the tower, where his study took up the ground floor. Dread renewed itself.

It was dark inside, for only two small windows illuminated the round room. Rex crossed over to the desk, where his papers were neatly piled in folders, his affairs legibly marked and purposefully categorized. The letter sat front and center on the leather inlaid desktop. He did not have to look at the postmark or the return address to know who it was from—her handwriting was despicably familiar.

The torment exploded in his chest. Stephen was nine years old now. The letter was late—it should have arrived in January. But then, that was Julia, sending him her account of his son's progress whenever she got to it. She had made it clear the task was one she felt below her.

How was Stephen? Was he still solemn and correct, and determined to excel so he might please the man he believed to be his father?

Did he still prefer mathematics to the classics?

Had they finally hired the fencing master he had recommended?

Rex choked, unable to breathe. He finally sat down on the edge of the desk, his crutch remaining loosely under his right armpit. No longer holding it, he reached for the envelope, trembling.

The memories began to return. He had arrived home after a long rehabilitation in the military hospital, his entire family there to welcome him, along with neighbors and friends. But Julia, his fiancée, had not been there—and she had only visited him twice in the hospital. He had immediately left his family to call on her, but she hadn't been home. Instead, he had found her at Clarewood, the Mowbray ancestral home—in Tom's embrace.

Since that long-ago spring day in 1813, he had intended to never set eyes upon either Julia or Mowbray again. He had been determined to ignore their very existence, as if the love-struck couple did not exist—as if she had not been his lover, as if he had not risked life and limb to rescue Tom from a certain death.

But society was a very small, incestuous place. A year or so later, he had heard that the Mowbrays had had their first son—in October. He hadn't wanted to allow his mind to go there, but the math was almost irrefutable. As he had left Julia just after the New Year, Stephen could so easily be his child, even though Mowbray had been sharing her favors then, too. And then he'd heard the gossip—that the boy was a changeling, adopted or even the son of one of Julia's lovers. Although both of his parents were impossibly fair, the boy was as dark as a black Irishman.

Stricken, he had sought out the boy at Clarewood, to see for himself. Rex had taken one look at the darkly complex-ioned child and it had been clear he was a de Warenne.

The de Warenne men took after one of two ancestors. They were either golden or impossibly dark, and usually, they had the brilliantly blue de Warenne eyes. Rex saw a child that could have posed for his brother Tyrell's childhood portrait—or his own.

They had reached an agreement long ago. It was hardly the first of its kind in the ton. The Mowbrays would raise Stephen, for Julia was insistent, and Mowbray would provide the kind of inheritance that Rex never could. In return for forsaking his child to the couple so Stephen would have a future of wealth and privilege, Rex would be sent annual reports and allowed an occasional visit. The truth, however, was to remain concealed. Mowbray did not want anyone to know that Julia had been with another man.

It was unbelievably ironic, because a decade had passed

and Stephen would have far more than a pleasing inheritance from Mowbray. When Clarewood passed on, Tom had inherited the dukedom, for his older brother had died in a shipwreck. More importantly, there were no other children. Apparently, Tom was incapable of fathering his own child. One day, Stephen Mowbray would be the duke of Clarewood, one of the wealthiest and premier lords in the realm.

He was doing what was best for his son. There was no doubt about that. But now, a knife was being twisted ruthlessly in his heart. Rex opened the letter.

As always, Stephen was excelling at every study and every endeavor. He was two levels ahead in his reading and undertaking advanced studies in mathematics, which remained his favorite subject. He was fluent in French, German and Latin, beginning dance instruction and already adept with a saber, enough so that his master wished to enter him in a tourney for those his age. His horsemanship was equally impressive and he had received a Thoroughbred for his birthday. He was already taking meter fences with ease. And recently, Mowbray had taken him on his first fox hunt.

The script had been blurring since he had begun reading the letter. Rex could no longer see—there was another short paragraph to read. Drops of moisture stained the page, which was shaking. He laid the letter down and gave up. Tears streamed but he could not stop them.

He was so tired of pretending that Stephen was not his. He hated these letters—and he wanted to hold his son. He wanted to teach him to jump those fences; he wanted to take him fox-hunting. But how could he? This was for the best. He did not want Stephen exiled to Land's End as he had been.

He fought for composure. God, if only he could see Stephen, even once. But he had never visited the boy. If he were going to go through with this arrangement, he knew he must keep the greatest distance possible between them.

Meeting Stephen as a stranger would be impossible—he was sure the anguish would rip him apart. He would probably wind up in an opium den, and God only knew that he drank too much as it was. Or he would meet the boy and change his mind. How selfish would that be?

And he could try to remind himself that one day Stephen would know the truth, but there was no consolation to be gained. It would be decades before he could ever approach Stephen and tell him the truth of his paternity, unless Mowbray died an early and untimely death. Rex despised Mowbray, but not enough to wish such a fate upon him.

Rex looked at the dark stone walls surrounding him, closing in on him, and felt as if he were being buried alive, there at Bodenick, where he had toiled so tremendously to turn ruins into a lucrative enterprise. But Land's End had become a place of exile from the moment he had realized he must forsake his son. It did not matter that he had chosen the exile. The day the yearly letter arrived was the day that he always felt the utter hopelessness of his life. It was the day there was never enough air, and that the weight of his life became crushing.

Rex seized his crutch and swung it viciously. The lamp fell to the floor, shattering, and his carefully organized papers flew everywhere. He stood, leaning against the desk for balance, and thrust the crutch violently at the remaining items on his desk. A glass, decanter, paperweight and more papers were swept to the floor.

He panted, closing his eyes, fighting for control. This day would pass. It always did. Tomorrow he would inspect his broodmares, return to work on the new barn, and begin to fill the pond he'd made in the gardens behind the castle tower. His body continued to shudder. His breathing remained hard and labored. The pain and despair clawed at his heart—he could feel talons inside his chest.

He glanced down at the decanter, which had not broken. He bent, the springs in his crutch allowing it to contract as he wished, retrieving the bottle. Long ago he had learned how to use the crutch in every possible way. It was custom-made, with springs and hinges, and he was no longer aware of its existence. It had become an extension of his body. It had become his right leg.

A quarter of the whiskey remained and he drained as much as he could in a single gulp.

A housemaid hurried into the chamber. "My lord!" She cried, taking in the mess he had created with a single, wide-eyed glance.

Rex finished off the contents of the decanter and then placed it on the desk. He slowly looked at his housemaid. There was a better way to forget.

Anne was on her knees, picking up his papers. She was twenty years old, buxom and pretty and very, very lusty. She had come into his employ two months ago, making it clear she wished to do far more than clean his house and launder his clothes. He refused to deny himself pleasure and passion— he could not survive without sex—and had been tiring of the affair he was having with the innkeeper's widowed daughter. He had instantly hired Anne. Her first chore had been to join him in bed and they had enjoyed themselves immensely—and had been doing so ever since. He hadn't been her first lover and he would not be her last. He had compensated her for her extra duties by providing extra stores for her family, who were tenant farmers in a neighboring parish, struggling to make ends meet. Her salary was also a generous one.

Recently, though, he had seen her flirting with the village blacksmith, a handsome lad her own age, newly arrived in Lanhadron. He sensed where that was leading and did not mind, as she deserved a home and family of her own. In fact, as long as he could find a new servant—and a new mistress—he would encourage the match and give them a handsome wedding present.

But she hadn't married the young blacksmith yet. And pleasure brought escape. He wished to escape into her body now. "Anne. Leave the mess for later."

She started, looking up, her eyes wide. "My lord, you care for your papers the way me mum cares for my little sisters. I know how important your papers are!"

He felt a new tension arise, there in his breeches, straining at the wool fabric. And it was as he wanted. "Come here," he said very softly.

She became still, understanding him. And slowly she stood, laying some papers on his desk, their gazes locking, a flush now on her full cheeks. She began to smile. "My lord, didn't I please you last night?" she murmured.

His breeches had become much tighter. He smiled back at her, reaching for her hand. "Yes, you did. Very much. But last night is over, is it not?"

"You're the randiest lord," she whispered as he reeled her in.

"Do you mind?" he asked, running his left hand down her back until he had clasped her very full buttock. He pulled her hard against his manhood, now raging, remaining perfectly and solidly balanced with the crutch.

"How can I mind when you're such a gent you take your pleasure after me, always?"

Her remark satisfied him. He had always tried to please the women in his bed—he couldn't imagine a satisfactory encounter otherwise. And then there was the obvious fact that he wished to compensate for his injury. No woman had ever thought about it a second time, not after the pleasure he gave.

"Do you wish to go up to your room?" she whispered, reaching down to stroke his thick length through his breeches.

His breath caught. "No. I wish to take you right here, right now, on my sofa." He pulled her around him and pushed her back onto the sofa. Fluidly he moved on top of her, using his thighs to spread her legs wide. He pressed against her sex and she whimpered, laying her hands on his bare, wet chest, her eyes beginning to glaze over. She gasped and her palms drifted down to the waistband of his breeches. And very deliberately, she traced the huge line of his arousal with her fingertips.

He grunted, reaching below her skirts. The best thing about a lusty maid was the utter lack of complication, the utter lack of pretense. How she appeared was exactly how she was. Anne wanted sex and pleasure—and food on her family's table. She wanted exactly what he had to offer and a bit of extra coin, nothing more. Treachery on her part would be impossible.

And she was very ready now. He rubbed his fingers against her wet, heated flesh until tears formed in her eyes and she was whispering for him to hurry. He rubbed her until she began to writhe in an impending climax. He bent, used his tongue, and felt triumph as she climaxed.

She didn't cling. Gasping breathlessly, she deftly opened the buttons on his breeches. He smiled with satisfaction now and became still, allowing her to do as she willed. The moment he sprang into her hand, she leaned toward him, eagerly seeking him with her mouth, his favor returned. Rex threw his head back. There was only pleasure now.

WHY HADN'T SHE COME to Cornwall sooner?

Blanche stared out of her coach window, awed by the stark desolation of the moors. Flat, pale and treeless, they seemed to stretch away into eternity. A freezing wind swept them, for she had her head out of the window, and her nose was ice-cold. But the skies were vividly blue and dotted with passing white clouds, the sun strong and bright.

She ducked her head inside the coach, her heart having picked up a swifter beat some time ago, when they had turned off the main highway at the sign pointing to both Land's End and Bodenick Castle. Leaning across the seat, aware of her maid staring at her from the facing bench, she lifted the other window, allowing more freezing air into the coach. The ocean was a shocking sapphire blue, reaching into an even vaster eternity, one belonging to the Lord. By looking somewhat ahead, she could see some of the coastline. It was breathtaking. Breaking white waves pounded the pale beach, strewn with huge black boulders at the base of soaring black cliffs.

"My l-lady," Meg chattered. "It's so c-cold."

Blanche closed the window, simply breathless. "I am sorry, Meg." Was she actually excited by this adventure? It seemed so!

Meg nodded at the other, still-open, window. Blanche was about to close it when she saw the sheep and cattle now grazing upon the moors. They had to be close to Land's End. As she was anticipating her arrival there, clearly, she had been in town for far too long.

She had yet to visit Penthwaithe, her father's estate. The moment she had realized that her friends were right and she must escape the crush of suitors, and that a holiday in Cornwall would be perfect—she had never been to the south—she had decided she would use the opportunity to call on Sir Rex. She was not interested in Sir Rex in the way Bess had suggested. That was absurd. Calling on him was socially correct—and a failure to do so was socially insulting. Of course, it was even more correct to go directly to Penthwaithe, settle in and then call at Land's End. However, the decision to take a holiday in the south had been made so spontaneously that they had not had a chance to send word to Penthwaithe's manager, informing him of her arrival. In fact, it was somewhat uncertain as to who that manager was. Her solicitors had only just discovered the manor's existence, as the title had been lodged between drawers, perhaps for years. Bess was the one who had decided they would go directly to Land's

End, spend the night there, and then settle in at the neighboring manor.

It seemed logical to go directly to Land's End and ask Sir Rex for lodging for the night. But Blanche was traveling alone except for her maid, Meg. At the last possible moment, Felicia had become ill—a ploy, Blanche knew, as she had no wish to leave Lord Dagwood. But Bess's daughter had taken a nasty spill from her hack. Bess had clearly wished to rush home and Blanche had assured her she wouldn't mind taking the holiday alone.

And she didn't mind. The solitude was striking, but it was oddly pleasing, too. She had been surrounded by friends and callers each and every day of her entire life. When she wasn't entertaining or making calls, she was immersed in her charitable duties, which involved numerous appointments and meetings.

They had spent two entire days traveling from London. Every day, the villages had become fewer and farther between. Every day, they had begun passing fewer travelers and fewer estates. Today, they hadn't seen a single vehicle other than their own. They had passed the last village several hours ago.

The isolation was magnificent, Blanche thought, and it was also a terrible relief. It wasn't just escaping the headache of entertaining so many single gentlemen every day—and deciding which one she would marry. There were no more meetings with her agents, trying to unravel her father's complex affairs. There were no callers and no calls. For this brief holiday, she had no duties and it was very enjoyable, indeed. She had the most surprising sense of freedom.

Blanche had been taking in every detail of the countryside for some time now. She was beginning to wonder if everyone was wrong about Land's End. They had taken the turnoff marked Land's End and Bodenick an hour past. The road they were now traveling on was very well maintained—and in far better condition than the main highway. Grazing cattle and sheep dotted the moors and they were fat and well fed, unlike most of the livestock she had previously seen.

Beside her, her maid shifted restlessly.

"Meg?" she asked.

Meg grimaced. "It's so cold, my lady. So cold and so ugly!"

Blanche shook her head. "It is a chilly day, but how can you say the moors are ugly? There is beauty in their stark desolation, beauty and power. And did you see the ocean, Meg? This is truly God's creation!"

Meg looked at her as if she were mad.

A number of buildings were coming into view and the hills were now crisscrossed with hedges. Blanche inhaled, suddenly glimpsing a castle with a single tower, its back to the horizon where the ocean blended seamlessly into the sky.

Land's End was not a manor home after all, she realized, glancing out of her coach window so she could see the castle as they approached. Several towering trees had emerged, lining the approach to the courtyard, where a single oak tree butted up against the dark castle walls. A herd of magnificent horses espied her coach and took flight. Blanche sat up with delight, watching a number of huge, dappled horses galloping alongside her coach. The herd wheeled and vanished over a rise.

As her coach approached the courtyard, she looked everywhere, at once. Wild rosebushes and vines crept up the castle walls, but they were obviously being tended. She was not a historian, but the castle had to be centuries old—and it was in perfect condition, on the outside, at least. There were a number of stone buildings, and the beginnings of a new structure, which she guessed might be a stable. She saw several carts neatly ordered between the buildings, and she now heard hammering. There were some bushes near the tower, cleverly clipped. In fact, everything was terrifically neat and well kempt.

Land's End did not to appear to be as impoverished as it

was rumored. It was impeccably maintained, Blanche thought. Oddly, she was pleased. And the countess did not have to worry—her son was clearly preoccupied with his estate and had no time for town or his family's matchmaking.

Her coach had stopped a short distance from Bodenick's front door. Blanche suddenly hesitated. She had not sent word and Sir Rex did seem inclined toward his privacy. Still, she was a family friend, and now, apparently, a neighbor. Sir Rex would never send her away. But she suddenly wished she had delayed her trip by a single day, so a note could have warned him of her arrival, never mind what Bess thought best.

And for the first time in a week, she thought about Sir Rex's failure to offer his condolences. If she truly dared admit it, that lapse in grace did bother her, and in a way, so did his failure to come forward as a suitor. On the other hand, she instinctively knew he was not a fortune hunter, even if his estate was modest enough to warrant his marriage for financial reasons. It had probably never crossed his mind to look at her as a prospective wife.

Blanche was uncomfortable with her thoughts. She hardly thought him suitable even as a candidate for her hand, much less as a husband, so there was no point in feeling a bit chagrined by his failure to come forward. She was a renowned society hostess and he was a notorious recluse, so they had a grave contradiction of character. And she did not want to think any more about it. But oddly, suddenly she wished Bess were with her. Suddenly she felt a bit awkward, calling like this. Suddenly, she was nervous.

Still, he had always been the perfect gentleman when their paths had crossed. She could not imagine him turning her away.

Blanche smiled at her footman and stepped to the ground. "Please wait until I have had a chance to ask Sir Rex for the night's lodging before you take care of the horses. Meg? Please stay here with the coach until we know that Sir Rex is home."

Meg nodded.

Blanche started for the front door, aware now of the litany that was the ocean echoing on the beaches below the castle. She knocked on the front door, and as she waited for a response, she glanced at the rosebushes growing against the castle walls. She had been right, they were wild, but Sir Rex clearly had a gardener tending them. She wondered when the last thaw was and when the roses would bloom.

She turned back to the door, knocking again, somewhat concerned. She had to have been standing there for a good five minutes.

"My lady?" Meg called from beside the coach. "Maybe no one is home."

Knocking a third time, Blanche thought about that. While she wasn't all that cold, Meg was chilled to the bone. If no one was home, they would go inside and wait while Clarence watered the team. Sir Rex couldn't possibly mind.

She knocked very firmly and gave up when no one responded. Her maid was right—no one was home. And Meg was shivering so much her teeth were chattering. It was several hours back to the village and it was growing late. Surely, Sir Rex would not mind if they waited inside, or even if they made a fire. But she was unsure now. Why hadn't a servant answered the door?

Blanche tested the door and it opened, allowing her to step inside a modestly sized front hall. She looked around. Much to her relief, a fire roared in the gray stone hearth, which looked to be as original as the castle. And that fire indicated that someone was certainly home.

She called out firmly. "Hello? Is anyone home?" But there was no answer.

She glanced around. The walls were freshly whitewashed, the furnishings modest but perfectly suitable and recently upholstered. There were only two seating arrangements, one in front of the hearth, making the hall seem far larger than it was. Only two rugs were present, but they were Oriental and of fine quality. She found the room pleasant. And then Blanche saw the display of sabers and firearms on one wall.

She intended to go outside and tell Meg to go to the laborers and ask after Sir Rex. Instead, very curious, she walked over to the display. She was certain that the weapons belonged to Rex and had been used by him in the late war.

She stared, unable to admire the collection. Two of the swords were ceremonial, their hilts filigreed gold, their sheaths gold and silver. She gazed at a long saber, with its dark, leather-wrapped, utilitarian hilt; and a shorter sword, its appearance equally as utilitarian and menacing. He had wielded these weapons in the war. She disliked the notion. She looked at the long carbine rifle, the butt dulled from use, and the shorter pistol. She was acutely aware that his hands had grasped the butts of those guns, just as he had wielded those swords. She didn't care for the display. It gave her an uneasy, uncomfortable feeling. But then, the war had been tragic not just for Sir Rex, but for so many.

A noise sounded.

It was quite the thud.

And then more thudding began.

Blanche was surprised. The rather rhythmic noise was coming from behind an adjacent door, which she assumed belonged to the tower room. Was someone home after all? And if so, what on earth was going on?

She hesitated, staring at the closed door. "Sir Rex?" She tried from across the room.

She cleared her voice and raised it, approaching. "Sir Rex? Hello! Is anybody home?"

The banging rhythm had increased. And Blanche thought she heard a man's voice, but without words—a sound of pain, perhaps.

Instantly alarmed, she hurried toward the door. But just as

she reached it, she heard the same male sound again. And she realized what it was.

It was a growl of pleasure.

Blanche went still.

The banging continued, fast and fierce now.

Oh, God, she thought, stunned. For she had just realized someone in that room was making love.

She had been to countless balls and even more country weekends. She was well aware of the trysts that occurred in the ton, both behind closed doors and in the corners of corridors and mazes. She had walked past embracing couples numerous times, pretending not to see. But she had never seen more than a passionate kiss.

Whoever was in that tower room, he was doing far more than kissing his lover. And her heart lurched unpleasantly—she had to leave now, immediately.

And surely, it wasn't Sir Rex in that tower room?

She clasped her face in her hands, aware of her cheeks burning. Who else would it be?

He prefers housemaids...his reputation is one of stamina and skill.

She knew that she must leave, instantly. This was a very private affair. Yet her feet would not move. The banging was reaching a terrific crescendo. Vague images danced in her mind of shadowy lovers, prone and entwined.

Blanche realized she stood a finger's length from the door and that she was listening acutely to the lovers. She was shocked with herself. *Was Sir Rex in there? Was he really such a skilled lover?* His image began to form, shadowy and naked, a woman in his embrace.

And then a woman sobbed in uninhibited pleasure.

Her mind froze. Her heart leaped as never before. She panicked. She meant to turn and leave, but she stumbled against the door instead—and it opened.

Blanche was confronted with so much masculinity that she froze. Sir Rex was making love in a frenzy to a dark-haired woman who lay on the sofa and she glimpsed his dark, slick gleaming back and shoulders, his hard profile and a tangle of skirts. She inhaled. He wore only his breeches and he had the physique of a medieval knight—huge shoulders, bulging arms, and his breeches revealed a high, hard, muscled posterior. His muscular thighs rippled, thick and full. She couldn't see much of his right leg, the lower half having been amputated from the knee down during the war, but his left leg was planted on the floor, and she was shielded from seeing what she should not.

Yet she couldn't turn away. Helplessly, her heart fluttering frighteningly in her chest, she stared. He was a dark angel—his hair almost black and wet, thick black lashes fanned out over terribly high cheekbones, his straight, not quite perfect nose flared. *He was beautiful.*

And she meant to go. This was shocking—she had seen too much! She ordered her feet to move, her legs to obey and carry her away. But she had never seen such a strained intense expression on anyone and he was driving hard and fast now, and as naive as she was, she understood. Rapture transformed his expression. He gasped.

She gasped.

And somehow, she knew he had heard her. Suddenly, slowly, he turned his head toward her.

She saw dark, unfocused eyes.

Blanche knew she had committed the worst faux pas possible. "I am sorry!" she cried, in a complete panic now.

She backed out, just as his eyes changed, becoming lucid, just as she saw recognition flare there, just as their gazes met.

His eyes widened.

She whirled and fled.

CHAPTER THREE

REX SAT ON THE SOFA, stunned. Lady Blanche Harrington, a woman he admired as no other, had walked in on him and Anne!

He breathed hard, praying he was in some terrible nightmare and that when he awoke, he would realize Blanche Harrington had not just caught him with his lover.

Anne whispered, "Who was that, my lord?"

Oh, God, he wasn't in a terrible dream—Blanche Harrington had caught him in bed with his maid! He covered his face with his hands and was overwhelmed with mortification and shame.

For one long moment, he succumbed to absolute horror and utter embarrassment. He did not know Blanche Harrington well, even though she had once, briefly, been betrothed to Tyrell. He had probably run into her half a dozen times since first meeting her eight years ago. But he had admired her instantly, as her grace, elegance and gracious behavior were truly remarkable, and had thought his brother mad and blind to have no interest in her. The few times they had conversed, he had done his best to be courtly, correct and polite. He had been determined to be a perfect gentleman in her presence. How in God's name would he face her now? And what on earth was she doing at Land's End?

"Is she your intended?"

He became aware that Anne sat beside him. He slowly

dropped his hands, aware now of the heat in his cheeks. Anne had arranged her clothing, but her braided hair was entirely mussed and she looked as if she'd been in bed with someone— with him. "No," he managed harshly. Why would she think that?

She was pale and stricken, apparently taking her cue from him. "I'm sorry, my lord," she began.

"You have no reason to apologize. The lapse of judgment— and good manners—was mine." And he began to despise himself. What had he been thinking, to dally in the middle of the day in his study? Oh, yes, of course, he had wanted to forget about Stephen. Well, that had certainly been achieved. Could this day possibly get any worse? And what should he do—and say—the next time he encountered Lady Harrington?

God, it would be the most awkward possible moment. He could not think of an encounter he wished to avoid as much. Perhaps, if he were fortunate, he could disappear off the face of the earth.

Anne had risen and was now gathering up the papers strewn about the floor. He saw, but couldn't really comprehend, what she was doing. He was never going to recover from this crisis, he thought. Because even though he was no one in comparison to such a great lady, he had always been the perfect gentleman around her—in the guarded hope of at least garnering her respect. Well, he had earned her utter reprobation instead.

And eventually, he had to leave Land's End. In fact, he was due in town in May. And he wasn't foolish enough to think that by then, she would have forgotten his little tryst.

But why had she been at Land's End?

And was there any possible way to excuse his behavior, explain it, so she might not find him so entirely loathsome?

Beyond shame, Rex reached for his crutch and stood. The moment he did so, he saw the large black Harrington coach in his courtyard. Disbelief began.

She was still at Bodenick.

He was breathless once again.

He swung rapidly to the window and saw her standing by her coachman and a maid. Her back was to the window and a conversation seemed to be in progress. He stared. Her carriage was always terribly correct, but her shoulders seemed even higher than usual, her bearing stiff and set. She was distressed—as she should be.

He fought the urge to hide until she left—the battle was over before it began. If she remained in his drive, he had to go outside and greet her and learn what brought her so far south. But he was amazed that she hadn't climbed in her carriage and driven off at a mad gallop. Whatever her reason for appearing at Land's End, it had to be important.

He cursed. There was no avoiding her now. An apology was in order, and there was no way around it. Except, such an apology would only bring forward even more awkwardness—and for him, humiliation. But if he did not apologize, it was even worse. And damn it, there was no graceful way to tender his regrets.

He wished he had offended anyone else, anyone other than Blanche Harrington.

He looked down at his bare chest. "Anne, please retrieve a shirt and jacket for me—quickly." And now he wondered how long she had been standing there—and how much had she seen.

Instantly, he chastised himself. Blanche Harrington was not a depraved voyeur. She could not have been standing there for more than an instant. Unfortunately, she had chosen the exact instant when his passion had been at its greatest. His cheeks flamed.

Anne laid his papers on the desk and fled the study to do as he had asked.

He continued to stare out of the window, deciding he must not dwell on what she had seen. He must not dwell on his shame. Instead, he must discover an apology that might, at least, smooth the waters somewhat. Oddly, not a single word came to mind.

Blanche suddenly turned and looked at the house.

Rex jumped away from the window, realizing that he now cowered behind the draperies, out of her sight. From depravity to cowardice, he thought grimly, and neither one would do. There was no damned way out of his predicament, he thought. She would never see him as a gentleman, not after this day. He could spend years atoning to her, years trying to reprise his character, but nothing he could say or do, now or in the future, would erase what he had just done.

Anne returned, carrying a beautiful lawn shirt with a ruffled collar and a severe, but elegant, navy-blue jacket. "Will these do?" she asked somberly.

"Yes, thank you. Help me, please." Although he could dress himself, as he could balance perfectly on the crutch without holding it, her help would speed him on his way. As she helped him with the shirt, she whispered, "Is she a great lady, Sir Rex?"

"Yes, a very great lady. Why do you ask?"

"You are so concerned."

He shrugged on the jacket. "I have known Lady Harrington in passing for years. There are ladies in society who would hardly care to witness such an event. Unfortunately, Lady Harrington's character is stellar and she is not of that ilk."

His time had run out. Rex hurried from the study and across the hall, feeling very much as if he were on his way to doom. The front door was open and his heart began to race erratically. The heat in his cheeks intensified and by the time he was crossing the single step outside to the shell drive, he knew he was crimson.

Her back was to the house again—she faced her carriage.

He inhaled, rapidly approaching. "Lady Harrington," he said tersely.

Tension rippled through her and she turned. She was smiling, but her cheeks were as pink as the ribbon in Anne's hair. "Sir Rex! How pleasant to see you again," she breathed. "Good day, sir. It has been some time!"

He halted before her. Did she really think to pretend she had not witnessed him making love to his housemaid? He stared, and for one moment, before she ducked her head, their gazes locked.

A fist seemed to land in his chest, hard. It winded him. She had always had the most beautiful blue-green eyes, tipped up wildly at the outer corners, and he had forgotten how petite and lovely she was. But he had never seen her like this—trembling and flushed with distress and dismay. It took him a moment to speak. "This is an unexpected surprise," he said harshly.

"I am on my way to Penthwaithe," she said, her strain evident in her tone and the fact that she now refused to look at him. "But knowing your home was so close by, I thought to call here, first."

Penthwaithe? He was confused. He had never been to the manor, but his understanding was that the owner resided in London and had left the estate in near ruins. Why would she be on her way to Penthwaithe?

She slowly looked up at him, her smile fading.

He became still, looking into huge eyes that were wide and mirroring so many turbulent emotions, he could not decipher any of them. Blanche Harrington always had the appearance of an angel—her smile genuine, kind and terribly serene, her grace unshakable. Suddenly he was looking at someone he did not quite recognize. She was an elegant woman of outstanding character, and he had to have distressed her greatly with his display of depraved lust. Other women might have enjoyed such a show, but she was not one of them.

"I must apologize for offending you," he said thickly. He truly hated himself.

"You have not offended me!" She was firm, but he caught a slight tremor in her tone. "It is a lovely afternoon and I should have gone directly to Penthwaithe and sent you my card, giving you some notice of my intentions. I must apologize for inconveniencing you, Sir Rex. But we were chilled through and through and when no one answered the door, we hoped to warm ourselves in your hall." She breathed. "Your home is lovely, sir. Just lovely."

He could not stand seeing her in such a state of discomfiture. And worse, she was now apologizing to *him*. "You could never inconvenience me," he said as firmly. "You must not apologize. Of course you should have come inside to sit by the fire." His mind raced. Should he play along with her as if he hadn't seen her watching him make love to Anne? It would be easier for them both, he thought grimly. They could casually converse, the kind of idle chatter he despised, until she went on her way.

His heart lurched with even more dread. They had conversed briefly no more than five or six times in as many years, and suddenly she was at his home in Cornwall. He despaired. He had never wanted her to see him as he truly was, and he wanted absolution, although he knew he would not ever gain it. But some noble part of him couldn't allow her to leave until she knew how sincerely he regretted his immoral behavior.

He inhaled. "Please, Lady Harrington, accept my most profound and sincere apologies—"

She cut him off, which was shockingly rude. "The fault is mine, to call so precipitously!" she cried breathlessly.

Aware of turning red, and in disbelief, he said, "Please accept my apologies…for not having seen your coach in the drive…and for failing to greet you properly…or having a servant at your disposal."

The fluttering smile vanished and she stared. He somehow stared back. Although disguised, he had tendered his terrible regrets and she knew it, but would never admit it openly. He desperately waited for her response.

She smiled oddly. "If you must apologize for...not remarking my coach, then I must accept that apology! However, I realize you are not prepared for company. I am not...distressed...that a servant failed to usher us inside. I am so used to the ton, or my group, anyway—we call at whim, without our cards...we are such a close circle of friends!" She laughed, and he realized he had never heard such a forced sound. "I simply forgot the country is so different!"

He could not decide how deeply she condemned him—and he could only be relieved that she would act so gracefully now. Her behavior was generous, but then, that was the kind of lady she was. She wouldn't stare coldly or sneer. She would not go home and gossip, either. Of that, he had not a doubt.

"It is so cold in Cornwall!" Her words jerked him to attention. And she smiled, shivering. "We will be on our way. Clarence needs to water the team, however, if you do not mind."

He breathed hard, relieved that the terrible subject was over. "Of course you may water the horses," he said.

He turned away to hail his own grooms to aid her servants. He felt her gaze on him as he did so, and his tension escalated impossibly. But an insincere round of graceful apologies was not going to mitigate any awkwardness. Surely he was now the object of her scorn.

He felt as if the irony might kill him. He had always wished to impress her with his manner, secretly wanting her to admire him in some small way, and instead, he had allowed her to glimpse his true nature.

When the team was being led to the stables, he returned to find her standing silently with her maid. Before she noticed him, he noted her grim, even glum, and very strained demeanor. And now, he noticed that the tip of her nose was red from the chill of the day.

He took one last breath, watching her. Somehow they had weathered this crisis, even if only superficially. Somehow the waters had been smoothed over, even if beneath lay huge, frightening currents. And they were on speaking terms. But now what? He remained terribly embarrassed. So, clearly, did she. He had no right to invite her in for some refreshment, but she was chilled, and that is what a true gentleman would do. He was afraid she might refuse the offer—and that would be a rejection he deserved but dreaded. On the other hand, what if she became ill, and all because of his uncontrollable virility?

He had never dreamed Blanche would magically appear at Land's End. He hadn't seen her in almost two years. He didn't have to even think about it to know he had last glimpsed her at the Carrington ball, when his sister-in-law had made her debut into society. Two years was a terribly long time. And now she was about to leave.

It was more than embarrassment. It was more than a fear for her catching a chill. He did not wish for her to go. Not now, not yet.

The sun had been pale and amber in the sky; now, it burned gold.

I am a fool, he thought grimly.

For what he really wished was to pass a pleasant call with her. But how could he possibly achieve that now?

Before he could debate any longer, he took his chances and spoke with great care. "Lady Harrington, it is late afternoon and you seem fatigued. Would you care for some refreshment? Perhaps some warm tea?"

She turned slowly, unsmiling. And she hesitated, clearly indecisive. "It has been a long journey from London," she said. "I am not that chilled, but my poor maid is frozen and has been so all day. If I am not imposing, I would love a cup, as would Meg." And her wide eyes gently met his.

And he thought he saw so much uncertainty there. "You

could never impose," he said gruffly, but he meant his every word. He managed a stiff smile. "Please." He gestured and she preceded him back into the house, calling for her maid to follow. And then Anne met them in the hall.

He knew he blushed. He was dismayed but his other servant was off the premises. He was careful not to look at Blanche now. "Anne, I will need tea for two and sandwiches, if you will. And please show Lady Harrington's maid into the kitchens, so she might take some refreshment, as well, and warm herself there."

Anne nodded before leaving with the other maid.

Rex watched Blanche stare after her. He didn't have to glance into a crystal ball to know she was wondering about his relationship with the housemaid—and possibly recalling what she had just seen. But when she realized he had noticed her gazing after Anne, she flushed and jerked her eyes to the window. "I had no idea the coast here is so beautiful."

"If you decide to walk upon the beaches, you must exercise care. The tides are strong and come in swiftly."

Her gaze skidded to his and darted away. "I will certainly remember that."

Apparently they would not get past the awkwardness of this disaster after all. Or at least, not with Anne about, as a reminder of his excessively virile and inappropriate needs.

But if she found him reprehensible, she hid it entirely. He decided that if she now despised him, she would take her tea and leave as soon as gracefully possible. The length of her visit might very well be a gauge of her feelings, he decided. "The best time to stroll the beach is an hour or two before noon."

Blanche actually smiled at him. "I will make sure to stroll along the beach before I return to town."

He tensed, surprised, because she seemed to have finally recovered her composure. Anne now out of sight, Blanche perused the great room and turned to him. The moment she spoke, he knew she was being sincere. "Your home is lovely, Sir Rex."

Blanche moved to a chair and he followed. His home was modest, but she had meant it—he was certain. "I have spent many years renovating not just the castle, but the entire estate. I find it pleasing enough. Thank you."

"I hadn't expected a castle," she said, and their gazes met and instantly danced apart.

His heart began an odd little dance, too. "Neither did I, not when I was first awarded Land's End and my title."

She looked up. His breath vanished. So did the terrible incident she had witnessed.

It was unbelievable, a dream. Blanche Harrington was sitting with him in his great hall. She lit up the room as the sun never had and never would. But then, hadn't his sisters-in-law and his sister begun to harp on him for his bachelor status? No fool, he knew they were determined to see him wed.

He would never find a woman like this one, he thought grimly. And he did not want to settle for less. For he did not have to know her well to know she was a lady to the core and as such, she was incapable of betrayal and treachery. His painful past had made him distrustful of ladies who wished for a relationship with him, but inexplicably, he knew Blanche Harrington was utterly trustworthy.

And of course, she was not for him. She would one day inherit a vast fortune, and she would marry a great and probably impoverished title, not a thirty-year-old knight who toiled like a common laborer on land no sane gentleman would ever wish to possess.

And he still couldn't grasp the fact that she had not looked at him with any condescension.

He cleared his throat. "May I ask why you are on your way to Penthwaithe?"

She smoothed her pale gray silk skirts with innate grace, a color that suited her eyes and her hair. "I have decided to escape my suitors," she said wryly. "Do you recall my friend, Lady Waverly? She suggested Father's estate."

He stared, mind racing. Everyone knew that Blanche Harrington had no wish to wed. He had always been certain that one day she would change her mind, and apparently, he had been correct. "What does Penthwaithe have to do with Harrington?"

She blinked. "I have just learned the manor is a part of the Harrington fortune. I am afraid Father kept me in the dark about his affairs, and now, of course, I must make sense of them."

He became even more perplexed. "I was under the impression that Penthwaithe belongs to a gentleman who so prefers the city that he has allowed it to fall into utter ruin. I am not sure there are even any tenants."

She sat up straighter. "You must be mistaken. Penthwaithe belonged to my father. My solicitors have recently found the title to the estate."

"You have used the past tense."

Her eyes went wide. "You do not know?"

He did not like this. "I do not know what, Lady Harrington?"

She hesitated, their gazes locked. "Father passed."

He was stunned. "I had no idea!" he exclaimed. And then, knowing how close Blanche had been to her father, how she had doted on him—and he on her—he was stricken for her. "Bl...Lady Harrington, I hadn't heard. I am so terribly sorry!" The urge to touch her—perhaps even take her hand— overcame him, but he would never do such a thing.

She continued to gaze at him, absolutely tearless, fully composed. "Thank you. He passed six months ago—he was stricken with pneumonia and it happened quickly. I have just come out of mourning."

He finally took a chair facing Blanche. He could not quite believe her composure. Her father had been the center of her life. Had she shed all of her tears, vanquished all grief, in six short months? He was doubtful.

And as much as he had always admired her, the one thing he had wondered was what it would take to shake her seemingly unflappable composure. He had always known great passion lay beneath the perfect exterior. He had even wondered, when thoroughly besotted, what she was like in bed.

Well, if Blanche still grieved, she would never do so in company. For all he knew, she wept privately every night, as was her right. And he had finally shaken her composure—with his little tryst. But she had bounced quickly back.

And he realized his admiration for her had increased. It was ironic, because he had little doubt that any admiration she had held for him, was now in ashes.

"I wish I had known," he said. "I would have come directly to London to offer my condolences personally."

She smiled at him. After a pause, she said, "I hadn't realized you didn't send your condolences." She glanced past him, out of the window.

Anne entered, bearing a sterling tray with a porcelain teapot, two cups and saucers. As she set the items down on the small table near Blanche, he told her he would serve. Surprise flicked in her blue-green eyes. "Sir Rex, allow me."

He tensed. "I will pour," he insisted. He knew the offer had been made because he had one leg and she did not realize he could get up and pour tea in spite of the injury. He despised pity and he adeptly served her first.

When he was seated with his own tea, he saw that the sun was now beginning to set. Outside of Bodenick, the sky was stained crimson over the darkening moors. Instantly he was concerned. "Lady Harrington, it is an hour to Penthwaithe.

And frankly, I am worried about there having been a mix-up in estate affairs. And even if not, I am certain you cannot possibly find decent accommodations there." If he offered, would she stay the night?

Blanche set her cup and saucer down. And she looked at him—right into his eyes. "I doubt I have a choice."

His heart turned over hard. How could he not offer her accommodations? She would refuse—she had to hold him in scorn now. And although gentlemen did not sleep with their servants, he did consider himself a gentleman, or at least, he had been raised to be one. "I may have a solution—although I do not know if it will interest you."

"I am all ears," she said softly, the angelic smile he so often recalled in his dreams finally appearing.

He hesitated, then plunged on, trying to sound casual. "Bodenick is rather spartan, as you can see. But I have several guest rooms, and one, the countess has furnished for her own comfort. It is yours if you so wish."

Her eyes widened.

He wet his lips. "And of course, there is a room for your maid and lodgings for your coachman and footmen in the servants' wing."

She smiled again, fully. "Thank you. I would love to spend the night here, Sir Rex."

BLANCHE KNEW she kept staring at the housemaid as the pretty woman set a pitcher of water on the table beside the four-poster bed. The chamber was very pleasantly appointed in shades of gold, green and beige. A small settee in gold brocade was at the foot of the bed, facing the stone hearth. The bed had dark green coverings and two gold floral Persian rugs covered the floor. The walls had been painted bright yellow and a cherrywood armoire graced one wall, while a secretaire adorned the other. There was one plush moss-green chaise.

The countess had clearly furnished this room, making it warm and inviting.

Sir Rex stood just behind her, remaining in the hall. Blanche was acutely aware of his presence. He cleared his throat. "I hope the chamber suits."

Somehow, impossibly, she had found most of her composure in the aftermath of her shocking discovery. Her composure and common sense had always been terribly important to her. But for the first time in her life, it felt fragile—as if it might vanish in an instant, with very little provocation. It felt as if she must fiercely cling to it, or face a vast, bottomless gulf of confusion. And in order to do so, she must *not* recall her memory of that tryst. She must not think about Sir Rex's extremely passionate—too passionate—nature.

She found a smile, anchored it firmly, and turned to face him. "The room is lovely—perfect, really. I cannot thank you enough."

"It is my pleasure," he said. "Supper is at seven, but if you need anything, simply send your maid." He bowed.

Blanche smiled, relieved when he turned to stride rapidly down the hall. His presence was simply too much to bear. Meg remained in the hall, wide-eyed, while Anne slipped past them both and hurried after her lord…and her lover.

Blanche instantly collapsed on the settee. *He was as virile as the rumors said.* All composure vanished. "Open a window, please," she managed.

Meg rushed to do so, her expression one of vast concern. "My lady, are you ill? You have been behaving so strangely!"

Blanche closed her eyes tightly and gave up all pretense. And all she saw was Sir Rex, impossibly masculine, terribly handsome, straining over that woman, a mass of wet, glistening flesh. *So much muscle, so much strength and so much passion,* she thought wildly. Opening her eyes, she tried to cool her cheeks with her hands and she tried to breathe. She was spinning in a whirlwind of confusion.

Meg handed her a glass of water, looking very frightened now.

Blanche accepted it and sipped until she had regained some fragments of composure. She must somehow forget what she had seen. She must never think of Sir Rex in a moment of passion.

"Find me a fan, please," Blanche whispered. If she did not erase the incident from her mind, how would she dine with Sir Rex at seven?

His dark, and yes, frankly handsome image came to mind. She softened then, because as embarrassed as she had been, she had seen the mortification in his eyes. Compassion began.

What kind of man isolated himself at the end of the world, rarely coming to town? What kind of man dallied with a housemaid in the middle of the day? Why did he prefer servants to ladies? Surely there was a plausible explanation, for Sir Rex was neither crude nor base. And most importantly, why was he unwed at his age?

"Do you have a fever?" Meg asked worriedly.

It was incomprehensible. Blanche handed her the glass. She hated gossip—as it was usually malicious in intent. But now, she wished to understand her host—and she needed a confidante. "I will tell you why I am distressed, if you swear you will tell no one what I have seen."

Meg nodded, clearly surprised that her mistress wished to speak with her in such a way.

"I intruded upon Sir Rex while he was with the housemaid—in a moment of indiscretion."

Meg gasped in comprehension.

"Do you think Sir Rex is fond of her?" And even as she asked, she knew it was not her concern, but she was rather dismayed by the notion.

Meg stared. "I don't know, my lady."

Blanche walked away thoughtfully. "Sir Rex is a war hero and a gentleman, Meg. I have known him for many years now. He is one of the most courteous and respectful men I know and I do not care what the gossips say. But his behavior is unusual."

Meg bit her lip.

"What do you think?" Blanche asked, wishing Bess were present to tell her exactly what was happening with Sir Rex and Anne even though she should not be giving the incident another thought. Bess wouldn't—and neither would Felicia. They would laugh about it and then forget about it. Blanche hoped she would soon forget what she had seen, too.

"You want my opinion?" Meg gasped, her gray eyes wide.

"I do."

Meg hesitated. "He's lusty, my lady, that's all."

Blanche stared.

"It's lonely out here," Meg continued. "Look around. We passed the village hours ago. Of course a handsome man like that would have a woman in his bed." She added, "When he tires of this one, there will be someone else. That's how these lords are. And, my lady? I don't know if he cares for her or not. He isn't bedding the maid because he cares for her." She blushed.

Blanche stared. Leave it to her maid to comprehend the situation, she thought. Sir Rex lived alone, in the middle of nowhere, and he was virile. Anne could ease his needs and it was as simple as that. She knew she was blushing now. And one day, he would take a new lover. His affair was not about affection, it was about passion. She felt more heat gather in her cheeks.

Bess fell in and out of *love* on a monthly basis. But she also freely admitted that her needs had nothing to do with love. The parade of men in her life was a parade of men Bess lusted after. The ton was filled with frenzied affairs. Sir Rex was having a passionate affair, as well. And now that she understood, she must stop thinking about it.

"Should I unpack your things? And what will you wear to supper?"

Blanche tensed. They had barely gotten past a terrible beginning, and as long as she kept a grip on her memory, as long as she remained composed, supper would be manageable, she thought. Perhaps by the evening, she could forget what she had seen, or dismiss it, and enjoy the evening. It was not her place to approve or disapprove of his choices, and she had always thought him an interesting man.

"Can you press my gray taffeta gown, Meg?"

Meg nodded. Blanche hadn't worn anything but gray since coming out of mourning. It didn't seem right to strut about like a fancy peacock.

As Meg began to unpack a trunk, Blanche walked over to a window. She faced the ocean below, pale gray now and sweeping into the horizon so it seemed to go on for an infinity, but directly below, violent, frothing waves now pounded the rock beaches. As magnificent as the scene was, there was no question now that she stood at the very tip of the realm, and she was acutely aware of it. An extreme sense of isolation swept her. Land's End was isolated, she thought. And with such awareness, she felt the enormity of the solitude.

The scene of endless ocean and dark rock, of pale beaches and towering cliffs, was stark, desolate and magnificent, very much like her host. And if she, one of society's great hostesses, felt such separateness upon gazing out at the view, if she could be so conscious of being so far removed from everyone and everything, what did Sir Rex feel when he went to his window? Could anyone live this far from society, on the edge of the world, so to speak, and not feel detached and alone?

Was Sir Rex lonely?

More unease crept over her, and with it, a sense of confusion. Blanche decided she was a bit too intrigued with her host. Still, she was a close family friend, and even his family was concerned about him. And she did not think Sir Rex could out-maneuver the countess, his sister and his three sisters-in-law, which meant his bachelor days were numbered.

He was hardly a perfect man. This afternoon had proven that. But he deserved more than a solitary existence on his Cornish estate, just as she deserved more than the Harrington fortune. Being kind and fond of his family, she wished him the very best. And she had not a doubt that when the day came that Sir Rex wed, he would give up his preference for house-maids. Somehow, she knew he would be a good, kind and loyal husband. All the de Warenne men were that way.

She didn't want to think it, but she did. He needed a wife, and she needed a husband. However, she had meant it when she said he would make a terrible husband for her. They were far too different, like night and day, and she sensed grave complications beneath his dark exterior. And his masculinity was far too overpowering for someone like herself. She didn't know why she had even thought about his future in the same breath as she had thought about hers.

She turned. Meg was shaking out the dove-gray. "Meg? I've changed my mind. I'll wear the green silk with my emeralds."

CHAPTER FOUR

HE HAD TWO SERVANTS in his employ. Frugal of nature, with no great economy to spare, he preferred to keep his household staff minimal. Now, Rex wished he had a chef. He wanted supper to be perfect. But Anne prepared his meals, while his manservant served as butler, majordomo and valet. Unfortunately, Fenwick had been attending to his errands that afternoon, preventing him from welcoming Lady Harrington properly and thus avoiding the fiasco of her stumbling in on him and Anne.

Rex never bothered himself with the day's menu. He did not care what was served—he never entered the kitchen. He could not even recall if he had ever done so. Now he swung in, perspiring with anxiety. Anne's meals were fair. And Anne was now bustling about frantically. Pots simmered on the stove. He could smell roasting lamb. He instantly noted a stable boy stirring one pot, and he was pleased she'd had the initiative to order young Jon to her side. He saw cold pheasant pies on the sideboard. "Anne."

She whirled, flushed from the kitchen's heat, never mind the two widely opened windows. "Sir!"

"Is everything in order for supper?"

"Yes, my lord," she said, wringing her hands and appearing anything but calm.

"Where is Fenwick?" He somehow managed to sound calm, but he'd had no help with his tie and cuff links and he'd been royally annoyed. And now, it appeared that Anne was in over her head.

When he'd had the countess as a guest, an elderly woman had been his housekeeper and she had been a good cook. There had been no other visitors since.

"I sent him to the village for a pie."

His tension did not ease. It was an hour to the village, another hour back, and he was afraid that Fenwick would not return in time to serve them. "When will he be back?"

Anne seemed nervous. "By eight, I think."

He just stared at her, wishing she hadn't sent the manservant to the village and that she'd planned to serve up custard instead. He could not imagine Anne serving them and hovering about while he attempted polite conversation now. It would be impossibly awkward. His temper sparked, rekindling the frustration he'd felt all day. It was as if one rotten incident after another was destined for him. However, Lady Harrington had agreed to spend the night and tonight they were dining together. His heart slammed. One good thing had happened after all. He prayed he'd seen the last of all disaster. He wanted to *impress* her.

"We will be dining à la Française," he said softly.

Anne looked helplessly at him, and he realized she was near tears.

He softened. "You will leave every course on the table. We will help ourselves." Then, "Do not worry. The lamb smells wonderful."

Relief covered her features.

Just then, Blanche's maid stepped into the kitchen. He was surprised; she curtsied properly at him. "Why are you not with your lady?" he asked, far more sharply than he intended.

"Lady Harrington is in the hall," she said softly.

His heart turned over, hard. He was going to have to control his anxiety and his excitement, he thought grimly, or she would realize he had an inappropriate attraction to her. He nodded at her and swung out, tugging at his necktie as he did so. He had almost donned tails, but that would have been absurd. Instead, he'd chosen pale breeches, a silver waistcoat and a fine, dark brown jacket. At least his appearance was impeccable, he thought.

He stepped into the great room and faltered.

Blanche stood by a window, gazing out at the night sky, which shimmered with stars. Clad in a silvery moss-green gown, with a low-cut bodice and small chiffon sleeves, her pale hair curled and swept up, she was impossibly delicate and impossibly beautiful. He was going to have to face the fact that he had always thought her beautiful, but he had done so in a very respectful way—most of the time. Now he simply stared, because they were alone in the great hall of his home. And in that moment, he wanted nothing more than to sweep her up into his arms, cover her mouth with his own, and damn, taste her very thoroughly. But that was never going to happen. Unfortunately, in that moment, the events of that afternoon entirely forgotten, his body betrayed him and he felt his loins stir.

She turned, smiling.

Her composure seemed to have entirely returned. His admiration for her increased. He would give anything if she had truly forgotten about his rendezvous with Anne—and if she thought it irrelevant to his character.

"Good evening. You look as if you have rested." He bowed very slightly.

Her cheeks were slightly pink, as if rouged, but he knew she used no artifice. "I did nap a bit. Am I early? I see your other guests have not arrived."

He hesitated. "There are no other guests, I'm afraid." Had she expected polite company?

She started. "Oh, I had assumed there might be company…

I am sorry. It doesn't matter." Although her tone was even, her flush increased.

He smiled grimly, wondering if she was dismayed that it would be but the two of them. "I am afraid I am not well acquainted with my neighbors."

"But you have been here for many years."

"Yes, I have."

Her eyes widened in surprise. Now she understood the extent of his reclusive nature, he thought even more grimly. He wished to somehow explain. "Having no hostess, I do not entertain." And that was not the truth—he despised polite, inane conversation, and hated being pursed by other men's wives.

Her smile returned. "I am sorry, Sir Rex, I simply assumed you would invite your neighbors. But this is better, is it not? You are the only de Warenne I am poorly acquainted with."

His heart accelerated. She wished to know him better? He was amazed…he was thrilled. But of course, she was simply making conversation, wasn't she? Or did she mean her words? "I can only hope I do not bore you with inept conversation."

She smiled. "I do not recall your ever being an inadequate conversationalist."

He decided not to point out that their conversations over the years had been extremely limited in duration. "Would you care for sherry or wine?" he asked politely.

"No, thank you," she said.

He swung on his crutch to the bar cart, aware of her gaze wandering the room. He poured a glass of red wine and faced her. He was startled to find her gaze locked upon him. She smiled and glanced aside; he wondered if his clothing was wrinkled, or in some other manner lacking. The silence became awkward and he worried about the supper that was to come. "Has everything been to your liking? Is there anything else that you need to make your stay a pleasant one?"

She quickly smiled. "There is nothing to complain about. Everything is perfect. Your mother made the chamber most accommodating."

There had been plenty to complain about, he thought wryly.

"I have noticed your collection of arms," she said.

He started. "They were my arms in the war."

"Yes, I realized that. It is an interesting display."

He stared. "You don't like it." And the words tumbled forth without his anticipating them. They were not a question. He somehow knew she disliked the collection.

"Oh, I did not mean to critique your decor."

"Lady Harrington, I am certain you would never criticize the most slovenly servant, much less your host. But I am curious. Why do you dislike my display?" He wanted to know. He wanted her opinion.

She hesitated. "I am hardly ignorant," she finally said. "I have heard many accounts of the war, and one of the charities my estate funds provides housing and many other services for veterans who, unlike yourself, can no longer make a go of it."

His brows lifted. "Are you referring to the Society of Patriots?"

"Yes, I am."

The society was a tremendous boon to those crippled and maimed by the war. He was impressed, and although it was impossible, his admiration for her grew. "I take it your father became fond of the cause?"

She shook her head. "Father allowed me to manage our charitable contributions. In a way, we had a partnership. I ran Harrington Hall and made the decisions for the allocation of all donations, while he managed all the Harrington properties and the Harrington fortune."

He hadn't realized she was more than a lady and a hostess. "Is that why you dislike my display of arms? Because it is a reminder of the war—and how it ruined so many lives?"

She inhaled. "That is one reason, yes. Unlike most ladies, I find nothing romantic about the war."

He stared. "You are right," he finally said. "There is nothing romantic or pleasant about war."

Their gazes met and held.

"And the other reason you dislike my display?"

Blanche hesitated. "I am not certain, but I do not feel pleasant when I look at that display. In fact, I feel saddened by it. Why do you wish to see those arms each and every day? Isn't the reminder painful for you?"

He flinched. Another man would have brushed her terribly direct comment off. He did not. "Men died under my command," he said. "Of course the reminder is painful."

Her eyes widened.

And Rex smiled politely at her and turned the subject to the weather.

THE LAMB TASTED like cardboard. She had no appetite, but she forced herself to finish half of her plate just as she willed herself to remain calm. But every time she looked down, she felt Sir Rex staring at her. She was accustomed to his stares, but not like this. At a ball their gazes might meet once or twice, a dozen people between them. She might even send him a smile, or he might do the same to her. This was entirely different. It was awkward. An odd tension seemed to fill the room. His stare was oddly masculine and terribly searching. It even seemed bold. She wished he had invited others to dine with them. It was simply too difficult, two strangers dining tête-à-tête like this, especially after the crisis of that afternoon.

How could one small incident unbalance her so?

They had managed to keep a polite, if stilted, conversation going; it was a miracle, from her point of view. Still, finally, a long and awkward silence had fallen.

From the corner of her eyes, she watched his hands. They

were darkly tanned, big and strong, the fingers long and blunt. Yet his hands moved with extraordinary grace—just as he did, in spite of the crutch he used. Watching his fingers touch fork and knife, she thought about his hands on Anne.

Her heart lurched and her body almost ached. She could not imagine what was wrong with her.

He said slowly, "I have been thinking about Penthwaithe."

Blanche swallowed, relieved to be discussing a proper topic. She tore her gaze from his strong hands and looked up. She was scorched by his dark, intent gaze, yet she smiled firmly.

"What will you do if you find Penthwaithe in the condition I believe it to be in?"

"I hope you are wrong. But if you are correct, I will begin some repairs." She noticed that he hadn't eaten a thing—but he had finished most of the bottle of wine. She'd taken a single sip from her glass.

The gossips also said he drank too much, sometimes before noon. She had always thought it an unfair accusation, and she suspected it was untrue. He was too industrious to imbibe without control and discipline.

"Would you allow me to join you on the morrow, Lady Harrington?"

She was stunned and their gazes met. She could not imagine sharing a coach with him. Before she could respond, he said, "I am concerned with the condition the manor may be in. I have a strong sense that you may need my assistance—assuming there has not been a bungled mess made of the titles."

The request was perfectly proper—and she might need his assistance. But could she manage an entire day alone with him when she was barely able to navigate her way through a simple supper? It would help if he did not watch her so closely. It would help if she could really forget seeing him with the maid. Unfortunately, that scene would remain etched on her mind for a very long time. And in the confines of her coach, they would be seated far too closely together, making the memory very hard to avoid. Besides, his presence was too masculine. It would be so much better to avoid it—him—at least until she felt more firmly in control of herself.

She glanced at his strong hands, willing herself not to open up her mind to any memory of that afternoon. "I hate to put you out," she somehow said. "You surely have many affairs to attend here."

"You cannot put me out," he insisted. "My own affairs can wait. I am very concerned, and as a family friend, I think I must accompany you."

She tensed. He was insisting. "Penthwaithe may be in a fine condition. I am assuming all is well and I will be moving my belongings there."

His stare was unwavering.

"Of course you may accompany me." She inhaled. The last thing she wished to ever do was insult him and there was no graceful way to refuse.

He nodded, his jaw flexing.

Their plates were cleared by a manservant she had not seen previously. She took the opportunity to attempt to regain a calm demeanor. But she was convinced that she must seek out a physician the moment she returned to town, as something was wrong with her heart. It kept beating far too rapidly.

Dessert was served. Blanche knew she could not manage a single bite and Sir Rex pushed his plate aside. He said, "Have you many suitors?"

Briefly, the question surprised her. "I have two hundred and twenty-eight."

His surprise was comical. "You are in jest!"

"Unfortunately, no, I am not." She smiled. "A shocking number, don't you think?"

His stare intensified. "A very shocking number," he said.
And then he turned to his wine.

Blanche wondered what he was really thinking.

He lifted his long, dark lashes and pierced her with his
stare. "Is there anyone you admire?"

Her heart skipped. For one moment, it was hard to speak.
"No, not really."

He smiled grimly. "I am sure the right prospect will
appear."

She avoided his eyes, trying to hold at bay an image of
gleaming, wet muscle, bulging arms and an expression of
rapture. "Yes, that is what I am hoping."

BLANCHE LEANED FORWARD as her coach turned onto the road
marked Penthwaithe. It was the following morning, an hour
before noon. She had left Sir Rex alone downstairs after
supper, wondering if he intended to imbibe alone, and
worrying if that was how he spent his evenings. And the
moment she had climbed into bed, never mind that it was only
nine o'clock, exhaustion had claimed her. She thought about
her enigmatic host, recalled the tryst she had witnessed and
fell promptly asleep. She slept deeply and peacefully and had
awoken only with Meg's encouragement.

Sir Rex had not joined her for breakfast. She had learned
he was busy with his grooms, apparently dealing with his
horses. And he was not sharing her coach now. He was riding
astride.

Blanche hadn't realized a man with half of a leg could ride
astride, but she had hid her amazement and pretended his
behavior was routine. She had quickly discovered that he rode
with great skill, as if a part of his horse, carrying a cane where
his right calf should have been. But of course, every cavalry-
man was required to attend the riding academy before ever
gaining admission into the service.

Now, she felt some trepidation. The highway had been rutted, but this road had severe holes and was strewn with rocks, some of such significance her coachman began to weave amongst them. Blanche wondered at the lack of upkeep, glancing now at the moors. She saw not a single grazing cow or sheep.

She glanced toward Sir Rex, who rode abreast of the carriage. His crutch had been folded in on hinges, and hung from a hook on his saddle. He rode with extreme ease, his mount a huge, magnificent beast. It was obvious he was a master horseman; she remained very impressed. Worse, that odd flutter remained in her chest.

He glanced her way, his expression somber. Blanche knew he did not care for the maintenance of the road.

Now, however, she saw some buildings on the right. As her coach came closer, she saw that they were mere stone shells, having been gutted long ago, but whether by fire or the elements and lack of care, she did not know.

It was beginning to appear that Sir Rex was right and Penthwaithe might be in a state of severe disrepair. The plan had been for her to holiday at the estate. But her plans might well be in jeopardy—and she was not ready to go back to London and face her horde of suitors. Blanche hesitated, aware that she could not impose upon her host for much longer, especially after the tryst she had witnessed.

"The manor lies ahead," he called to her.

Blanche poked her head entirely out of the carriage window to glimpse it. She saw a square stucco building, plain and unimpressive in appearance, unadorned by trees, hedges or ivy. A small water fountain graced the courtyard, but it was not functioning. A small stone building was in the distance, probably serving as a stable. Now she saw some sheep grazing behind the barn, and two very thin cows appeared, wandering into the front yard. Blanche suddenly saw a pair of young boys, one hauling a bucket, the other carrying a basket. They were barefoot, their pants too short, and they went into the house.

Penthwaithe was not a thriving estate. The contrast to Land's End was glaring. Worse, she did not have to step inside the manor house to know she was not going to stay there.

Her coach halted. Blanche waited for her footman and alighted, joining Sir Rex, who had dismounted and was glancing around. From the front courtyard, she could see piles of animal droppings everywhere and a cart left almost in the path leading to the front door. Scum adorned the water in the fountain. Not only was it stagnant, the statue of a fish from which the fountain should have run was seriously broken. She saw a sparse vegetable garden on her left. She grimaced. How had Father left the estate in such a condition? Her father was meticulous when it came to attending to his property. She couldn't believe he would allow tenants to stay on if they cared so little for the manor.

Sir Rex swung over. "You will not be staying here." He was firm.

Blanche continued to grimace. "Obviously not." She hesitated. "I had no idea…this is terrible."

"It is slovenly," he said abruptly. "The estate is not my affair, but had I tenants such as these, I would terminate the lease."

Blanche hesitated. She thought about the two small barefoot boys.

His stare was unwavering. "You have had a long journey from town. You may stay on at Land's End as long as it suits you."

She was very surprised. "I can hardly impose upon you."

"Why not?"

And before she could react, he swung rapidly to the front door. As he knocked, Blanche followed and paused beside him.

A nursing woman opened the door. Her eyes widened.

"This is Lady Harrington," Sir Rex said firmly. He didn't look at the suckling infant. "I am Sir Rex de Warenne of Land's End and Bodenick. Where is your husband?"

Terribly surprised, the woman removed the infant, closing up her dress. "He may be in the stable, or out in the fields, plowing."

"Summon him, please. We wish a word."

The woman turned. "James! Go get your father, now! Tell him a lord and lady are here. Hurry!"

Blanche was peering past Rex. She had seen such squalor in London. While working with the sisters of St. Anne's, she had attended some very impoverished and ill women in their homes. But the manor looked as if it hadn't been repaired or even cleaned in years. The wood floor in the entry and hall was coming up in sections, or missing entirely, there was very little furniture, and paint was peeling from the walls, which were blackened in some places. Blanche now saw two young girls and one of the boys she had seen earlier. The boy who had gone off to fetch his father was probably eleven or twelve years old. The three children facing her from behind their mother were between the ages of two and eight. She saw wide eyes and pinched faces.

This poor family was in dire need. She reached out, instinctively touching Sir Rex's hand. He started, looking at her.

Blanche dropped her hand but held his gaze. Something had to be done.

"My lord, my lady!" a man cried, huffing and out of breath, coming up behind them.

Blanche turned, as did Sir Rex. A tall, thin man approached, eyes wide and fearful. Instantly he bowed.

"You are?" Sir Rex asked.

"I am Jack Johnson, my lord."

"Sir Rex de Warenne, and this is Lady Blanche Harrington."

He blinked. "Please, come in. Bess, boil up some tea."

His wife rushed to obey.

"Please, we are not in need of tea or anything else," Blanche said firmly. She would not deprive them of their spare provisions. "I have merely come to inspect the estate."

He plucked nervously at his collar. "Are ye buying it? Is that why you've come to inspect it?"

Blanche started. "My father passed, Mr. Johnson, and the fact that this manor is a part of my inheritance just recently came to my attention."

Johnson shifted uneasily. "We're good people, my lady. But…" He stopped.

Sir Rex was staring at the man, clearly thinking there was no excuse for the squalor. "But what?"

He inhaled. "I mean no disrespect, but I am confused. Lord Bury has owned the manor for years. I didn't know he was dead—or that there are heirs! He was so young and a bachelor himself!"

Blanche tensed and glanced at Sir Rex. "I do not know any Lord Bury, Mr. Johnson. Now I am confused. Are you saying that Lord Bury owns the manor? For my solicitor recently found a document indicating that the manor is a part of the Harrington fortune."

"Lord Bury inherited Penthwaithe from his father, perhaps six or seven years ago. In fact, he was here three months ago to inspect it and collect his rents. I thought you might be his agents, come to see if I have improved it as I swore I would do! But he sold the estate to you? I didn't know."

Blanche froze.

Rex faced her. "Blanche, are you certain about the title you saw?"

Blanche shook her head. My God, there had been a monumental mix-up. For it no longer appeared that her father had owned the estate for years. But if Lord Bury had been out to collect the rents three months ago, how could her father have purchased the estate from him? Her father had been dead.

She began to have an inkling, and she tensed, thinking, *Bess?*

And she quickly thought about the events leading to the title's discovery. The solicitor who had told her of the title had been surprised by its existence. He had been very frank: he hadn't heard of Penthwaithe in all the years he'd been employed by Harrington. But Harrington hadn't owned Penthwaithe for years, Bury had. And Bess had been with them and she'd remarked that this kind of mix-up happened all the time. Oh, how casual and certain she had sounded! And there had been an odd gleam in her eyes!

Blanche became convinced. They had been discussing Sir Rex at some length. Bess had asked her if she wished for him to court her. She hadn't, and she had said as much, but when Bess had an idea, she was like a terrier with a bone. Clearly, Bess intended to send Blanche to Cornwall on a wild-goose chase—and arrange a match with Sir Rex.

Her heart lurched wildly. She stared at Sir Rex, stunned. He might need a wife, but they had nothing in common! Yes, he needed additional income, and he was very attractive, but he was wedded to his Cornish lands. And he certainly wasn't interested in her as a possible spouse—he'd had eight years to come forward, if that were the case. *What was Bess thinking?*

And why was her heart galloping madly—why was she so stricken?

He didn't even like ladies; he liked solitude and housemaids.

"Are you beginning to believe there has been a mistake?" Sir Rex asked her quietly.

She managed a bright smile. She couldn't reveal to Sir Rex that her best friend had conspired to send her to him by falsely implying she owned the neighboring estate! On the other hand, he'd laugh uproariously if he knew Bess thought to throw them at one another. Wouldn't he?

She should laugh! Shouldn't she?

"Lady Harrington?" He clasped her shoulder, steadying her.

She forced the words, stiffening now. His hand was large, warm and firm. It was unyielding, like the man. "It seems the title might be as bungled as you believe."

"A dead man cannot purchase a manor, and apparently the Bury family has owned Penthwaithe for years," he said very seriously, studying her very closely. "You are distressed."

I am very distressed, she thought, *and when I see Bess, I intend to set her straight.* "The logic is inescapable, then, there has been a mix-up," Blanche somehow agreed. *A mix-up and a misunderstanding,* she thought.

A match between her and Sir Rex? It was madness, sheer madness!

Except, Bess Waverly was one of the most astute women Blanche knew.

CHAPTER FIVE

JOHNSON WAS GLANCING rapidly between them now.

Blanche had almost forgotten his presence. She turned to soothe him, relieved by the distraction. "We are not agents for Lord Bury, Mr. Johnson. And apparently, I do not own this estate."

He sagged with relief. "I do not mean to deny Lord Bury. But I got five children to feed!"

"I understand."

"If you see his lordship, please tell him I'm workin' as hard as I can," he cried.

"I have never met Lord Bury, but if you wish, I will seek him out in London and plead your case," Blanche said, meaning it.

Johnson seemed incredulous. "Could ye, please?"

Blanche nodded. "I am more than happy to help."

"Good day," Rex said firmly, lightly clasping Blanche's arm and glancing closely at her. As she walked beside him down the stone path to the coach, she glanced back to see Johnson and his boys staring after them. She waved. They paused beside her coach.

"Are you all right?" he asked.

She made up her mind; she shook her head. "I am never well when confronted with those who are so needy."

"I can see that." he added, "Most of the families in the parish are impoverished."

"So that makes it acceptable?" she asked frankly, their gazes locked.

"I did not say that. What do you wish to do?"

"If you do not mind, I wish to proceed to the village. And there, I wish to purchase provisions for them. Johnson seems sincere. Maybe with a little help, he can get Penthwaithe on its feet." She was distressed for the Johnson family, but kept calm, smiling at Sir Rex instead. "As his landlord is hardly helping by collecting the last of his funds for rent."

Sir Rex stared as if he knew some anger lurked beneath her facade. "That is what landlords do, Lady Harrington."

"Not all landlords," she said seriously. "Would you collect Penthwaithe's rents?"

He stiffened. "No, I would not."

Blanche hadn't thought so.

"My program is different from that of most landlords. I have actually deferred rents frequently, as I prefer to see the farms thrive. In the long term, everyone benefits from such a program. The farms prosper, the tenants can pay rents and I can receive them."

"Your policy is impressive." She hadn't realized he was such a benevolent landlord.

"It is logical." He hesitated. "And apparently we share some common ground. You are distressed by the plight of the Johnson family. I am often distressed by the same circumstance, which unfortunately, one encounters everywhere in the parish—and in most of Cornwall. But charity only goes so far. Our poorer families need more than charity—they need livelihoods."

She stared directly into his dark eyes, which she realized were flecked with gold. Sir Rex was a compassionate man. She knew many noblemen and women who were indifferent to the plight of those less fortunate than themselves.

"Most ladies of the ton lack such compassion," he added. "They are too involved in their own vanities."

She hesitated. How odd, they had been thinking almost the same thing. He was right—very right—but she wasn't about to condemn all London noblewomen. "That is a broad indictment."

"Yes, it is," he agreed with a slight smile. "Have no fear, I am not asking you to agree with me—you would never throw stones at your friends."

"No, I should never do so."

His regard was oddly warm. "I admire your compassion, Lady Harrington, not just for the Johnsons, but for the war veterans." He hesitated. "I am not sure I have said so. It equals your generous nature."

Blanche was surprised. Sir Rex had never offered such flattery before. "You are being far too kind."

"I think not. Let's make those purchases. I can help you with them, if you wish." He smiled at her.

He became a very attractive man when he smiled, she thought uneasily. "Sir Rex, I am somewhat involved with the Johnsons, but you are not. Please, I can manage to provide a few necessities for them." She was certain he could not afford to indulge in the luxury of more charity.

His smile vanished, as if he knew she did not care for him to spend his modest resources on Penthwaithe's tenants. "I am glad to contribute. I'll have Fenwick drive the stores over and we can be back at Bodenick in time for a late dinner." He was firm.

Blanche nodded. He was clearly determined to show her that he was generous, but she already suspected he was just that in spite of his modest estate. Why had he flattered her? He wasn't a gallant and he did not flirt. And why was she pleased? She was used to flattery and flirtation. She could not enter a salon without some rogue accosting her with his mundane, insincere praise.

Following Rex to the coach, she stole a glance at his strong, classic profile. There was more to this man than met the eye.

He was reclusive and he did drink a bit freely, but she could not condemn him for such behavior, as he was industrious, resourceful, honest and astute. It was not as if he wasted his life away; to the contrary, his life was filled with improvements and accomplishments.

She had always been somewhat aware of him. He had a charisma, and whenever he was present and she entered a salon, she had noticed him instantly. She had never thought about it, but now, she wondered if she had always instinctively liked him. He certainly had a strength of character which she found attractive in a man. He was the kind of man one could undoubtedly depend on.

He caught her staring and smiled.

IT WAS THREE in the afternoon when they finally returned to Land's End. Blanche walked up to the house, pleased with the purchases she had made for the Johnson family. It had been impossible to dissuade Sir Rex from making an equal contribution.

She was at present thoroughly preoccupied. Once, she had had a vague interest in Sir Rex de Warenne. If anything, that interest had been a result of their being family friends. She was thoughtful now. They were becoming well acquainted in a very short period of time. Clearly she was becoming somewhat intrigued with her host. She wasn't certain what to make of that, as she had always been a bit intrigued, but from a very safe distance. Nothing felt safe any longer, especially when she allowed herself a vivid recollection of the previous afternoon. That tryst was unforgettable. But it wasn't as shocking today as it had been yesterday.

Meg came running out of the house, followed by Anne, who was walking more slowly. Meg was beaming; Anne sent Blanche an odd, sidelong look. Blanche didn't quite care for it, but she couldn't decipher it, either, and she dismissed it.

"My lady, did you have a pleasant day?" Meg beamed. "Did you enjoy your box lunches?"

"It has been an unusual day," she told Meg. "We will not be going to Penthwaithe after all." She hesitated. "Sir Rex saved the day."

Meg's eyes widened; Anne glanced her way.

Sir Rex, who had been speaking to her coachman, now came forward. "I had Anne pack us boxed dinners, in case we needed them." He turned to the maid, who had retrieved a wicker basket from the coach. "Please take our luncheon inside to the dining room. Lady Blanche must be famished and we will dine there immediately."

He was thoughtful, she realized, and meticulous. Blanche stared at his handsome face for so long that his brows lifted. "Lady Harrington?"

Her heart flipped disturbingly. "I am ravenous." She hesitated. "It's a beautiful day. Can we dine al fresco? Meg mentioned you have a magnificent view from the tower gardens." Supper had been awkward last night, the dining hall somehow too small for them both. With her sudden interest in his character, it would be better to dine outside. It wouldn't be as intimate.

He seemed mildly surprised. "One can see all the way to America, or so the locals claim, but the gardens are dormant now."

"I don't mind."

"Are you certain you will not be cold? You have been outdoors most of the day."

If she hadn't intruded on him in his tryst yesterday, she would still consider him a perfect gentleman. "I am enjoying the brisk air." She smiled, not looking at him.

Had Bess thought to match them because she knew he had the strength and integrity of character to help her manage her fortune?

Sir Rex was staring closely, but she refused to meet his gaze. He said, "Anne, bring Lady Harrington a warm throw."

He gestured and she preceded him around the castle and past the tower. She paused. He was right. Here, one could see all the way to America, or, it seemed that way.

For the gardens ended where the land vanished into the ocean, and while she knew cliffs were below the final precipice, they could not be seen. Today the Atlantic was as gray as steel, but shimmering with iridescence. Gold and orange sparkled on the water's surface. "Oh," she breathed.

"A school of fish has passed. They leave a metallic display in their wake," he said softly.

And he stood so closely behind her that she felt his breath feather her neck. Blanche leaped away, putting a polite distance between them, her heart suddenly thundering in her chest. His body hadn't touched hers, but it might as well have, for she had felt his heat.

She was undone. She could hardly breathe and she didn't understand such an intense reaction to his proximity—which had certainly been a mistake.

"I am sorry, I did not mean to startle you," he said, turning away. His tone was rough.

She refused to let her mind release her memory of him with Anne. She refused to even begin to consider what that rough tone meant. Instead, she quickly perused the gardens. Blanche saw rosebushes, wisteria and beds for daffodils and tulips. Meg was laying out a plaid blanket; Anne was opening the basket. Rex smiled casually at Blanche and swung over to the maid. "Bring a bottle of white wine and two glasses," he said.

"This must be beautiful in the summer."

"As I said, you must return." He smiled at her.

Blanche felt her heart turn over now. She didn't know what was happening to her, but he had a beautiful smile and it was a shame it was used so rarely. If he spent more time in London, he would not be single; some beautiful young lady would have snapped him up. She had not a doubt. His fortune was modest, but he had other attributes and not every debutante was a fool for charm. In fact, it was really odd that he had yet to marry.

Had Bess really thought to match them?

She stared at his strong profile as he watched her maid laying out their luncheons, and briefly an image flashed, one of bulging muscles and powerful shoulders, of the wet glistening skin of his back, his chest. Not entirely insistent, a tension began, accompanied by an odd ache. She deliberately looked across the dormant gardens, trying to imagine what she would plant if she lived at Land's End. She might try lilacs, she thought firmly.

She felt his gaze. She glanced up and caught him staring boldly at her. The look was almost seductive and far too male. For one more heartbeat, as if unaware of her gaze, as if deeply in thought, he did not smile; he simply stared.

He preferred housemaids to ladies; he was industrious and resolute; Bess thought to match them.

He flushed, glancing away. She hurried to the blanket, sitting so swiftly she lost her balance, but then, she felt entirely off balance now. Fussing with her skirts, she felt her cheeks flame. A picnic now seemed to be the very worst idea, but how could she possibly escape?

And what had that direct and potent glance meant?

She had probably imagined it, she thought breathlessly. And damn Bess for her little conspiracy, anyway!

"Lady Harrington?" He sat beside her, laying his crutch carefully on the grass.

She summoned up a bright smile, aware that escape was impossible. She must find a stimulating subject! "Wine is a splendid idea!" And now, too late, she wished to recover her composure and wear it like armor.

He stared searchingly. "Sometimes when I look at you, I see worry written all over your face."

Her eyes widened. He was not a gypsy and he could not read her mind.

"I would like to take that worry away. The Johnsons will get on nicely until the spring. If you wish, I will make their welfare my personal concern."

He assumed she was worrying about the family, she thought, relieved. "Thank you. I am worried about their welfare. It would be very noble if you kept an eye cast their way."

His stare skidded over her and she knew he thought her behavior odd. He handed her a plate of cold chicken and salad. She focused on her food. But it became impossible to eat, because he sat very closely by her. In fact, sharing a small blanket was far more intimate than being seated across from one another in his dining hall.

"I heard that the earl and the countess will be celebrating their anniversary in May," she managed.

"Yes," he said, pausing as Anne appeared with an open bottle of wine and two glasses. He thanked her and she left. After pouring, he handed Blanche a glass and lifted his plate. "It will be a family affair. I am looking forward to it."

"They seem as fond of one another now as they ever were," Blanche remarked, after taking a small bite of chicken. Her interest in food had waned.

His appetite seemed fierce, however. But he did look up. "They love one another deeply. They were both widowed when they met, so it was a love match—and it remains such."

Blanche stared. It was impossible not to think about the fact that everyone in his family was happily wed, he being a glaring exception. She could never ask why he remained single. But now, she wished to do just that. "Marrying for love seems to run in your family."

"Yes, it does." He glanced oddly at her.

Blanche knew that she was prying and it was inexplicable. Surely, this wasn't why Sir Rex had yet to marry? He did not seem at all romantic. "Perhaps you will be next."

He glanced aside, reaching for his wineglass. "A romantic notion." His gaze lifted. "Are you a romantic, Lady Harrington?"

"No." She was hardly romantic. She added, "Not only have I never been in love, I will marry for economy and convenience."

His stare intensified. "Marriage is usually convenient. I am afraid I do not comprehend how economics might affect your choice."

She breathed. This was a perfectly suitable discussion. "Last month, I began to sit with my father's agents and lawyers in an attempt to unravel my father's financial affairs. It is all so terribly complicated! There are overseas ventures, shares in companies I have never heard of and odd partnerships, as well. My mind is not mathematical. I am suited to managing our charitable donations and that interests me. I cannot understand account ledgers, much less his various investments."

"So you need a husband." He finished his wine. "I happen to agree. Harrington's reputation was that he was a brilliant entrepreneur. I have friends who schemed to learn of his latest ventures and investments, in the hopes of copying him. He kept his affairs secret, of course. Why should you have to cope with such a vast inheritance alone?"

He agreed that she needed a husband. That wasn't odd, as everyone thought so. But now, she kept thinking about how industrious he was. How meticulously he kept his own affairs—and his estate was a shining example. She was uneasy but had to admit that she did need someone with some of Sir Rex's more stellar attributes. However, Sir Rex was not the right choice for her, no matter what Bess seemed to think. For his mere presence was too disturbing.

"How will you choose?"

She tensed. "How will I choose?"

"How will you decide which suitor will make the best husband? You have just said you will not marry for affection, but for economy and convenience. That requires some standard which your prospects must meet."

She became uncomfortable. "My best friends are advising me."

More surprise covered his handsome face. "Lady Waverly and…I cannot recall the brunette."

"She is Lady Dagwood now. Felicia is newly wed."

"And what do your lady friends advise you to do?"

Blanche stared, their gazes locked. And this time, she could not seem to look away. She felt warmth creep into her cheeks. She could not imagine telling him what Bess and Felicia advised.

He leaned forward. "They are aware, are they not, that of your two hundred and twenty-eight suitors, two hundred of them are fortune-hunting rascals?"

She wet her lips, for they were terribly dry. "I beg to differ. Of my two hundred and twenty-eight suitors, I am certain that two hundred and twenty-eight are fortune hunters."

Relief covered his features. And he began to smile. "Thank God you are a sensible woman. So what do your friends advise and how will you choose from such a lot?"

"They hope I will choose someone young and handsome, and they do not care if he is interested only in my fortune."

"Surely you will not heed those two!"

"I am not really interested in a buck years younger than myself and I do not care if my husband is handsome or not." She stared at the blanket. Sir Rex was also handsome— sometimes she thought him excessively so.

He calmed. "I hope you will remain this sensible in the face of a charming rake who whispers his undying devotion in your ear—appearing to mean his every word, when every word is insincere."

"I doubt I will be fooled, Sir Rex," she said, their gazes once again meeting.

"I must warn you, Lady Harrington," he finally said.

"Why?"

"Because in spite of what you may think, I am a gentleman." He flushed. "You are a ripe mark for every scheming rogue. You do not need a husband who will waste your fortune instead of guarding it. And even if there is some amusement the first year or two, he will cause you years of grief afterward. The kind of rogue I am referring to, will spend every cent and penny and then wander when he wishes."

She stared and he stared back. "I am aware of that scenario," she finally said.

"Good." He poured more wine for himself, appearing somewhat angry.

She was aware of how terrible a mismatch could be. "Do you care to offer your advice?"

He did not look away, his dark stare shockingly intense. "I advise you to cast your net outside the current pool," he said instantly. "The kind of gentleman you are looking for will not step forward. He will consider himself beneath you—and he will consider stepping forward, considering your wealth and his lack thereof, beneath him."

She had never received better advice, she thought. He was right. She must discard all 228 suitors and find new ones. And was this the reason Sir Rex hadn't come forward?

Her heart hammered yet a third time, which she could not comprehend. Of course this was the reason—he was not a fortune hunter—and he would never put himself in the position of appearing to be one.

On the other hand, that didn't mean, had she possessed more modest means, that he would step forward, either. And she hardly wished for him to court her! She had recovered from seeing him in such a private encounter, and she certainly admired a great many qualities he possessed, but he was far too manly for a woman like herself.

Blanche realized she was breathless. This was the crux of the matter. It was far more significant than her being a society hostess, and him being a country recluse. She hadn't even been kissed and Sir Rex was clearly a man with huge appetites and vast experience. They would never get on.

"You haven't eaten," he said.

Blanche picked up her plate, aware that her hand trembled. She was careful to avoid Sir Rex's regard now. "Thank you. I think I will follow your advice," she said. "Or at least attempt to do so."

SHE WAS NEVER going to sleep now.

Blanche stood at the window in her bedroom, the night sky sparkling with stars, the ocean gleaming black and silver. Because of the late luncheon, Sir Rex had taken a light repast in his study while he went over his paperwork, and she had taken a tray to her room. It was almost midnight, and she had been tossing and turning for at least an hour, entirely preoccupied with her host.

She must discard all of her current suitors; she had made up her mind because such advice was inherently right. But then what?

Should she consider Sir Rex as a prospective husband, after all?

And why, at his age, was he still unattached?

She listened to the ocean's roar, but was not soothed. No amount of cold ocean air could cool her cheeks. So much had happened in the past day and a half, she felt as if she had been gone for a year. Her world felt entirely different now, as if she had been poised on a precipice, and one false step would lead to a vast fall. It was so unnerving.

But hadn't she dreamed of a day when her heart would race, when she would feel something other than calm and peace?

She just hadn't anticipated that day ever coming, and then being filled with so much confusion. Sir Rex had somehow tilted her world, making her feel uncertain and unsettled. But it was better than her world being so perfectly flat and even that she never missed a stride, wasn't it?

If they had separate bedrooms, Sir Rex might be the right choice for a husband. He would honestly and meticulously manage her fortune and her estates. They seemed to enjoy one another and were becoming friends, and Blanche knew that the few successful marriages in town were based on a deep affection. Still, she had many reservations about him. His drinking worried her. That display of arms worried her even more. Whatever had happened in the war, it haunted him and was causing him great unhappiness. She would dismiss his reclusive nature; he could come and go in town as he pleased. The truth of the matter was that his virility caused her the most hesitation.

He obviously had extreme needs. She had none. He undoubtedly required a passionate partner, and Blanche knew that woman was not herself. Many couples had separate bedrooms. However, if they had separate bedrooms, he would wish for a mistress, and of course, she would have to look the other way, with absolute indifference. She would be indifferent, wouldn't she? And what about children?

She was jumping ahead of herself. She was considering Sir Rex as a candidate, in spite of the reservations she had about him. And she still didn't know why he remained a bachelor, and she certainly didn't know if he might be persuaded to enter a union with her even if she decided to ask him for one.

And if she did tender a proposal, and he accepted, then what?

Anne had wept in pleasure in his arms. She had wept in ecstasy and it had been shocking. The rapture on Sir Rex's face had been even more shocking.

Blanche turned from the window. Not too long ago, she had been immune to a handsome face. But Sir Rex had always made her look up when he entered a room, and now, he made her heart race. Was she finally becoming aware of a man?

Was this desire? Blanche tried to imagine what she would do and how she would feel if he actually touched her, not a polite grasp upon her elbow, but a tender caress. And just considering that made her heart beat harder, made her skin tighten and tingle, and that odd little ache began anew.

Her color had increased. She could feel heat in her cheeks. *She wouldn't mind him taking her hand, or even his attempting to kiss her.*

Blanche sat down abruptly, stunned. She was almost twenty-eight years old, and for the first time in her life, she was aware of a man and thinking of his kisses. How had this happened?

She took a moment to clear her mind. Attraction and desire were not good reasons to marry. She was never going to sleep now. She decided she wished for a brandy. She would make a list of pros and cons tomorrow. There was no rush. She had waited this long to marry, and she had to make the right choice.

She opened the armoire and pulled out the dress she had worn that day. She shed her nightclothes, as she was not about to wander about Sir Rex's home dressed for bed, and slipped on a chemise and the pale gray gown.

As Blanche left her chamber, she glanced at the closed doors she passed. Unless the master suite was in the tower, one of those doors belonged to her host. She realized, as she tiptoed in her slippers down the hall, that she was tense now and straining to hear. But the hall was so silent she could have heard a hairpin drop.

The great hall was empty when she came downstairs, the fire in the hearth dying to a small, flickering flame and glowing embers. Two wall sconces had been left on, but both were by the front door, leaving the great room in dancing shadows. Blanche went to the bar cart, stumbling into a footstool in the process. It clattered as it skidded away from her shin and she winced, hoping she hadn't woken anyone up.

She saw several decanters on the cart and poured the one she thought was brandy. Then she realized she was being watched.

Blanche turned and saw Sir Rex seated on the sofa, so indolently he might have been asleep. But he wasn't asleep. In spite of the shadows, his gaze was unwavering upon her and he was very much awake. In the firelight, his dark eyes had turned gold and amber, and were as watchful as a lion's.

She froze but her heart leaped.

He slowly sat upright, reaching for his crutch, which he'd laid on the floor. He had shed his jacket and waistcoat, and was wearing only the ruffled lawn shirt with his trousers and shoe. But it was unbuttoned almost to the navel.

She stared, knowing she must not, but she couldn't force her gaze to move upward. He reminded her of Michelangelo's sculpture of David.

He stood. "Lady Harrington?"

She finally jerked her gaze to his face. "You must think me a secretive drinker," she said hoarsely.

He swung forward. "I think no such thing. You are trembling. Are you ill?"

She shook her head, careful not to glance at the two sculpted slabs of his chest. She didn't have to; the memory was engraved on her mind. "I can't sleep. I thought a brandy might help."

With one hand, his gaze relentless, he buttoned his shirt, but only to the hollow of his chest. "You are welcome to all the brandy you wish," he said softly, the firelight playing over his face. "But that is port you have poured."

"I am afraid I did not realize the difference."

"Allow me," he said, moving closer.

And Blanche's tension escalated. She really didn't want him to come closer, because his presence was so powerful and agitating. He took the glass from her and set it down, standing so close she now smelled his cologne—it was the ocean blended with the woods and something slightly citrus. And it was man. His arm brushed her as he handed her the drink.

"Thank you for being kind."

His gaze settled on her mouth, then moved back to her eyes. "Do you wish to talk about what is disturbing you?"

She didn't know what to say. It was hard to think. Her mind was racing, and trying to comprehend her every unsettled feeling. This moment was too daringly intimate. She realized that her racing heart and trembling limbs were evidence of desire. But she was afraid as well as excited. She felt as if she had been suspended over a cliff by an unraveling rope.

And when she dared to meet his eyes, she flinched and her heart pounded even more rapidly. His dark gaze smoldered in a way she had never seen before.

"The fresh air," he said, "usually puts one to sleep." And his thick, dark lashes lowered.

Blanche knew she should either converse lightly or go back to her room. She was utterly confused now and it did not help matters that Sir Rex might be a candidate for her hand. But she couldn't think of a thing to say when polite conversation had always been second nature for her. And worse, she could not bring herself to leave the hall. Her slippers felt glued to the floor.

"In the candlelight," he said softly, "you appear as innocent as a girl of fifteen."

Her heart erupted into a thunderous pace. She was as inexperienced and innocent as a fifteen-year-old, she thought. She was as timid and as anxious as a girl of fifteen! But he could not know that. "I will soon be twenty-eight."

He gave her an odd, sidelong look. It was as if he said, *I do not care.*

She struggled with herself. He was unusually loquacious, and maybe this was an opportune moment after all. "Why do you remain awake, Sir Rex? It must be close to midnight."

His dark gaze met hers. He did not look as if he was inclined to answer.

And suddenly she realized he must be waiting for his lover. She felt her cheeks fire. "I am sorry; I will leave!" She turned to run.

He caught her wrist. "You are not intruding."

She was somehow turned back around.

"If you cannot sleep, we can share our insomnia together," he added softly, releasing her.

Her wrist burned. An odd tension filled her body. A part of her did not wish to go; he was simply too compelling. This was what she had hoped for, wasn't it? Except, she had dreamed of someone less disturbing, someone far lighter in nature, someone not inherently threatening.

And the sensible part of her knew she must flee before it was too late—because that rope was unraveling—she could feel it. Sir Rex was too dark. But her feet did not move, not even an inch.

A long moment passed.

"Do you suffer from insomnia often?" she breathed, clutching the glass to her bosom.

A beautiful smile flitted across his face. "It depends."

It took her a moment to decipher his meaning. Somehow, she envisioned him with Anne and knew that if she were not his guest, he would be in bed with her now. Her heart thundering, even her ears feeling hot, she quickly said, "I really must go to bed."

"Don't."

Blanche froze.

"Please," he added. "I do not mind the company," he said softly, sending her another astonishing glance. "I like it."

She trembled. Was he inebriated? Or was he being terribly bold and frank? "I have been enjoying your company, as well, Sir Rex," she said as lightly as possible.

He seemed amused, in a heavy-lidded way.

She swallowed and tried to find a suitable topic of conversation, a nearly impossible task, given the hour and the circumstance. "I envy you this place."

His smile reappeared, wry but achingly beautiful. "How can you, the lady of Harrington Hall, envy me Land's End?"

"Perhaps for exactly that reason…it is the end of the world. I have no privacy at home. I am enjoying the solitude here."

"How long will you stay?"

And that melodic tone stirred her flesh in ways she had never before experienced, as if a spring breeze had drifted beneath her skirts. "I don't know. I can hardly impose."

"And if I wish for you to impose?"

She started and their gazes locked.

"Maybe I will confess," he said slowly, and she tensed in anticipation, "that it can be lonely here."

She was stunned. *Sir Rex was lonely.* But she had sensed that, and now, it was confirmed. Her compassion swelled. "You should come to town more often."

His lashes fluttered, hiding his eyes. He murmured, as if he hadn't heard her, "You do not have to decide this minute."

Her mind raced. He had been awarded the estate. So in a way, he hadn't chosen this life at all. But he had chosen to avoid town. And why, oh why, did he remain without a wife?

"Blanche?" he murmured.

She faced him, aware of his intimate and silken use of her name. She knew he had not realized the slip.

"I realize we do not meet your standards here," he added softly. "But if you tell me what you require, I will move heaven and earth to please you." He smiled slowly again, his gaze roaming her face before drifting to the mere edge of her bodice, where it lifted.

He meant it, she realized, feeling dazed. But why would he want to accommodate her so fully? "You do meet my standards!" Her passion shocked her. She didn't know where such emotion had come from. "I love—I like Land's End, very much. I should like to stay on...a bit longer." She was going to ask him, she decided, very boldly and improperly, why he was not wed.

"Midnight is always the best time for confessions."

"Do you have another one?" She could not imagine what he might confess next.

His smile flickered. "You have seen me in my worst light, yet you do not run for the woods. You do not even run from my great room—or from me."

She licked her lips now. What should she say to that? And was he going to converse about his afternoon affair?

"You have an amazing grace, Lady Harrington. I sense you are thinking about running, even now."

He was right. She breathed hard. "It is just odd...I have never conversed with a gentleman like this, at such an hour. It is very...intimate."

His gaze narrowed, assessing her. "This is intimate?"

Blanche laughed nervously. "You know I am impossibly proper," she said. And prudish, she added silently.

His regard was searching. "Why have you stayed? Why didn't you run away yesterday?"

She inhaled, trembling. And her memory of his tryst loomed, graphic and vivid. "You have every right to your private...affairs."

A long moment passed. "Have I just shattered your composure—again?"

"My composure," she said thickly, barely able to breathe, "vanished yesterday. I am not sure I ever retrieved it."

He stared, his eyes lingering on her throat, where she knew her pulse was visibly pounding. "Then your pretense has been admirable. I am distressing you yet again. I never meant to distress you. I am ashamed that you know the truth about me."

She started, wide-eyed. "Have you been drinking, Sir Rex?"

A very beautiful smile formed. "I am entirely foxed."

This explained those long smoldering stares and his shocking confessions. He didn't desire her, not really—he was inebriated. But what was not explained was his need to find inebriation.

"What? No gentle persuasion that I must retire…no gentle reprobation for such overindulgence? No obvious scorn, no mocking disdain?"

Blanche folded her arms to her chest. "You know me well enough to know I am not malicious or unkind. And the truth is—" she hesitated "—you have every right to your love affairs." She was aware of turning red. "Unlike others, you are not deceiving a spouse."

His eyes glittered. "I would have never imagined having such a discussion with you. And I was referring to my excessive fondness for wine and whiskey."

She avoided all eye contact now. "I mean—" she breathed hard "—of course you may sit up at night, enjoying a glass of wine!" *Ask him,* she cried silently. *Just do it!*

"That isn't what you said. So you refuse to condemn my affair…. It is not a love affair, but you do know that."

His candor was shocking. She didn't know what to say. Nervously she whispered, "I have no wish to condemn you."

A silence fell.

He stared so interminably she began to squirm. "Why do

I have this unshakable feeling, that there is something you wish to say—or ask?"

Dear God, he was too perceptive! "I have been wondering," she breathed, "but really, I hardly wish to be impertinent…I think I should return to my room!"

He grasped her wrist, and his gaze intensified. "Now I am intrigued. You can speak freely, you can ask me anything," he said very softly. "Come, it is midnight, we are alone, confessing our most intimate thoughts and desires."

She struggled as he stared. "Why haven't you taken a wife?"

His eyes widened. "That is what you wish to ask me?"

She simply nodded.

And he glanced away, his long dark lashes fanning out on his high cheekbones. "You already know the answer."

Blanche was breathless. She did not know the answer, not at all.

"The de Warenne men marry for love—or so it is claimed."

CHAPTER SIX

SHE WAS STUNNED. Her mind repeated what he had said, again and again—he would marry for love. It was romantic. Sir Rex was a romantic. He hadn't married because he was waiting for love.

"You seem surprised—and dismayed."

She smiled brightly. "I am surprised. I hadn't thought you to be as romantic as the rest of your family."

"Should I be insulted?"

"No!" she cried. "Of course not, you are the last man I should ever wish to insult."

He started, unsmiling. Then, "I am surprised that you would give my wedded life—or lack thereof—a single thought," he said smoothly.

She helplessly shrugged. "I recently chatted with your mother and Lizzie. The subject of your bachelor status came up."

A gleam entered his eyes. "Really? And did you participate in the conversation?"

She tensed. "They care for you, Sir Rex. Obviously they wish to see you wed and with a family of your own."

"And you agree?"

"I am thinking that you will soon find your lady love," she said lightly.

He made a harsh sound. "Love is highly overrated."

She was simply stunned. "But you said—"

"I am drunk," he said. "And by the way, I did not find your question impertinent."

"Then I am fortunate," she said, her mind racing. What had Sir Rex just meant?

"I believe it is my turn to ask you another question." His gaze was bold.

Blanche stiffened. "Are we playing a game now?"

His smile returned, terribly lazy. "Why not? You have asked me for my advice. What if I ask you for yours?"

She felt as if they were sparring. She had to find a seat; it was that or collapse, and she took the closest chair. "I should return the favor," she said thickly.

"Is there a reason I must cater to the women in my family?"

She tried to comprehend him. "Everyone is better off with a family," she finally said, feeling as if he were somehow circling round her and coming closer and closer.

"So I am better off married to a harpy or a shrew?"

She knew she flushed. Now what did she say? "You might find love—as the proclivity runs in your family."

"Perhaps I am the exception to the rule," he said smoothly, "or, perhaps I already have."

Her heart lurched.

His expression became hard and bitter. "Love is highly, vastly, grossly and absurdly overrated." He limped away.

She simply sat there, gaping. Sir Rex had a broken heart. And it explained *everything*.

Then he whirled, effortlessly. He smiled, but coolly now. He was no longer seductive; he seemed angry. "What really kept you awake tonight?"

His abrupt change in mood disturbed her. "A dream," she said instantly. Heat crept into her cheeks as she was not inclined to telling lies, even harmless, white ones.

He knew; she saw it in his slow smile of amusement. "I hope it was a good dream."

She did not like his seductive tone or what it implied. She made certain to look past him, so he would never guess she had been debating her future marriage—and considering him as a prospect. And what should she do now? She could barely comprehend that his heart was scarred, and perhaps, broken.

"And who were you dreaming of?"

"Sir Rex!" she gasped.

"I thought so." He seemed satisfied, but cool. "You are an extraordinary woman—I have always thought so. I used to simply accept the fact that you are one of the rare and true ladies of the ton, but recently, I have wondered about you."

She decided he was very drunk. And she did not like this turn. "I must retire for the night," she said quickly.

"You are a great lady, but you are human. You have red blood in your veins, like everyone else. Like us all, you dream. I cannot help wondering what you dream of—and who you dream of." He took one step closer. He did not seem drunk, yet he had to be, for he never would ask such a question otherwise. Worse, his gaze was terribly intent.

She failed to breathe. And finally, "Sir Rex, I am discomfited!"

"Because I am a boor—a drunken boor. Come, do not deny it, I am aware of what they say behind my back, just as you are. Why, Blanche? Why have you chosen to stay here for two nights, when you could have stayed, out of sheer necessity, for one single one? We both know I shocked you yesterday. If I ever had your admiring regard, it was forever lost." His expression was twisted and odd. "But you said you had no wish to insult me, so I am beyond confusion! In fact, your exact words were, 'I am the last man you wish to insult.' Is that a gracious pretense, Lady Blanche? For you could not mean such words."

Blanche realized she was emphatically shaking her head. "I have always admired you, Sir Rex."

He stared at her, allowing a huge silence to fill the great room.

"So please, do not presume to know my thoughts."

"Are you sincere?" he demanded.

"Yes!" She bit her lip mistakenly and tasted blood. "I am so impressed by your industrious and resourceful character! I never expected such a well-run, well-kempt estate!"

His eyes widened.

"Your help today at Penthwaithe was so generous. You are a generous and noble man!"

"But I am sleeping with my serving maid."

She clasped her hands to her flaming cheeks. "It is not my affair—and I would have never known if I hadn't intruded, and I so regret that lapse!"

After a moment, he demanded, "How can I recover a small modicum of your respect?"

She felt moisture gathering in her eyes, which shocked her. But she could not stop now. "You have my respect. I do not know the details of your life, but I feel certain you have remained in some pain, not entirely physical, from the war. I sense, strongly, that pain causes you moments like these—and your affairs." And she would add his broken heart to the equation, too.

He stared at her, a terrible silence falling.

She put her glass down and hugged herself, near tears, when she never wept, and so dismayed and distressed she was shaking. When the silence continued, she had to look at him. She wasn't certain she had ever seen a man as grim and unhappy.

"You are right," he said flatly. "Is there anything I might do which would cause you to criticize me?"

She shook her head. "It is not my nature to criticize anyone, and I will certainly not begin by criticizing you." She took a trembling breath. "But I might suggest you remove the display of arms from your wall."

His eyes widened.

"But you wish to torture yourself with a constant reminder of your pain—whatever it is—do you not?"

He made a harsh sound. "You are shockingly astute."

"I know you are a hero. Everyone knows you saved the Duke of Clarewood's second son from death—and Mowbray is now the duke, himself. Heroes deserve respect not censor. Heroes deserve approval and affection."

"I am not a hero," he said harshly. "For if I had to do it all over again—if Mowbray lay there, close to death, I would leave him to the devil."

She cried out, "You cannot mean it!"

He was shaking. She saw him grapple with huge emotions, emotions she could not understand. "You know a lot about me, Lady Harrington."

She realized he was suddenly, dangerously annoyed. Her tension escalated wildly. It was time to leave. She said, "Everyone knows that much about you, Sir Rex."

"My family knows I rescued Mowbray—no one else recalls it."

"You recall it." The moment the words slipped, she wished she had not spoken.

He turned furiously away—losing his balance.

Blanche cried out, racing to him, but as she caught his arm they crashed together into the wall. And for one instant, she was in his arms. In that instant, his entire hard body pressed her against the wall and her fear for his becoming injured vanished. He was so large that she was engulfed by a mass of muscle—making her aware of being vulnerable and small and so terribly female. She had never been in a man's arms, not like this. A shocking tremor passed through her loins. Stunned, she looked up—and found him staring at her mouth.

And in that moment, she realized that Rex de Warenne wanted her.

In that moment, she realized that Rex de Warenne, the most virile man she knew, was going to kiss her.

Excitement and fear merged helplessly. For this was truly desire.

But he did not bend over her and press his mouth to hers. He gave her a very dark look instead, swinging a step away from her, breathing hard.

Blanche leaned on the wall, incapable of movement, suddenly trembling again. Her knees felt useless, and that stabbing continued, although fainter now, like the pinpricks of needles in her suddenly swollen flesh.

"There is a saying. One does not confront the lion in his den."

It took her a moment. "I came downstairs for a drink. I did not expect for you to be here." She somehow met his eyes and was shocked to find them blazing with anger.

"Yes, just as you walked into my study yesterday."

She flamed. "I…"

"Confront the beast and you will get bitten," he cried, frustration written all over his face.

She tensed, dismayed. But he was right. She had been asking terribly intimate questions and offering advice on his most private affairs. She deserved his anger, but not to this extent. "I am sorry." She turned to go—the night had become a disaster.

He suddenly barred her way. His face terribly close to hers, impossibly beautiful, he demanded, "So tell me, really, truthfully, the thought of which young stud has kept you up tonight? Which paragon of manhood do you really wish to wed—and bed? It is your turn to confess, Blanche," he purred.

She was aghast. No man had ever spoken to her with such anger—and somehow, she knew that desire was wrapped up in his rage and frustration. It crossed her mind that she could blurt out that she was considering him as a possible husband—

with separate bedrooms, of course. "I will make a sensible decision," she gasped.

"Without any romantic consideration?" He demanded.

"I will choose sensibly," she cried.

He made a harsh sound. "You deserve more."

Her eyes widened.

"I am foxed so I will tell you exactly what I think. You deserve an honest man, a man with innately good character." His eyes blazed. "You deserve a man who will admire you, defend you, respect you…and cherish you."

What diatribe was this? She gasped.

He reached up—and stroked his fingers against her cheek. Blanche went still. Panic assailed her—and so did the needle-like pricking of desire. "You deserve a man who can make your heart race—and who will make you weep in pleasure."

She failed to breathe.

He dropped his hand. "I wish you luck in finding your paragon of manhood."

Blanche cried out.

Sir Rex left.

SIR REX HAD ALMOST KISSED HER.

Blanche stared at her tea, which was cold. She sat alone at the breakfast table, recalling every moment of the previous evening in utter detail, her heart fluttering uncomfortably in her chest. Sir Rex had been inebriated, brazen, far too masculine and terribly bold. He had a broken heart, he was haunted by the war, and he thought she deserved admiration, respect and passion.

You deserve a man who can make your heart race—and who will make you weep in pleasure.

Blanche was so dismayed she reached for her cup, and her hand trembled so badly that the china rattled. She quickly set it down. She was not capable of the kind of passion he had referred to.

How could he have said such a thing to her?

How could she have said all the things she had said to him?

Blanche stared at her ice-cold tea. She had never been so confused. She was so sad for Sir Rex. She was overflowing with compassion, but there was no way to offer it. He was not a child whom she could embrace and caress.

Last night he had kept sending her those dark, smoldering glances.

Last night he had been on the verge of kissing her.

She did not have to be experienced to know it. But he had been terribly drunk. His attraction came from the bottle, not from any real desire, didn't it?

She trembled wildly. Last night she had wanted his kiss! And it hadn't been mere curiosity.

She was never going to forget that brief moment in his arms, when she had been overwhelmed by his power, his masculinity and his strength. She had been stunned and afraid; there had even been panic, but Blanche now understood desire. Her body had ached with it.

After all these years of believing she would never feel passion, the womanly part of her had finally awoken. How could this be happening? Sir Rex was not for her and last night had shown her that. He was dark, dangerously, frighteningly so. His virility was equally as threatening. He had many wonderful qualities, but these were overshadowed by his torment and male nature. She must cross him off her list of one, mustn't she?

What if he had kissed her?

If she stayed on at Bodenick a bit longer, would he kiss her?

Blanche didn't know what to do and what to think. She could accept the astonishing fact that she was interested in a kiss. It was about time. Bess and Felicia would encourage her. But what if it led to something else, something more?

Wanting a kiss in the dark of the night was entirely different from wanting passion fulfilled. And she wasn't the kind
of a woman to take a lover, especially not now, when she was
trying to find a husband. The best thing, she decided, would
be to leave Land's End immediately. Before one thing led to
another, before there was any more intimacy, before there
was no way out.

But couldn't Sir Rex take those weapons off the wall
before she left?

If she had her way, if she could help him at all, she would
get rid of that display so he might eventually forget the war
and whatever ghosts were haunting him. And who was the
woman who had broken his heart?

Lizzie had once said, very proudly, that when the de
Warenne men fell in love, it was once and forever. Blanche
believed it. She knew the family so well. She had watched
Tyrell's love for Lizzie blossom after she had broken off the
betrothal, and it was still in full bloom, years later. She had
heard the shocking news when Eleanor had been abducted at
the altar by Sean O'Neill, and their romance continued
unabated. Two years ago Cliff de Warenne, the most eligible
bachelor in the ton, and the most notorious one, had come
home with a homeless pirate's daughter—only to marry her.
While still in the royal navy, Devlin O'Neill had defied the
admiralty and abducted Virginia to gain revenge on his
enemy—and they were now in Paris on their ninth anniversary. They adored each other as much as ever. And of course
there was the earl and the countess.

Sir Rex was going to pine for some paragon of womanhood
until the day he died, she thought. And she was so saddened
for him. He deserved so much more than the hand life had
dealt him. Now she began to realize why he toiled so endlessly.
In the light of day, he left his ghosts behind through hard
labor, and at night, with his bottle of wine or brandy.

She should probably leave Land's End, and focus on a proper list of suitors who were interested in more than her fortune, but she had to do *something* before she left, something to make Sir Rex's life easier and even, perhaps, to infuse it with some joy.

A shadow fell across the dining hall. Blanche tensed.

She did not have to look up to know that Sir Rex stood on the threshold. His presence was huge. In that instant, her blood raced and she became breathless and she forgot his demons, instead recalling being in his arms with utter clarity.

She summoned a smile, hoped she was not flushing, and looked carefully up at him.

His gaze was terribly, uncomfortably direct. He also appeared no worse for wear, and she would have never guessed that he had been foxed last night. "Good morning. I am surprised to see you." He flushed.

Blanche couldn't speak. Her heart fluttered madly as she stared into his eyes, which shimmered with remorse and regret. He recalled their conversation last night. She wished he had not. She looked at his mouth, which was pressed in a firm line. But no amount of tension could change the perfect bow or the fullness of his lips. "Good morning," she managed, hoping he would not continue on with this subject. "It is a lovely morning," she began firmly.

"I hadn't noticed." His stare did not waver and he was clearly determined. "I realize I have committed yet another unpardonable offense, or rather, a series of them." The pink stain on his cheekbones deepened.

She bit her lip. He looked so unhappy and clearly, he was condemning himself yet again. "Sir Rex," she offered, "shall I pour tea for you?"

He made a harsh sound. "I thought you would have already left, but I realize you are leaving now—I saw your coachman readying the team. I must offer my sincere apologies once again.

You have suffered the rudest remarks possible—as well as brazen behavior. I had no right to address you as I did. I had no right—" he hesitated, and she could not look away "—to toy with you."

Her heart slammed. His words should have been rude, but they were not—they conveyed too much sensuality. Had he "toyed" with her last night? Had he intended to discomfit her with his aggressive sexuality?

"I didn't realize," she managed, very undone now, "that the honest conversation we shared was something else for you."

"Didn't you?" His gaze blazed. Then, "There is no adequate excuse to make for my behavior."

Blanche knew a terrible distress. She stood, trembling. "The truth is that I should not have intruded last night." She found her voice and was firm. "This is your home. You have every right to enjoy your great room after supper."

"You are my guest. You had every right to join me. I asked you to stay—or do you not recall it?"

She tensed, wanting to defend him. "Please, Sir Rex. Do not castigate yourself. I haven't given last night a single thought." And as she lied, she felt her cheeks flame.

He stared darkly, with disbelief, and she knew he did not believe her.

She looked at her teacup. "We had an unusual conversation." She inhaled. "It was remarkable—refreshing, nothing else." And she glanced up.

His gaze widened. "Surely you do not believe that. Surely you will condemn me now."

"There is nothing to condemn. Bess and I discuss all kinds of subjects. She is very frank—shockingly so, at times." She managed a smile when she was so nervous her knees were weak.

"I am not Bess."

"Friends speak frankly. I am certain you meant to advise

me, not offend me. You did not offend me," she added with conviction. "I have never had a male friend before."

"A male friend," he repeated flatly. "I am now a male friend?"

She hesitated.

Very slowly, he said, "You are impossibly gracious. You set an example everyone—ladies and gentlemen—should follow."

She blushed, terribly thrilled by his praise. "Not really."

"I am more certain than ever that your kindness is without peer. I wish I had let you enjoy your nightcap alone."

She bit her lip, as she had last night. "You wished for company. That is not unusual, Sir Rex."

She saw recollection flare in his eyes and he glanced aside—she felt certain he was remembering confessing to her that he was lonely. Her heart ached for him now. He was lonely—he needed a true friend. "Besides," she said softly, "did I not offend you? I also pried. And I did so deliberately, Sir Rex, and you cannot deny it. Perhaps I should be the one to apologize to you for my behavior?"

He emitted a short, harsh laugh. Incredulous, he shook his head. "Once again, you try to turn the tables and make your behavior seem faulty. You are trying to spare my feelings."

She dared, "I meant what I said last night. You are a good and honorable man. I have always and will always hold you in high esteem."

He started. "I feel as if we have somehow survived another storm, one of hurricane proportions."

She smiled, relieved. "So do I."

He finally smiled, but briefly, his gaze searching. "So we will part company on good terms?"

Blanche stared into his dark, enigmatic eyes and realized she didn't want to leave. Not today, anyway. Maybe tomorrow she would feel differently. "We have known one another for a very long time."

"Yes, we have. It has been eight years."

Her heart jumped. Why did he remember the date? "I do not wish to jeopardize our friendship."

"Neither do I," he said instantly. His intense tone startled her.

But she smiled. "Besides, friends often share their secrets."

He sent her a sidelong glance, not quite as potent as the night before, but a stare direct and probing enough to make her breathless. "I believe it was one-sided."

She flushed. "Perhaps. Sir Rex, it is a blessing to have a true confidante."

"Women are different. Men do not speak as openly—unless under the influence." And finally, she saw his guarded stance shift and relax slightly. "But apparently I am forgiven."

"There is *nothing* to forgive." It was odd, but she meant it. She shrugged, but was aware of miraculously having passed onto safer ground.

Until he smiled disarmingly at her. "Do you have secrets that you wish to share?"

She started, and knew she had paled. *If she ever changed her mind, if she ever approached him for marriage, she would have to reveal the truth about her defective nature.*

His eyes were wide. Then he turned aside. "Obviously you do not. " A pause ensued. "I'll have Anne ready a meal for your trip back to town."

She tensed. They had just agreed upon an odd friendship—how could she go? Had Rex needed a true friend even half as much as Bess and Felicia needed her, she wouldn't hesitate to stay. "Are you asking me to leave? If I have overstayed my welcome, I understand."

He started. "I have assumed you were preparing to depart."

"I was planning to go into Lanhadron. The Johnson boys were barefoot and so was the little girl. I really hadn't thought about my eventual return to town." And she smiled directly at him. "Now I must confess, in broad daylight. I am not ready to return to the hordes of suitors at Harrington Hall, Sir Rex. I dread the choice I will eventually make." And she smiled again, hoping he would let her stay. If she had known how to bat her eyelashes at him, she would have done so.

His intense gaze made her feel as small and feminine as she had last night. "I cannot say I blame you. There is obviously no rush. Your fortune will hardly vanish overnight and therefore, neither will your slew of suitors." His gaze became bland. "You are welcome to stay on as long as you like."

She wondered if he truly meant it. "If I ever become an imposition…" she began.

He held up his left hand. "You could never impose."

Her heart leaped and then raced. He could be as gallant as the best of them, she thought. "Thank you. I should love to stay on a bit longer."

He gave her another long, searching glance, one that made her tremble.

Why was she dismissing him as a candidate for marriage? In that moment, it was so unclear. In that single moment, his flaws seemed irrelevant. What seemed relevant was the way he kept looking at her, and the odd and insistent dance in her heart.

His gaze moved to her mouth. "I have a meeting in the village at noon. If you will wait another hour, I will be delighted to escort you."

Blanche murmured how lovely that would be.

CHAPTER SEVEN

HER HEART FEELING strangely light, Blanche handed her purchases for the Johnson family to her coachman. "Have you seen Sir Rex, Clarence?"

"I am afraid not, my lady."

She had been shopping in the quaint village for close to two hours, and she had even purchased a new hat in the haberdashery. She hadn't seen Sir Rex leave the meeting he was attending in the village church. He had ridden into the town on horseback, so there was no pressing reason to wait for him, but she wanted to do just that.

She kept thinking about their conversation that morning, and the odd friendship that had arisen from the ashes of last night's encounter. She kept thinking about Sir Rex's character, both his attributes and his flaws. No one was perfect. She was hardly perfect. Her flaws made his seem delightful.

She wished Bess could come down to Land's End. She so needed her advice. But she knew what Bess would say and do, at least partly. She would encourage Blanche to rush into Rex's arms and experience her newfound passion.

Blanche blushed. The more she thought about it, the more she knew she wouldn't mind a kiss.

"My lady?" a woman asked uncertainly.

Blanche turned. The young woman who had addressed her had been shopping in the haberdashery, too. Blanche had been aware of her indiscreet glances earlier, while she had been purchasing her hat. "Hello," she returned pleasantly.

The plump brunette curtsied, her cheeks red. "I pray I am not offending you," she cried, "but I couldn't help overhearing that you are a guest at Land's End."

Blanche's attention was riveted now. "Yes, I am an old family friend. I am Lady Blanche Harrington," she said carefully. The village was small, the size of no more than two London streets, and in such a town, everyone probably knew or knew of everyone else. What did this young woman want?

She curtsied again. "I am Margaret Farrow. My husband and I are Sir de Warenne's neighbors."

Blanche's surprise crested. "Then I am very pleased to meet you," she said seriously. This was so opportune, she thought. She now noted that the flushed and breathless woman seemed to have a pleasing look in her eye, never mind her nervousness. She did not seem frivolous or vain; she seemed like a young gentlewoman of both good character and some means.

Relief covered Margaret's face. "We live but a half hour from the castle, you know. I just thought that visitors are so scarce and I should meet you."

"So you must be well acquainted with Sir Rex," Blanche said, her interest keen.

Her eyes wide, Margaret hesitated. "I'm afraid not."

How was that possible? Blanche wondered. "I know he does not care to entertain, but you are close neighbors, so surely you are acquainted," she said.

Margaret flushed. "I married Mr. Farrow five years ago and we have never been invited to the castle. We invited him to Torrence Hall a few times, just after we were wed, but he declined the invitations."

Blanche was disbelieving.

"But we admire Sir Rex, very much! We know he prefers

to keep to himself. He is a very civic-minded gentleman. He has done great deeds for the parish."

It was shocking, Blanche thought, that Sir Rex had not invited his closest neighbors to dine, and that he had failed to accept even a single invitation from them. Blanche had to defend him. "He is lacking a hostess and has admitted it." She smiled. "Once he marries, which he will inevitably do, he will begin to entertain. He was probably in London when he received your invitations. He must be well acquainted with your husband, however. Surely they fish and hunt?"

Margaret smiled anxiously. "We have a mine at Torrence Hill, so they do have some matters in common, like the meeting today. But otherwise, they do not know one another and they have never gamed together, not to my knowledge. But I have only been in the parish these five years," she added in haste.

Blanche felt as if she were reeling. This young woman was of a very pleasing disposition. Was her husband an ogre, then? It was more likely that her host was the ogre, she thought grimly.

He was lonely. He had confessed. Well, there was certainly a way to do something about that.

"Sir Rex did not tell me about the meeting."

Margaret said eagerly, "Once every month or two, Sir de Warenne asks the miners for an assembly. He is very interested in the conditions of the local mines. There are eight in the parish. We had a terrible cave-in three years ago. Ten men died that day. Ever since, Sir Rex has demanded that the mines be carefully maintained."

Blanche was not surprised that Sir Rex would wish to oversee the mines in the parish with the notion of securing the welfare of all the miners. "Yes, Sir Rex has a charitable nature."

"Oh, he does—he gives a percentage of his profits to the

hospice at St. Jude's," she said breathlessly. "And it was his idea to refurbish the old Norman church, which the village had let lapse into ruins. Our poorest families know they can always find something to eat behind his kitchens."

"Is that where the meeting is now, at the refurbished church?" Blanche found it very interesting that Margaret Farrow held Sir Rex in such high esteem, when she could have so easily held him accountable for his social failures.

Margaret pointed down the block. "It is at the end of the street. You can just see the steeple from here. Will you be with us for very long?"

"I haven't decided," Blanche said. "But I do hope our paths will cross again, and soon. Perhaps they will cross at a supper at Bodenick?"

Margaret Farrow gaped. Then she said eagerly, "Oh, we should love to come to supper. Mr. Farrow truly admires Sir Rex. He said he is a war hero—his cousin was in the 11th Light Dragoons, too, on the Peninsula."

Blanche's heart sped. "Was that Sir Rex's regiment?"

"That is what Mr. Farrow believes."

Blanche felt a moment of excitement, followed by a moment of doubt. Margaret's husband might know what haunted Sir Rex. On the other hand, Sir Rex might not care to have any discussion of the war at his supper table. She knew she must proceed with great caution. "I will plan an evening, if I can," she said frankly. "May I call you Margaret?"

"Oh! Please, do!"

"But do caution Mr. Farrow. Sir Rex does not care for talk of the war."

"Yes, I will advise him."

A moment later, the two women parted company. As there was still no sign of Sir Rex, or any miners on the street, Blanche decided to proceed to the church. She wasn't sure how she would get Sir Rex to agree to a small supper affair, but she was going to introduce him to the Farrows, one way or another. He might claim he liked living in complete isolation, but it was not conducive to his welfare, not in any way. Blanche had never so boldly interfered in anyone's life before. It was not her nature. Bess and Felicia would be shocked to know what she was planning. But she had never been more certain that what she was doing was right for Sir Rex.

Blanche had reached the small walk leading to the old stone church. And as she arrived at the front door, she heard many voices, raised and heated, arguing at once. Tension assailed her.

A huge debate raged inside. She told herself not to worry— a fervent discussion was probably common in a village meeting. She really wouldn't know, as she had never been to a village meeting of any kind. She did not especially like crowds. She had fainted at a May Day festival when she was eight years old, and at a circus a year later, and she had avoided raucous crowds—common crowds—ever since. But that had been a long time ago.

It was silly to feel uncertain now. Besides, she was very curious about the meeting—and about Sir Rex's part in it.

But from inside, someone started shouting and he was angry.

Blanche froze, suddenly afraid. The desire to turn and flee was instantaneous and overwhelming. And for one second, she recalled waking up at that May Day celebration, on the ground, in her father's arms, surrounded by a dozen farmers and their wives, fear like talons inside her. She had experienced the exact same painful feeling of fear upon awakening after her swoon at the circus, too. Those claws were in her belly now.

She tried to shake it off. There was no cause for anxiety or even panic. It was only a meeting, she reminded herself. And she did not need to avoid crowds. She had never had a problem with the crowds in a ballroom or a museum. What was wrong with her?

And suddenly she was aware of the dark, unfocused images in her mind, images she had lived with for years, ignoring them the way castellans ignored castle ghosts. But the images weren't dormant now. They were somehow demanding her attention, as if waving at her urgently, and she knew that these images were frightening and violent. Blanche felt a pain stab through her head.

What was happening? More panic began. Why did she have the terrible feeling that if she tried very hard, those images would finally become clear, after so many years of being indistinct? She had no interest in recalling that long-ago riot.

Then she heard Sir Rex speaking, calmly and quietly.

It was as if he had reached out and caught her before she fell, bringing her back to firm ground. She breathed. The clawing eased. He was a man anyone could depend on. She could certainly depend upon him now. She took a deep breath and walked up the steps and entered the end of the knave. How silly to think that the ghosts of over twenty years past might suddenly demand her attention.

Blanche glanced around. Perhaps fifty or more miners filled the church. It could not possibly be more crowded—every pew was filled and men stood in the aisles. Sir Rex stood with four other gentlemen before the altar. And the moment she espied him, he saw her, too, and their gazes met.

His surprise vanished, he smiled.

She smiled back, relieved. But it remained difficult to breathe.

And a dozen men began speaking at once. Blanche's tension not only renewed itself, it escalated wildly. She glanced around at the passionate crowd. Instantly she knew she should not have come inside.

Those jumbled dark images now danced in her mind, as if about to come forward.

What was this? What was happening? She couldn't breathe. There was no air. There was so much shouting!

Blanche felt faint. She had to escape this crowd. She reached blindly out, and her hand touched a wool-clad shoulder. She jerked away. Across the men, she looked for Sir Rex, trying not to give in to a severe panic.

"The shaft collapsed! He won't tell ye, so I will! It bloody collapsed and it's only God's will that the last man was out!" someone shouted.

A dozen furious voices began shouting out in agreement.

The ground seemed to tilt wildly. Blanche knew she had to escape before she fell or swooned.

A hand closed on hers as she turned. She met a pair of pale eyes—and saw hatred there. She screamed. For the man was leering at her, about to seize her, and there was blood everywhere.

"Blanche!"

She fought to free herself. Chaos erupted. So many bodies, so many men, she pushed and shoved and turned, but was seized from behind. It was too much. *They had taken Mama. Mama!*

"Blanche!"

Blanche staggered against the wall, imprisoned by arms that would not let her go, looking wildly at the mob. Fists pounded the air. Features became blurred. Saliva dripped from teeth and gums. Pitchforks and shovels waved.

Somehow she pulled free. She tripped on the steps and fell into the street, rocks and gravel biting through her gloves and the skin of her cheeks. *So much hatred and blood was everywhere, she was lying in it, and Mama was gone…*

She fought to breathe but it was too late. The shadows loomed over her, shadows of violence and death—and then there was only darkness.

HE LET HER GO when he realized she was out of her mind. She ran from the church and fell down the steps. In horror, he rushed after her. The men knew him and parted instantly for him. He charged outside, at an impossible speed given his handicap, and somehow crashed down the stairs and landed on one knee at her side. "Blanche!"

Rex tossed the crutch aside, pulling her into his arms. She was as white as a sheet. Her cheek was scraped.

Fear joined the horror. He found her pulse and it was strong but much too rapid. "Blanche, wake up," he said harshly.

"Sir Rex."

He realized his foreman was handing him salts. He held them to her nostrils and she coughed instantly, her lashes fluttering. He embraced her more tightly, and as her eyes opened, he became aware of a terrible relief. "It's all right," he told her quietly. "You have fainted. Lie still for a moment."

But it had been far more than that, he thought grimly. He had seen terror in her eyes.

Her blue-green eyes met his. Color began to return to her cheeks. Then she looked past him and he saw fear widen her gaze. He glanced up—every man from the assembly encircled them. "Stand back! She needs air."

The men obeyed at once.

Blanche started to sit up; he helped her. "I fainted?" she asked hoarsely.

He became aware of how intimately they were entwined. In that moment, he didn't care. He had never felt a fiercer need—and it was the urge to protect her. His grasp tightened. "It seems so. Sit still for another moment, please."

She inhaled. "I am so sorry," she began. And he saw a tear track down one cheek.

"Do not dare apologize now!" he cried. He glanced at his foreman, Jack Hardy. "Have the Harrington coach brought up."

Hardy ran off to obey.

And although worried, he smiled reassuringly at her. "Rest for a moment. Please." He removed the tear with the blunt tip of his forefinger.

She smiled weakly at him. "The church was so crowded. I couldn't seem to breathe properly."

He simply smiled. Every window had been open and there had hardly been a shortage of air. "Are you feeling better?"

She nodded; she looked better, as her coloring was now normal. "I am fine, really."

He hesitated.

"Sir." A miner held out his hand.

Rex slid his arm under Blanche and with the miner's help, stood. Someone handed him his crutch, which he instantly leaned on. He refused to release Blanche. It was impossible not to be acutely aware of how small and slender and feminine she was, tucked against him. Was she claustrophobic?

She stared at him, and then at the men milling about the church. She seemed apprehensive and anxious, but of course, she smiled.

He knew her well enough now to know when her smiles were a pretense, aimed at him, to please him. "Blanche, do you faint often?"

"No."

He did not like her reply. "I am going to summon Dr. Linney to Bodenick."

"I am fine, Sir Rex." She pulled away from him and he had to let her go. "Was it my imagination or was everyone so angry?"

He was surprised. "These discussions are usually heated. Every issue raised can be a matter of life and death. These men toil long and hard, usually for very little compensation. Yes, they are angry, and who can blame them?"

She shivered. "Will they hurt you?"

He did not understand. Was she afraid for his safety? "I pay my laborers well. I also keep my mines well lit and properly ventilated. The shafts are inspected every single week. I would rather lose profits than lives. I trust the men in my employ."

She stared as if she could not decide whether to believe him or not.

He somehow smiled at her. "It was an assembly, Lady Blanche. It was a debate. We have never had a violent confrontation, not since I opened the Bodenick mines a half a dozen years ago. The whole point of these meetings is to avoid just such a conflagration."

She shuddered again. "I thought violence was imminent," she said, low. "I thought you might be in danger—that we both might. But I imagined it?"

He saw how distressed and uncertain she was. He would have never expected Blanche Harrington to come apart this way. He had wondered what could strip away the facade, but he had never expected it to be something like this. He did what would have been unthinkable a few days ago; he laid his hand on her shoulder and clasped it, hoping to reassure her. "You imagined it," he said firmly.

She hesitated and he was aware that she was deciding whether to speak or not.

Do you have secrets that you wish to share?

She started, becoming pale.

That morning he had been very surprised to realize Blanche had a secret—or secrets. She was a perfect lady with a perfect life, and he would have never guessed. Was this her secret? Was she ashamed of her claustrophobia? For surely that was what it was.

The coach had paused on the street before the church. "You are distressed. I will ride back to Land's End with you—if you do not mind."

"Of course I do not mind. My coach is undoubtedly far more comfortable than the back of your horse."

He smiled, when he was distressed. "I have always preferred the back of a good horse."

Her smile fluttered, and it was insincere.

He helped her into the coach. When they were both seated inside the coach, his mount tied to the back, she said, "I am very sorry for causing you some alarm."

"Do not apologize for a swoon!" he exclaimed.

She met his gaze very directly. "You do know I am not hysterical."

"Of course I know that." He wasn't trying to be gallant. "I have never known a woman as level-headed as you, Blanche. You are graceful in every occasion."

She studied him searchingly, as if what he thought mattered, and then she smiled and relaxed. She turned to gaze out of her window.

He gazed out of his window, too, determined to give her some more time to recover her composure. Something was wrong. It was more than the occasional fear of a crowded room. He sensed it with every fiber of his being and he was terribly concerned.

They left the last of the village houses behind, traveling now through the moors, which were currently treeless and bland, on both side of the highway. The village being inland, they would not see the coast for another half hour, at least. The silence in the coach remained tense and awkward, but he was determined not to break it. He hated insipid conversation anyway, and Blanche seemed as absorbed with her thoughts as he was with his.

She murmured, "The clouds are gathering. Will it rain?"

"Undoubtedly." Instead of being irritated by her opening remark, he knew it was just that, an opening. Her next words proved him right.

"I owe you an explanation." Her hands fluttered on her lap. She didn't—but he wanted one. It could wait, however.

"Why don't you rest until we get to Bodenick? We can speak later, when you are feeling better."

Her cheeks were flushed. "You have told me your secrets. There is something I wish to tell you, too."

He forced a negligent expression. "You need not reveal yourself, Blanche." He was firm. "I am concerned that you fainted, but that hardly means you must bare your soul."

"I am not claustrophobic," she said harshly. "Have you not seen me at a half a dozen very crowded balls?" She barreled grimly on. "There is an issue, Sir Rex. But I hadn't realized it remained. I haven't fainted since I was nine years old."

He stiffened. What was this about?

She looked at him. "You will think me mad."

"I know you are not mad." He could not begin to imagine what she was about to divulge.

"I dislike crowds because my mother died in a crowd when I was six years old."

He hadn't known. He sat up straighter. "I am sorry."

"Balls don't bother me—everyone is so pleasant at a ball." She bit her lip. "I was with her. It was election day."

He was instantly stunned—and horrified. For election days were often days of mayhem and violence. They were an excuse for angry, impoverished mobs to form and attack the well-to-do. On election day, Harmon House had its windows boarded up, as did every one of their neighbor's. On election days, the innocent could be beaten, trampled to death, hanged. And the mobs did not discriminate between their own and the wealthy and privileged. Often the poorest were their victims, too.

Blanche smiled grimly. "Of course, I don't remember. I don't recall anything about the incident, or the day."

"It is a blessing that you cannot recall your mother's death!"

She suddenly met his gaze directly. "When I turned thirteen

years old I asked Father for the truth. He said my mother tripped and fell, hitting her head so badly, death was instantaneous." She shrugged, glancing past him now. "I do know there were many riots that day."

He did not have to be brilliant to know that her father had lied to her. He knew Blanche knew it, too. He leaned forward, reaching for her hand. It was bold and untoward, but damn it, he didn't care.

Her eyes widened as he clasped her palm. "What are you doing?"

He smiled. "I wish I had known. But your dislike and distrust of common crowds makes perfect sense." He spoke lightly. "Leave the past in the past, which is where it belongs, as you cannot change it. And do not fear the miners, Blanche. They are good and respectable men—I swear. They mean no harm to you or me or anyone."

She finally smiled.

He added seriously, "I would never let harm befall you."

Their gazes locked.

"I believe you," she said on a breath.

He became aware of the change in them both. She had confessed a very intimate detail of her life, allowing him a glimpse she had allowed to so few, just as he had done, perhaps without deliberation, last night and the afternoon of her arrival. A new and different bond had been forming between them, and it was becoming tangible now. It wasn't just a bond of respect or admiration or friendship. And he was certain she was as aware of him as a man as he was of her as a woman.

No good could come of it.

He released her hand.

BLANCHE WAS RELIEVED when Meg left her, as Sir Rex had told the maid about the fainting spell and she had been fussing incessantly. Alone, a fire now warming the bedchamber, she went to the window and stared out at the ocean. The day had turned heavy and gray and she was certain it would soon rain.

She was uneasy. She wasn't certain she should have told Sir Rex about the riot that had taken her mother's life, but she hadn't wanted him to think her a hysterical female. His admiration had become important to her. His friendship had become important to her. And why had she fainted, when she hadn't fainted since she was nine years old? Had she really had that inkling that she might remember the riot, if she tried?

The incident in the church now bewildered her thoroughly. Why had she panicked as she had? And for one moment, before her spell, she had actually seen—or imagined—men waving pitchforks.

She didn't want to remember anything about the day her mother had died. If that mob had welded pitchforks, she didn't want to know. The monsters who inhabited the depths of her mind needed to remain buried there forever. She couldn't understand why she had lost control, panicked and fainted. But she was in control now.

And Sir Rex didn't seem to think any less of her for that silly episode. She had always been proud of her genteel nature. She would hate it if he thought of her as hysterical or frivolous.

By glancing to her right, she could see a part of the coastline curving into the ocean. The black cliffs were damp and glistening, soaring powerfully high, while the ocean frothed and pounded the shore, the currents deep and dangerous. In a way, Sir Rex belonged here, she thought. He was as powerful as the ocean, as strong as the rocks, and his character had the same hidden depths. Who would have ever imagined him to be so kind and gentle?

So much had happened since her arrival the other day, she thought. Her heart no longer felt like the smooth glasslike surface of an iced-over pond; it sped and leaped and lurched in anticipation, confusion, distress, dismay and even happiness and desire. Blanche smiled at the window and hugged herself. It was a bit frightening to be so off balance, to race through so many emotions, but she didn't want to go back to that safe place where she used to dwell, either. She wasn't certain how this miracle had happened, and she was beginning to think she owed this miracle to Sir Rex.

A knock sounded.

Blanche knew who it was. She turned, smiling. "Please, enter."

Sir Rex paused on the bedroom's threshold as Meg came inside, carrying a sterling tray. Instantly their gazes locked and he smiled. Still, she saw the concern shimmering in his dark eyes. "I learned you take a single slice of toast for breakfast. Anne has pulled together some refreshments. You'll feel better if you eat."

She smiled at him, her heart feeling so light that she wouldn't be surprised to watch it drift from her chest to the ceiling, like a balloon. "I am hardly a small child, to be coaxed to dine." But he had held her hand in the coach as if she was just that.

And oddly, he was making her feel younger than her years.

As Meg set the tray down on the table by the chaise, he smiled at her, revealing his single dimple. "You are hardly a small child, but you eat like a bird—a sparrow, actually." His smile vanished. "Lady Blanche, I am somewhat worried about you. Please, humor me now."

"Will you join me?" she asked, arching a brow, hoping he would accept the invitation.

He started—then slowly glanced aside.

Blanche felt her pulse race. She had never been coy, not once in her entire life. But the sultry invitation had somehow slipped out of its own accord. Perhaps because she so wanted his company. Then she heard a chair scraping the floor. She saw Sir Rex move the chair belonging to the secretaire not far from the chaise.

"Of course," he murmured. "No one wishes to dine alone." He gestured at the chaise.

Her heart thundered now. He dined alone—all the time—and apparently, he had done so for at least ten years. She settled on the chaise, thanking Meg for the tray, as Sir Rex took the adjacent chair. As she nibbled a cucumber sandwich, she thought about being in his arms a few hours ago. Last night, his embrace had been powerfully and almost frighteningly male. Today, it had been shockingly and wonderfully gentle. He was such a good man and he deserved so much more than his current life. He did not deserve to be alone.

But she was going to change that, somewhat, at least. Her agenda had never been as clear.

She realized he was watching her. She met his gaze, smiling at him. "I do not think I ever thanked you properly for rescuing me today." Even her tone had changed; she sounded happy.

His gaze became hooded. "There was nothing to thank me for—and you did thank me."

"There was everything to thank you for."

He lifted his gaze. "Are you saying that you thought I might leave you unconscious on the street?" But he smiled wryly now.

She laughed. "Maybe I will go home and set the gossips straight."

He hesitated, then laughed. "Yes, you have the courage and audacity to do so."

Blanche became still, her tiny sandwiches forgotten. She had never heard Sir Rex laugh with mirth. The sound was warm and beautiful.

His smile vanished. "Have I grown a second head?"

She realized she was completely breathless. "I am the least audacious woman in the *world*."

His dimple appeared. "You underestimate yourself. But

you need not defend me to the ton, Lady Blanche. I gave up caring what society thinks long ago."

Blanche cared. She despised the rude gossips. And the first gossip she would set straight was her own dear friend Felicia.

A silence had fallen, one with a distinct weight. He said, "You are not eating."

She finished the quarter sandwich. "I have never had a large appetite."

"That is terribly obvious. Do you ride?"

The question surprised her. "I ride rather well, although not as well as you, of course."

A beautiful smile, entirely seductive, unfurled. "Come with me tomorrow. We'll ride across the moors. I'll show you the haunted ruins of a Norman castle. You will be famished," he added, "when we return."

Her pulse leaped and her skin tightened, warming everywhere. She liked this man. She liked him very much. And the moment she was alone, she would write Bess and beg for her advice. If Bess had thought to match them once, she would probably still think it a good idea.

"You are staring."

She blushed. "You must be used to ladies who stare."

There was no reply. Blanche looked up—his gaze was steady and unwavering upon her. "Is that a compliment?"

"Of course it is!" Had he thought she was insulting him? It crossed her mind that strangers might stare at him because of his leg. "You are a handsome man—women surely stare— I know Felicia has admired you and I have heard other ladies doing so, as well."

"Really."

She was at a loss. "I meant to flatter you, Sir Rex."

His mouth quirked. "I do not care what the ladies of the ton think."

She shrugged. "Most men would be pleased—"

"I am not most men. I care what *you* think. What *do* you think?"

She looked up into his eyes, disbelieving. Was he asking her if she found him handsome? And if so, what was she supposed to say?

His gaze was fixed, a slight smile on his face.

"You are fishing, Sir Rex," she said lightly and nervously.

"I am." He relaxed in his chair. "And it is not very gentlemanly of me, now is it?"

"No, it is not."

He smiled at her.

She smiled back. A new, even higher ground seemed to have been achieved. "I should love to hack the moors," she said softly. "With you."

"Good. Then it is decided. The weather permitting, of course."

They both glanced at the windows and the rapidly darkening skies. Blanche prayed it would be sunny on the morrow. "By the by, I have met your neighbors."

His smile faded.

"Or rather, I met one of your neighbors, Mrs. Farrow of Torrence Hall." Her sense of well-being vanished. His expression had become one impossible to read. Worse, he now refused to speak.

"She is a very pleasant young lady. We had such an interesting chat. I hadn't realized you had neighbors a mere half hour away by coach." Blanche now stared grimly, for his lack of interest was obvious. "Sir Rex? Do you wish to comment?"

"Not particularly." He stood, adjusting his crutch. "What do you intend, Lady Blanche?"

She tensed. "I am not intending anything," she lied.

His lips twisted into the semblance of a grim smile. "I see she was a fountain of information."

Blanche thought about an instant retreat. But he needed

some small social life. "It is remarkable, really. She has been wed and in the parish for five years, but has never dined at Bodenick."

"I thought so," he said harshly. "Have you forgotten? I am a recluse and I prefer the company of my brandy to that of pleasing young ladies."

She was beyond dismay and she stood, stumbling. "Am I not pleasing? And a lady? And you have asked me very forwardly for my company!"

He threw up his left hand. "Unfair!"

She had just raised her voice. He had raised his. Blanche was stunned. "I am not trying to be unfair," she said very quietly. "I simply thought to arrange a very pleasant evening for us all."

A smile of distaste formed. "I see."

"I don't think you do," she said. "But I hadn't realized that merely mentioning your neighbors would cause a crisis."

He stiffened. "It hasn't."

She felt his retreat and seized the opening. "Can I not comment if I am taken with a neighbor?"

"Of course you can."

"Perhaps you would be taken with them, too!"

He stared, nostrils flared. "I doubt it."

Blanche felt like taking him by the shoulders and shaking him silly. She felt like telling him that if he acted like a recluse, he would be labeled one. Yet he knew all that—and he didn't care. She was the one who cared about the stones thrown at him.

"Now what?" he demanded. "You are staring—I have earned your displeasure!"

He cared very much about her respect, she thought. "Yes, I am disappointed."

His eyes widened. "It is important to you that I meet my neighbors?"

She bit her lip, afraid to hope. "Actually, it is."

"Why?"

"Because I think your life might find some improvement from just a bit of social intercourse."

He stared at her as if she had lost her mind. "You wish to improve my life."

She winced. "Yes, I do."

"Why? You are merely my guest. Why bother? Why put yourself out? Why now?"

"We have become friends!" she exclaimed.

His chest rose and fell, hard. He stared and so did she.

"Fine. Invite them." He wasn't angry; he seemed resigned. He inclined his head and turned to leave.

She ran around him, barring his way. He halted abruptly and she gripped his arm instinctively.

"I am off balance," he said softly, and his eyes smoked, "but not because I am missing half of my leg."

She inhaled. "If you plan to sulk—like a child—I will not invite the Farrows for supper."

His gaze probed hers. "So now I must promise to be charming?"

"Yes."

"Very well. I will be all charm—I promise." His gaze swept her face.

She smiled, thrilled and very aware of that prickling sensation beneath her garments. "I daresay, you might even enjoy the evening."

His jaw flexed. "At least with you at the table, it will not be an evening from hell."

She shook her head. "Such drama! Now I will make you a promise, Sir Rex."

He became still. "I am waiting."

"If you are not amused, I will never interfere in your life again."

His chin lifted. "Then I will be amused."

Blanche started.

"And by the way, you are *very* audacious." He bowed and stalked out on his crutch.

CHAPTER EIGHT

Dear Bess,

I hope this letter finds you and the children well. I am afraid I am greatly in need of your advice. I have been at Sir Rex's manor for a full week now, as you must know. It was very shocking to discover that Penthwaithe is not a part of my fortune! I am certain you are smiling now in smug satisfaction. So I must ask if you seriously thought to match me with Sir Rex.

He has many stellar qualities. He has the strength and integrity of character to manage the Harrington fortune. His attributes far outweigh his very few flaws. I believe we have developed a genuine friendship, based on mutual respect and affection. And I will dare to write that I also find him quite attractive. Bess, I am considering asking him for a union.

Please respond in absolute haste and tell me what you think! And if you would still encourage a match based on friendship, affection and a strength of character, please advise me exactly as to how I should proceed.

Finally, I have not a single clue as to whether he would be receptive to such a remarkable advance on my part. I would not care much for his rejection.

BLANCHE FINALLY PAUSED, dread knotting in her stomach. Oh, she would so hate his rejection! She would rather go on this way, as somewhat more than casual friends, than to put herself out so boldly and suffer such a painful dismissal.

She had also glossed over his faults. But Bess really didn't need to know everything. For as dear as she was, she did love to gossip. Trembling, she dipped her quill.

Your devoted and loyal friend,
    Blanche Harrington

Then she sat back in her desk chair, relieved she had penned the letter. The post was swift—Bess would have the letter in two days. In four days, if Bess responded immediately, Blanche would have her reply.

She was hoping Bess would tell her to rush forward with such a match.

I must be mad after all, she thought, smiling, *to want to rush such a monumental decision.* But before she dared to contemplate actually going forward with a proposal, pandemonium raged outside in the courtyard.

Men were shouting with urgency and fear. Someone cried, "Open the bloody door!"

Blanche leaped to her feet and ran to the window, but by the time she looked down, the courtyard was empty.

"Lady Harrington! Lady Harrington!" her maid screamed from downstairs.

Alarmed, Blanche ran from the room. She stumbled down the stairs and before she even made the ground floor, she saw into the great room. A handful of men were standing in a circle, blocking her view, but she saw one booted foot, and she knew.

Fear overcame her. *Something terrible had happened to Sir Rex.* "Stand back!" she cried, rushing into the great hall. The men leaped away and she saw Sir Rex lying prone on the floor, half of his white shirt crimson. He was unconscious—he could not be dead!

Blanche shoved past the men and knelt, aware of his shocking pallor. And now she saw the source of blood—his shirt had been ripped open and his chest was gashed raw and bleeding. Terror replaced the fear. She looked up, saw Meg. "Get me clean linen to stop the bleeding," she said calmly. She wadded the clean hem of her underskirt and pressed it swiftly to the wound.

There was so much blood.

"Hardy, correct?" she asked, not taking her gaze from Sir Rex's pale countenance.

"Yes, ma'am."

"Summon the closest surgeon, now." Her quiet tone amazed her, considering she was terrified Sir Rex might die. But then, the world had stopped turning, time stood still, and there was only Sir Rex as he lay there, bleeding and pale.

He must not bleed to death.

She heard the man racing out. "Young man," she said, gesturing at a boy she had vaguely noticed standing with the men, "I want you to press as hard as you can on my petticoat, so I may take Sir Rex's pulse." His chest was moving; she was certain she had seen it rise.

The boy dropped to his knees and took over the task of stanching the wound.

Blanche leaned over Sir Rex's face but did not feel his breath. She willed more calm and laid a fingertip on the carotid artery in his throat. She found his pulse instantly. It was weaker than she would have liked, and it was very rapid, dangerously so. But his heart was working furiously to pump his blood when he had lost so much of it. She smoothed her hand over his face, hoping he might somehow know that she was there and she would care for him—that she did care for him. "Anne?"

"Yes, my lady," Anne gasped, stepping forward. She was as white as a laundered sheet.

"Boil water, thread, needles. And I need soap, warm water, clean cloths and whiskey—lots of whiskey."

Blanche heard Anne rush off as Meg knelt with clean linens. Blanche looked up at the five men. "What happened?" She asked hoarsely.

They all started talking at once.

"One at a time!" she begged.

"He was working with the young stud, my lady. The stallion is usually quiet. Something must have startled him—it happened so quickly—the stallion struck and Sir Rex just barely avoided it, but it being so muddy, he went down! And the stud took off—a horse will never trample a person, my lady, never!"

"Damn it," Blanche cried. "Are you saying he was run over by the horse?"

"Nicked," the groom cried, flushing. "He got nicked by one of the hooves."

Blanche felt murderous. She fought for calm and smiled at the wide-eyed, worried boy. "What's your name?"

"Jimmy," he whispered.

"I'm going to take over now. Can you go find Anne and help her bring me all I have asked for?"

When he had eagerly run off, she lifted the hem of her underskirt, which was as crimson as the right side of his shirt. She fought fear and despair and took a good look at the wound. Nick or kick, it was a deep gash on his upper chest and it would need many stitches. She felt certain the surgeon would not arrive soon enough. She was also afraid of infection. There was no doubt she saw dirt sticking to his raw flesh.

She reminded herself that Sir Rex had had half of his leg amputated in a military hospital in Spain. He would survive a kick to his chest, assuming he had been kicked and not trampled.

He moaned.

She hurt so much for him. "Please take him carefully upstairs." There was no avoiding moving him. He needed to be in bed and she needed to attend him immediately. As four men hoisted him, he grunted, and tears finally filled her eyes. She brushed them furiously away. This was not the time to find the ability to weep, damn it to hell, she thought, furious with herself. Sir Rex needed her.

"He's a big, strong man, my lady," Meg whispered. "He'll be fine."

"He has lost so much blood," Blanche said. Then firmly and with a deep breath, "Boil my tweezers, too, in case I see any debris in the wound." She clasped Meg's shoulder, forestalling her. "I am counting on you, Meg. Do you have a strong stomach?"

Meg hesitated. "I'll do my best."

"Good. Now, I need the whiskey, soap and water *immediately*." Blanche lifted her skirts to her knees and ran up the stairs.

Sir Rex had been laid in his bed. She did not bother to look around his bedchamber, but she did see a brandy bottle on the night table. She seized it and sat, removing the linen. The wound oozed more blood. "Hold him down," she said.

When the four men had done so, she poured.

He shouted, eyes flying open, lunging up with all the power such a man should possess. Briefly, his dazed eyes found hers, incredulous and accusing.

"You have been kicked—or trampled—and I am sorry, but I am not done," she said.

Accusation vanished. Comprehension filled his gaze. "Hell," he said, collapsing. Sweat now beaded his brow but he stared at her.

Blanche felt ruthless. She had to be ruthless. "Hold him," she said. "And I would appreciate him not being able to rise up."

Rex looked at her.

"Lie still," she smiled, and she poured the rest of the bottle over the wound.

He grunted and then gasped.

She took Meg's clean linens and pressed them down. "I'm sorry." She wished he would faint again, but saw that he was trying to stay conscious. "Can you breathe properly? Does it hurt when you breathe?" She had to wonder if he had been stepped on, and if so, if he'd broken a rib.

He somehow managed to shake his head. She knew he meant he could breathe without pain.

"Let go, Sir Rex. It's better if you pass out."

He panted and then opened his eyes. "How bad…is it?"

"You need stitches. And I still intend to clean the wound with soap and water."

Pain rippled in his eyes, which were a pale blue now. "Do it," he gasped. And he fainted.

Blanche had never been so relieved. She reached for his hand, grasping it tightly, aware of the tremor in her own palm. Even unconscious, his face was a mask of pain. Meg returned, carrying the soap and water, and Blanche released him.

Meg was also carrying a pair of scissors. "I thought you might need these," she whispered.

"I do." Blanche was glad Meg had kept her head on straight. She nodded at the men to back off and she cut his shirt into enough pieces that it could be easily dislodged from his frame. She blotted the wound—it seemed as if the bleeding had finally stopped.

She paused, feeling a moment of despair. She was not a surgeon or a nurse. She had nursed some impoverished women and children as a part of her efforts for St Anne's, but that had consisted of icing feverish brows and bodies or spooning broth into the mouths of those too weak to do so themselves. At Harrington Hall, her housekeeper had taken care of small injuries and wounds, but Blanche had seen her stitch up the stable master's son.

"How can I help, my lady?" Meg breathed.

Blanche realized that everyone was staring at her. She

looked grimly at the five men. "Has anyone ever sewn up this kind of wound?"

They all shook their heads. "You can wait for the surgeon, my lady. He'll certainly be here by nightfall."

Blanche felt more despair. She went to the basin and began washing her hands thoroughly with lye soap. Meg followed. "You are very skilled with a needle," she whispered.

Blanche smiled grimly. "I have never sewn up a man before."

Meg smiled miserably.

"I am afraid to wait for the surgeon. The one thing I do know is that the longer that wound is open, the greater a chance of infection."

Their gazes met in understanding. Meg whispered, "Maybe you should have a sip of whiskey, too."

Blanche was horrified. She walked back to Sir Rex. "I'll clean the wound thoroughly—if he should awaken, you must hold him down." The men nodded somberly.

One said, "You'd better give him some whiskey before you put those stitches in."

Blanche agreed. "If he doesn't awaken, we'll wake him before I sew him up and see if we can't force a bottle down him then."

She pulled up her chair and began rinsing the wound.

BLANCHE PULLED THE NEEDLE through Sir Rex's skin for the twenty-third time. She could barely believe it was done and she knotted the thread. She willed herself to stay calm and steady for another moment or two. Meg handed her the scissors; Blanche snipped the thread neatly, handing all of her instruments to the maid. Sir Rex remained unconscious.

She sat there, completely incapable of movement now. All she was capable of was drawing deep, shaky breaths.

He had been unconscious for hours. But after she had cleaned the wound—and, God, there'd been sand, dirt and even gravel inside—his men had awoken him and forced half of a bottle of whiskey into him. She was never going to forget the way he'd looked at her, as if he trusted her to make him well.

She began to tremble wildly. Tears spilled down her cheeks. How had she managed to clean that horrid wound and sew it up?

What if she had missed a pebble?

What if he got an infection?

Where the hell was that damnable surgeon!

"It's all right, my lady, he can't feel a thing," Meg whispered kindly.

Blanche put her hands over her face and fought for control and composure. It was impossible. Tears burned her closed lids. She had never wanted to cry like this, and she wasn't sure why she was crying. The worst of the crisis was over, wasn't it?

Tears managed to escape her lids. She realized she was crying because she was so afraid. She couldn't recall ever feeling like this or shedding such tears, but she was terrified that Sir Rex, as big and strong as he was, wasn't going to survive the kick.

"He'll be fine, my lady," one of the men said, shuffling by.

"He's strong like a mule,'" another added, following his friend to the door.

"A little kick won't hurt him, not at all," Hardy said as he left.

Blanche nodded at them as they left the chamber. "Thank you," she gasped. Then she turned to Sir Rex, who looked like death barely warmed over. He remained pale, but with a jaundiced reflection, and his stitches were red, swollen and angry. Blanche caressed his cheek.

"You will be fine," she managed, praying her words were true. She clasped his cheek, which was stubbly now, and thought she saw his lashes move.

"It's your turn to rest, my lady," Meg said firmly.

Blanche smoothed her fingers over his strong jaw one final

time. Even ill, he was as beautiful as a dark angel. His lashes seemed to flutter this time and she withdrew; she did not want to wake him. He would not feel particularly well when he awoke. He would be feeling the effects of both the wound and the whiskey.

"My lady, please," Meg said.

Blanche looked up at her, realizing that Anne stood near the door. Both maids had been very helpful, rushing to bring clean water and linens as needed— everyone had been helpful, a testimony to the respect one and all seemed to hold for their employer. "I cannot thank you both enough," she whispered hoarsely. And now, her stomach ached and felt sick.

"Anne and I will take turns sitting with him. Anne can stay with him first and I'll draw you a hot bath and bring you a fine supper," Meg implored.

Blanche finally found a semblance of self-control. She wiped the moisture from her cheeks and sat up straighter as she looked at Sir Rex. Although seriously injured, he was resting quietly now. The sheet was drawn up to his waist, revealing his navel. And for the first time that afternoon, she looked carefully at his sculpted body. The man was all male muscle with not an ounce of flesh to spare. No woman could be immune to that figure or that face.

She glanced at Anne, who stared at her, unsmiling. "I'll sit with him," she said, curtsying. But there was no genuine deference in the action. But then, Anne had never been particularly deferent to her since her arrival. Until then, Blanche had assumed she was imagining it. But she felt certain Anne didn't like her—and maybe, absurdly, considered her a rival.

They were not rivals. Blanche was an aristocrat, Anne a servant. On the other hand, she had been thinking of marriage—and Anne would lose her place in Sir Rex's bed if he ever accepted a proposal from her.

She was feeling oddly possessive now.

Blanche pulled the sheet as high as she dared, to just below his chest, very careful not to cover the stitched wound. She would leave it undressed until the surgeon arrived. She touched his brow, which was warm, but not hot. If he had a fever, it was very low. Then she turned to Meg. "I'm not hungry and I am not leaving him, not yet. However, you may bring me a glass of wine and something to eat, because I should nourish myself. And where is the surgeon?"

Anne walked out.

Blanche stared after her, then faced Meg. "What is taking him so long?"

"I'm sure he'll be here at any moment," Meg said. Then, "I can sit with him. And I'll send Anne home. My lady, at least take a short rest. And look at your dress! It is stained."

Blanche stiffened. Did Meg guess that she was fond enough of her host to want to keep his lover away from him? And was that what was happening? Was she worried about Sir Rex's affair? "If Sir Rex becomes feverish, we will need her help." She smiled then, but felt as fragile as a butterfly. "If he becomes ill, I want to attend him. He has been nothing but generous and kind when I have done little but impose." She avoided Meg's gaze, turning to touch Sir Rex's cheek briefly.

"He's done so much for me—I have to stay."

BLANCHE AWOKE.

She was seated in the same chair beside Sir Rex's bed and the sun was shining brightly, indicating the beginning of a new day. She had fallen asleep around midnight and could barely believe she'd slept for so long, curled up uncomfortably in the chair, her head on the wood frame. Her neck was so stiff she winced as she straightened.

But she was already reaching for Sir Rex's brow. It was cool—if he had ever had a fever, it had been low and insignificant.

So much relief began. And he didn't look ill now; his complexion had returned to normal, in fact, he seemed to be resting very comfortably. She wiped her eyes, which were suddenly moist, realizing that in spite of the rest, she was beyond exhaustion. Her anxiety had known no bounds and she could admit it now.

She allowed the relief to flow over her in waves, but then she began to stare at Sir Rex.

The sheet and thin wool blanket had somehow been pushed down to his hips. She assumed he had tossed and turned at some point in the night. She reached for them to pull them higher, but hesitated. And in that instant, she was acutely aware of how masculine he was and that the two of them had shared a room for most of the night and remained alone now.

Her mouth felt dry. Her heart raced. Her gaze moved slowly over the protrusion of his navel and the square that his muscles and tendons had etched in his tight, flat abdomen. It moved higher, of its own accord, and she was acutely aware of what she was doing—she was openly admiring him. But she simply could not deny herself this opportunity. She felt mesmerized by the sight of so much masculinity. His chest was broad, not quite flat, entirely muscular and just barely dusted with dark hair. Even in sleep, his biceps bulged. His shoulders were three times as wide as her own—and maybe twice as wide as his narrow hips. She glanced down—and saw the sheet stirring.

For one moment, Blanche stared, but without any confusion at all. A ridge had formed, impossibly, but she knew what it indicated…. She started to leap to her feet. Was such a thing even possible?

He seized her wrist, holding her in place.

Her gaze flew to his.

His regard was steady and intent.

She realized he was not only awake, he had been watching

her ogle him and was now having a male reaction that only a well man could have—or so she assumed.

"Don't go."

Blanche inhaled and sat. She felt dazed—and was terribly aware of his grasp. His palm was warm and strong on her wrist. Their eyes remained locked.

She swallowed, trying to look only at his face, except, her vision seemed to have its own accord. From the corner of her eye, she saw his flat belly and a tented sheet. Finally, heat crept into her cheeks. "How are you feeling?" The moment the words were out, she wished she'd asked a different question.

But he didn't smile. He released her. "I feel as if I've been on a binge."

She swallowed again. "We made you drink over a half a bottle of whiskey. The surgeon never came. There was a breech birth at Tythwrithgyn. But the wound has been cleaned and sewn up and you haven't had a fever."

His gaze moved to his chest then back to her face. Then he glanced at her skirts. "Thank you."

She hesitated, aware that he had remarked his blood which stained her skirts. "I hope you shoot the horse."

His face tightened. "I will if you wish me to, but it was an unfortunate accident."

She somehow nodded. "How does your chest feel?"

"It hurts. But the whiskey is continuing to numb the pain. How many stitches did I need?"

"Twenty-three," she whispered.

He absorbed that. "May I have some water?"

She jerked. He must be terribly thirsty, considering. She quickly stood and poured a glass of water from the night table, then paused by his hip. "Can you sit up?"

His gaze drifted aside. "I may need some help," he said softly.

Of course he needed help, she thought. It would probably hurt terribly to use his right arm—and that meant it would be a while before he would be able to use his crutch. She set the water down, sat down by his hip and put her arm around him. The moment she did so, she felt his warm skin and his breath.

Her skin heated. She did not know what to do with her hand.

He didn't move a muscle.

She put her hand on the side of his lean, hard back, her shoulder now against the left side of his chest, her breast nestled lower. Blanche could no longer breathe. She reminded herself that this was necessary, but she was in a nearly naked man's embrace. Not just any man, but Sir Rex.

He slid his left arm around her, his grasp so powerful she felt faint. She slowly looked up.

She started, becoming impossibly still, because he was staring at her with that distinctly male, smoldering look and his face was inches from hers. For one heartbeat, she was certain he would kiss her.

And her heart fluttered wildly, hopefully.

He said roughly, "You may have saved my life."

It took her a moment to find her voice. "Can you sit?"

He did not answer. His right hand, which she hadn't realized he could use, lifted, and he touched her cheek. Blanche gasped. His gaze unwavering on hers, he stroked her face, pushed her hair behind her ear and smiled roughly at her. She breathed hard, very certain he would lower his mouth to hers. His hand lingered on her cheek for another moment. Blanche felt her eyes drift closed. She felt herself lean toward him. Her heart was trying to beat its way out of her breast.

He released her and sat up, quite by himself.

She stood, too, flaming, aware now of what his caress had done—a new, very insistent and very definite ache had begun, pounding in unison with her pulse.

He smiled grimly at her, but he had turned pale once again.

"Why didn't you let me help you sit?" she exclaimed. "Did you hurt yourself? Let me look at those stitches!" And she forgot the near kiss, if that was what it had been, because she dreaded having to replace a popped stitch.

He lay back against the pillows and she quickly saw that all the stitches were intact. Suddenly she was furious. Tears came to her eyes. "Sir Rex! Enough is enough!" She brushed her eyes with her sleeve while he started, wide-eyed. "You have no idea what I went through to sew you up! You are not healed and until you are, I insist you behave like a proper patient!"

"I'm sorry," he said. "I forgot about the injury."

"You forgot?" Disbelief mingled with her fury. "Well I haven't forgotten cleaning your raw flesh and sticking a needle into you—many times! I am not a surgeon! I have never wanted to be a nurse! Until you are healed, you are to lie still—and sit still—no matter how difficult that is for you." She wiped her eyes again. "If you need to sit up, someone will help you…. Anne can help you!" she cried.

"I'm sorry," he said, looking ashamed. "I am genuinely sorry. Blanche, you are clearly exhausted. Did you spend the entire night at my side?"

She sniffed, reaching for the glass of water. "Yes, I'm afraid I did." She sat beside him on the bed, refusing to feel anything other than objective concern for him, and held the glass to his lips. Their gazes met; he drank, draining the glass.

Her hip was perilously close to his thigh. She stood, briskly refilling the water glass.

"I am fine," he said. "Why don't you go to your bed and rest?"

"You are dehydrated from loss of blood—and the whiskey." Standing this time, she helped him drink. She was, unfortunately, so close to tears once more.

"I have distressed you," he said softly. "I am sorry!"

"You should be sorry. " She trembled now. He hadn't even needed her help to sit up. Had he asked for her help just so he could get her into his bed? And how could she think of such a thing now, after the trauma of his accident?

How could he?

Their gazes locked.

"Blanche." He sent her a smile—it was thoroughly disarming. "I promise to rest…and behave as a proper patient. But only if you promise to lie down in your own bed."

She didn't hesitate, even though that single look caused her heart to dance, disarming her even more. "You're right, I'm exhausted." She hesitated, because she needed to ask Meg to sit with him. And then she boldly whisked the sheet and blanket to his chest, aware of his narrowed stare. But he could not possibly guess that she didn't wish for her maid—or Anne—to view his splendid physique.

"There. Meg will check in on you." She gave him what she hoped was a cool glance. "Anne is busy in the kitchens," she said, having no idea if it was true.

And he smiled at her as if he knew she intended to keep them apart. "I have one more request."

She paused at the door.

"In return for my good behavior, you must also promise to sit with me later." His dimple flashed.

She froze, her heart beating with urgent and rhythmic force. "It is hardly proper, now that you are on the mend."

"I don't care if it is proper or not," he said. "And no one will know except for the servants."

She stared, wide-eyed, and he waited, smiling. "I will know."

"But if I suffer from ennui, I will wish to leave my bed."

"Are you negotiating with me, Sir Rex?"

"I am trying to *charm* you to my wishes."

"You may charm me," she trembled, "in a few more days,

when the physician says you can be up and about." He was flirting with her!

"I can accept that bargain," he said softly, appearing rather pleased.

A small thrill raced through her. "I will check in on you later. Rest, Sir Rex, please."

CHAPTER NINE

FOR ONE MOMENT, she was so surprised to find a lion staring
at her from the doorway of her bedchamber. Vaguely, she
realized she was so tired, and as vaguely, that she must be
dreaming. Because a lion could not be in her bedroom. The
beast was magnificent, and he was staring at her with such
familiar, amber-flecked, smoldering eyes—and even though
she saw a predatory intensity there, she wasn't frightened.
Instead, an odd excitement began.

Then its face changed, becoming impossibly bestial, partly
monstrous and almost human, and it growled, revealing huge,
white, glistening fangs. Blanche jerked in fear, and blood
began running from the fangs. The white fangs turned black,
becoming the metal tines of a pitchfork. Blood ran from them
now, too....

She screamed, sitting bolt upright in her bed.

Blanche realized she had been deeply asleep and dreaming.
Terrified, her heart thundering so violently that it hurt her
chest, she turned to stare wildly at the window. It was bright
outside—the middle of the afternoon. She had been sleeping
for several hours and she recalled why—she had been up all
night with Sir Rex, taking care of him.

Blanche threw the covers aside, shaken and trying to
recover from such a threatening dream. She now remembered
that Meg had helped her out of her ruined gown, corset and
petticoats and she had collapsed in her bed in her silk chemise

and cotton and lace drawers. She ran to the window, shoving
it wide-open. Why had she had such a nightmare? And why
was it so terrifying?

Nothing had actually happened!

But there had been so much blood....

It was *only* a nightmare, she told herself sternly, and it
meant nothing, nothing at all!

Her door slammed open, and Sir Rex stood there, clad
only in his breeches, his expression one of alarm. "Blanche?"

For one moment, she simply stared at him, seeing the
golden lion again. And then her mind began to work. "What
are you doing out of bed?" she cried, and it was an accusation. Concern for him began to chase the fragments of her
dream away.

He glanced around the room, then back at her. And now,
his gaze swung to her hanging hair and then down her very
scantily clad body, right to the tips of her bare toes. He looked
up. "I thought a highwayman was murdering you in your
sleep." Then, "You will catch pneumonia standing by the open
window like that."

Blanche realized she was standing in her undergarments,
which were very revealing. She ran to the armoire and threw
a wrapper on, suddenly flushing, wondering just how transparent her chemise was. "I had a dream." She belted it firmly,
aware that she was still feeling ill, and her heart had not
returned to a normal pace. But a different and acute awareness had arisen. Sir Rex's presence filled the bedchamber,
dominating it. "You should have knocked."

"You screamed as if someone was murdering you," he said
sharply. "It was bloodcurdling—just like your scream the
other day in the church."

She tensed and slowly faced him. That dream had frightened her just as much as the miners in the church, she thought.
Now she was disturbed and uncertain. But she was calmer this

time, calm enough to notice that Sir Rex remained clad in the same breeches he had worn when he had had the accident, and they were muddy and bloodstained. But his wound had now been properly dressed.

"Was the surgeon here?" she asked, jerking her gaze from the dressing and the hard slab of his chest.

"Yes, he was. And Dr. Linney also called." Two spots of pink now colored his high cheekbones. His gaze had drifted to the bodice of her pleated wrapper, as if he might be capable of seeing through the fabric. It shifted upward. "Tom Hamilton approved of your handiwork and said I am certain to be fine."

She tried not to notice his near nakedness. Someone was going to have to help him change his clothes. "Did he also say he approves of your running around the house, just hours after my surgery?"

"If I hear you scream like that, I will come running," he said flatly. "And do not doubt it."

She hugged herself. A part of her was thrilled. "And if a highwayman was here, I doubt you could fight him in your condition, Sir Rex," she said firmly, finally in a firm grasp of her turbulent emotions.

His tight expression softened. "Where there is a will, there is a way. Are you all right?"

His soft tone sent a frisson of desire through her, chasing away the last remnants of revulsion and fear. "It was only a dream." She somehow smiled. And she did not want him concerned with her welfare when he had to mend his own body. "Can you get yourself back to bed? *You* need rest."

"Of course," he said, staring.

She looked as closely at his face. His recuperative powers were amazing, because he did not look pale, ill or close to fainting. But he made no move to go. "Well?" she said, rather imperiously. She began to think about his seeing her in a state of undress a moment ago. His gaze had lingered where it should not have. But that only made her heart skip, and she had to wonder if he had been admiring her. She touched her hair. Meg had taken the pins out and it hung past her shoulders. She hoped it was not entirely disheveled. There was probably little to admire right now.

"What were you dreaming about?"

"Lions and monsters," she said sharply. She had no intention of ever discussing this nightmare with anyone, much less him.

His eyes widened.

She flushed. "I am sorry. I did not mean to shout." The lion had been so very much like Sir Rex. She was certain it had symbolized him. As for the rest, she had to forget about it.

"Good afternoon, Sir Rex," she said firmly. But her mind twisted and turned. If she did not know better, she would think the monster had been a man—one of the villains wielding pitchforks in the mob.

But she did know better. Her father had never said anything about the mob having pitchforks. It was absurd to be dreaming of monsters as if she were a child, but that was what she had done.

"Please stop apologizing to me when there is nothing to apologize for." He nodded curtly and swung out, not bothering to close her door.

She had insulted him, or damaged his feelings, she thought, by being so abrupt. But she was not going to share the rest of her secrets with him. She hurried to the door to shut it, but paused to watch him limping down the hall to his own room. His gait had slowed—he was fatigued, no matter his display of masculine strength, and so evidently pushing himself, never mind his recuperative powers.

It must hurt terribly to use his crutch now, she thought. The right side of his chest had to pain him every time he used his right shoulder and arm.

More concern arose. What was she thinking, to be so caught up in the aftermath of a child's nightmare? She wasn't a child, Sir Rex had been seriously injured, and she was not certain he was entirely out of danger.

She went back to her room and threw a pale blue dress on, along with stockings and shoes. She twisted her hair into a knot and stuck a dozen pins into it. Then she hurried to his bedroom. The door was open, but she knocked anyway.

He eyed her from the bed. He had tossed the covers aside. He was as still as a perfectly sculpted male statue. But his gaze narrowed with speculation and something else, a regard very similar to the preying lion in her dreams.

"May I?"

He nodded.

She hurried in. "I must apologize for being rude to you when—"

"Accepted." He cut her off.

She stared. Then, "Did Mr. Hamilton say that you were out of all danger?"

"He said it was unlikely an infection would set in if it hadn't already. Dr. Linney agreed."

"Did he tell you to stay in bed?" She knew he had. She poured him a glass of water, waiting for his reply.

He didn't answer, accepting the glass. He took a sip, then said, "Do you frequently have nightmares?"

"Never," she said, more sharply than she had intended. But once again, he seemed determined to pry.

His gaze was searching.

"I never have nightmares. I am a very sound sleeper," she said in a more controlled tone. Then she gestured helplessly. "The night was endless. I am still tired. I was very worried." She forced a smile. "I was probably dreaming about you, Sir Rex, and my having to sew up your wounds. I doubt I will ever recover from such a trauma!" she added lightly.

"I don't want you to ever worry about me," he said firmly, unsmiling. "I am dismayed you had to attend me. I am dismayed you were reduced to nursing me. And I certainly do not want to be the cause of your nightmares."

"You are not," she said grimly. But the more she thought about it, the more convinced she became that the dream had begun with the lion, a symbol for Sir Rex, for a reason. Why he should turn into a monster she feared and dreaded, she had no idea. "I was not about to let a farmer sew your wounds."

"I am adding tenacious to your list of attributes," he said softly, their gazes meeting.

She softened. "I can admit to some tenacity. If I believe something is right, I cannot be dissuaded."

He smiled, dimpling. "Are you stubborn, too?"

"No." She had to smile back, at last. "I am very open-minded and reasonable."

"Then that makes one of us." He took her hand.

She started, and then so much desire began. "Are you stubborn? Because I have seen a very reasonable and rational man."

"Really?" He looked around the room. "Where? I should like to meet him."

She gave in and laughed. "Very well, you can be determined, but I do not mind."

"Why not? Everyone else minds."

She stared and he stared back.

"Why not?" he repeated very softly.

She removed her hand from his. "Because I understand more than you might know. Now—" she became brisk, fluffing his pillows "—are you hungry?"

He just looked at her, his gaze dark, the lids heavy.

She felt a tremor. "I'll bring you a tray," she said, shaken by such a certain regard. At midnight in the great room, she had thought his desire to be the result of liquor. She had thought the same thing that morning. There was no possible explanation now, except, perhaps, that he truly admired her, as a lady and a woman.

"Bring enough for two," he said softly, "and we will share."

BLANCHE MOVED SWIFTLY downstairs, her body feeling heavy and far too warm for comfort. She was so pleased Sir Rex was well on the way to recovery. As she approached the kitchens, she heard a male voice, and assumed it was Fenwick. But when she reached the open door, she saw Anne standing by the back door, speaking quietly with a tall, blond fellow in the clothes of a laborer. He was most definitely not Fenwick—he was Anne's age and very attractive and they were speaking in hushed tones.

Blanche went still. There was almost no doubt in her mind that the young man was Anne's lover. She had her hand on his bare forearm and their conversation was earnest. She tried to tell herself that he could be a brother, a cousin or simply a friend, but he was looking at her in a very male way. She gave up. Anne was having an affair, and she was oddly dismayed, because somehow, she felt that it was a betrayal of Sir Rex. He did not deserve to be betrayed even if she did not really care for his having an affair—or having had one.

Suddenly the blond man saw her. His eyes widened, which confirmed Blanche's suspicions, and he turned and left. Anne whirled, and for an instant, she seemed very angry. Then her lashes lowered and she curtsied. "My lady."

Did Sir Rex condone his lover having an affair with another man? Somehow, Blanche didn't think so. And it wasn't right. She shouldn't judge, but she was appalled. At least she knew Anne's true nature. Clearly she had no concept of loyalty.

She crossed the large kitchen. "Who was that?" she asked coldly.

Anne looked at her with no expression. "The farrier. He's come to shoe some of Sir Rex's horses."

Blanche stared at her, sensing a lie. "Is he family?"

Anne's chin lifted. "No, my lady, he is not. Why do you ask?"

"You seem familiar with one another," Blanche said as coolly.

Anne smiled and it was brittle. "He's new to Lanhadron. I hardly know Paul." She shrugged dismissively and walked away, which was an act of rudeness, as she had not been dismissed.

Blanche tensed. She had never had an issue with any servant before. She was fair, at times kind, and when appropriate, generous with her staff. But she hadn't particularly liked Anne from the moment of discovering her relationship with Sir Rex. Still, she had been polite until now. Anne walking away from her without being given leave was not deferent at all.

Blanche finally said, "Please prepare a meal for two and bring it to Sir Rex's room."

Anne smiled, or grimaced, not looking up. "What will you be having?"

"A cold meat, some bread and cheese, I think." She thought about wine and decided against it; Sir Rex drank enough as it was and had certainly been given far too much whiskey last night. "And hot tea, please."

Anne grimaced again, moving across the kitchen to the pantries.

"Where is Fenwick?" she asked, speaking to the maid's back and becoming dismayed because she did not turn.

Anne didn't pause. "I sent him to the village for groceries."

Blanche almost demanded that she look at her when speaking to her. But Anne disappeared into the pantry, leaving Blanche shaken.

Anne did not care for her rank and was letting her know it. They weren't rivals, but she felt as if they were just that. But

Blanche wasn't about to compete with a servant. She followed Anne, pausing on the threshold of the pantry, which was dark and cool. "I am not pleased that I have to follow you around to speak with you," she said, trying to keep her tone neutral. "I am sure you show Sir Rex far more respect."

Anne had been opening an icebox and she straightened. "Oh, I beg your pardon. I thought he might be hungry, considering all he's been through." She smiled.

There was nothing Blanche could say to that. "When Fenwick returns, Sir Rex needs his breeches removed. I assume he will wish to lounge in bed in a nightshirt."

Anne blinked innocently at her. "I can certainly help him change his clothes…my lady."

Blanche felt a terrible tension. She spoke slowly, in an even but firm tone, and with care. "When Fenwick returns, he will aid Sir Rex. Your duties, Anne, are here in the kitchen." She was firm.

"Of course," Anne said, her eyes flickering. "Except when Sir Rex has other duties for me."

Blanche gasped. Flushing crimson, she turned so swiftly she stumbled, and she left the kitchen. Glancing back, she saw Anne staring coldly. The maid was horrid. No, she corrected herself, the truth was horrid, if she dared to dwell on it.

Sir Rex should not have taken advantage of his housemaid, even if she had been utterly willing. She had managed to gloss it over, but it was so terribly inappropriate. Yes, she now knew he was lonely and virile, but surely there was someone in the village who could serve as a mistress.

And she must find some sympathy for Anne. Of course Anne would dislike her. She was a simple housemaid and her employer's lover, a very impossible and difficult position to be in, and she probably resented Blanche in every possible way. But her rudeness and lack of respect were intolerable. Blanche was shaken.

She hurried upstairs, forcing a pleasant expression on her face. Sir Rex's door remained open and as she paused there, he put down the book he was reading and smiled at her. He had put on a shirt, but it was open. She lowered her hand; she had been about to knock.

"Anne is readying a small meal."

His smile faded. "What is wrong?"

"Nothing." She smiled very brightly at him, thinking about Anne. "Your blacksmith is here."

His expression changed. "I have no blacksmith. I shoe the horses myself."

Blanche stared in disbelief.

TWO DAYS LATER, BLANCHE SAT in the great room, going over correspondence from her solicitors. When the post had arrived, even though a reply from Bess was almost impossible until the morrow, she had been disappointed to realize that the reply was not in the mail. She was reading the first of two very long reports, when she heard Sir Rex coming downstairs.

Her heart skipped with an excitement she could not deny and she smiled, looking up.

He entered the room, meeting her smile with one of his own. "I assume I am now allowed out of bed? I have been a proper patient," he said pleasantly.

She stood. "I would have never dreamed you could be such a model patient. How do you feel?"

"I feel," he said, limping closer, "like taking you for that hack across the moors." His gaze locked with hers, his smile gone.

Her heart turned over, hard. "It has only been three days since the accident," she began softly, but more excitement swept over her, because Sir Rex looked very fine, too fine, in fact.

"I have stayed in bed, doing all of my paperwork there. I

refuse to become indolent, or God forbid, fat. My body is aching for vigorous activity. I am fine, Blanche," he said firmly. "Certain movements cause a mild ache in my chest, that is all."

Blanche had to repress a laugh. "You will never be overweight."

"If I sit on my posterior all day, I will become just that. Look." He took her arm and turned her toward the window. "The day is perfect."

Their bodies touched from shoulder to hip. Her heart slammed. Her skin hummed. Elsewhere, it tightened, swelled. "I need some outdoor activity, too," she said softly.

"Good." He shifted. "Anne, go round to the stables and have my mount readied, and Isabella for Lady Harrington."

Blanche whirled to see Anne on the great room's threshold. Anne curtsied and left.

Sir Rex touched her shoulder. "What is disturbing you? Is something amiss with the maid?"

Blanche hoped she was not flushing. "Why would something be amiss with your servant?" She shrugged. "I will change. I actually brought a riding habit." She hesitated, lifting her gaze to his. "I am so pleased you are fully recovered, Sir Rex."

He simply stared back at her and tension knifed between them.

BLANCHE THOUGHT her mare lovely. She was quiet, sweet and willing. Sir Rex pointed ahead as they paused on a high rise on the moors. The sky was blue, filled with faraway white clouds, and the sun was brilliantly shining. Winter seemed to have left Cornwall; it was warm and mild out.

"Can you see those stones?" Sir Rex asked, turning his gray gelding to face her.

"The ruins?" she asked, seeing a lone tower rising against the horizon.

"Yes. Are you up for a canter?" he asked eagerly.

She looked at his handsome face, his eyes filled with warmth and happiness. "Yes."

He gestured for her to gallop off first.

Blanche lightly tapped the mare with her crop and she set off at a canter. She laughed, pleased, because the mare was as smooth as a sofa. Sir Rex caught up with her. "She is like a rocking chair, is she not?"

"Very much so," Blanche called to him.

The tower loomed as they approached. Stone hedges criss-crossed the moors, which were dotted with the first of spring's wildflowers, and she saw the remnants of the castle's walls. The tower was three stories high, but clearly lacking an interior or a roof. They slowed their mounts to a walk and then halted beside it. It had become amazingly silent, as if ghosts truly haunted the place.

Blanche could see past the ruins, which were perched on a high slope. Below was a lush wooded valley and a picture-perfect village. "It is so lovely."

"Yes, it is," he said. "The local myth says that just after Hastings, my ancestor erected the original fort here. But Rolfe de Warenne was then sent to harry the north, and he never came back. The fort was passed into the hands of one of William's other lieutenants." He smiled at her. "Even in those days, the de Warenne men found and claimed true love. You do know he fell for a Saxon princess—who was not his wife."

Blanche beamed, wondering if the story was true. "And did he end up with his lady love?"

"He most certainly did, for she is the matriarch of our family. Her name was Ceidre."

"An unusual name," Blanche said, now studying Sir Rex closely. His humor had become lighter and lighter with every passing day—ever since the accident, or even before it. He was more smiles than not. She had not seen any sign of anger or frustration. When he had been bedridden, she had checked on him every night. He had been soundly asleep early every evening. And she had not seen him drink more than a single glass of wine with his supper.

She still wondered who had broken his heart. If family legend was true, he would pine for her forever. But he did not seem to be pining at all now.

He slid from his mount, crutch in hand, landing on his left foot and then settling onto his crutch. If his chest pained him, there was no sign. He dropped his mount's reins onto the ground and the animal stood obediently there. Blanche watched him move to her left side with some surprise. He raised his left hand. "Come down."

She hesitated, but he was smiling and her heart was melting into a pool, somewhere below her, on the grassy ground.

"I won't fall over and I won't break," he murmured softly.

So much tension arose that her mare snorted. Sir Rex instantly laid his left hand on her neck, fingers splayed, caressing her. He murmured a soft word and Blanche saw her mare drop its head. She could almost hear the animal sigh in pleasure.

Even my mount is affected by his touch, she thought, trembling.

Sir Rex looked up slowly. His eyes were very dark and they gleamed. In that single lazy moment, he appeared so much like the lion from her dream—indolent but intent, predatory and watchful and oh so certain. "Come down," he murmured again in that silken and impossibly intimate tone.

Blanche took his hand and as their palms locked, her heart pounded wildly, urgently. She slipped down from the mare, landing lightly on her feet and in Sir Rex's arms.

He smiled at her as if this was exactly what he intended, and she knew it was.

She couldn't smile back. Her skirts covered his good leg from thigh to toe, and they stood so closely, she felt his hard knee against her thigh. No more than a few centimeters separated her breasts from his chest. And although he held her loosely, she felt his left hand on her waist, his right hand on her back.

"Have you enjoyed our hack?" he murmured, his gaze heated now and searching.

She tried to swallow. "Yes."

"Can I give you Isabelle as a gift?"

Her eyes widened. "You do not have to do such a thing," she gasped brokenly. She could barely think, standing like this, in his carefully controlled embrace.

"But you get along famously. And you are a perfect match. She's a beautiful horse—a beautiful horse for a beautiful woman."

Blanche felt faint. "Are you flirting…Sir Rex?"

"Yes, I most definitely am."

She couldn't think of a thing to say to that. She looked at his full and now-still mouth. She swallowed hard again. Could he hear her heart pounding? For it was deafening in her ears.

His voice softened. "I have come under the impression that you might not reject my advances."

Her knees buckled and she swayed against him, her breasts flattening against his chest. His arms tightened around her. "Am I correct?" he whispered.

She somehow nodded. She couldn't speak. Desire was drumming through her.

"I wish to make advances, Blanche," he said roughly. His hands splayed out on her back and shoulder, pulling her more closely against his hard, powerful body. "I wish to kiss you," he said, his tone now thick. "May I?"

She inhaled, nodding. She raised her face, realizing she was ready to cry.

"Don't cry," he said softly, his face tightening. "Just allow me this kiss," he breathed.

She saw his lashes lower sensually; she saw him drift his mouth toward hers. In disbelief, in hope, she waited, and she felt his lips ever so barely feather against her mouth.

She gasped at the sensation, eyes closing, as he began to slowly, gently, brush his mouth back and forth against hers. Blanche felt her heart explode frantically, and with it, a shocking pulse began, beneath her skirts. She clasped his shoulders and pressed closer and the moment she did so, his mouth firmed, the pressure increasing.

She cried out.

His mouth opened hers, his hand now on the back of her head, and he began to kiss her with hunger and need. Blanche felt him stabbing against her hip and a terrible excitement began. She hung on to him more tightly and he swept his tongue deep. He was kissing her as if he could never do so deeply enough.

The world spun.

Air failed.

His huge hard body, his mouth, his embrace, consumed her entirely. His hands moved low, almost to her buttocks, and the pressure between them grew. Blanche felt shocking moisture dripping and for the first time in her life, she wished he would slip his hand beneath her skirts and touch her to ease her aching.

His tongue thrust deep. He grunted, the sound male, sexual and intent. Blanche gave up and cried out softly.

He tore his mouth from hers and held her tightly, pressing her face to his chest, his cheek against her temple. She was aware of her heart, pounding wildly in her chest, and his heart, pounding even more furiously beneath her cheek. He was breathing harshly, but so was she.

Desire, Blanche thought, so much desire.

Tears began.

She had never dreamed that this day would really come.

She wanted Sir Rex. She wanted him to kiss and touch her and she wanted to kiss and touch him back. And she wanted more than that, no matter how shocking it was.

"Blanche," he finally said somewhat breathlessly. He tilted up her face. "Why are you crying?" His eyes went wide with alarm.

She didn't hesitate as the tears rolled down her face. "I did not know a kiss could be like that."

He started. Then, "Neither did I."

CHAPTER TEN

IT WAS VERY DIFFICULT to stand there like a gentleman. He had never dreamed Blanche would be staring at him with dazed eyes, swollen lips and mussed hair. He had never dreamed he would ever kiss her. But more importantly, he had never dreamed he would want a woman as desperately as he wanted her.

A soft breeze sent tendrils of pale platinum hair against her cheeks. He summoned a smile, as if they had not just shared a devastating kiss, as if his loins were not straining the confines of his breeches, as if he did not wish to crush her soft, small body in his arms again and do far more than kiss her. "Shall we?" he gestured toward the ruins.

She swallowed and breathed, her soft lips opening. He vividly recalled their moist texture and sweet taste. Everything had changed that day at the church. Or had it been the result of her stumbling upon him at midnight while he was foxed—and refusing to condemn him? He had been stunned again and again by her kindness, her admiration, her respect. Maybe their relationship had changed because of the accident. Or was it every single moment combined, rolling together like the rocks in a landslide, gaining momentum and growing in force, since her stunning appearance at Land's End?

He knew when a woman was receptive to him. She had begun to flit about him nervously...and steal glances at him when she thought he was not looking. And that had begun in the great room at midnight when he had been anything but a gentleman.

Subsequently she had been filled with gratitude for his concern after she had fainted outside the church, and somehow, he knew she had wept over him when he had been seriously injured by the stud colt. Most importantly, he would never forget awakening after her surgery to find her openly staring at his body, hunger in her blue-green eyes.

He was never going to define the precise moment in time when Blanche Harrington became aware of him as a man, but it had happened, and with every passing moment, he had become more certain of it.

And now, there was no doubt. He had kissed her, meaning to remain rather chaste, but his passion had spiraled almost uncontrollably until he had taken her with hunger and need. And she had kissed him back, not quite as wildly, but wildly enough; she had also shed tears in his arms.

Now she nodded and smiled tremulously at his suggestion that they stroll among the ruins. He was aware of a distinct aching in his heart, as well as his body. Desire was one thing, any other yearning another, and therefore, forbidden. He could imagine taking her to bed, but he must not go further than that. He limped carefully after her, as the ground was both uneven and strewn with rocks.

And he smiled inwardly. He had somehow known that she was a fiery woman, never mind her infallible grace.

But her single remark still seemed strange.

I did not know a kiss could be like that.

What, exactly, had she meant? Was it at all possible she had enjoyed his kiss that much more than anyone else's? It was unlikely—he'd have better luck betting his entire fortune on the nag with the worst odds at Newmarket, than having such false hope here.

Blanche paused, glancing up at the tower. She smiled hesitantly at him, over her shoulder. "If there are ghosts, they can't be your ancestors."

He marveled at how elegant and lovely she was, even after such an interlude. "My ancestors haunt the far north if they have bothered to linger at all."

She reached down and picked a small purple flower, lifting it to her small, delicate nose.

"The gorse rarely bloom until midsummer," he said. "This is an unusual turn of the weather."

She faced him, her cheeks pink.

He felt his own color increase and he stared at her, unable to think of a thing to say. He kept recalling her taste and feel and how wildly she had trembled in his arms. He reminded himself that they had shared a simple kiss, even though it didn't seem simple to him. It could not possibly lead anywhere. Could it?

"Will the horses run off?" she asked softly.

His entire body had stirred. It was not a good idea to think of her in his bed. "No."

"Do you think the ruins haunted?"

"I don't believe in ghosts."

She nodded. "Neither do I." She drifted toward the tower wall. This gave him the opportunity to openly admire her face and figure. But the moment she glanced at him, he lowered his gaze. He had to get a firmer grasp on his raging desire, he thought. A kiss between two adults their age meant nothing. It certainly did not signal the beginning of an affair.

He had only begun to consider actually kissing her since he'd awoken after her surgery. Her concern for his welfare had indicated she would be receptive to his advances, if they were made in a proper manner. He had never considered an affair, and he should not do so now. She would choose someone else, someone lighter in nature, someone younger, someone who was whole, and not just physically, but in spirit, too. Her kisses did not indicate a willingness to go further with him.

His tension knew no bounds.

"You are so deep in thought," she exclaimed softly.

He jerked and felt his cheeks heating. "I have been admiring the scenery," he heard himself say.

She colored. "I am somewhat advanced in age," she began.

"I meant it." He limped over to her, more swiftly than he should have, and his crutch hit a rock. He stumbled but righted himself—she seized his arm, alarmed.

"I have fallen a hundred times learning to use this crutch," he said flatly.

"Falling cannot be pleasant."

"It is hardly pleasant, but neither is losing one's leg."

"It must be difficult, walking on this kind of terrain."

"It is…but not impossible. Blanche."

She started at the familiar use of her name.

"I meant my every word. I do not speak lightly. I am not a flirt by nature. I was admiring your silhouette."

She inhaled. "I do not know what to say…thank you." She glanced away, but she was smiling. "This is silly, for I am flattered all the time." She looked up. "I truly appreciate your admiration, Sir Rex."

He hoped so. "I am going to be incredibly bold." He did not pause, even though her eyes widened. "I did not quite understand your meaning earlier. You said you had never known such a kiss. I cannot imagine what you meant."

She glanced away, toying with the strands of her hair. "Do you really wish to discuss this subject?" She asked, her voice low.

"Yes, I do. We are both adults, and obviously we are rather fond of one another. There is nothing wrong with our sharing a kiss—even a heated one."

Her gaze flew to his. "Sharing a kiss, and discussing it, are two distinct matters."

She was right; he was wrong. The topic was sensitive and

intimate. But he wanted to know if she had meant that she had felt more for him than any other man. "I have admired you for a very long time. I have wanted to kiss you for a very long time," he said bluntly.

"Oh…I didn't know." She sat down on the edge of the stone hedge, seeming stunned. "Really?"

He limped closer. "May I?"

She nodded and he sat beside her. "Really."

She glanced at him with confusion. "But we rarely spoke, and then so briefly."

"By now, you know I do not get on in society. And the truth is, the gossips are right. I have no charm…I am boorish."

"They are wrong!" she cried passionately. "You have been charming to *me*."

He did smile. "It is easy to be charming around you. Your grace makes it so."

"I wish," she said slowly, "that you thought better of yourself." He started.

She stared at him very directly now. "I wish whoever broke your heart, that she had never done so."

He flinched, aghast. It took him a moment to rearrange his expression, and in doing so, he looked away. "I beg your pardon. I hardly have a broken heart."

"The way you spoke of love that night," she said, her voice low and husky, "makes me firmly disagree."

He felt breathless. How could she know, when no one did, not even Ty, that Julia had hurt him all those years ago? But the blow had not been inflicted solely by her, it had been equally inflicted by Tom Mowbray, now Clarewood. And with the passage of a decade, he wasn't sure either one of them had done more than wound him deeply. If his heart was broken, it was because of young Stephen.

He spoke slowly, and with great care. "I cared for someone once, long ago. She betrayed me. But it has been over for years. I do not recall how I spoke that night, but I do know that my heart is not broken." He looked at her for emphasis.

"You said love was grossly overrated."

"I don't recall," he said firmly, but now, he recalled his exact words.

She looked at her lap. "Well, as I am prying, that is convenient. But it seems obvious to me that is why you linger at the end of the world."

He was incredulous. "I am the earl's second son! My choice was to join Her Majesty's forces. I was awarded this estate, Lady Blanche, as you know. Of course I linger here. I have lingered here to make Land's End thrive."

She flushed and he saw the glint of tenacity in her eyes. "You could come to town more often, do not deny it."

He sighed. "I concede defeat. I could come to town more often, but the truth is, I do not care for polite society, outside that of my family. I am sorry. And that," he spoke with a triumphant edge, "is why they call me a boor."

"Yes, they know you do not like them, that you scorn them, and they throw stones in return," she said calmly.

He had to smile. But he was relieved they had gotten past the loathsome subject of his possibly broken heart. "Is it so terrible, for me to linger here at the end of the realm and make a modest living for myself?"

She clasped his forearm and he stiffened. "In many ways, it is admirable." She looked at her palm on his jacket sleeve for one moment and then removed it.

It was a matter of great control not to touch her. And he gave up. He laid his fingertips on her cheek. Their gazes flew together and held. "Tell me what you meant. I think I have misunderstood."

Her mouth opened and there was no mistaking the throbbing tension between them. It thickened the air; it thickened him. It made him savagely satisfied.

"I am afraid I do not recall the topic."

Oh, he did like this tangent. He leaned toward her. "Shall I help you remember?" He took a good long look at her mouth and then, unable to help himself, at the hint of cleavage exposed by her very modest bodice.

She trembled and lifted her gaze, her regard beseeching and dazed.

He slid his hand around to her nape, clasping her firmly, and as he lowered his mouth to hers, so much desire swelled, he could not bear it. He exhaled harshly, pulled her closer and touched her lips with his own. A savage need to possess began and he gave in, claiming them fiercely, opening them wide and pressing deeply inside her with his tongue, and all the while, with the back of his mind, knowing what it would be like to have his male body pushing deep within hers, again and again.

She gasped, and then she kissed him back, using her tongue.

He told himself to stay in control, no simple task, because he saw red, and he was terribly close to giving up and allowing himself a frenzy of desire. He could not stand the pressure of his breeches now. Gasping, he somehow pulled her closer, somehow went deeper into her mouth, until she was shaking and gasping in his arms. He pulled back, dazed and dizzy, yet he murmured her name. "Blanche."

Her blue-green eyes met his.

He wanted more. He was a man, he admired her so; he could not help it. But he breathed and murmured, "Have I re-freshed your memory at all?" And because he could not keep his hands to himself, he rubbed his knuckles against her jaw.

"I didn't know," she said, tears shimmering in her eyes.

He started, for she began to cry yet again.

She touched her lips, as if stunned.

"Why are you crying? Have I hurt you?"

She shook her head, breathing hard, wiping the tears from

her cheeks. "How could you hurt me with a kiss? Even a kiss like that?"

He felt like telling her that kiss was a bare shadow of the kind of kiss he wished to give her. He felt like also telling her that, given the opportunity, he would put his mouth everywhere he could on her slender body, savoring every possible inch of her flesh. Given that opportunity, he would worship her until she begged for mercy. And then maybe he would continue, anyway.

"I have only been kissed two times," she said breathlessly. "And those kisses were chaste and dutiful. I had no idea!"

He was stunned. *"What?"*

She shrugged, glancing aside and briefly closing her eyes. "Do you really wish to know?" she cried breathlessly.

"You have only been kissed twice?" His mind raced furiously. If she had only been kissed twice, *two single times,* she had never been with a man. He stared at her in disbelief.

"We should not discuss this," she cried in determination.

Shock shifted to tension. She had not been with a lover, but the man who had kissed her had to have been his brother Tyrell.

She turned her head away, continuing to tremble, clearly distressed. He finally breathed. Of course Tyrell had kissed her. They had been engaged for a few months, long ago—eight years ago. He had assumed Ty had kissed her during their engagement, but he had refused to think about it. Now, he did. "Ty was in love with Lizzie."

"Yes." She looked at him in dismay. "We were both doing our duty," she said tremulously. "There was no attraction."

He kept staring at her. Ty had only kissed her twice—chastely. Blanche Harrington had never known a real kiss until a moment ago.

And she had never known the pleasure—and the ecstasy—a man could give her in bed.

She had never known the pleasure he could give her in bed…. He could be the first.

He looked down at the grass, trembling. A savage sense of triumph arose. He had made a sensible but erroneous assumption. Blanche Harrington, at times, acted as inexperienced and anxious as a fifteen-year-old girl, and now he knew why.

And, dear God, there were two hundred and twenty-eight rakes lined up in town, waiting to prey on her. The thought sickened him.

He could not let her be ravaged by a single one of them. But how on earth would he protect her? God, she was a sheep about to be put out in a pasture infested with wolves.

"Why are you so dismayed?"

He slowly looked at her, quickly recovering from the shocking swing of his emotions. He would debate her future later—and find a way, perhaps with the countess's help, to protect her best interests. For now, he would concentrate on the impossible revelation she had just made.

"I am sorry," he said softly. "I assumed that a beautiful woman of your age had surely enjoyed several discreet encounters."

"I do not take passion lightly."

His heart foolishly soared. "Neither do I."

She gave him an incredulous look.

Instantly, he realized that she would never believe him. But she did not understand the difference between lust and passion. He wasn't certain that this was the time to explain that difference, either. Especially as he continued to reel as if struck by lightning.

"Are you dismayed that Tyrell kissed me?"

He tried to smile. "When I first glimpsed you at Adare, I thought him mad to be so indifferent. I had assumed there were many moments you both shared. I did not really think about it…until now."

She relaxed. "He was so terribly in love with Lizzie."

"I know." She was regarding him closely, even anxiously, and he stared back. "The truth is," he said slowly, "I am honored you allowed me such liberties."

She blushed. Hesitantly, she said, "It was about time, don't you think, that someone finally kissed me?"

His errant heart soared yet another time. "Yes, it was."

She added, "Besides, it felt right to allow you the moment."

"MY LADY? Did you need something?" Meg asked.

Blanche whirled. They had returned from their hack an hour ago, and she had been pacing her chamber ever since— her mind racing frantically, her body feverish. She stared at her maid, who started, her eyes widening. "Come in," Blanche said tersely. "Meg, I need your advice."

Meg quickly entered the bedchamber, closing the door. "You want my advice?" She was disbelieving.

"Yes, I do."

"Are you all right?" Meg asked with worry.

Blanche inhaled, shaking. "I do not think I can wait for Bess's reply. I sent her a letter, hoping for her advice. Meg! I am considering asking Sir Rex to marry me."

Meg started to smile. "Really, my lady?"

"You are not stunned?" Blanche cried.

"I am a bit surprised, perhaps, but the two of you seem very fond of one another. And he is handsome, and solid, if you know what I mean. All those suitors in town, not one of them is as solid as Sir Rex."

Blanche allowed herself a deep breath, hugging herself. "You are so astute," she cried, meaning it. Leave it to her maid to get to the heart of the matter so swiftly. Reclusive or not, dark or not, Sir Rex was solid. He was the kind of man she could count on even now, when they were just friends.

But that had changed, hadn't it? She touched her mouth, still stunned by what had happened on the moors. She hadn't realized a kiss could be so consuming—so intense—so wonderful!

"So you will propose marriage to him?" Meg asked eagerly, grinning.

Blanche inhaled. "You do know he drinks…and he hates town. In some ways, we are very opposite."

"Most men drink. As long as he doesn't mistreat you, as long as he can manage his estate, why should it matter? Besides, I think he is lonely. I haven't seen him drinking recently." Meg shrugged. "If he dislikes town, he can spend more time in the country while you entertain there. Many couples reside apart for some of the time."

"Yes, they do, and it would be considered normal for us to have our separate lives, too," she said, but she somehow disliked the notion. But separate lives would be required in such a union. She knew Sir Rex would never spend an entire Season with her in town. "I don't even know if he will accept me," she said hesitantly.

"He looks at you as if you were a fairy princess," Meg smiled. "I can't imagine why he would refuse your offer."

Blanche could think of a dozen reasons why, including the fact that a woman whom he had loved had broken his heart—and he was a de Warenne. His denial had obviously been a falsehood. However, their marriage was not going to be based on love. It was going to be based on friendship, convenience and economy, among other things. She wet her lips, which still seemed swollen from his kisses. And it would also be based on desire. "He kissed me."

Meg stifled a smile.

"It was wonderful," Blanche said, and more tears came. She realized they were tears of happiness, and perhaps relief—she had hoped the kiss would last forever. She had been consumed with desire, just like any other woman. Although she still felt certain she would never be as passionate as he required, she no longer thought separate bedrooms a necessity. "I never thought I'd want a man's passionate kisses," she added in a whisper. "I never thought I'd wish for a man's passion, either."

"Maybe you're in love," Meg said, smiling. "My lady, you are the kindest lady I have ever met—of all ladies, you should marry for love!"

Blanche simply stared at her maid, her heart lurching. Surely Meg was mad now, for she was incapable of love. Wasn't she? "When Sir Rex walks into the room, I am so pleased to see him." She trembled. "When he is not in the room, I am thinking about him anyway. I have worried about his life, his past, the way he lives, his being alone…. I was terrified when that horse hurt him!"

"That sounds like love to me," Meg said cheerfully.

Blanche stared at her, seeing Sir Rex instead. Her heart danced and she touched her chest. She cared about Sir Rex, terribly, and she would not deny it. But love? Was she falling in love after all these years?

Was she like other women after all?

She dared to do more than hope; she prayed it was so. She so wanted to be an ordinary woman, capable of heartfelt passions and deep emotions. But the notion was also frightening—for she still feared Sir Rex's rejection. And now she trembled with uncertainty, for once again, she was sliding off the precipice of a cliff. But hadn't it been that way from the moment of her arrival at Land's End?

What should she do? What could she do? Sir Rex had become so dear to her.

And as she trembled, overcome with confusion, shadows infested her mind. She tensed, knowing what was within the darkness inside her head—a monster waited there, and he wielded death.

A pain knifed through her head.

It was so debilitating that she sank to her knees, cradling her head in her hands, blinded by the pain.

Meg cried out, rushing to her.

All thoughts of Sir Rex were gone—her head felt cleaved in two. And she saw the monster, half beast, half man, his teeth yellow and dripping saliva, his eyes filled with vicious hatred. Behind him was a vague, shadowy crowd of other vicious monsters. The knife stabbed into her head again, through her right temple. Blanche screamed, clasping her hands to her ears.

Meg cradled her. "My lady, what is it? Oh, God, what's happening?"

The monster leered at her, holding up a pitchfork which dripped blood.

Panic consumed her. Blanche couldn't breathe. She fought for air. The world swam. She somehow saw Meg peering down at her—and then she saw Sir Rex, staring down at her instead, entirely alarmed. She wanted to beg him to save her, but when she opened her mouth to speak, everything went black.

CHAPTER ELEVEN

"DR. LINNEY IS HERE," Sir Rex said from the threshold of her bedchamber.

Blanche sat in her bed, fully dressed, on top of the covers. Sir Rex had apparently carried her to her bed while she remained in a dead faint, and then he had revived her with salts. He had insisted she cover herself with a cashmere throw, which she had dutifully done even though she was not cold. He had then left to summon the doctor, less than an hour before.

Blanche smiled tremulously at him. "He must have been close by."

"He was," Sir Rex said, striding into the room. His gaze was dark with concern. He seemed distressed, and worse, dismayed. Did he think her mad? Blanche wanted to reassure him, but she could not. She had fainted for the second time in less than a week, and she was alarmed, too. What was happening to her?

Dear God, was she actually beginning to recall something from the riot? Those images had been real, even if for so briefly. And she didn't want to recall a single detail of that day.

Dr. Linney followed Sir Rex into the room. A small, dapper man, he was smiling cheerfully. "I wish we were making our acquaintance under other circumstances, Lady Harrington," he said with a smile.

"Thank you for coming," she somehow said.

"I very much admired your handiwork the other day," he said, his eyes twinkling.

Blanche could not relax. "I wish it had been the surgeon's handiwork," she said truthfully.

He smiled, standing over her, Sir Rex beside him. "If you ever wish to become a nurse, you need only let me know."

Blanche finally smiled. Then she looked at Sir Rex, whose face was so tight, his skin seemed about to crack. She felt her own smile vanish, her tension escalate. How ill was she?

"Sir Rex said you fainted—for the second time in five days. Why don't you tell me about it?" he asked kindly.

She somehow tore her gaze from Sir Rex. "There isn't much to tell. I fainted earlier in the week when I walked into the miner's assembly at the church. I simply could not breathe. I have always disliked crowds."

He nodded. "And today?"

Images flashed—their ride upon the moors, her first genuine kiss, her body's feverish longing, and her frantic debate over whether or not to ask Sir Rex for marriage. And then the monsters had appeared in her head. They had appeared amidst blood and pitchforks. What could she possibly tell Dr. Linney? It was unclear if she was remembering the past or not. Her father had never said a word about the mob being armed with pitchforks. He had not mentioned there being blood.

Mama had stumbled and fallen, tragically hitting her head. Hadn't she?

Blanche closed her eyes tightly. She had dared to tell Sir Rex about the riot and her fear of crowds, but she would never tell him the entire truth. She wasn't going to allow him to know that she had an odd, defective nature and that she had lived an entirely emotionless life until recently. And she didn't want the physician knowing any such thing, either. Those were very private matters.

But she was afraid. She was afraid to have those violent images reappear…and she was afraid of what they might mean. She was afraid of that pain in her head. And if those monsters weren't memories, what were they? If they were memories, why were they returning now?

Blanche reluctantly smiled at the physician. She would tell him what she could and hope her headaches had a medical explanation. "Sir Rex and I had been hacking across the countryside," she said, aware of her host's unwavering stare. "It was a pleasant ride. I had returned a half an hour before and I was chatting with my maid when I had a terrible pain in my head. It was very much like a knife cutting into me. And the next thing I knew, I had fallen, because I could not stand the pain. I saw Meg and Sir Rex, and then everything went dark."

"Have you ever had such a headache before?"

She stiffened. "I have had the occasional headache, but rarely. This was not a headache. It was far greater than a headache."

"So you have never had this kind of head pain before?"

"Never," Blanche said emphatically, glancing at Sir Rex.

He looked displeased, dismayed and distressed. Their gazes held. She knew he was thinking about what she had said and the passion they had shared—and suddenly she wondered if he was blaming himself for her episode.

"And how is your health, generally?"

"I am rarely ill. My health is good," Blanche said.

"She barely eats," Sir Rex interrupted. "She takes a single slice of toast for breakfast. And we rode before dinner."

Blanche looked at him. "This is not your fault."

He stared back, clearly blaming himself.

"Maybe you fainted from hunger," Doctor Linney said pleasantly. "Many ladies do. You are a slender woman, Lady Harrington. You do not need to starve yourself."

"I have never had a hearty appetite," Blanche defended

herself. "I do not follow a regime as my friends do—it has never been necessary."

"Her father died six months ago," Sir Rex said harshly. "I have known Lady Harrington for years. He was her only family...they were very close. Since then, she has been deluged with suitors, as she has a great fortune. She came to Land's End for peace of mind." He grimaced. "Yet my household has not been peaceful, I'm afraid."

"Are you suggesting the toll of these past months has caught up with her?"

"It is only a suggestion, as I am not a physician," Sir Rex said tersely.

"Is there anything else you wish to add?" the doctor asked Blanche.

She hesitated. Was Sir Rex correct? She had taken her beloved father's death in stride, without even shedding a tear over his passing. She had wished to grieve, but hadn't been able to do so. Had his death caused a severe strain upon her? Having to tolerate 228 suitors was certainly a burden, and she was very worried about her future. She had lived her entire life in a serene and pleasantly dispassionate manner—until now. Suddenly she was in a whirlwind of passion. But did she dare confess to the rampant confusion which now ruled her days? Was this the strain that had caused her to faint?

And was her anxiety over whether or not to choose Sir Rex as a husband a part of that strain?

"Lady Harrington?"

She avoided his eyes, and as she stared at her clasped hands, she felt Sir Rex's sudden attention, as if he knew she was not revealing what she should. "No, there is nothing else. Sir Rex is right. There has been a great strain these past months, and it has continued, and, in some ways, it is even greater, now."

But he stared at her until she looked up. His gaze was

searching, as if he wished to discover the answers she had refused to give. "I know you wish to examine Lady Harrington, but can I have a private word with her?" he asked the doctor, his regard unwavering upon Blanche.

"No, you may not. I have other patients, Sir Rex. Go and loiter in the hall." Dr. Linney smiled at him and reached for Blanche's wrist. "I am going to take your pulse," he said.

Sir Rex strode out, his expression harsh. Blanche flinched as the door closed—he seemed angry. She then sat patiently as Dr. Linney took her pulse, listened to her heart, and asked about her urine. Dr. Linney closed his black doctor's satchel. He smiled at Blanche. "I can find nothing wrong with you, Lady Harrington. Your health seems exemplary, in fact."

Blanche smiled grimly at him.

"I am inclined to think that Sir Rex is partly right—the strain of these past few months has finally taken its toll on you. That strain, coupled with your delicate eating habits, has resulted in your fainting spells."

Blanche nodded. How she hoped he was right. How she prayed she would never recall those monsters again.

Sir Rex knocked and thrust open the door.

"Come in, as you are hovering as anxiously as a husband over his wife." Linney's eyes sparkled with amusement as he glanced between them.

Sir Rex swung rapidly back to Blanche's side.

"He says I am under a strain and that is why I fainted," she said softly.

He made a harsh sound.

"You may be acquiring migraines," he said. "Let us hope not. I am not going to worry about it, as the pain vanished as suddenly as it came. But I am prescribing a remedy to help you remain calm and restful. Sir Rex can send a servant to the apothecary."

Sir Rex seemed furious now.

"Meanwhile, improve your regime, my dear, and get more rest. I'll leave a dose or two of laudanum, in case the head pain returns. And try not to fret," he said, patting her hand.

"That is your diagnosis?" Sir Rex exploded.

"Her health seems fine," Dr. Linney said, his smile vanishing. "But send for me if she has another episode."

Sir Rex went with him to the door, and then swiftly returned.

Blanche tensed.

"I will take you back to town. You can see a London doctor there. The pain you described is not a migraine."

Blanche said carefully, "I do feel better. Dr. Linney is probably right. I have been under a strain and—"

"I have added to that strain." He cut her off. "Do not deny it."

She stared at him beseechingly. "Sir Rex, you have been a wonderful host."

"Isn't that what you neglected to tell Dr. Linney? That I have distressed you since the day of your arrival here?"

She cried out.

"I frightened you in the great room that night, and do not deny it!"

She shook her head. "Only a little," she offered.

"And I pushed too hard this afternoon! I added to your strain today!" he cried.

Blanche hugged herself. "Do not even begin to say that the afternoon we shared caused me to faint, hours later. I so enjoyed this afternoon."

"You are not well, Blanche. You are a tiny, delicate woman, too kind for your own good, who gives generously to everyone but yourself. You care for everyone else, do you not? You have even cared for me, when a servant could have done so. Who cared for you after Lord Harrington passed?" he demanded. "Who will care for you now?"

"I have a huge staff," she tried.

He stared at her. "Your father died, you are deluged with rakes and rogues, and then you come here, and I must insist upon making advances. I am frankly not surprised that you fainted. I believe I am the very last straw, for you cannot tolerate any more pressure."

Blanche felt her temples throb, but with a very normal headache, not that brutal, frightening pain of before. She was ready to tell him the truth. She was under a great strain, but not for the reasons he thought. It was the strain of so much emotion when she was so unused to it. It was the strain of making a decision that would change her entire life—if he did not reject her.

"Anne is preparing a supper tray." He turned to go. Then he turned swiftly back. "You cared for me when I was injured, and now it is my turn. Do not deter me! You will rest for a few days and we will forget about this afternoon."

Her eyes widened. She did not want to forget. "Sir Rex, this is not your fault," she protested. "I am not so fragile that I will break if I am looked at the wrong way."

He gave her a dark, long look. "I am sensing something in you that I have never sensed before. I have always sensed your vulnerability—I even remarked on it that night. But there is more. And it is fragility. I do not know if it is your person or your sensibilities, but you are very fragile beneath that facade of grace and perfection. Am I wrong?"

She could not speak. Because somehow, she knew he was right—that if her composure was stripped from her, contrary to her statement to Sir Rex, she might break. The monsters told her that.

"I thought so." He nodded harshly and left.

Blanche had the urge to weep. This time, the ability to cry was a curse. She did not want it! It hurt! She flung the cashmere throw to the floor, when she wished to crash a glass instead.

The monster leered.

Blanche froze, terrified, his image vivid and clear in her mind. The knifelike pain began. "Sir Rex!" She screamed.

REX HEARD HER piercing scream and he whirled, losing his balance. He hit the wall and regained his stance, pushing the door open with his left hand. Then he tore into the room at great speed.

She held her head in her hands, her face almost in her knees. He sat beside her but she said, "Don't!" Her tone told him she was on a terrible brink.

He clasped her shoulder, using all of his self-control not to hold her. She breathed harshly, trembled and looked up. Tears stained her face.

"You had another head pain?"

She nodded and said, as if she was afraid speaking might bring more pain, "It's gone."

He nodded, his heart now thundering in his chest. He did not know what to think, and damn it, terrible worst-case scenarios were flashing through his mind—he knew someone who'd had terrible head pains, and he'd become gaunt and thin and had finally died. "It only lasted an instant?"

She nodded, sighed and finally smiled. Her smile was so tremulous he had the urge to weep. "I'm fine."

He did not refute her, but she was hardly fine. Her scream had been bloodcurdling—again. He knew he had uncovered the truth when he had accused her of hiding a vast fragility beneath her exterior airs and manners. He stared at Blanche. He wished he could decipher the cause for such delicacy. He wished he knew what made her so vulnerable, and by that, he did not mean inexperienced.

"Why don't you take a dose of laudanum after you eat something?" He kept his tone carefully neutral.

She smiled again. "I think that might be a good idea."

She knew he was afraid to leave her. Their gazes locked.

"It is a migraine," she now said, softly. "I have no doubt."

She had fainted, she had head pain, she was in tears, and she thought to reassure *him*. "Yes," he lied smoothly. "I am sure it is just that." He would send Fenwick to town to bring a doctor back. Tyrell was there, Tyrell could find the best physician, a specialist of some sort. But they didn't even know what kind of specialist she needed. Maybe, if there was any justice in the world, Linney was correct and she simply needed rest.

And he had to keep himself in check. She did not need his attentions now. *Damn it.*

He stood, aware of so much disappointment—and how selfish it was. "Let me have a tray sent up. Please humor me and eat something before you rest."

She touched his hand. "Sir Rex." Her smile wavered. "Do not worry so. I am *fine*."

He would not argue that point now.

"I feel terrible putting you out," she added. "Meg can prepare a tray—"

"You are not putting me out. You could not put me out, not under any circumstance. In spite of my behavior, in spite of everything, you nursed me through my accident, perhaps even saving my life." He realized his tone was brutally harsh. He tried to soften his expression, too. "Blanche. I owe you a great debt. Let me return it."

She stared at him.

"Please," he added, incapable of summoning a smile. "Let me take care of you now."

She finally nodded. "Thank you."

"HOW DO I LOOK?" Blanche asked the next morning.

"A body would never know you were ill yesterday," Meg said, standing behind her as they stared into a mirror. "You are so beautiful, my lady."

Blanche trembled. She was going to ask Sir Rex to consider marrying her.

It was almost noon. The dose of laudanum had been exactly what she needed—she had slept through the entire night without even moving once. And the moment she had awoken, she had thought of her host.

He was not only the kind of man who could manage her considerable fortune, he was kind and considerate, a rock of towering strength, and after yesterday, she was certain they could make a go of it. She had spent the entire morning bathing, dressing and doing her hair while trembling with anxiety and excitement. She was wearing a lavender gown with a lower-cut bodice—it was an elegant dress, suitable for any supper party in town. She had adorned it with amethysts and diamonds. A diamond clip even decorated her hair. Sir Rex was fond of her, he desired her, and she desperately wished for him to accept her proposal.

"I am so nervous," Blanche whispered, but she kept thinking about how Sir Rex wished to blame himself for her illness yesterday—and how concerned he had been. Meg had told her he had spent the night in a chair in her room. Blanche had been thrilled at the thought. On the other hand, she tried to hold that emotion in check. He had specifically said he owed her. She did not want his acceptance of her suit as payment for any personal debt.

As if reading her thoughts, Meg said, "He will be a good husband, my lady. He is so caring of you!"

"He is, isn't he?" Blanche smiled, and as she did, her heart leaped for the hundredth time. She could not manage his rejection. She dared not think of it. She was so fond of him, all of him—in spite of his periodically dark humor. "I have decided to be blunt. In most matters, we suit. This will be a marriage of convenience and friendship, and what is wrong with that?" She thought about the two kisses they had shared.

It might even be a marriage of passion, she thought, and she inhaled, as more moisture gathered in her eyes.

Blanche could barely believe she would suddenly cry at the drop of a hat. But she was wary now, as well, for her tears yesterday had brought that terrible head pain. And it had brought an image of that half beast, half man, and while she had no wish to recall it, unfortunately, the image was engraved on her mind.

Blanche hurried to the bed stand to take a sip of water, but no pain came. She breathed more deeply and when nothing foul occurred, she finally relaxed.

Meg patted her arm. "Be yourself, my lady. Tell him that you care." She smiled.

Blanche had to smile back, her heart racing wildly again. "I will see how it goes. Wish me luck!" She hurried from the room and downstairs.

In the great room, she paused. The tower room door was open and she felt certain Sir Rex was there. She slowly approached, trying to marshal her arguments. He was a very rational man, so she intended to persuade him with logic. After all, such a union was meant to be beneficial to both parties.

He was seated at his desk, but he was staring at the open doorway as if aware of her approach. His gaze met hers when she paused on the threshold there. His eyes flickered and he looked at her hair, her entire gown, her bodice and then back at her face. He slowly rose to his foot and crutch. "Are you going back to town?" he asked.

She started. "No!"

Relief appeared on his face. "You are dressed for town."

She flushed. "Am I? Meg insisted on the lilac, I cannot recall why."

His gaze narrowed.

"Actually," she swallowed, suddenly ill with nervous fear,

"I was wondering if you had a few moments. There is a matter I was hoping to discuss with you."

He straightened. "Of course. I take it you are feeling better?" His gaze roamed her face again slowly, feature by feature.

She closed the door and then came forward, aware that he had remarked the unusual action. His gaze appeared suspicious. "I had a very good night's sleep and I feel wonderful today. I even had an omelet for breakfast."

He nodded, watching her closely, as if he sensed an assault was about to be launched. Blanche reminded herself that he was very perceptive and he now knew her well. She sat down in the chair facing his desk, fussing with her skirts, her heart thundering far too loudly. Maybe she should delay such a proposal, she thought. She hadn't expected to be so nervous.

He was staring oddly at her.

She realized she should have sat on the sofa.

But he sat down in his desk chair, the large desk between them. "You seem uneasy. I cannot imagine why. Is this a business matter?"

She smiled brightly. Marriage was usually a business arrangement. "Yes...for the most part."

He leaned back.

She took a breath for courage.

"What is wrong?"

She smiled brightly again. "There is a matter I wish to discuss, but, I am not sure I can. I have never raised such a matter before."

"I will help if I can," he said swiftly. "You do wish to ask me for my help in a business matter?"

"Not quite," she managed. "But in a way, yes."

He seemed wary. "That clarifies matters."

"Sir Rex." She somehow smiled. "In a way, you were right about yesterday. There was some excessive strain, but it had nothing to do with our hack on the moors."

He was entirely attentive now. His gaze did not flicker, once.

"And, really, I did not object to your advances—as you know." She looked carefully at him.

"Then what possible strain arose yesterday after our ride?" he asked bluntly.

His eyes were as watchful as the lion's in her dream, she thought uneasily. "I have been thinking about my future," she said on a long breath. "I have been giving it a great amount of thought and even internal debate."

He sat up sharply.

"I was thinking about it yesterday after we returned from our hack. My fears about my future did cause strain, Sir Rex. I believe that is why I fainted, or at least, that is partially why."

He stared during a long pause. "Where are you leading?"

She wet her lips. His gaze moved there. "I am not going to consider any of my current suitors for my hand."

He was silent.

He wasn't making this easy, she thought. "I mean, that was your advice when I first came to Land's End, and it had seemed correct to me, even then."

"Are you hedging?" His tone remained blunt.

She inhaled and nodded. She was about to blurt out that she was so fearful of what she must ask! Instead, she trembled, sought composure, and said softly, "Sir Rex, it seems clear to me that we have developed an unusual friendship in the past week, even though we have known one another for years."

Confusion flitted through his eyes. But he remained watchful. "Yes, I agree."

"I am aware that you hold me in some esteem, and I also hold in you in the same regard, but I have said so already."

He began shaking his head. "What are you trying to say?"

"We have gotten to know one another as never before," she

managed. "And there are wonderful qualities to your character…. You are clever, astute, industrious, honest and resourceful!" she cried.

His eyes widened.

"I have been impressed with your management of this estate."

His surprised expression intensified.

She saw that he had no clue as to where she was leading. "I am aware of our differences, of course, but after carefully considering the subject, I was wondering…" She stopped. She wanted to marry Sir Rex. She had not a single doubt. She did not know if she could fashion a proper proposal. She was foundering when she should be persuasive and firm.

"What subject?" he demanded. "Because I am lost."

"The subject of marriage."

His eyes widened impossibly.

"I thought we might suit," she gasped. "And I was wondering if you would consider a marriage proposal from me!"

His brows jerked upward. He was clearly shocked. He stood, incredulous.

Oh, God, she thought, ill to her stomach. Is he horrified, too, or just stunned?

He opened his mouth, but no words came out.

Blanche slowly stood. "I see you are somewhat surprised—"

"Are you suggesting a marriage between *us?*"

"Yes," she whispered, aware of becoming crimson. He seemed to think it a terrible idea!

"You and me." But his harsh tone was somehow a question.

"Yes." She swallowed, dismayed by his reaction, aware she must either rush to save the day or flee. "You need a wife and I need a husband. You need a fortune and I need someone with the strength and integrity of character to manage my fortune. Clearly, such a marriage, one of convenience and economy, with the additional value of friendship, would be mutually beneficial!" she cried.

"A marriage of convenience and economy," he echoed, in disbelief.

"We do seem to have conjoining needs," she tried.

"We do?" A dark shadow fell over his face. "If I wished to marry a fortune, I would have done so long ago."

For one moment she stared, incredulous and dismayed. Then she reeled. "You are refusing me?"

"Have you even thought about this?" he retorted, seeming angry now.

"Of course I have," she responded, shaking. He was displeased, he was angry, he was *refusing* her.

"I prefer the country, and you, town. You are a great hostess, I admit I am a complete recluse. Am I supposed to move to town? How long will I last at your supper table, at the head reserved for the host of the affair?"

She had not thought about supper parties, but she had certainly thought about this particular problem. "Many couples lead separate lives," she tried, aware of moisture filling her eyes. They were arguing about her proposal.

"Separate lives," he echoed. Disbelief widened his eyes. "I see—I will manage your fortune. You will live in town, I will live here."

She stiffened. "I have made a horrible mistake." She turned to go, stumbling, tears blinding her.

She heard his crutch thumping. She stumbled to the door but he barred her way when she got there. "Blanche, do not walk out now! You cannot shock me with such a proposal and simply leave!" he cried harshly.

She looked up at him and saw emotions that were far too familiar to her now—she saw anger, frustration and a torment she did not understand. "But you seem distressed by my offer—when there are over two hundred gentlemen in town, of whom each and every one would be thrilled and flattered to receive such an offer."

"They are fortune hunters—I am not." His gaze blazed. "Or have you misconstrued our friendship—and my advances? Do you now think me the kind of rake to scheme and intrigue and whisper words of love in your ear, all so I might attain your fortune?"

"Of course not!" She trembled.

"Then explain what you are thinking, because I do not understand. I mean, if we are to have a convenient marriage with separate lives, why not simply ask me if I would manage your fortune for some compensation? After all, in the end, it will be cheaper—and it will save me the scorn of your friends."

She blinked. "My friends will not scorn you."

"I will never succeed as a society host."

"I am not asking you to stay on in town. I assumed you would continue to spend most of your time in the country, and that you would come to town now and then, when estate affairs demanded it."

"Ah, yes, the coup de grace. Separate lives—and separate beds?"

She flushed. "I don't believe the subject of bedrooms is appropriate at this point."

"I think it is very appropriate—considering the passion we shared yesterday."

She tensed. Her mind felt scrambled and it raced. "I want children, Sir Rex," she finally said.

His hard stare became searching. A terrible silence ensued. He finally said, "I see." He limped away from the door.

She staggered against the wall, aware he was not looking at her, and hugged herself. She had never thought a furious tempest would ensue from her marriage proposal. "My intention was not to insult you," she whispered, recalling Meg's parting advice. "I am too fond of you to ever wish to insult you—or hurt you."

His crutch thudded like a sledgehammer as he turned to face her. His expression was twisted with anger and anguish. "I will think about it."

She was stunned.

"I never expected a proposal from you." He was terse. "I also never thought to marry—*ever.*"

Oddly, it had never occurred to her that he might wish to consider her idea. She had expected him to be flattered and to accept instantly. She hesitated.

"Surely you will give me a day or two to consider such an offer?" His tone was sharp—and even mocking. "Unless, of course, you are retracting the offer. Are you?"

She stared. She did not like his dark anger, and she never had. She did not know why he would find her proposal insulting. She did not know why he was angry now. A sensible woman—the old Blanche—would withdraw the offer. "I am not withdrawing my offer, Sir Rex."

He nodded, unsmiling and grim.

"Have I misconstrued our friendship?" She had to ask. Maybe her feelings of affection simply were not returned. Her heart lurched painfully now.

"No, you have not." He now stared into her eyes.

She swallowed, remaining impossibly shaken. "Then I cannot understand this conversation. I cannot understand you, Sir Rex."

"No, you cannot." His mouth turned down. "I must question the kind of future we will share. Not because I have reservations about you—but because I have grave reservations about myself."

CHAPTER TWELVE

WHEN BLANCHE HAD LEFT, he limped to the door and shut it. Then he simply stared blindly at it, his mind reeling.

He had never expected a marriage proposal from Blanche Harrington. She had to be mad to even begin to think him suitable as her husband. He was dark, she was light. She was good—too good for him. And she could do so much better!

He realized he could not breathe adequately. He was undone. Because a marriage to such a woman was almost a dream come true—except he did not harbor such dreams, not anymore.

Shaking and shaken, but not as angry, he swung to the window and stared blindly outside. Here in the country, they got along well. Clearly, the friendship they now shared had caused her to think so insensibly. But in town? They would not get along there. He would disappoint her, let her down.

And a marriage of *convenience?* A marriage of *economy* and *separate* lives?

His temples throbbed. His disbelief grew. He did not want a genuine marriage much less one of convenience or economy! And only a fool would think to lead a life separate from a woman like Blanche Harrington—and he was no fool. If he accepted her offer, he would wish to be with her as much as possible, these past few days told him as much.

He tried to analyze the situation with some calm. He despised society and he always had. It was not a secret;

everyone knew. That would never change—he was a simple man, with simple tastes. And Blanche knew it! She had not been thinking clearly.

Yes, they were friends. He was pleased to know she was fond of him—she had just stated so. He was more than fond of her. And there was passion. It had only just begun, but clearly, she felt an attraction for him. But friendship and some desire on her part, as well as his desire, did not indicate a successful future. For if he chose to stay in town, if he somehow defied his very nature, if he forced himself to fit into society, no matter how he tried, eventually he would fail. There was no way he could please the ladies and gentlemen of the ton. Even if he wore a facade of charm, it would only last so long. He was not a conversationalist and he was neither charming nor witty. Besides, everyone already knew the truth about him.

And he would hate his life if he lived in town. He was already bitter—he could not imagine becoming more so. But he wouldn't hate it entirely, because she would be the bright spot in an otherwise dark existence. She would be that drink of water in the midst of a hot desert.

He suddenly imagined being the lord of Harrington Hall. He imagined a conversation with his steward in the library, and then his wandering through the endless rooms and halls, only to come upon Blanche—his *wife*—as she conversed quietly in a salon with her callers. And he smiled. His heart raced.

The truth was, he would give up his right arm to marry a woman like that, when he was already missing half a limb.

But Rex was not deluded. There was so much temptation to accept her offer and try to make a go of it. If he dared to accept her proposal, they would have to lead separate lives. The matter would be one of his sanity. He would never last more than a month in town. He carefully thought about it now. He would spend most of his time in the country. Blanche would be his wife, entertaining in town, while he lived very much as he did now. They would exchange letters, of course. He would probably live for those letters. He was used to being alone, but he already knew that when Blanche left Land's End in a few more days, his sense of loneliness would increase. So what would it be like to leave her to return to the country after they were wed, and after they had shared a household and the kind of affairs a married couple did? After they had shared a bed?

She wanted children.

He leaned against the door. He could be the father of her children—and while he would not love Stephen any less, and while the loss of his son would always haunt him, he knew there would be so much joy to have such a family.

He trembled. He had never thought to have other children. He was the most cautious of men with his lovers, terrified at the thought of begetting another bastard—and losing her or him. If he accepted Blanche's offer, not only would she be his wife, there would be children and he would have a family.

He felt ready to collapse. This marriage would be difficult, and for every pleasure, there would be pain—he had not a doubt.

Blanche Harrington was the ideal, perfect woman; the ideal, perfect wife. Except this match was entirely imperfect. He had never intended to marry. The de Warenne men married for love. He had realized long ago that love was not for him; he had intended to remain single. For love involved trust, and that word was not a part of his vocabulary—it had been erased in the spring of 1813. Except…Blanche Harrington was different. He already trusted her—he always had.

Which meant he was in the gravest danger of falling in love—and that, he knew he must not do.

How could he accept her offer?

How could he refuse?

BLANCHE RUSHED into her bedchamber, trying to remind herself that he had not refused her yet. But she remained terribly shaken. Worse, an actual tear tracked down her cheek—his reaction to her offer hurt so much.

"My lady!" Meg cried in shock. She was kneeling before the hearth, taking the old ashes out.

"I am fine," Blanche lied, smiling so brightly it hurt, too. "Really!"

Meg stood, stunned.

Blanche covered her face with her hands. "My offer dismayed him—enraged him, really—and I hardly know why."

"Oh, come sit down," Meg cried, taking her to the closest chair.

"He did not refuse me, actually. He is considering my offer of marriage."

"I am so sorry! I thought he loved you...shows you how much I know."

"Sir Rex did not act like a man in love, or even a man fondly disposed toward me." Blanche sat. "I must be frank. I fear a rejection. He is going to reject me!" And pain lanced through the vicinity in her chest where her heart lay.

"Let me get you a cup of tea," Meg said, sounding angry herself now. "You do not need such rudeness, nor such strain."

The words were barely out when Blanche felt that knifelike pain in her head. She cried out, clasping her hands to her ears.

"My lady!"

Blanche didn't hear her; she couldn't. She balled up over her knees, unable to breathe, the pain blinding.

The monster appeared, but his face had become that of a thin, gaunt, angry man—with bitterly high cheekbones and a bony chin, and he leered—his eyes wide, wild and hate-filled.

"I'll get Sir Rex!"

Blanche couldn't speak. The monster was drawing the

knife slowly from her skull. She began to breathe deeply and harshly, as the pain lessened, until only a slight shadow of it remained. She straightened, trembling and aghast.

And now, the monster had a face.

I don't want to remember anymore, she thought. Her stomach lurched—she realized she might vomit.

And then she realized what Meg had said—and where she was going.

A part of her wished for the safety of Sir Rex's presence, another did not. That proud half won. She leaped up and ran into the hall. "Meg! Come back! I am fine!"

Meg was about to race down the stairs. She hesitated, her face ashen.

Blanche began breathing more normally. "Come back," she said firmly. "The episode is over."

Meg returned fearfully. "My lady, you are ill."

She wasn't ill, Blanche thought. It was far worse than that. Her worst fears were coming true—she was remembering details from the riot.

She was almost certain that man had been the man, or one of them, who had murdered her mother.

She tensed in dismay. Her mother had died from hitting her head while falling. She had *not* been murdered. She did not know why she had just thought such a thing.

She somehow smiled. "Dr. Linney is right. It is just the onset of a migraine. I am hardly the first woman to suffer from a headache. There is no need to worry."

But even as she spoke, she recalled the devastating encounter with Sir Rex. I am under too much strain, she thought. And grief rose up. She was anticipating his rejection—she was certain of it—and she was so fond of him, it hurt.

And Meg voiced her very thoughts. "Maybe we should return to town. Maybe we've been in the country for too long."

"I think you may be right," Blanche said. She closed her

eyes, because her heart was protesting and she realized she did not want to leave. But this strain was intolerable—and even more intolerable was the advent of some of her lost memories.

"MY LADY," Meg whispered, behaving as if someone had died, "Sir Rex has asked you to meet him in the gardens."

Blanche sat on the chaise, staring at the fire. Had he made his decision so swiftly? He had said he needed a day or two, and it had only been a few hours. She looked grimly at Meg. "He is going to refuse me."

"If he is such an arse, good riddance to him. You can do better!" Meg cried furiously.

Blanche stood, breathing rapidly. She felt light-headed, but knew she would not faint. "You like him."

"Not anymore, I don't! Not with what he's putting you through! He's selfish, he is, choosing his lonely life of melancholy to a life with you. I thought he was a gentleman. Gents take care of their women."

"I am not his woman."

"He's been acting like you are. He's been acting like the ground you walk on is holy!"

"He despises society," Blanche said, and realized she wished to defend him still. "You can see how much he enjoys his life here."

"He doesn't like town? So what! He likes you, and that should be enough. But I guess it's true, you can't teach an old dog new tricks."

Blanche stared at Meg, for the first time shaking off her hurt and beginning to realize what was, possibly, driving Sir Rex. She had been so immersed in his rejection and her hurt, that she hadn't stopped to think about his feelings. "In town, they gossip about him ruthlessly—even Bess and Felicia do."

Meg met her gaze, some of her hostility fading.

"I have always hated the gossips—and especially, the

gossip about him," she admitted. "He told me he will fail in society," she added quietly. "I have just realized he is a man who never fails—look at this estate."

"What are you saying?"

"He told me his decision wasn't about me—but his doubts about himself. He is afraid to fail. But what he doesn't know is that I have entertained more in ten years than most ladies do in a lifetime. I don't care if I never entertain anyone except my family and friends again—and I don't care what others think, either. And I certainly don't care if he cannot tolerate the ton!"

"Then you should tell him so—if he gives you the chance."

Blanche grimaced. "He is going to reject me…and I am certainly not going to argue then." She glanced at the mirror. She looked as stressed as a woman on her way to some terrible fate. She picked up an ivory shawl, saddened now for Sir Rex as much as for herself. But she must stop wishing to meddle in and improve his life. If she could, she should stop caring about him, too. Her thoughts had never felt so dismal.

"It will be too awkward to stay here—you should start packing our things." The hurt welled up again, turning into grief. His rejection was bad enough, but now, she realized she would miss him the moment she left.

"Oh, my lady," Meg whispered.

"It is better this way. Maybe he is right, and if not, it is better he refuse than force himself into a marriage he has no interest in." Blanche smiled again and went slowly downstairs, her heart fluttering, perspiration gathering between her breasts. She stepped outside and noticed that the day had turned as heavy and gray as her heart felt. It was going to pour, she thought. How absolutely appropriate.

Sir Rex was silhouetted against the steel-gray ocean and the equally pale horizon. As she approached, her heart turned over, and she was certain that leaving him now would not change her newly found affection. He was a formidable sight—a handsome, powerfully built man. He turned, one hand in the pocket of his brown wool jacket, the other resting on the bar within his crutch. From a distance, across the gardens, their gazes met.

He left the edge of the precipice and started slowly toward her, entering the bare gardens. Blanche paused, incapable of taking another step. His slow pace made her wonder if he was filled with his own dread.

His expression was somber as he paused before her. "You have shocked me," he said quietly.

"I am aware of that." She trembled, wishing they could avoid this encounter and somehow go back to a previous time.

"Blanche, I am honored that you would think me a suitable candidate for your hand."

She made a sound. "You are not honored. You seemed dismayed and angry, but not honored." She could not believe her blunt words. Then, "I realize you are about to refuse me."

His expression became twisted. "No, I am honored. And I have felt many emotions this afternoon, but dismay was not one of them."

She had no idea of how to respond, and she felt perilously close to tears.

"Actually, I wished to discuss the matter with you a bit further." His regard was direct and searching.

She began breathing hard. She felt her own anger spark—and it was entirely unfamiliar. "Are you toying with me, Sir Rex?"

"No, I am not. I would never do such a thing. I meant everything I said earlier, and I will add this—I believe you are far too good for a man like me. However," he cut her off, "I wish to accept your offer if you have really thought about what a marriage between us would mean."

She was so surprised, having expected the worst, that she

lost some of her balance. He lightly steadied her. "You are not refusing me outright?"

"No, I am not." He hesitated. "But I do not want to accept your proposal and disappoint you one day."

"You won't."

He lifted his hand. "Blanche, are you certain? I realize that, for the most part, we get along famously here at Land's End. But have you considered, really, what it will be like to reside together, even if for a mere month, in town? Have you envisioned me at the head of your table during a supper affair? Will you be unhappy when I must return to the country? Will you be annoyed, or even disappointed? And what will you do if you overhear gossips behind your back, condemning me, or even us both?"

Blanche was stunned by his tangent. "Are you trying to protect me?"

"Of course I am. I have felt the urge to protect you for some time now. I wish to protect you from a future of unhappiness— from me, if you will."

"How can you predict such a future? I happen to think it will be an amenable one."

"If I had a crystal ball," he said tersely, "and saw the kind of future you envision, I would not hesitate to accept."

Blanche gasped.

"I prefer your happiness to my own."

"I am becoming aware of that," she managed. "So you really feel some of the affection for me that I feel for you?" She began to reel—with happiness and hope.

"I do not lie and I do not dissemble. I said I care for you, and I do."

She was moved, and there was the swelling of joy. She reminded herself that he hadn't accepted her suit yet. "I have seen you in your worst moments, Sir Rex."

"I was about to bring that up. Can you blame me for being

surprised by your proposal when you have seen me dallying with the maid—and drinking alone at midnight? That night I was foxed, my comments were inappropriate—and some, highly suggestive. Yet, instead of condemning me, you offer me marriage."

"I have begun to comprehend you, Sir Rex."

His mouth finally shifted, tilting up ever so slightly at the corners. "Really?"

"Yes, and do not deny that the war and a woman are responsible for a great deal of your torment."

He stared, his mouth suddenly turned down. "I will admit no such thing. We are both entitled to a few secrets."

She did not like his choice of words—or the direct stare that followed it.

"I do not want to disappoint you," he said firmly. "I do not want, a year or two from now, for you to find me alone at midnight with my demons and despise me, regretting this day."

"I could never despise you," she gasped.

"You mean it."

"I do!"

He nodded grimly. Then, "Blanche, I cannot promise you I will be able to linger as long as you would like in town. I cannot promise you I will not be stricken with insomnia, and sit up drinking well into the night. Nor can I promise you that I will be polite or pleasant if you dare to confront me at such a time."

She bit her lip, her heart racing madly now. He was on the verge of accepting her offer, yet he insisted on defining his every flaw. "I am aware that if I confront the lion in his den, I may get bitten. However, like a small dog, your growl is far worse than any bite."

"I cannot dissuade you? You realize the pitfalls awaiting us in such a marriage?"

"I do, and no, I will not be dissuaded," she cried.

He stared and she stared back. He still refused to smile; if anything, he seemed more intense and uncertain. "Then I must make a final confession."

Blanche started. Fear began, bringing dread. Hadn't there been enough confessions? What could he possibly admit to?

He wet his lips—a nervous gesture she had never before seen. "I will understand entirely if you decide to withdraw after you hear what I am about to say."

"You are frightening me."

He grimaced. "In all conscience, I cannot go forward without a declaration. Blanche, I have a child—I have a son."

Her surprise began—she hadn't heard a word, she hadn't guessed!

"He lives with his mother in an arrangement made almost a decade ago." His mouth twisted into severely unhappy lines.

And lightning struck—she knew. His broken heart was wrapped up not in the war, but in this woman, the mother of his child, and in his son.

"There are no other heirs," he said as if reciting rehearsed lines. "I realized some time ago they could offer my child the kind of life and inheritance I never could."

They, she thought. "Another couple is bringing your son up?"

He nodded. "His name is Stephen and he is nine years old." He suddenly stiffened and turned away. His profile had become a mask of self-imposed control. In that instant, she saw that he was battling a profound grief.

Blanche's heart broke for him. He mourned the child he could not acknowledge or raise. She wanted to comfort him, but did not dare—and she sensed that even if she touched him, he would break down before her. She knew his pride must not be compromised.

He inhaled raggedly. "One day, he will inherit a great title, one of the greatest in the land, and with it, a great fortune." He slowly faced her.

His agony was expressed in every deep line in his face. "Tell me about him," she whispered. "Is he dark, like you? Is he fair?"

"I cannot." He limped away.

Blanche inhaled, hugging herself. After nine years, the subject of his son remained raw and painful. She knew she dare not ask the questions she wished to…but one day, she would.

He finally faced her, a dormant flower bed between them. "I believe I am doing what is best for my son. He does not know that I am his father. Until he inherits, he never will."

"What you are doing is selfless," she said softly, "and it is what any good parent would do."

He nodded curtly. "Thank you. And no one knows. This is a secret I have borne alone. It is hard enough to accept without sharing it with my prying, opinionated family."

"Of course. Your secret is safe with me."

He faced her directly. "I see no shock on your face. And again, I see no condemnation."

"I will not condemn you for having an illegitimate child. My God, half the ton has illegitimate children." She somehow smiled, hoping to encourage him.

His face tightened. Then he reached out. Her heart soared and she gave him her hand. His fingers closed tightly around her palm—as if he was afraid to ever let go. "You are, without a doubt, the most generous woman I have ever met."

"This is not a matter of generosity, Sir Rex. Friends do not judge, accuse or condemn one another. Friends are loyal."

"Do you wish to rethink your offer? We have had a frightfully open conversation. I would encourage you to think about it."

"I do not have to rethink anything." She tightened her grasp on his hand. "My affection remains—as do my hopes for a future together. I am not dissuaded," she added.

He nodded and then lifted her hand to his lips. She felt faint as he kissed it. "There is one promise I can make you. You will have my loyalty, Blanche, in every possible way. I will do my best to defend you and your interests, protect them, uphold them and cherish them."

His vows made her sway. He caught her, placing his left arm around her waist. "That also means I will never stray, Blanche. I will never be unfaithful."

She thought of Anne and hesitated. How could she let him make such a promise?

"What?" he asked sharply. "Do you doubt me? The de Warenne men are notorious for being rakes as bachelors—and then being ridiculously faithful as husbands."

"I know," she whispered. "I have always known you would be faithful to a wife."

"I will be faithful to *you*," he said firmly. He hesitated. "I want to be faithful to you."

Blanche let the tears fall and they were tears of happiness. "And what if it becomes impossible for you to keep that promise?"

He slowly became incredulous. "What does that mean, exactly? Are you suggesting I will want to stray? Why would I wish to be unfaithful? Are you implying that you will bar your door to me?"

She turned away, pulling free of his hand. If only she could confess the entire truth to him! She owed him the kind of confession he had just made to her. If only she could tell him the truth about her life—and how odd she was, compared to other women. If she could somehow explain that she had never felt half of what she had felt this past week, that angst and joy, desire and despair were all new emotions for her, he might understand that she was not an extremely passionate woman.

He might realize they were not as well matched as he might hope in one certain area. At some point in time, she was going to disappoint *him,* not the other way around.

But she couldn't reveal any of this. It was too humiliating.

He stalked around her, crutch thudding. "Will you bar your door to me? Is that what you intend to do, after a child is conceived?"

"No," she whispered. "I haven't any such intention."

"Then what are you saying?"

Blanche hesitated, aware of her cheeks flaming. "I have lived in society for most of my life—and all of my adult life. My best friends are notorious for their love affairs. I understand them and do not condemn them, even if my nature is not at all like theirs." She paused, hoping he would begin to understand.

He shook his head in confusion.

And she found a way to try to tell him what she really meant. "We will be spending months apart from one another. If the time comes, and you feel you need a mistress, I prefer not to know, but if I do, I will look the other way." Hating what she had said, knowing she would hate any other woman, she was also, impossibly, relieved. She did not want pressure from him, not in this case. She walked away from him and paused to stare at a mound of dirt.

His crutch thundered as he swung around her. "That is the most generous—and absurd—statement I have ever heard. If I marry, I will be faithful, and I do not care what the marital circumstances are. I do not care if years go by before we cohabit! In fact, the mere *idea* of infidelity in a marriage is repulsive to me."

She looked up. Sir Rex would never betray her, she realized, no matter what happened in their bedroom. Even if she disappointed him in their bed, he would be faithful. She had to wipe her eyes.

"I am not sure if you are stricken or thrilled," he said harshly.

"I am overcome," she finally said, reaching for both of his hands. "I know you think yourself a very dark hero, but you are a hero, plain and simple."

And he seemed overcome, as well. She saw so much light flickering in his eyes, and she thought she saw hope and the beginning of joy, but she still saw torment, doubt and pain. "I am a war hero, perhaps, but not a dark hero or any other kind," he said slowly. "Are you certain you do not wish to go to your rooms—or even back to London—to think about everything we have just said to one another?"

She shook her head. "I want to stay here with you."

He nodded. "Tenacious," he breathed. "And stubborn."

She almost smiled. "I am feeling very stubborn now."

"Then I concede." His gaze held hers. "Your tenacity exceeds mine. I wish to accept your generous offer. I will be your husband, and do everything in my power to make this marriage a strong and pleasant one."

Blanche clasped his shoulders, her heart thundering, and finally she smiled. "Oh," she said, "oh! We are engaged!"

He tilted up her chin, his gaze finally moving to her mouth. "I will do everything in my power to please *you*," he added softly. "In every possible way."

She knew exactly what he meant. And desire was instantaneous—a response she could barely believe. But this entire week was like a wild dream.

"May I?"

She nodded and she smiled from her heart. "I do not think you need ask anymore, Sir Rex."

He half smiled as his mouth closed on hers. And he murmured, kissing her, "Rex. Although it is unofficial, you must call me Rex now."

CHAPTER THIRTEEN

SIR REX HAD BEEN CALLED AWAY by a stable boy. Blanche walked to the edge of the gardens and then to the cliff, which dropped to the ocean below. She was beaming; she was so entirely happy! She hugged the shawl closer to her body, but she was hardly cold. It was unbelievable; she and Sir Rex were going to marry.

She didn't think she had ever been so pleased or so thrilled. Who would have imagined that her life would undergo so many changes, and so rapidly, from the moment of her arrival at Land's End?

And what to do first? They had a wedding to plan, and although they hadn't discussed it, she felt certain he would not mind a small affair restricted to his family and her few dearest friends. And she had to write Bess, immediately—Bess would faint—and then she would shout with glee! And of course, she had promised the Farrows a supper invitation, and there could be no better time. They could even announce their engagement then.

Blanche started back to the house, her mind racing, envisioning the wedding ceremony, the reception and the supper party and all the while imagining what she would write Bess. She needed a wedding dress, something perfect—and they had to set a date. And when would be a convenient evening to entertain? Did she have something special to wear for the first event they were holding as a couple?

Blanche was passing the tower and her smile faded; her steps slowed. What was she doing? What was she even thinking? Sir Rex had just accepted her proposal, and they did have a wedding to plan, but did she have to entertain immediately? He had made it very clear that he was not interested in doing so. It had been a very reflexive reaction to instantly plan an affair. That is what she did—it was one of the things she excelled at. And she realized now that she could not wait to announce their engagement to the public.

But she had a lifetime to convince Sir Rex that some small social life was indeed pleasant, and they did not even have marriage contracts drawn up. There was no rush. Besides, he was not going to be as lonely once they were married, even if they lived apart more than they lived together. She could send a note to Mrs. Farrow, offering some excuse while inviting her to call, instead. Sir Rex would surely prefer that.

Blanche paused not far from the tower. She smiled again, realizing she was taking a better course of action, as far as her fiancé was concerned. Her smile deepened. *Her fiancé.* How she liked the sound of that.

And, dear God, was that love swelling her heart? She was very fond of Sir Rex, but just then, her affection for him felt suspiciously consuming.

She clasped her warm cheeks. First confusion and desire, and now, possibly love. After all these years, a miracle had happened. She was becoming a normal woman, with normal passions—and she was about to have a normal life.

She was, in fact, deliriously happy.

And fear seized her.

It was terror. Blanche stiffened as all of her tender feelings vanished, an acute fear suddenly clawing her, as if talons wished to rip her apart. She had no reason to be afraid—she did not know where such a huge, consuming fear had come from—and then she saw him and she knew.

She cried out, that terrible knife stabbing into her head, while the gaunt monster-man towered over her, holding a lethal object in his hand—something black, metal, with tines. His eyes blazed with hatred and he reached for her.

She choked in terror. And she saw a hundred such men, shadowy and indistinct, behind him, around them, screaming and shouting in rage and hatred, wielding pikes and knives. A horse screamed. Blanche turned. The animal had been cut from its harness and was on the ground, legs flailing, being beaten by the mob. Blood ran…

Blanche covered her ears with her hands, sobbing. This wasn't real—it was a memory! She didn't know how long she struggled to believe that, but she found herself fighting the men, the sounds, the smells, the fear, the ground now spinning wildly. Shadows fell. Blanche welcomed them. She wanted nothing more than to embrace the darkness; she wanted oblivion.

But the ground steadied and the shadows grayed, receding. Blanche realized she lay still, the mob having vanished. But the memory was there now, etched firmly in her mind, a single bloody scene, and there was no more doubt that she was re-calling the events of that terrible day. She blinked up at the gray, ominous sky and realized it had begun to rain. Her clothes were becoming wet.

"My lady?"

Blanche met dark eyes—and realized Anne was standing over her, staring.

Dismay roiled. She sat up. How much had Anne seen? How long had she been there, watching her, while she was reliving the past?

For this memory had become *real*. She had actually thought herself surrounded by a mob of raging men—no, she had been in a mob of raging men. She had seen that poor horse beaten to death, and it had lay on the ground, thrashing, inches from her. She had heard those men shouting at her, at everyone.

But it hadn't been real, she reminded herself. It had been a memory, and now she knew her father had lied to her about that day. She could imagine why—she could forgive him for it, but she must not ever recall anything else! And she must not allow herself to feel as if she were a child again, lost in that mob.

"Shall I get Sir Rex?" Anne asked.

Blanche swallowed, feeling ill, aware that she was very wet now, but so was Anne. She met the maid's unblinking, unsympathetic stare. In fact, there was no possible way to read the housemaid's thoughts. But Anne was the least of her problems.

She was so afraid, and not just of what her mind might tell her about the riot. Recalling a forgotten day was one thing, and actually believing oneself to be back in the past, another. Was she going mad?

"My lady, can you hear me? Should I get Sir Rex?"

"No!" She did not want Sir Rex to ever see her like this. *How could this be happening now?*

Why was this happening now?

Blanche looked at Anne again, who simply stood there, staring, her face an impassive mask. And Blanche sensed that she was pleased. In that instant, she was certain the maid disliked her, even envied her, and wished to see her fall. And now, Anne knew more than she should.

"Shall I get your maid, then?" Anne asked.

"No. Help me up," Blanche said harshly. She reached up and took Anne's hand. But even standing, she felt off balance. It was as if she stood on a slippery, dangerous slope.

She was getting married. She was, possibly, in love. A wonderful future lay ahead. She did not need this! She had to stop these memories—and she must never allow herself to feel as if she was in that long-ago riot again.

"I'll help you inside," Anne said. Her eyes flickered. "Before his lordship sees you in such a state."

Blanche whirled to stare at the servant.

Anne smiled.

REX STRODE INTO the tower room, trying to restrain his turbulent emotions. It was impossible. He felt light and buoyant; he felt happy. He was happy. And he could not recall the last time he had felt this way.

He reminded himself that this marriage was not going to be an easy one, no matter what Blanche seemed to think. She was an optimist, and he was glad, but he must remain cynical and cautious. This was not a fairy tale or a romance novel; a long road lay ahead, the territory uncharted. But God, he did not want ever to disappoint his wife.

Overcome, he sat down at his desk, smiling. *His wife.* He was marrying Blanche Harrington and he could barely believe it.

It was time to consider improving himself.

But he had to share such good news. He reached for a parchment and quill and quickly dipped it into the inkwell. "Dear Tyrell," he began. And he smiled again; Ty would be astonished. He wished he could see his face when he read the letter.

I am aware that you remain in London with Lizzie and the children and I hope all is well. I have some rather extraordinary news that I wish to share with you. Blanche Harrington has been my guest at Land's End and I have had the good fortune of becoming engaged to her. It is currently unofficial and we have yet to set a wedding date, but we will, soon. You, my brother, are the first to know.

He laid the quill down, smiling. He felt like hollering like a boy. He did not feel like writing the letter with any restraint. Once again, he picked up the quill.

I assure you that I am very pleased with this sudden and unexpected turn of events. I have always admired Lady Harrington. In a very short period of time, we have developed a deep affection for one another, as well as a genuine friendship. My only concern is that she can do so much better, but she assures me that I am the man she wishes to wed. I am determined to make her happy.

He smiled again. When had he ever smiled so often?

I imagine we will be returning to town soon, as there are so many plans to make. You are more than welcome to convey the news.

He signed the letter simply with his first name, then waved the parchment gently to dry the ink. He remained somewhat disbelieving—and he still felt as if he could float to the ceiling. Ty was going to be stunned, but so would his entire family—so would all of town.

His smile faded. The gossips would have a field day with their betrothal; he didn't care. He had learned long ago to ignore their every malicious word. Blanche had claimed that she didn't care, either, but he didn't believe her and he never would. Ladies had far weaker sensibilities than men. He had to decide on a way to shield her from any harmful whispers.

The best way would to be to appear in town as if he had been miraculously reformed. He wasn't sure he could carry off such a pretense, but he was going to try.

He slipped the missive into an envelope and addressed and sealed it. Then he opened up the desk's center drawer, removing a small portrait of his son. Tom had sent it to him on Stephen's sixth birthday.

Blanche was going to be his wife and eventually—sooner, not later, considering their ages—there would be more children. His heart ached as he stared at the young, handsome face in the portrait, but not as terribly as it so often did. Stephen would soon have a brother or a sister. Maybe he should reconsider his arrangement with the Mowbrays. He would never try to take his son away from Julia, and he did not want to jeopardize Stephen's future, but it seemed that he would soon have a family. If so, how could Stephen not be a part of it? On the other hand, how could he reveal that he was his father and not jeopardize Stephen's future?

"Sir?"

He looked up at the sound of Anne's voice. She stood in the doorway, smiling at him, and instantly, he recalled the many moments they had shared in his bed. All levity of mood vanished. He was now engaged to Blanche and Anne's presence in his household was shameful. He stood, forcing a smile. It felt grim. "Come in, please."

She came in, her gaze searching. "I am about to prepare supper and I was wondering if a rabbit stew would please you?" She smiled again.

He swung out from behind is desk. "We must speak."

Her eyes widened slightly.

He no longer tried to smile. "Lady Harrington and I have just gotten engaged."

Her expression froze…and then it became an expression of mild interest. "Congratulations, my lord."

He grimaced. "Anne, please. We have been lovers and this must be a shock. That is not my intention. You have been a devoted servant and I have enjoyed our liaison, but everything must change now."

"Of course." She curtsied, glancing aside.

"I am going to have to dismiss you," he said, "but I will do so with a full month's wages and a letter of recommendation."

He thought she smiled wryly; it was hard to tell, as she stared at the floor.

"I know you must be distressed," he said quietly, wishing she would say something.

She looked up. "I have always known you would marry one day, my lord. All men do." She smiled at him. "I never thought to continue on here this way."

"You do not seem dismayed, distressed or even angry."

"I am not a foolish or stupid woman. I am happy for you, my lord, but I must wonder, is her ladyship ill?"

He tensed. "She is delicate—most ladies are. Why do you ask?"

She shrugged. "I heard about her headaches, that is all."

He had the instant notion that she was lying—and that she knew something he did not. "Is there something you wish to add? Something I might wish to know?"

"Of course not, my lord." Her eyes flickered. "Do you wish for me to stay on to help with the house until you can find someone else to replace me?"

He was, finally, relieved. "That is generous of you, Anne. But I think it best you leave immediately. Fenwick and Meg will have to manage for a bit." He hesitated as she looked up, directly into his eyes. "I am glad you are so sensible. You are a passionate woman; I expected a scene."

"I am not surprised. I have noticed you admiring her ladyship several times."

His gaze narrowed. She kept staring, boldly, and he knew it best to end the interview now. "Let me draw up a bank check," he said.

He went to his desk, took the checks from a drawer, and drafted a generous sum. She had followed him to the desk and watched while he wrote it out and signed it. He straightened and handed it to her.

She folded it and slid it into her bodice, between her breasts. "I am a very passionate woman, as you know."

He tensed.

"And we both know you are a very passionate man. I imagine it has been hard for someone like you, who likes his bed warmed every night, to go so long without." Her eyes gleamed and she reached for his hand. "I don't mind giving you a proper farewell, Sir Rex. I should enjoy it very much."

Her tone was throaty and signified the potential for so much lusty sex. As she laid her hand on his chest, he said softly, "I am sorry, Anne. I cannot. Such behavior would be shameful—on my part, not yours."

That light flickered in her eyes again, and he wondered if she was not as accepting as she seemed. He wondered if he had seen a flash of malice. "It is not shameful to be lusty, Sir Rex," she whispered. "And you are not wed yet."

He removed her hand, becoming annoyed. "Why don't you gather up your things?"

Now she stared, her face not quite impassive, and while he could not read her emotions, he felt them. He felt the malice he had thought he had seen.

But she curtsied and turned to go.

And he saw Blanche standing in the doorway, staring at them with wide eyes, her skin ashen, her hair wet.

He was horrified.

Anne hurried from the room, brushing past Blanche as she did so, and Blanche's cheeks turned pink. "I did not mean to interrupt," she said hoarsely.

"That is not what it appeared to be!" He thudded over to her. "Blanche!"

"No!" She backed up, appearing breathless. Then she

smiled. "I mean, we aren't married, she is right, and you have every right to your privacy—"

"Like hell!" he cried. He seized both of her hands. "I made vows. They were effective the moment I made them. I will not break them! I won't deny the maid made an advance, but I have just dismissed her."

"If you wished to be with her, I would understand," Blanche gasped, trembling.

"Did you hear a word I said?" he cried. How could this have happened—already? "Blanche, I dismissed Anne. I have given her a month's wages and she is gathering up her belongings."

Blanche met his gaze. "Oh." She wet her lips and pulled free of him.

He followed her. "I don't want her," he said harshly. "I want *you.*"

She turned and smiled uncertainly at him. "I am behaving very foolishly."

"You are not. I have already disappointed you."

Blanche inhaled. "Sir Rex, stop. I overreacted...I had a headache."

He froze. "How bad was it?"

She smiled quickly—falsely. "It wasn't half as bad as the others."

Was she lying to him? He refused to believe it. Blanche could not lie if her life depended on it—he had always been certain of her honesty and integrity.

"I was a bit shaken," she added, "when I walked in. Anne's presence here merely added to my confusion."

He nodded. "I hope you mean it. Because I am not tempted by a housemaid, how could I be? I have you." He didn't smile, he couldn't.

But she finally smiled. "I am glad you dismissed her."

He held out his arm. "Come into the great room with me. I see you were caught in the rain. We can sit before the fire and you can tell me what it is you wish to discuss." He finally smiled, too.

"Am I so obvious?" she asked with another, even lighter smile.

"You are." They strolled into the hall and sat on the sofa. "But I can guess. You wish to discuss our wedding."

She smiled widely. "What woman does not wish to plan her wedding?"

"I will agree to everything you want."

"Just like that?"

"Just like that."

"I would like you to enjoy our wedding, too."

He had to smile and he took her hand. "Oh, I will. You may count on that."

Their eyes met. "I was thinking of a very small affair. My few dearest friends and your very large family."

His heart soared. "Are you trying to please me? Because if so, I am pleased. But I had expected you to want a society wedding—a very large, elaborate affair."

She shook her head. "We are thinking alike," she exclaimed.

"Apparently so." He could not resist. She was as delighted as a child. He took her face in both his hands and kissed her. He meant to be gentle, but the moment his lips touched and tasted her, he felt a conflagration of desire. In that moment, he wanted to plunge deeply inside her, and his loins swelled, confirming a desperate need. This great woman was going to be his wife. He wanted to possess her now—and show her so much pleasure. He released her.

Her eyes sparkled. Her smile was shy but pleased.

He had almost ruined everything a moment ago, he thought. But miraculously, he had not. Because, apparently, Blanche trusted him—and would think the best of him no matter what. Her nature was simply too generous.

He had to match her. "Have you planned our supper party yet?" he asked casually.

She started, eyes wide. "I was thinking about it, but then I decided there was no rush. After all, we have our wedding to plan."

He smiled, still dreading such an evening, but now, he was determined to make that evening a success for her. "Our wedding is what? Six months from now? A year? A supper party can be tomorrow if you wish."

She stared at him, unsmiling. "Sir Rex—"

"Rex!" he corrected, smiling.

She bit her lip, hesitating. "Sir Rex, we don't have to rush into entertaining—"

"But I want to. As you said, it is overdue. And now I have a hostess." He took her hand again, simply because he wished to touch her.

"Well," she said, clearly debating, "I know the Farrows would be thrilled to receive such an invitation. We could invite Dr. Linney, too, and his wife. Just to round things out," she told him.

"Whatever you wish," he said firmly. "You tell me the time and what I should wear, and I will be here to greet our guests." *Our guests.* The words echoed in his mind pleasantly.

Blanche sat back, clearly thinking. Then she looked at him. "I will have to ask Anne to help with the supper. Meg doesn't cook. Fenwick needs to serve."

He knew that Anne should not stay on, not for even a single affair. "Can't you find someone else in the village?"

"I can try. But Sir Rex, you have paid her handsomely for an extra month, she knows the kitchens inside and out, and her cooking is passable."

He hesitated, aware of a distinct sense of foreboding.

Then she said, "Why don't we simply wait until after we are wed to entertain?"

He loved that idea. He thought about what she had walked in on—and not just that afternoon. He wanted to please her with a successful supper party. "I will tell Anne she needs to stay on until after the supper affair."

BLANCHE HAD DECIDED to dress for her first supper with her fiancé. She had brought one other evening gown to Land's End, a pale ivory-and-rose creation. She was making a final inspection in the mirror, trembling with anticipation, as if a girl of sixteen. Her heart soared.

And then the monster leered at her, revealing yellow, wet teeth.

The horse screamed in torment and anguish, somewhere close by.

Blanche cried out, clasping her hands to her ears, all of her happiness vanishing, replaced with terror. The memory had become engraved on her mind earlier that afternoon, but now, it wasn't a memory. The man was reaching for her and she knew, without a doubt, he was about to seize her. In that moment, she was a small child, alone and terrified. Where was Mama?

They had taken Mama away, dragging her from the carriage.

The pale-eyed monster reached for her. She jumped away and ran, not across the room, but through a seething crowd, on a London street, slipping on bloody cobblestones. As she ran, the horse's screams dimmed. The leering image of the man faded, and she looked back, but he wasn't real now—he was just another terrible memory, etched forever upon her mind. Blanche realized she was clinging to the banister at the end of the hall, panting, her heart thundering painfully. Tears tracked her cheeks. She didn't dare release the rail to wipe them. She didn't know how she had gotten from her bed-chamber to the top of the stairs.

She breathed hard but continued to hold on to the post for support. Total comprehension began. She had just been flung back into the past—but she wasn't in the past, she was at Bodenick, on the verge of marriage to Sir Rex. This had to stop. She had to find a way to stop this horrific recall. And why was she experiencing bits and pieces of that riot *now?*

Was she truly mad?

Sane people did not forget who, what and where they were! Sane people did not suddenly travel into the past, as if through time, with no awareness of anything else!

"Blanche?"

She flinched as she realized Sir Rex stood at the bottom of the stairs, waiting for her. However, he was smiling—he had not seen her fit of insanity. And as she looked fearfully into his eyes, the roiling panic eased slightly. He had dressed for supper in a white dinner coat and he had never been as compelling or as handsome. Standing below her, it seemed terribly important that she rush to his side. Somehow, he was a safe harbor, a certain destination, a place she must go.

But he had every right to know what was happening to her.

She came downstairs, quickly rearranging her expression and slowing her breathing, so he would not suspect anything to be wrong. "I see we both thought to dress," she said. She must not tell him a word of what had just happened; he would think her as mad as an inmate in an asylum! Her shame would know no bounds.

His gaze was searching. "Is anything wrong?"

She hesitated. But how could she not tell him? He was her fiancé. He had every right to know. In a way, it would be a relief to tell him that she was beginning to remember that long-ago riot. It would be a relief to fall into his arms and confess that something terrible was happening, and making her feel six years old again. But he would think her mad and he would leave her—as he should. Because if these fits didn't cease, he deserved far better than what she had to offer.

Blanche stiffened. She was *not* insane. There was an explanation for what was happening; there had to be. And soon, dear God, it would all go away. The memories would vanish and be forever forgotten and she would never relive another moment from that day. It had to cease, because she was finally in love!

Fear and panic clawed at her. What if she was on an irrevocable path? What if the fits continued? "Nothing is wrong," she somehow said.

She reached his side and he took her arm but did not move. She wanted to press closer.

"You look frightened," he said softly.

Blanche tensed. And she lied, when she was not a liar, when she would rather lose everything than lie to Sir Rex. "I am a bit nervous about the supper party."

He smiled, but it did not reach his eyes. "Sometimes, I have the very strong feeling that you are keeping secrets." His tone was light.

Her smile remained firmly in place with an effort. "I do not have any secrets worth keeping," she said as lightly. But until then, there had been one secret, and now there was another one, far more significant than that of her defective nature.

"I did not mean it in a derogatory way," he said swiftly. But his penetrating stare did not waver. "Blanche, are you in trouble?"

"I'm not sure what you mean," she said. "The only trouble in my life is the complicated fortune my father left me—and that is about to be placed in your hands, making my life quite carefree."

His smile was uncertain. "I was hoping we might go to town soon. I know you will probably wish to announce our engagement, and there will be many plans to make, even for a small wedding."

Blanche couldn't smile now. "You hate town—and now, you wish to rush there immediately?"

He shrugged far too casually. "The countess will be over-joyed to hear our news."

She stared at him.

"Very well." He was grim. "I want you to see a physician there. I am worried about you."

Had Anne told him what had happened that afternoon? More panic set in, and with it came the unfortunate images of the dying horse and the leering monster-man, reaching for her. How could a doctor help her if she did not confess everything? And how could she confess to being reduced to moments of near madness? Somehow she was going to control the memories and never go back to that day again. And she would be a good wife to Sir Rex—not a sickly burden. All she had to do was find a great strength, somewhere deep within herself.

"I am fine, Sir Rex. There is no need to rush back to town, not for the purpose you have mentioned. I am famished! I wonder if supper is about to be served?" She pulled away from him.

And from the corner of her eye, she saw his dark, search-ing stare.

He knows I am lying, she thought miserably. He knows something is terribly wrong. And it occurred to her that this was not the right way to start a marriage.

She knew in her heart that Sir Rex did not deserve an ill or insane wife. If push came to shove, she would leave him before they had even begun.

CHAPTER FOURTEEN

BLANCHE RAN into the kitchen at half past five. Her hair was done and she was donning her diamonds, but she was clad in a simple day dress, her dove-gray wool. The Farrows would arrive at half past six, and while she should be putting on her moss-green satin gown, a sense of foreboding had arisen. And once in the kitchen, she halted. The aroma of fish was overwhelming.

Dismay began. "Anne!" The maid was nowhere to be seen.

Becoming angry, Blanche hurried to the roasting pans lined up on the counter. They were filled with cod fillets and potatoes. She had specifically suggested local Cornish hens and shanks of lamb. She went to the ovens, which were warm, but nothing was inside. On the stove she found more potatoes and green beans.

She began to shake. "Anne?" Surely, surely, the maid had not dismissed her menu. She went to the pantry, but it was empty. Then she saw Anne outside—with the tall blond blacksmith. They were having a pleasant, unhurried conversation, as if a supper party, the very first at Bodenick, was not scheduled to commence in an hour. In fact, there was no doubt a flirtation was in progress.

Blanche lost her temper. As she never became irate, much less furious, she was shocked, but too angry to stop herself. She ran outside. "Anne! I wish a word with you this moment!"

Anne turned and looked at her; so did the young man. He

then smiled and doffed his wool cap. Blanche nodded tersely. Anne strolled over, in no apparent rush.

"Where are the Cornish hens and the lamb?" Blanche asked swiftly.

Anne blinked. "My lady, I beg your pardon, but I told your maid no hens were available at the market, and we have no shanks in the meat house."

Blanche began to tremble. "Meg did not say a word."

"She must have forgotten."

"Cod is a common fish! No one serves cod and cod alone at a supper party."

Anne simply stared benignly.

"Is this our meal? I asked for a dinner salad of wild greens, too."

"I'm afraid I only have beans and potatoes—and the cod."

Blanche had never been so angry. She shook with her rage. If Anne had not already been dismissed, she would let her go on the spot. "The meal you have prepared is unacceptable," she said stiffly. "I wanted everything to be perfect for Sir Rex's guests!"

"I do have a custard, just like you asked."

Blanche tried to breathe. Vaguely, she knew she should not be so undone by the changed menu, but she was undone—completely. In fact, she felt perilously close to tears. "Are you trying to sabotage this meal?"

Anne gasped. "Why would I do that? Sir Rex has been nothing but generous with me, my lady, and so terribly kind."

Blanche stared, certain Anne was throwing her affair with Sir Rex in her face. "Then do you wish to sabotage me?"

"I would never think to cross a great lady like you, Lady Harrington," Anne said, and while her words felt mocking, her tone was bland.

"I think you wish to hurt me, for marrying Sir Rex!" Blanche heard herself cry. And she could barely believe she would speak in such a heated manner to anyone, much less the housemaid.

"I am happy for you both," Anne said. "And if you wish for a meal to be served at seven, then I had better get back to the kitchen."

Blanche stiffened as Anne simply walked away from her, leaving her standing outside the kitchen. Then she clasped her throbbing temples, for she now had a headache, one she feared. She tensed, waiting for the onslaught of another memory, but all she saw were the images she had previously been confronted with. When she realized a knife was not about to stab into her skull, and that a new memory would not sweep her into the past, she relaxed, but only slightly. Maybe, finally, she was getting better.

Last night, she had dreamed of the horse being beaten by the mob while she watched, a terrified child of six. However, it had been a dream and she had known it. She had awoken and spent the rest of the night in front of the fire, afraid to go back to sleep, afraid of another dream, one so vivid, she would think it real. As a result, she was exhausted. But twenty-four hours had passed without a new memory arising or her slipping into the past. For that, she was grateful.

She prayed it was finally over. Because yesterday she should have told Sir Rex the truth. But if the memories had finally stopped, if she was no longer being jettisoned into the past, her lie would not matter, not in the course of the long future she would share with Sir Rex.

Now, though, she did not know herself. She had become volatile instead of rational and calm. Was Anne hostile? Did she seek to thwart her—and even sabotage her first party? Or was she so unnerved and unbalanced, that her suspicions were unjustified? Blanche could not decide. She remained high up on that seesaw, but her balance was precarious, at best.

Shaken, she entered the kitchens, noting that Anne was busy at the stove, and for that she was grateful. She hurried back upstairs, trying to find the composure which had served her so well for most of her life. Her moss-green satin was laid out. At least her gown was suitable, she thought. Blanche stepped out of her gray dress, suddenly certain that the evening might not go as well as she intended.

She froze. Why would she have such a thought? She had entertained hundreds of times, she was a practiced hostess, very skilled at conversation and putting her guests at ease. Of course the evening would go well. No one would remark on the poor choice of menu and she would make certain plenty of wine was served. There was no cause to worry, none.

Meg knocked and stepped into the chamber. As Blanche was helped into her gown, she asked, "Meg, why didn't you tell me there were no hens at the market—and no lamb in our meat house?"

Meg looked at her. "My lady, I didn't know."

Blanche faced her. "Anne didn't instruct you to tell me that the menu had to change?"

"No, she did not. In fact, I haven't spoken to her even once today."

Blanche simply stared.

Meg said softly, "She's a cunning one, she is. I don't like her and I don't trust her, my lady."

"Yes." Blanche inhaled. "I think you may be right." Then she adjusted the diamond necklace at her throat. "It doesn't matter. We will survive tonight's menu. If she is thinking to thwart me, so be it, she has succeeded, but it is only a matter of annoyance. Her days at Land's End are numbered and she can't change the fact that I am the mistress here now."

Meg smiled in agreement. "She cannot change that you will soon be Sir Rex's wife."

BLANCHE THOUGHT that the evening was a success, in spite of the modest meal. The Farrows were so clearly delighted to be at Bodenick that the both of them complimented her on the repast numerous times. Doctor Linney was affable and his wife an incessant but pleasant chatterbox. Mrs. Linney kept redirecting the conversation to Sir Rex's exalted family. She had raved about the earl and his heir, although she did not know either man personally, and was currently discussing the countess.

"And of course, everyone knows the countess is as lovely as she is generous. She is renowned for her charity. You must take after her, Sir Rex! I do wish I had met her when she was visiting! I was so disappointed we did not meet, not even in Lanhadron on the street. You will let us know when she comes again, won't you, Sir Rex?" The plump matron asked eagerly, beaming.

Sir Rex had been polite but reserved throughout the meal, acting no differently than he did in town, when they had come face-to-face as vague family friends. Blanche saw that he was simply a reserved man, not given to frivolous chatter. And it didn't matter, as Mrs. Linney and Mr. Farrow had kept the conversation alive. "I will do my best."

"Oh, your best isn't good enough—is it, Margaret? Lady Harrington, don't you agree? Sir Rex must inform us when the countess is in residence so we can call properly. She will receive us, won't she?"

"I am sure she will be pleased to do so," Sir Rex said, glancing down the length of the table at Blanche. He smiled at her and she smiled back.

"The countess is a delightful lady," Blanche told the doctor's wife. "She has no airs, in spite of her great station, and she would never turn Sir Rex's neighbors away. In fact, when I am in town, I will make a point of telling her to expect your call the next time she is in Cornwall."

Mrs. Linney beamed. "You are such a dear lady, Lady Harrington. I can see why Sir Rex is so taken with you."

Blanche started, mildly surprised, as a silence fell. Sir Rex caught her eye again, appearing amused. Paul Farrow leaped gallantly into the breach. "I am very taken with Lady Harrington, too. We have heard so much about you, my lady, but never imagined we would dine with such a gracious hostess. And you must compliment the chef!"

Sir Rex said softly, "I am very taken with Lady Harrington."

Blanche flushed in pleasure. Mrs. Linney seemed very surprised, her husband seemed pleased, and the Farrows looked back and forth between them, not for the first time. Blanche felt certain the young couple suspected that she and Sir Rex were very fondly disposed toward one another.

Margaret Farrow said quickly, "You have not indicated how much longer you will stay in the country with us."

"I have made no plans to return to town," Blanche said, still smiling at Sir Rex. "I have never been to Cornwall before and I am very taken with the clime." She wondered if they might tell their company they were engaged.

Margaret simply smiled, as it was pouring now, the rain pounding on the windows and roof.

A small silence began. Then Mrs. Linney said, "I cannot stand the clime here, if the truth be known. Except in the summertime, of course. You must return in the summer, Lady Harrington."

Blanche and Sir Rex exchanged glances. "I intend to," she said softly.

And he understood. "Actually, there is some news we wish to share."

Everyone started, glancing between them. Blanche beamed as Sir Rex said, his gaze unwavering and potent on her, "Lady Harrington has agreed to become my wife. Although it is unofficial and the contracts have not been drafted, we are engaged."

The uproar was instantaneous. Both men turned to Sir Rex

to congratulate him, at once, while the ladies faced Blanche in delight.

"I thought something was going on," Margaret cried, smiling. "Oh, this is so wonderful. We will be neighbors, at least some of the time!"

"And you may call on me at Harrington Hall," Blanche told her as they clasped hands.

Margaret nodded happily.

"I never thought I'd see the day." Mrs. Linney leaned close, whispering. "I thought he'd remain a bachelor until the end of his days. Oh, how fortunate Sir Rex is, to catch a sweet lady like yourself!"

"I am the fortunate one," Blanche corrected her without rancor.

"He does have his dark humors," Mrs. Linney warned.

"I do not care," Blanche said, smiling.

"You have snagged a great war hero," Paul said from across the table. "My cousin says he carried the duke of Clarewood from the battlefield on his back, with only one leg. If it weren't for Sir Rex, Clarewood would be dead." He beamed.

Blanche tensed and looked at Sir Rex. His gaze had lowered and she saw a flush on his high cheekbones.

And Paul Farrow instantly understood his mistake. He jerked, looking from Blanche, who could not even imagine what Sir Rex was now thinking or feeling, to his host. "Sir Rex, I am sorry! My cousin was in the 11th Light Dragoons, too, but I should not have mentioned the war."

Sir Rex took a sip of red wine. He glanced at Paul and shrugged. "I have done my best to forget the war. It was a lifetime ago."

"Of course you have," Paul cried nervously and in obvious dismay. "It was a bloody awful war, but thank God, we did win, thanks to heroes like yourself."

Blanche stood abruptly, filled with anxiety, as Sir Rex was

staring into his glass as if it were a crystal ball, relaying images of his past. "Why don't we ladies adjourn to the hall? The men can take their cigars and brandies here."

Doctor Linney winked at her. "An excellent suggestion, as I am overdue for my brandy."

As Margaret and Mrs. Linney rose, Blanche hurried to the head of the table. "I'll tell Fenwick to bring the brandy in," she said softly.

Sir Rex didn't quite look at her. "Thank you."

She was dismayed. Whatever demons haunted him from the war, she knew they had their talons in him now. She turned to the ladies. "I will join you in a moment."

Blanche hurried into the kitchen where Meg was helping Anne and Fenwick was sitting at the counter with a news journal. "Anne, supper was a success. Thank you."

Anne started.

Blanche then asked Fenwick to serve the gentlemen brandy and left the kitchens. As she passed the dining room she glanced inside, but Sir Rex seemed affable enough, as he was nodding at whatever Paul was saying. Still, he saw her instantly and as instantly, their gazes met. She was relieved he had recovered from his own memories, whatever they were. Doctor Linney saw her and gave her a reassuring wink.

Before entering the great room, she realized that the women were whispering, and instinctively, she paused. Why were they whispering? What could they possibly wish for her *not* to hear?

Before arriving in the country, Blanche would have smiled firmly and interrupted them as if she were not really doing so. Now, instead, she walked closer to the door, but hovered there to eavesdrop, remaining out of sight.

"I feel so disturbed—and so sorry for her!" Mrs. Linney whispered.

"I am certain it is not true," Margaret said firmly.

"Her mother's sister is employed by Squire Deedy. It is true—poor Lady Harrington doesn't have a clue that Sir Rex is having an affair with his housemaid...right under her nose! It is shameful! *Shameful!*" she cried.

Margaret was now silent. Blanche was in disbelief. Then Margaret said, "I will not believe it."

Blanche pressed into the wall, aghast and dismayed. Sir Rex had warned her that there would be gossip against them—and he had been right. But she had never anticipated such malicious gossip—and the worst part was, it was true. She was trembling. And for once, she couldn't decide what to do.

There was no way to quell the hurtful rumor. And if Mrs. Linney knew, so did most of the gentry in the parish—and maybe, everyone else, too.

Her heart sickened with dismay. She could manage this hateful gossip, but Sir Rex did not need any more whispers behind his back.

Once, she would have sailed gracefully back into the room, pretending nothing was amiss. Now, unable to smile, she strode into the great room, beyond determination. Both women turned, Mrs. Linney smiling, Margaret appearing uneasy. When they saw her, they paled. Blanche realized she must appear fierce.

"I do not appreciate gossip in my home," Blanche said bluntly.

Mrs. Linney blanched even more.

She turned to Margaret. "It is *not* true." Blanche told one of the few great lies in her life. "Sir Rex has had problems with Anne from the beginning, and she has started those rumors to get back at him, even though he has been so generous to her." She confronted the ashen and wide-eyed matron. "Sir Rex is a *gentleman* and I will not have *anyone* saying otherwise. My future husband would *never* dally with a servant."

"I am sorry," Mrs. Linney gasped. "I did not mean to be so rude!"

Blanche stared, thinking about the ton. She was the only woman she knew who did not care for gossip at all, although she heard it all the time, as Bess loved gossip. Gossip was always ugly, it usually hurt the victim, and it was the rage. Her temples hurt her now. She had spent her entire adult life entertaining, somehow ignoring the slander and half truths and half lies swirling about her salon. She had never taken any gossip to heart. Suddenly it wasn't so easy to dismiss. Suddenly the gossip was as painful as a real wound. And she became confused. Why had she enjoyed entertaining—or had she? It had been her role as Harrington's daughter. She had never questioned it. There had been three or four supper parties every single week.

This supper party had been pleasant enough until now, but the private suppers, shared solely with Sir Rex, had been far more enjoyable, she thought.

She took a calming breath but could not smile. "I would appreciate it if you set the gossips straight, Mrs. Linney."

"I will do my best," Mrs. Linney said slowly. "You know I will refute this entire matter! After all, we are dear acquaintances now."

Blanche knew she had hardly convinced her of Sir Rex's innocence, but Mrs. Linney was no fool. She wanted another invitation to Bodenick, and it would not be forthcoming if she did not comply. "Thank you. And yes, I treasure our new friendship, which is why I am certain this foul subject will be swiftly laid to rest."

Margaret sent her a worried look. "Do you wish to sit down, my lady? Should I ask for tea?"

Blanche smiled. Margaret Farrow was a very decent and sweet young woman. "I was disturbed with such slander, but I am fine now." Then she realized Sir Rex stood in the doorway, just where she had been eavesdropping a moment ago. She didn't have to wonder how much he had overheard;

from the dark look on his face, she knew he'd heard everything.

He limped into the great room. "I know you are tired and I suggested the evening end prematurely." His face was so tight Blanche suspected he was holding a vast fury in check.

"Of course! " Margaret cried nervously. "Lady Harrington has so much on her mind, she must be overcome." Margaret turned to her. "I would love to be of help, if I can. Please, do not hesitate to ask, and thank you so much for supper. It was lovely."

Blanche thanked her as the gentlemen came into the hall. Mrs. Linney took her hands. "I do hope I did not offend you. I am so thrilled for you and Sir Rex! I will call later in the week," she said quickly, "if you do not mind."

Blanche forced a smile. "Of course not. Good night."

A moment later, she watched Fenwick closing the front door behind the last of their guests. As Sir Rex swung back into the room, she firmed her smile. "That was a very pleasant evening, wasn't it?" she said lightly, hoping he would agree. She did not feel up to an intimate and frank exchange now.

He gave her a dark look.

She felt her anxiety escalate. "It went *well*," she stressed.

"Did it?" he mocked dangerously.

In that instant, she knew his mood was black. "I am sorry you had to hear that! But you were the perfect host!"

"No, you were—and are—the perfect hostess. But you agreed to marry me...and this is what you get. Vicious truths."

She inhaled. "But I have already accepted that truth, Sir Rex. We have gotten past it. Somehow, we have developed a deep affection, in spite of certain challenges."

He gave her a hard, sidelong look. "I will hand this much to you. Margaret Farrow is a pleasant young woman and I hope you two become friends."

A very small relief began. "And Paul is a pleasant sort—"

"He is weak and ineffectual. I can tolerate him for an evening, if I must."

That was boorish, she thought helplessly. "I don't want to argue over the evening—or anything else. I am tired."

He limped to the bar cart. She watched him pour a brandy. He did not seem foxed, but she worried now about how much he was drinking. He turned. "I warned you I have no tolerance for such foolish frippery."

Blanche hugged herself. "Are you angry at me for wishing to foist this evening on you? Or is it yourself you are angry with—for succumbing to your needs with a servant?"

He stiffened, incredulous. "So, finally, you condemn me."

She realized she had done just that. But that was not what she wished to do, ever. "No. I only know that if the affair hadn't happened, there would not be such malicious gossip."

He stared at her, his gaze dark and hard.

"I am not condemning you," she tried desperately. "And I did think the evening a success!"

"You are right," he said bluntly. "I should have had an affair with Mrs. Farrow—or one of her friends—for that would be acceptable."

Tears came to Blanche's eyes.

"And I regret my *needs*. And even more than that, I regret not caring that I was defying society. I regret my indifference to the damned gossips. But I care now. *Now* I care what the gossips say and what they think. I care now because of *you*."

She wiped an errant tear. "It doesn't matter. There is always gossip. They will gossip about us at first, because we will be a source of speculation and entertainment. But in a year or so, they will set their sights on someone else."

He swung to the hearth and drank his brandy grimly, downing the entire glass.

Blanche hesitated. She was exhausted and she hated this confrontation, but she also wished to comfort him. She did not want to go to bed with any unresolved conflict, either. "Sir Rex? The evening was pleasant, in spite of Paul's lapse—until Mrs. Linney started to gossip."

He turned slowly to her. "You are right. However, there are numerous skeletons in my closet. And every evening might turn out like this one. Are you certain this is the life you wish for yourself? Because you need only say the word, and I will release you from the engagement."

Blanche stiffened, unpleasantly surprised. She did not know what to think or what to say.

He made a harsh sound.

"No!" She cried quickly. "Do not misconstrue my hesitation. I am so fond of you—and I want to marry you, I do. But Sir Rex, when you are dark like this, I become confused and I do not know what to say or do! I don't know if I should hold your hand or run from you!"

"Then you should think long and hard on the future we are planning," he said tersely. "Because I never promised you that you would not find me brooding at midnight."

Blanche bit her lip in dismay.

He refilled his drink and went into the tower room, his crutch thudding with his displeasure. She stared as the door shut behind him.

Blanche began to shake. How had they gotten to this place, a dangerous crossroads where one false word or move might break them apart? She was falling in love with Sir Rex. Did he want her to end things? And how would they manage if one single simple supper party could so disrupt them?

Her distress abruptly changed. Grief flooded her. It was so much like a rising tide that briefly, she could not breathe and it felt as if the air alone was smothering her.

And she knew she could not lose Sir Rex. Her heart broke at the notion. She would seek him out in the tower and tell him how much she cared. But the anguish intensified. It was stunning, paralyzing and unbearable. In that moment, Blanche knew it was not grief over the prospect of losing Sir Rex.

Somehow, she knew it was far more.

Her father's image danced through her mind. And it was followed by an image of the portrait of her mother, which continued to hang over the staircase at Harrington Hall.

She cried out, sitting, holding her chest. She had not shed a tear when her father died, and she could not recall her mother at all, much less her death, but now, suddenly, she wanted to weep and sob and scream in outrage. The sense of loss was acute. The sense of being lost was even worse. She felt six years old, not twenty-seven.

"Blanche?"

She turned as Sir Rex thudded rapidly over to her.

His eyes widened. "Don't cry!" He sat, pulling her into his arms. "I am sorry; I am a bastard."

She moved into his arms, helplessly crying, helplessly grieving; he cradled her face.

"I am sorry. Please don't cry!" He was aghast.

She wanted to tell him this was not his fault, not at all, but she couldn't. She wanted to beg him to help her find happiness and joy, so she might escape the anguish, but she couldn't. She could only shake her head, incapable of speech, and try to bury herself in the circle of his arms, against his large, powerful body, a place she knew was secure and safe. His grasp tightened.

Images danced through her head—the dead horse, its eyes wide and sightless, its body bloody and battered, the leering monster-man, with his dripping yellow teeth, the bloody tines of a pitchfork, and Mama's portrait-perfect face, smiling just as she had done for the painter.

Father had died six months ago and she couldn't even remember one moment with her mother. Why did she have to grieve now? It was too much to bear! Everything was happening at once, and she couldn't handle so much emotion. She began to understand what was happening to her. Upon coming to Land's End, her heart had been awakened. First there had been confusion, then desire, then love. Her heart was a whole, beating, functioning organ now. And its experience would not be limited to a few positive, kinder emotions. For there had recently been anger and fear. Now, her heart hurt with grief.

In that instant, she would give anything for the placid existence she had known for most of her life.

"Blanche," he whispered, caressing her back and holding her tightly. "I am so sorry! Forgive me!"

She turned her face into the warm skin of his neck and jaw. She breathed there, inhaling so much male scent. Her lips touched his skin and her own flesh fired wildly; the grief diminished, an urgency arising in its stead. Blanche clasped his shoulders, marveling at his breadth and strength, rubbing her face against his throat. She felt his body tense.

He was so large, so strong and somehow intoxicating. She ran her hands down his biceps, which instantly flexed beneath her palms. She moved her mouth tentatively against his throat. She heard him exhale. Her heart jumped wildly and a pulsing began beneath the many layers of her clothing.

"Blanche," he said thickly, one large hand clasping her waist.

She breathed in his scent and pulled her face reluctantly from the crook of his shoulder and neck. His gaze was wide and bright, meeting hers. She took a deep, trembling breath as she glanced at his firm, bowed mouth. More desire lanced through her as she thought about what his mouth felt and tasted like. She lifted her gaze back to his. "Make love to me."

His eyes widened.

Blanche just sat there, heart pounding, body thrumming.

He touched her cheek. "You are distraught. You don't mean it."

"I do mean it," she breathed. "I'm twenty-seven years old

and I am still a virgin. But my body is somehow begging for yours."

His eyes darkened. Then his hand clasped the back of her head and he pulled her close as he lowered his mouth to hers.

Blanche's heart went wild as he feathered her mouth. She felt him shudder and knew he was exercising great restraint and control. She kissed him back, hard, wanting his lips to open. When they did, she heard herself moan—soft, feminine, breathless.

The kiss deepened. Blanche fell back onto the sofa, Sir Rex on top of her, their mouths fusing hungrily. She was vaguely aware of spreading her thighs. And she felt his manhood, hard and huge, against her inner thigh and pelvis, through her skirts.

He broke the kiss and she lay back, gasping for air, her heart pounding so swiftly it was almost frightening.

"It's late," he said roughly, but he kissed her throat, and then he kissed the skin below her diamond necklace, and went lower, kissing the hint of cleavage revealed by the bodice.

Blanche gasped with pleasure, stunned by the heady sensation of his lips between her breasts and his manhood against her thigh. "No, it's not late. Sir Rex…take me upstairs."

CHAPTER FIFTEEN

REX HESITATED, his pulse pounding, the small, delicate and somehow fragile woman who was to be his wife in his arms. He could barely think straight. It was so hard not to shift his weight and push himself where he wished to be, instead of remaining against her thigh and hip, where he throbbed dangerously.

She smiled tremulously at him.

She wanted to go upstairs. She wanted him to make love to her. Why not?

He breathed hard. "Blanche…I would like nothing more than to take you to my bed. But I do not want you to regret this tomorrow."

She shook her head and clasped his cheek, unspeaking.

His heart thundered. He leaned low and took her mouth, no longer able to control the pressure of his lips. He opened her and sparred with her tongue. He wanted to taste every inch of her, not just her mouth. He shifted and pushed directly between her thighs, over her skirts. She gasped softly, arching for the pressure he could give her—and the release.

His male lust escalated. It was determined, intent, predatory. She was a virgin. She was more than ready. They would be married, sooner, not later. She wanted his children and he wanted to make her his….

He tore his mouth from hers. Smiling, he said roughly, "Come. Come with me."

She gasped, her gaze riveted to his. He saw so much trust and so much innocence. A savage exhilaration arose.

Why not? He was a man and she was the woman he wanted. She was the woman he had always wanted. He was still in some disbelief. But the urge to possess was rapidly chasing away any lingering disbelief.

He found his crutch, took her hand and stood. In another moment, Blanche Harrington would be in his bed. Impossibly, more blood filled his painfully erect loins. Rational thought vanished. Urgency raged.

But as they went upstairs, he looked at her carefully. "You may change your mind at any moment," he said thickly.

She paused on the landing, staring. "I don't want to change my mind," she murmured. Her gaze fell to the obvious bulge in his trousers. Her cheeks were already pink but the flush deepened.

"Any time," he stressed, taking her hand and leading her toward his bedchamber. His heart kept pumping his blood into his lower body, sure and rhythmic. "But sooner," he said, entering the room, "would be better than later."

She stared at the four-poster bed, shaking her head.

He closed the door and pulled her into his embrace. She was trembling but not as violently as he. "I want you so badly," he murmured, caressing her cheek. "I feel like a green boy again. Blanche, I won't hurt you, I promise."

Her gaze held his. "I like it," she whispered, "when you are gentle."

He hesitated, as he wasn't certain of his ability to be gentle, but her message was clear. She did not wish for a frenzied barbarian in her bed and he did not blame her. He smiled and feathered her lips once with his. Then he led her to the bed.

A small fire blazed in the hearth so he did not light a lamp. Swiftly, he shed his jacket and unbuttoned his shirt. Then he pulled her into his arms and to the bed, remaining aware of her uncertainty. As they sank onto the mattress, he kissed her earlobe and then her neck. She shivered and sighed.

That raging urgency instantly renewed itself. The anticipation was in the forefront of his mind—that precise moment when he would be so deeply inside of her, coming. He smiled at her and kissed her gently, stroking her arms, her waist. She sighed again, longer and lower this time.

"I want to touch you everywhere," he whispered, running his shaking palm over her bodice and breast. He palmed her, showering soft kisses on her throat and chest. She trembled and began writhing, throwing her head back.

He reached behind her and began unbuttoning her dress. Her eyes flew open and he smiled reassuringly, no easy task. She glanced at the fire. He understood. "You are beautiful," he whispered, "and I want to look at you." He wished he could stop shaking.

"Sir Rex, how can I be beautiful when I am ancient by most standards?" she protested very seriously.

He was actually amused and he chuckled. "You are not ancient and I want you to stop thinking." He wrapped his arm around her waist and kissed her slowly and deeply. "I want you to feel." He slid the dress down to her waist and tried not to inhale harshly. But her chemise was transparent, her stays ivory lace. He slid his hand over her breast and heard himself groan. His arousal leaped erratically.

Her eyes closed, lashes fanning out. He could not think and he did not want to; he tugged the chemise down over the corset and bent and tongued her very erect nipple. She gasped wildly.

Rex saw only a red haze. He pushed her against the pillows, fumbling with her stays. She gasped again. He threw the stays aside, wrapped his arms around her and turned to lave and play with her other nipple. She shuddered convulsively and he knew.

Her bodice and chemise were all bunched up around her waist; he lifted her skirts and petticoats and slid his hand up her smooth, slim thigh. She cried out as he rotated inward, stroking her inner thigh, and finally brushing her sex. She was hot and swollen and wet.

He cried out. "Blanche, darling." And he slid his hand firmly over her, spreading her folds and she gasped and writhed, arching. He didn't hesitate. He jerked down and sent his tongue feathering over her. She stiffened, undoubtedly in shock, but he pressed more intimately, laving all of her that he could. She shuddered again.

"Give over to me," he whispered, and it was not a request. "Relax, Blanche, and let me pleasure you."

There was silence. He felt her body soften and heard her cry, "Oh God."

And then she gasped, shuddering, and he felt her coming against his tongue and cheek. He smiled, triumph surging in his red-hot blood.

When she lay still, he moved away, took some water and shed his shirt. He turned and saw her gazing at him and he smiled, just once. She pulled a sheet over her breasts and then reached out, touching his chest. Instantly he caught her palm and pressed it more firmly there.

She didn't speak.

He smiled, still holding her hand against his bare skin, leaning over her. "I am going to pleasure you again—and again."

She breathed hard. "Sir Rex." She swallowed.

He pulled her up into his arms, her bare breasts against his naked chest. She cried out, clinging to his shoulders. She was small and perfect against his larger frame, he thought. He held her more tightly, kissing her hair. "I would like to get rid of that dress," he said softly. "Unless you have changed your mind?"

Her mouth moved, her lips brushing his chest. "If you will get rid of your clothes, I will, too."

His heart soared. He smiled against her hair. "A bargain that is mutually beneficial," he murmured. And because he could not resist, he lifted her chin and kissed her deeply, then bent and kissed her nipple.

She gasped and arched upward for him.

He sucked her slowly into his mouth, then pulled.

"Ohh," she whispered.

He flung the sheets aside and meeting her gaze, reached for her skirts. In a moment, they were gone. He then tugged away chemise and petticoat, and finally, her silk drawers.

She slid under the sheets, but he had seen her slim, lovely body. "I am too thin," she whispered, blushing.

"You are perfect," he returned, tossing one shoe and stocking aside. He unbuttoned his trousers, his hands trembling. "Will the sight of my amputated leg offend you?" he asked casually, but the question wasn't casual at all.

Her eyes widened. "I have seen you in nothing but your drawers, Sir Rex."

His eyes widened.

"You have a habit of tossing all the covers aside when you sleep." She was blushing now and staring not at his face, but at his hands—or what stood straining beneath them. "I nursed you, or have you forgotten?"

He paused, hands on his fly. "I recall waking up and finding you regarding my body with a singular intensity." He was aware of how rough his tone had become, but his need was explosive.

"I was admiring your figure," she said. Her tongue flitted over her lips. He knew it was a nervous and hungry gesture that she was entirely unconscious of.

"Good," he said flatly. He slid his trousers and drawers down together, tossing them onto the floor. Then he lay down beside her. Her eyes were huge. He pulled her into his arms, but loosely. "I cannot help myself. I want you passionately. Is my passion offensive?"

She slowly lifted her eyes. "No." She breathed hard, roughly. He felt her mind racing wildly. Her glance skidded down between them again. "Oh."

He cuddled her, kissing her cheek, her temple, her hair. As he did, he quivered against her thigh, helpless not to. "If you are worried," he whispered.

"No! No, I am not worried…." And she looked up, seizing his shoulders and kissing him wildly.

He was stunned, but only for a moment. He took over the kiss, rolling her beneath him and pushing her thighs apart with his good leg. He shifted against her inner thigh, trying not to groan and thrusting his tongue deep. She kissed him back and there was no mistaking her urgency now.

Holding her, he buried his face against her neck and began rubbing her loins with his erection. She cried out as he met wet, hot, distended flesh. Trying to caress her, he moved slowly, as lightly as possible, his massive head probing against her swollen lips.

"Oh dear!" she cried.

He wanted to smile but couldn't. Sweat rolled off his temples and down his chest. He pushed his entire length beneath her, several times, when he wanted desperately to push into her. She gasped as he stroked the cleft of her buttocks, too.

And then he reared up over her and pressed flat against her belly, breathing hard. "I want to make love to you. I want to come inside you." He kissed her ear. "But I do not want to rush you, Blanche."

She wrapped her arms around him and he felt her calf move over his hip. "Sir Rex, yes!"

Desire surged. He shifted and pressed home. Her flesh was

wet but tight. He gritted, trying to go slow. And as he pressed inside, there was so much pressure, he could not stand it. In that instant, he knew he was lost.

"Hell," he gasped, and he thrust past her membrane, exploding uncontrollably. Somehow, in the throes of a violent climax, he stopped moving, buried deep inside her now and spilling so much seed and reveling in the glory of the huge release.

For he was with Blanche and it was glorious.

But when the last convulsions had ended, he was horrified. His grasp tightened, but he didn't look at her. He remained fully sheathed and erect enough to stay that way. "Blanche, I am sorry," he managed.

She was trembling. Her hands slid over his back, a shaky caress.

"Did I hurt you?" he asked roughly, now aghast at his premature ejaculation. But he had wanted her desperately for years. Still, his performance had not been impressive. Worse, she had not climaxed with him.

"Only for a moment," she said hoarsely.

And he felt her throbbing against him.

Red passion blinded him. She still wanted him; she needed him. He breathed hard and moved slowly, deeply, and she gasped with pleasure. He smiled, a savage determination beginning, mingling with triumph. He would show her so much pleasure now, he thought, the blood racing to his arousal and stiffening it once again. He thrust slowly again and again, holding himself up so he could watch her now. Her eyes had closed. Her cheeks were pink. She was breathless, turning her head from side to side. He moved deeper, more swiftly and more purposefully; she cried out. Their gazes met.

And he saw from the dazed and unfocused look in her eyes, that she was spiraling toward the pleasure he wished for her. He smiled and withdrew. She protested, he entered her again, slowly and deeply, watching her closely now. She seized his arms, and he felt her nails cutting his skin.

"More?" he asked, lust consuming him.

She nodded.

He moved swiftly, pulled out, tongued her and entered her again. She clawed his arms, gasping. He stroked his head, now terribly swollen, over her cleft lips. She cried out, shuddering. And as he plunged deep, again and again, her eyes flew open and blindly met his.

She arched wildly, her nails slicing into his skin, her soft cries filling the night.

So much lust, desire, passion and pleasure consumed him. He arched back, deep now, exploding and crying out, loud and hoarse, with triumph. The euphoria was consuming and complete.

Blanche.

BLANCHE SLOWLY DRIFTED back to Sir Rex's bed. She began to realize she had just experienced true passion—and tears of joy filled her eyes. She was lying naked in Sir Rex's strong arms, her cheek in the crook of his shoulder and chest, her hands between them against his chest. He had his calf over both her legs. Oh dear lord, he had just made love to her, and she had found so much rapture.

Her heart swelled with love. Smiling, feeling uncertain and shy, she slowly looked up.

He was regarding her with such a tender expression that her smile faltered and her heart leaped wildly. He smiled, revealing his single dimple. His dark eyes, gold flecked, were searching and so wonderfully warm.

Blanche knew she flushed, as she now recalled not just his incredible male prowess, but how he liked to use his tongue. Oh, but she did not mind! And she loved being in his arms this way. She rubbed her cheek against his chest and felt a stirring against one of her thighs. Her gaze flew to his.

His dimple deepened. "You seem pleased," he said softly.

"I am pleased...very much so." She felt her cheeks warm as that very male part of him became stiff against her leg.

"I find you stunning and I cannot help wanting to please you again," he whispered.

She hesitated, and then laid her hand on the hard, bulging muscle of his chest. "You are the stunning one."

He chuckled.

Blanche had never heard such a warm, wonderful sound. "Are you pleased, Sir Rex?"

"I am beyond pleasure, Blanche." He reached up to clasp her face. "Darling, you must call me Rex."

She smiled. "It sounds so odd...Sir Rex."

His smile faded.

She felt hers fade, too. "What's wrong?"

He shook his head. "I never thought to see this day, you and I, lovers, and soon to be wed."

She reached up to touch his cheek. "Nor did I." Then she saw a red scratch on his bicep. Her eyes widened—she was stricken.

"It doesn't matter," he said softly. "I am pleased to see that there is a wildcat in you."

Blanche could not believe she had scratched Sir Rex and drawn his blood.

He pulled her closer. "I want to make you insane with passion." He nuzzled her and she felt that large tip against her belly. Her blood quickened and she felt a very delicious tingle between her thighs.

"I cannot believe I did such a thing. I am sorry."

"Do not apologize for losing your head while in my bed," he said thickly, but with laughter. He slid his hand in a stunning caress down her back and over her buttock, where he clasped her. She met his gaze and saw the question there. "Am I being too manly and too forward? If you are tired or sore, simply say so. Otherwise, I wish to pleasure you again."

She trembled, aware of the heat and moisture gathering now. She stroked the scratch on his bicep instead of answering, relishing the feel of his skin and muscle. Then she slid her hand over the equally hard tendons in his forearm. He became still.

"Your physique is amazing," she whispered, moving her hand over the other side of his chest. His nipple stiffened as her palm slid over that pectoral muscle.

He didn't speak.

Blanche swallowed, sliding her hand over his ribs, amazed again that he should have no fat to spare. She paused when she reached his belly button. Even his abdomen was tight and hard.

He moaned.

Surprised, she looked at his face and saw that he had closed his eyes and flung his head back. He lay back against the pillows, the invitation clear and compelling.

The sheets were at the bottom of the bed. Blanche stared at his manhood, so much desire flooding her that she couldn't move or think. Sir Rex was breathing hard.

She wanted to touch him the way he had touched her, but she hesitated.

His eyes still closed, he took her wrist and moved it lower, then released it.

Blanche inhaled and slid her fingers over the ripening tip. He gasped, his eyes flying open, and she saw that she was giving him the kind of pleasure he had given her. And she saw he desperately wished for her to touch him.

Her heart thundering, she ran her fingers down his length and to the heavy sacks below. He grunted and Blanche gave in. She gasped at the velvety feel, at the shocking heat, and at the steel hardness.

He sat, eyes blazing, pulling her into his arms and claiming her mouth with his. Blanche welcomed the assault, kissing him back, and as they went down onto the mattress, she slid her calf over his hip, running her hand down his back to his high, hard buttock. She didn't want to wait. She wanted to feel him inside her; she wanted to be a part of this wonderful man. Rex seemed to understand exactly; he grunted, pushing her thighs apart with his, and then he was sliding into her.

Blanche felt so much pleasure and so much urgency she could not stand it; she grasped his shoulders, wanting him to hurry his invasion, and arching for him so she could take more of him inside. He gasped and hesitated, buried so deeply now that it was shocking, and she felt him pulsing there, almost inside her womb, and she felt her own throbbing response. He looked at her, eyes smoldering, and he slowly withdrew, inch after inch, until she was spread wide on him, and Blanche felt the wave cresting. He knew. He plunged and began thrusting and the wave broke. Blanche wept in pleasure this time.

And so did Sir Rex.

BRIGHT SUNLIGHT finally awoke her.

Blanche blinked, oddly aware of being deliciously happy, so much so that she felt as if she were floating. She sighed, and then she remembered the night she had just spent with Sir Rex.

Her eyes opened and she turned her head, but his side of the bed was empty. She glanced toward the window and saw that it was well into the morning, for the sun was high and bright in a brilliantly blue sky. She began to smile. Oh dear, she'd had no idea passion was so wonderful; Sir Rex was wonderful!

She cuddled into her pillow, recalling his passion and his affection—recalling her own shocking passion, her own outbursts and boldness. Even after the night they had shared, she felt hollow with need and desire. Dear, dear God, she was a woman of passion now.

Who would have ever thought it possible?

She smiled, thinking of his touch, his kisses, and his powerful lovemaking, which she knew he had kept somewhat restrained. She thought of his glorious body—and how he seemed to find her terribly attractive. They had made love many times—maybe she was with child. Oh, she prayed she was with child now!

And vaguely, she recalled his leaning over her and whispering that he had affairs to attend to but that she should sleep late. She felt certain he had kissed her hair before leaving the room. Suddenly tears began. He was a kind, gentle man, but only she knew it. And she was so deeply in love. Their marriage was going to be a successful one—there was simply no more doubt.

Joy swelled in her breast—and instantly, grief surged.

Blanche stiffened, as all of her happiness vanished, replaced with such despair and grief, such loneliness, she could not breathe. Images instantly appeared before her—her father as he lay in bed stricken with pneumonia, and her mother, but not as she appeared in her portrait at Harrington Hall. Blanche sat bolt upright, horrified, recalling her mother as their coach was besieged by the mob, her face stark white with fear. And the men had ripped the door from its hinges....

"No!" Not now, not today, she didn't want to ever recall that horrific moment!

But the memory was there, and there was no disputing it or chasing it away—her mother had been holding her tightly until those men had torn the carriage door open, reaching inside to drag them into the street. Blanche cried out, reeling and dizzy. She clasped her head as the pain began, but it intensified, a butcher knife going through her skull.

She had to stop this now! She did not want to know what had happened next! She staggered from the bed when her mother screamed. *Don't kill my daughter! Spare my child! Please spare my child!*

Blanche straightened, stunned to hear her mother begging the men for her life. A dozen men separated them, blood was everywhere, and Mama was begging again as they grabbed her and dragged her away, so that Blanche could not see her....

Blanche screamed. "Mama!" The child begged, terrified, "Mama!"

But she could not see her mother, as dozens of men wielding pikes and pitchforks were between her and the carriage now. The pale-eyed monster leered at her, holding up his hand. "Come out of the carriage, girl," he said roughly, and it was an order.

She was so afraid she could not move, and his fury intensified.

"Don't make me come and get you," he warned.

She wet her drawers. "Mama!"

And the screams began.

Mama screamed—the screams of a woman being brutally tortured....

He reached for her, grinning. Blanche shrank back into the carriage as far as she could go. He cursed and leaped inside, seizing her. She fought uselessly and was dragged out to the street and thrown down onto the rough stone.

Mama wept and screamed, begging for her life, for Blanche's life.

"Mama!" Blanche screamed.

"Blanche! Run! Hide!"

The monster loomed over her, reaching for her now, to torture her, too. Blanche twisted away and fell onto her hands and knees, cutting them on the cobbled street, crawling away as fast as she could, between and beneath so many raging men. Someone stepped on her hand. Pain exploded and she collapsed. Mama screamed endlessly.

"Got you!"

She covered her ears with her hands. Something terrible was happening to Mama and she knew it. She gave up, curling into a ball. Please stop, please stop, she thought desperately. "Mama, Mama, please stop, please stop, Mama, please stop!" She was frozen with terror, chanting until her own voice drowned out the screams of Mama dying and the shouts of the men, glorying in her death.

"Please stop," she whispered, and suddenly she realized that the cobbled stones had vanished, and Mama's screams were gone, too.

Blanche blinked. She was no longer in the London street, she realized, and she wasn't six years old, either, but she was afraid to stop rocking herself, and the chant had become a soothing prayer of some sort. She knew she was an adult woman; she knew she was at Land's End. She remained so frozen with fear that she couldn't care. And she didn't dare get up. She did not dare move from the far corner of the bedroom where she now sat, curled up in a ball.

The monsters lurked in the shadows of the morning, waiting to come back.

And she rocked and chanted for a long time, desperately.

"MY LADY, WHY DIDN'T you call me? I would have helped you dress but his lordship told me you were not to be disturbed," Meg cried.

Blanche stood before the open armoire, which was mostly empty now, as she had carefully taken most of her clothing out, laying everything on the bed. His lordship...Sir Rex. She did not want to think about him now. She knew her hold on her sanity was fragile, at best, and certainly temporary. She turned and smiled at Meg.

Meg's eyes widened. "My lady?"

Blanche had never been so calm, so composed—or so

detached. She felt as if she had been given a dose of some miraculous drug, or as if she were floating in a peaceful, stagnant pond. It didn't matter. She had found a safe and quiet place inside of herself, and nothing was going to ever change that. However, every step had to be placed with care. She was terribly aware that she stood on the edge of a cliff.

"Good morning, Meg," she said quietly. Sir Rex's image loomed, his eyes dark and bold; she dismissed it. She must not think of him now. It would hurt, and God only knew what would happen if she allowed herself to feel pain. She did not want to go down that road or any other one. Every other road was dangerous and threatening. "Can you swiftly finish packing? I will order the coach brought round."

Meg stared, unmoving.

"Please, Meg, do make haste," Blanche said quietly.

"We are leaving?" Meg gasped. "But…what about Sir Rex? My lady, are you all right? You seem…strange!"

"I am fine," Blanche said. She walked to her bedside table and poured a glass of water with steady hands. "I am afraid I am breaking things off with his lordship."

There—it was better not to say his name. She couldn't go forward as planned. No amount of joy was worth the pain and fear. No amount of passion was worth the pain. It had all started upon her arrival at Land's End. She wasn't blaming the place and she would not blame her host, even if both were huge factors in her insanity. She had been awakened as a woman at Land's End, body, heart and soul. But she could not pick and choose her emotions. And somehow her emotions had led her to those terrible, forgotten memories. Her memories had made her mad.

She wasn't going to remain at Land's End, not after what she had survived that morning. She couldn't wait to leave. Whatever had happened in the past week and a half, it was over, all of it. She had found calm. It was what she wanted.

She never wanted to ride that seesaw again. In fact, she must remain in this impassive limbo for the rest of her life.

And while she did not want to think about Sir Rex, she had to face him directly to explain that their engagement was a terrible mistake. She felt certain he would be disappointed when she broke it off. But he would manage, and he would find someone else, someone prettier, younger and far more passionate than she could ever be. And she would return to her quiet existence at Harrington Hall. He would marry a sane woman, not a mad one. She was doing what was best for him in the end, too.

But her heart lurched, as if with dismay. Blanche drank more water, refusing to entertain dismay or any other emotion. A slight throbbing had begun in her temples, so she shut off her thoughts. Thinking about Sir Rex was dangerous. Every thought and every action was dangerous. She must remain composed at all costs. She must not allow her heart any leeway. So she thought about the agents and affairs awaiting her in London. She could not imagine how she would ever sort out her father's finances. She would have to hire someone to help, she thought. And then there were her suitors. She wasn't marrying anyone now. But it wouldn't be all that difficult to get rid of the entire lot.

In fact, if ever a whisper of her insanity surfaced, they'd all flee.

"Oh, my lady, what happened?" Meg whispered, hugging herself.

Blanche started and smiled. "I have come to my senses, Meg. That is all. Do not be so distressed. I cannot wait to go home. I have had enough of the country—haven't you?"

Meg simply stared at her with confusion and pity. "But Sir Rex," she said slowly. "He will be crushed."

Blanche felt tension stab through her. *She did not want to hurt Sir Rex.*

She clasped her cheeks, breathless now, an aching in her chest. *Please stop.*

Please stop, please stop, please stop.

Blanche breathed naturally. She had found that calm, gray place again. "I will speak with Sir Rex now. Hurry, Meg." This was best for herself and it was best for Sir Rex.

Blanche had no doubt.

HE THUDDED into the tower room and sat down at his desk, smiling. His favorite broodmare had foaled last night, but that wasn't the cause of his extremely good mood. He stared at the papers spread before him, but saw Blanche instead. So lovely, so kind, and even now, so innocent that she touched him as no woman ever had. He was fiercely glad he was the first man to make love to her—and he would be the last.

He glanced at the desk clock. It was noon and she should be up by now. On the other hand, they had made love four times, so maybe she remained abed. He hadn't meant to be selfish, and he had been concerned he might hurt her, but she had been as eager last night as he. In the end, he had insisted they sleep and she had fallen asleep in his arms, her small hands pressed against his chest.

He stirred, just thinking about it. He was, without a doubt, the most fortunate man on this earth. And it was too late to regroup or retreat now. He was head over heels in love with his fiancée, and maybe, if he dared admit it, he'd been in love with her these past eight years.

His door was widely ajar, but a knock sounded there. He looked up, saw Blanche and began to smile. And then he stood, his smile failing. Her expression was so odd, and for a moment, he didn't recognize her. She reminded him of a very beautiful porcelain doll.

"Sir Rex? May I have a word?" she asked quietly, unsmiling.

In that instant, he knew everything was about to go up in

smoke. In that instant, his heart stopped and there was a peculiar certainty that his life was about to implode. There was knowledge and there was dread.

He moved around his desk, calming himself. Something was wrong, he could see that, but maybe she was just tired. And if that was not the problem, whatever was amiss, it could be fixed. They were lovers now. Not only were they engaged, but last night they had shared passion and love. He had not been mistaken, had he?

"Good morning," he said, his heart now thundering unpleasantly.

She smiled. "Good morning, Sir Rex. Do you have a moment?"

"I always have a moment for you." He wasn't trying to be gallant. He stared, but could not see a single emotion in her eyes. They had become cloudy and dull. She did not look like a woman who had been well pleased last night—who had cried out in passion several times, for the first time in her life. She did not glow like a woman in love.

She was having regrets.

Hadn't he known there would be regrets if he made love to her? "You are unhappy," he said bluntly, sickened.

She smiled briefly. "I have realized I must return to town."

He felt his stare widen. And then he looked out the tower window, and saw her coach coming into the courtyard. He whirled. "You are leaving me."

She smiled again—a plastic smile, the kind of smile that was carefully placed upon the perfect face of a beautiful china doll. "Sir Rex, you have been the most gracious host. I never expected such generosity, but I have surely imposed long enough."

She was leaving him. He felt dizzy. He clutched his crutch, but felt himself reel anyway. "You are leaving me."

She did not smile again, and for that, he was grateful. "I

do not want to cause a scene. But I have given this some thought and our engagement is a mistake. I am so sorry. But you can do better—you will certainly do better—"

"Get out." He couldn't breathe. There was only the beautiful woman standing before him, discoursing so dispassionately, proof that she did not care, proof that here was one more treacherous society bitch.

She started. "I beg your pardon."

He fought for control and lost. There was only pain, rage and hatred. "Get the hell out!" he shouted.

She gasped. And something flickered in her wide eyes.

He hefted his crutch and swung it at the closest object at hand—the desk lamp. "Get out!" he roared.

Blanche fled.

He crashed into his desk and managed to seize onto it, and he swept every other item from it, then he took his crutch and began beating the desktop. When the crutch broke in two, he gave up and sank to the floor with a single bestial roar.

And he was still sitting there stunned, his face on his one knee, consumed with rage and pain, when he heard her coach departing.

CHAPTER SIXTEEN

AS SHE WALKED through the vast, luxuriously appointed rooms and long corridors of Harrington Hall, Blanche knew she had been right to return home. Although she passed a servant in almost every chamber, the house was quiet and peaceful—and she had never needed such peace more. But it wasn't what she had expected. She had somehow thought to return home and to the old life she'd had before venturing to Land's End. Yet her old life was oddly elusive.

For while she was no longer standing on the fatal edge of a dangerous cliff, she was acutely aware that a single misstep might send her back to a terrible brink of madness. She had to remain in a gray, cloudy space—floating, not feeling—cloaked in her composure. She was afraid to feel even the slightest frisson of pleasure—or regret. Yet in her heart, those emotions were screaming at her, demanding to be let loose. Blanche simply knew it. The effort was vast, but somehow, she had been able to remain unfeeling and there had not been a single episode since she'd left Cornwall three days ago. She wasn't relieved—she was determined. She was not going to go mad.

But ghosts lurked in every corner of her home. Every step she took, every gesture made and each uttered word, somehow seemed to conspire to bring forth the ghosts she wished to avoid. If she passed the library, she could see her father hunched over his desk, as he had been wont to do when he

was alive. Her heart would tense but she held the grief at bay.
Her mother's portrait remained on the wall above the stairs,
almost life-size. She would glance at it and see her mother as
she had been in the coach, before being dragged out to her
death. That image had to be savagely shoved aside, as well.
And in the recesses of her mind, Sir Rex lurked, too.

He threatened to split apart her composure, as well.

Now, she glanced out of the windows in the marbled foyer.
Eight carriages lined her drive, each containing suitors waiting
for the clock to strike noon so they could call. Word had
spread rapidly that she was back in town, she thought grimly,
as she had arrived late last night. She was used to callers and
it would be odd if no one came. But was she supposed to
consider one of these men as a prospective husband? She
knew she could not do such a thing, not now, not after the past
two weeks. If she dared to reveal any truths, she'd admit to a
broken heart. But she must not go there. She could not admit
to such a thing sensibly and calmly, without feeling. One
crack would lead to a dozen fissures. She had a terrible secret
now and she did not want it ever exposed.

She passed through one of the grandest rooms in the house,
the gold salon, where she could entertain fifty or sixty guests.
As she crossed the room, the floors covered with pale
Aubusson rugs, three huge crystal chandeliers hanging from
the high ceilings, every chair and sofa in shades of cream,
beige, sand and gold, her butler appeared at the far threshold.
"Yes, Jem?"

"My lady, Lady Waverly and Lady Dagwood are here. I let
them in, assuming you would wish to entertain them privately
before your suitors."

Blanche was pleased. She smiled, aware it was her first
genuine smile since leaving Cornwall, but she so dearly
wanted to see her two best friends. And as she had that
thought, Sir Rex's image tried to come forth, but she quickly

refused to allow it any space in her mind. In spite of her will, a small unpleasant frisson rippled through her. Once, she would have told Bess and Felicia everything. Now, they must know nothing. "You are right. In fact, I am very eager to see my two dearest friends." Maybe Bess and Felicia would be able to help her retrieve her old life entirely—a pleasant, placid, serene existence with no cares.

"They are in the Blue Room," Jem said, bowing.

Blanche thanked him. Bess stood by one arched window in the small blue salon, beautifully dressed in bronze and green. Felicia lounged on the slate-hued sofa, sipping tea. Bess whirled and Felicia stood when Blanche entered the room. "You are back!" Bess cried, rushing to her and hugging her, hard.

"Yes, I am, and I am happy to see you, too," Blanche said, smiling. She turned to embrace Felicia, who had a glow she instantly recognized—the glow of a woman in love. "How are you both?" she asked, her heart lurching in a strange manner. It was hard not to think about Sir Rex, but she was so happy that Felicia liked her new husband.

"We have missed you," Bess exclaimed, her green eyes bright. "Blanche, what happened at Land's End! Did you ask Sir Rex to marry you? I almost died when I read your letter!"

Blanche tensed, turning away. "I had forgotten that silly, impulsive letter."

Bess and Felicia exchanged looks. "You sounded besotted," Felicia exclaimed. "Bess let me read it!"

"I was not besotted," Blanche said harshly. And Sir Rex's image assailed her vividly, against her very will. His gaze smoldered with passion and heat as it had when he strained over her in his bed. Her heart lurched hurtfully as she had not allowed herself such a painful recollection for days. And then she saw him, enraged, roaring at her to get out.

Her heart turned over hard and sped wildly. The room

seemed to tilt. Grief stabbed through her breast. And it was all muddled up—Sir Rex, her father, her mother—they were all there, in her head, jumbled together!

Blanche turned, clasping her cheeks and closing her eyes, fighting the grief. *Not now, not when everything is perfect. Please, not now!* She had found a way to navigate the darkest corners of her life, but such a simple moment had become threatening and dangerous instantly. *Please stop,* she cried silently.

She simply must not feel. Not now, and not ever. Sir Rex was a part of the past, as was her father and the mother she could not—and did not want to—remember.

She breathed hard.

"Blanche, what is wrong?" Felicia asked with concern.

Blanche knew the moment she had regained her calm and composure. She felt as if she were floating in a gray, empty space. Those faces in her head had receded and blurred. She turned and smiled. "I wrote that letter so precipitously. I am hardly marrying Sir Rex."

Bess seemed bewildered. "I received your letter a week ago, and suddenly you do not care for him, when you have never cared for any man before?"

"I am not discussing Sir Rex," Blanche said, far more sharply than she had intended. But the dismay began and it was potent. Her heart sped and thundered all over again, refusing to obey her mind. She felt ill now, heartbroken and ill.

Bess put her arm around her. "Well, I can see that something is wrong. We have never kept secrets—"

"Nothing is wrong!" Blanche exclaimed vehemently.

Bess flinched and Felicia gasped.

Blanche realized she had become undone—and so easily. Somehow she sat on the seesaw once more, far too high up. "I need air," she cried, rushing to the window. She fought to open it. Her temples were throbbing now—and she was terrified of that mild aching becoming the head pain that signaled recall.

"Those windows don't open," Bess exclaimed. "Come, let's go outside. Felicia, get some salts."

Blanche didn't dare move, clasping her temples now.

Get out!

She had never dreamed Sir Rex would ever shout at her with such anger and hatred.

Get out of the coach, lady, get out now.

The monster was reaching inside for Mama. Blanche began to shake, Mama squeezing her hand so hard that it hurt.

Get out of the coach now! he shouted.

And suddenly Mama was being wrestled from the coach, and then hands were grabbing Blanche, too.

Mama screamed. "Blanche, run!"

She somehow broke free and fell to the stone street. Mama was screaming again, but in torment now.

The cobbled street spun. "Mama!" she cried, trying to crawl to her. But the ground tilted terribly, spinning even faster, her mother's screams now deafening.

Blanche gave up, curling into a ball, frozen with fear. She held her ears, and began to focus on the blue-and-beige rugs on the floor and not the rough stones of the street. The rugs were spinning. She was spinning. And Bess was speaking to her.

She inhaled, realizing that the episode was over. She was crouched on the floor in the Blue Room, the way she had crouched on the street after being seized and taken from the coach. There had been no memories since leaving Land's End, and now, the moment Bess had begun discussing Sir Rex, she'd had a fit.

Bess tipped a glass of water to Blanche's mouth, her arm around her. "Take a sip."

Blanche nodded, aware that her cheeks were tearstained. She drank, realizing her friends must think her mad. She slowly looked up at Bess.

Bess was wide-eyed. "Are you better?" she asked quietly.

Blanche wet her lips and nodded. "We must never discuss Sir Rex."

Her eyes widened impossibly. Then she held out her hand. "Come, let's sit on the sofa. You will tell me what just happened."

Blanche stood, glancing around the small, charming parlor. She closed her eyes and tried to send the last of her fear and dread away. It wasn't easy, especially as this latest memory was now engraved upon her mind. She looked at Bess. She had trusted her since childhood, and she desperately needed a confidante. "I am beginning to remember the riot."

Bess gasped, aware of Blanche's memory loss. "The riot that took your mother's life when you were a child?"

Blanche nodded. "The memories seem determined to come back. They are terrible—I don't want to remember—and I am determined to do anything to stop them."

Bess put her arm around her and went to the sofa, where they sat. "I didn't think you'd ever remember—and I didn't think it mattered."

"It matters! Did you see what the memories did to me?" Blanche cried.

Bess nodded. "You were screaming and crying on the floor, curled up like a small child. Felicia had left for salts, and I'm the only one who saw." She was pale. Bess was never pale. "Thank God no one else saw. What happened to you?"

"It's not just memories," Blanche whispered. "I am reliving the riot, moment by moment." She started to cry. There was no room for shame now, she was too afraid of what was happening to her.

Bess gaped and then held her. "Surely you don't mean it."

"I do. I become six years old again. This room became the London street. I wasn't aware of you—I was lost in that mob!" Blanche cried.

Bess was silent, and Blanche knew her well enough to know she was horrified but trying to be rational.

"This all began at Land's End," Blanche whispered, and heartache stabbed through her. "We were going to marry, Bess. I fell in love, and then this happened!"

Bess pulled away to stare at her in disbelief.

Her temples hurt all over again. Blanche held them tightly. "I want my old life back. I don't want to feel *anything*. And I do not want to remember one more detail of that terrible day."

Bess stroked her back. "Your remembering now is so strange. Yet oddly, I feel it is healthy. Let's put that aside for one moment. Blanche, I have always hoped you would one day fall in love. I had a notion about Sir Rex."

"You do not understand," Blanche gasped, distraught. "With love and passion comes the pain I just lived through—again! Falling in love was a mistake. Look at what it is doing to me!"

Bess stared. "How can the two be related? Blanche, if you care for Sir Rex—"

"No! It is *over!*" she cried, meaning it. Panic began.

Grimly, Bess said, "There is a rumor in town that the two of you are engaged. I ran into the countess on Bond Street, and apparently Sir Rex wrote his brother to that effect."

Her headache intensified. Blanche moaned. "I am going to remember more, I know it. Every time I feel happy or sad, a new memory sweeps in. I broke it off. I need peace, not passion! And Sir Rex now hates me—as he should!" she cried, trembling. "Bess, we must stop this conversation before I wind up on the floor in the midst of another fit."

Bess paled. "How can a conversation cause such a fit?"

"I don't know. But every little thing is a terrible threat—to my peace of mind!" she cried passionately.

"I have never seen you so passionate," Bess said quietly, after a pause. "Or so emotional. It is a shock."

"I do not wish to ever discuss *him* again."

Bess stared for a moment. "And what makes you think you can avoid feeling, anyway, now that you are capable of tears and grief? The moment we began discussing *him,* you were undone."

"I have to try," Blanche cried uneasily.

Bess stared. "What are you really afraid of? Maybe you should face your memories. I can't help thinking that if you did, you might find the peace of mind—and the happiness—you want."

"Now you are the mad one," Blanche snapped, furious. "For you have no idea what they did to my mother!"

Bess stiffened. "You are angry."

"Yes, I bloody am! And if you don't retreat, I am going to start recalling that damnable day!"

"All right. I will back down. But I am very uncertain that this plan of action is the right one."

"Didn't you see what the memories do to me?" Blanche cried. "They make me a child of six years old, in the midst of a London riot—they turn me into a madwoman."

Bess was silent and grim. "How often have you had these fits?"

"Four or five times. In the beginning, there was only a recollection. Now, every time I recall a detail, I am thrust into the past."

"Maybe you are right. Maybe recalling that day is a terrible idea." She paused abruptly.

Blanche hugged herself. "What is it?"

Bess flushed. "I don't want anyone, not your personal maid, not even Felicia, to ever see you the way I just did." She then smiled, but grimly, and took Blanche's hand. "No one will understand. You know the ton. It is not a tolerant place."

"They will think me mad and the gossip will fly,"

Blanche cried with nervous dread. "And the truth is, I am mad. Aren't I?"

"No! You are not mad. But you're right. This must be our secret."

"Of course it is our secret," Blanche said swiftly.

"Does he know what is happening?"

Blanche shook her head. "I fainted twice—I believe he thinks I am claustrophobic and that I do not eat enough to nourish myself."

Bess said, "You need a physician. Someone we can trust to tell the truth. Someone who can prescribe some medication to help you through these fits. I will do some research. But until I can locate the right doctor, why don't you take a dose of laudanum and sleep? You'll feel better when you awaken, I am certain." Bess smiled encouragingly. "You have been through so much in a week and a half! You must be exhausted and rest won't hurt you."

Blanche stared at her best friend.

Bess's smile faded. "Why do I have a distinctly bad feeling about this?"

"I heard a physician once say that he doesn't prescribe laudanum to women who are bearing children. He said a very unpopular study showed it disadvantageous for the unborn child."

Bess was bewildered—and then her eyes widened in shock. "What are you saying?"

"There is a chance I could be with child," Blanche cried. And the tears began all over again.

Bess gasped. "You and Sir Rex were lovers?"

"It was only one night—one very long and passionate night—oh, Bess! I pray I am with child!"

Bess stared grimly. Then, "Do you realize what you are saying?"

"Of course I do."

"May I assume you will tell Sir Rex—and change your mind about marriage to him?"

Blanche stared back, her heart filling with fear and dread. "I can't tell him…and I can't marry him…because this will get worse."

"Are you certain that your feelings for him are the cause of this?" Bess stood. "Although I don't know him well, I am certain he would stand by you, even if he saw your fits, even if they recurred."

Blanche leaped up. Her heart raced painfully now. "No one must ever see. He must never see me this way. And he deserves a sane wife—not a mad one! I had thought myself in control, but I am not. That has just been made obvious. I am not going to entertain at all if I can avoid it—and I am not going out unless I have no choice."

"Oh, God," Bess said.

"I can't take any chances," Blanche cried.

"Then you had better set your sights on one of your current suitors. Obviously you will have to marry, and soon, if you are carrying a child."

Blanche twisted her hands. Even she knew she would be ostracized if she had a bastard child while unwed. She had been trying to avoid that dilemma, as she was hardly certain she was pregnant, anyway. But Bess was right. She would have to marry if it became certain that she was carrying Sir Rex's child. "As long as this future husband is someone I do not care for, I can manage." And she felt ill.

Tears finally came to Bess's eyes. "Maybe this will pass. Maybe the memories will stop, and so will the fits. Maybe this has nothing to do with Sir Rex."

"I cannot allow myself any emotion, much less love," Blanche stressed.

Bess was grim. "Oh, God. Blanche, what will you do? How will you get on?"

"Don't despair. I will manage, somehow."

"LADY HARRINGTON? A Mr. Carter is here to see you."

Blanche was in the library. She had removed her father's large desk from the room, purchasing a smaller Portuguese-style desk for herself. Then she had rearranged the furniture, placing her new desk in a different place. She had decided to redecorate the library completely, beginning by changing the color scheme. Just that morning, she'd had all of the furniture draped with white linen covers and tomorrow she'd meet with an upholsterer and painter.

But her chest ached.

She was reading papers left for her by her agents. She could barely understand this last venture which her father had invested in. Apparently, however, the returns were excellent—to the sum of well over a thousand pounds per year. She would have to ask Geoffrey Williamson to explain exactly what this company did.

A week had passed since her arrival in town. Bess had kept her suitors at bay and they had avoided all discussion of both Sir Rex and the possibility that she was pregnant. Blanche had trodden very carefully, taking every carefree moment as a huge accomplishment. There had been no sorrow, no anger, no sudden recollections and no fits. Instead, her attentions were focused on, in addition to the library, redecorating the Gold Room. And outside, her gardens were also being entirely re-designed.

With things going so well, yesterday Bess had asked her if she wished to finally entertain. Gossip was already raging. The ton wished to know why she had come home and secluded herself. Bess had reluctantly told her that everyone was speculating wildly. Some of the gossips seemed to think she was engaged to Sir Rex and preoccupied with her wedding; others felt she had a broken heart; while a few gossips merely insisted she had gone back into mourning. It was time to step forward and lay all gossip to rest.

Blanche laid her papers down. She noticed that her hands were trembling slightly. She dreaded the afternoon, but kept reminding herself that she was a hostess *sans pareil*. She was glad of another diversion. "I do not recall a Mr. Carter, Jem. He has no card?"

"My lady, he is a rough sort and I will be pleased to send him away."

Blanche was bewildered. "Did he say what he wishes?"

"He said it is an urgent matter, pertaining to your holiday at Land's End."

Blanche went still while her heart leaped erratically. "Send him away," she finally said. But she was almost desperate to know what Mr. Carter wanted.

Jem bowed and left. Blanche pulled another folder forward, this one pertaining to mundane estate affairs, such as the tenant farms on their manor in the middle of the country. She began to browse the report when Jem returned, appearing grim. Blanche was seized with a foreboding. "Jem?"

"He will not leave. He says you must see him and he will sit on our front doorstep until you do."

Blanche stood, trembling. What could be so urgent? And Sir Rex's dark, handsome and terribly unhappy image came to mind.

She had not allowed herself to think of him, but now, there was no choice. Was he hurt? Ill? Drinking excessively? She should not care—she must not care, but dear God, she did. And her temples throbbed for the first time in a week.

Blanche tensed, filled with absolute dread. "Did he say anything else?"

"Yes, my lady, he did. He said the matter is in regard to Sir Rex de Warenne."

Blanche hugged herself. She did not want to lose her mind and thinking about Sir Rex—feeling anything for him—might cause her to do just that. But her worry knew no bounds. *What if something was terribly wrong at Land's End?* "Send him in," she whispered.

Jem nodded and hurried out.

Blanche went to the sterling tray on the low table before the dark green striped sofa and poured herself a cup of tea. She had recently discovered herbal teas, and unlike the Darjeeling tea she so preferred, it seemed to soothe her. Footsteps sounded and she turned to see Anne's blacksmith standing on her threshold.

She started in surprise.

Carter held his wool cap in his hands and he smiled at her, inclining his head. "Thank you, my lady."

Blanche couldn't begin to imagine what the blacksmith's call could mean. She went to the door, smiled at Jem and shut it firmly. "Mr. Carter, this is quite the surprise. Is Sir Rex all right?"

Carter smiled and it was sly. "I think so. Nothing seems to have changed up at the manor since you left."

Dread clawed at her. Did he mean what she thought he meant? "Is Anne still employed there?"

"Yes, she is."

Blanche felt ill. Had Sir Rex continued his affair? Or had she remained there as a convenience? She felt a terrible jealousy—and bitter dislike—and she was hurt and angry, too. The throbbing in her temples increased. In another hour Bess and Felicia would arrive and her doors would be opened to her callers. She had to find out what this man wanted, so she could send him away and rest.

"You seem distressed," Carter said wryly.

Blanche did not like his tone. She glanced at him and saw satisfaction in his cold blue eyes. "If I am distressed, it is not your affair."

"You are right—it is your affair—and that is why I am here." He smiled. "To discuss your affair…with Sir Rex."

Blanche went still. "I beg your pardon?"

"Come, Lady Harrington. I know you were enjoying Sir

Rex's bed on your little holiday—and I know you broke it off with him. Apparently you remain in the market for a husband. I can't say I blame you for wishing a different one, maybe someone who's not a drunken gimp." He grinned.

Her fury blinded her. "How dare you refer to Sir Rex in such a disrespectful manner! He is a hundred times the man you are—and he is not a drunkard!" she cried, enraged.

"He's in his cups every single night—or so Anne says." He winked.

"Get out!" Blanche cried, so angry there was no hope of any control. And pain began stabbing into her skull.

"Get out!" Sir Rex roared.

Get out of the coach now, lady.

Mama, white with terror, clutching Blanche's hand so hard it hurt.

Blanche cried out, refusing to go back to that day. "Get out," she panted wildly.

He didn't move. "I bet you don't want your suitors to know you've been whoring for Sir Rex. I'll keep my mouth shut—and so will Anne—as long as we are fairly compensated."

It took Blanche a moment, as she was so furious. *"What?"*

"A hundred pounds—for each of us—and we are sworn to take your little dirty secret to our graves." He grinned.

"You dare to blackmail me?" she cried.

"I do."

Blanche was shaking wildly. She paced away then whirled. "Tell the world! I don't care! I'm twenty-seven years old—twenty-eight in another month—and no one will blame me for my affairs!"

"Your new fiancé might." His eyes had turned dangerously dark.

"Get out," Blanche gasped, reeling from such an ugly confrontation.

"You'll be sorry," he snapped.

Blanche watched him heading for the door, that knife stabbing. She clasped her temples, fighting for control, her head now filling with memories. Sir Rex, enraged, ordering her to go; the monster, dragging Mama from the coach; the dead and bloody horse.

Anne knew.

Anne had seen her in the midst of a fit.

"Wait!" she cried.

Carter turned.

She did care about her private affairs being aired publicly, though not enough to pay Carter's price. But what if he also revealed her most sordid secret—that she was slowly but surely going mad? He would go home to Anne and tell her Blanche had refused to pay them off. Anne would be hateful, vengeful. Anne would do whatever she could to hurt Blanche. She was certain. It would take Anne all of two minutes to start spreading the truth.

"Fine. Come back tomorrow and I will have your payment in coin."

He smiled at her

SHE HAD DRUNK THREE CUPS of the calming tea and was surrounded by her admirers—or rather, the bucks and rogues who so cherished her fortune. Before that, Blanche had also spent a half an hour lying motionless in her bed, thinking not of the blackmail but of a stagnant pond, while imagining herself floating in it. She was floating now. She was perfectly calm. She knew she could get through this afternoon without a misstep.

"Your holiday in Cornwall suited you, Lady Harrington," a very handsome tall, brown-haired young gentleman said, his blue eyes direct. Blanche tried to recall his name. He was the third son of an earl and penniless—and a reputed rake. Bess said, however, that otherwise he had no faults. He did not gamble and did not spend what he did not have. "You have never been as lovely." He smiled, dimpling.

Blanche smiled back, recalling his name—James Montrose. She carefully looked at him—he was handsome and well built, tall but muscular, and now, she could imagine the body that lay beneath his clothes. He had no fat to spare on his frame. He probably spent a great deal of time on a horse. She was unmoved.

Not a single thread of desire arose. "I enjoyed my respite," she said lightly. "I had never been so far south before. It is actually lovely."

"Have you been to the north—the far north?" He grinned. "My father has a hunting box in the Highlands. I would love to take you there."

"I have never been farther north than Stirling," she said, when she saw the countess of Adare entering her salon. Blanche froze. Lizzie was with her, and so was the countess's stepdaughter, Eleanor O'Neill.

"Is something amiss?" Montrose asked, turning to follow her regard.

Did they assume her to be engaged? Bess had spent a week telling everyone that there had never been an engagement. Bess had told her she must insist the very same thing, otherwise, there would be questions, questions which might "upset" her. No one was asking questions now—and she was distressed.

Her temples throbbed.

Please, not now, she silently begged.

"Lady Harrington? Do you wish to sit down?" Montrose asked, sounding kind and concerned.

Instantly, Blanche knew he would not do. "I am fine. Lady Adare is here and I must greet her." She smiled at him—or tried to—and ignored his suddenly piercing regard. She inhaled, gathered up her composure like a heavy wool cloak, and went forward. "Mary!"

Mary de Warenne beamed and embraced her. "I have been waiting for the day when you were receiving," she exclaimed. "I almost sent you a note."

Blanche tried to smile at her, aware of her wildly pounding heart. Could Mary possibly think her engaged to her son? She turned and hugged Lizzie. "How are you, Lizzie?"

"I am fine—but perhaps not as fine as you." Lizzie also beamed.

Blanche could not summon up another smile as she faced Eleanor, a tall, statuesque honey blonde with amber eyes. "I hadn't realized you had come to town, my dear. How are you? How is Sean? How are the boys?"

"Sean is fine—and so are the boys." Eleanor clasped her hands. "Are you engaged to my brother or not?" she asked excitedly.

Blanche stared at her, overcome with so much heartbreak she could not bear it.

Still holding her hands, Eleanor cried, "Rex wrote Ty and said you are engaged. Is it a secret? When is he coming to town? What happened! You must be in love—otherwise, you could not snare my brooding brother!"

Blanche's head pounded. Raw grief rose up. She had loved Sir Rex. She still loved him—she always would. She tried to breathe and she tried to pull her hands from Eleanor's.

"Eleanor, dear, you are distressing Blanche," Mary said quietly, her expression grave.

"It was a mistake," Blanche somehow whispered. Tears filled her eyes. And from the corner of them, she saw Bess watching, pale and wide-eyed. She felt moisture trickle down her face. "I am sorry, we are not engaged."

The three ladies stared, stunned and disappointed.

This has been a mistake.

Get out!

Get out of the coach, lady!

A knife stabbed cruelly through her skull. And the screams began.

The room tilted wildly, her mother's anguished screams filling the chamber. The well-dressed crowd changed, becoming a mob of common laborers; the chandeliers vanished, becoming gray skies. The screams were screams of pain and terror.

Blanche knew she must not become that six-year-old child, not now, not while surrounded by her callers. But the screams would not stop and the rug-covered wood floors became cobbled stones. The Gold Room finally vanished completely, replaced with a London street and the raging mob. She clasped her hands over her ears and ran.

"Blanche, run!" Mama screamed—and then her screams changed.

She saw Mama falling, the men on top of her, stabbing her with pitchforks and pikes. She screamed, afraid to run away and afraid to stay. They were hurting Mama. And Mama's screams stopped just as hands seized her....

She tried to curl up and protect herself from the men, sobbing. But she was lifted up and she met the pale gaze of the monster. Her terror escalated—and instantly, darkness came.

She floated through clouds for a long time, aware that she was waking up and not wanting to. If she could, she would stay this way forever, blissfully half-conscious. But the gray receded. Bright light burned her closed lids. Blanche inhaled the salts, and the obnoxious odor made her cough and she started, fully awake.

She lay on the sofa in the Blue Room. Bess and Felicia were with her—and the door was firmly closed. She heard her guests beyond that shut door. In that moment, she recalled what had happened.

"Oh my God," she gasped, sitting.

Bess restrained her, deathly pale and as grim. "You only fainted for a moment. Lie back down."

Blanche ignored her. "Please tell me I did not do anything I would regret."

Felicia stood behind Bess, wide-eyed with shock. "You started screaming bloody murder, then you ran across the room—and fell. You curled up on the floor screaming and weeping!"

Blanche sat very still, not even trying not to feel. "I am doomed."

"Lady de Warenne is calming your callers and making certain they all leave," she said quietly.

Blanche realized Bess was avoiding her eyes. She seized her hand. "How bad was it?"

Bess finally looked at her. She seemed near tears. And she was, in a very rare moment, incapable of speech.

"Blanche, it was ghastly!" Felicia cried. "What is going on? Was that a fit of madness?"

Blanche tried to find some dignity and a shred of pride. "Is that what it seemed to be?"

"I have never seen anyone act in such a manner." Felicia pulled up an ottoman and sat, taking her hand. "I have sent for your physician, Blanche."

Bess said suddenly, "Blanche had a migraine. They started recently—and they are so debilitating, you saw what happened."

Blanche looked at her friend with sheer gratitude. Bess smiled reluctantly and met her gaze, but only briefly. She stood. "I will go reassure everyone, as well."

Bess walked out. As she did, Blanche saw the countess Adare standing in the corridor with Lizzie and Eleanor, all three of them ashen. All of her suitors seemed to be gone, except one. James Montrose stood leaning against the wall, his hands in his jacket pockets, appearing thoughtful. Bess approached the small group and everyone came to attention. As she started speaking, they all turned and looked into the Blue Room.

Blanche looked away. "Close the door, Felicia," she whispered softly.

And she prayed Bess would convince everyone that she was ill, not mad.

Blanche looked away. When she does before.", she was persuasive.

And she knew these subtle emotions were one that she was all too used.

CHAPTER SEVENTEEN

THE MOMENT HE RECEIVED the letter, foreboding overcame him. Rex laid the unopened envelope down, and although it was noon, he reached for the bottle of Irish whiskey and poured himself a drink.

The letter was from his sister-in-law Lizzie. His family wrote him frequently, but he was due in town at the end of the month for his parents' anniversary. A letter from Lizzie just two weeks before his arrival now seemed strange. He was loath to find out what news Lizzie wished to share.

Blanche's image came immediately to mind. He was furious with himself for allowing her into his thoughts, so he drank. He never thought of her; he refused to do so. He was too busy to do so—the new barn was complete and he was finally restoring the old ruined tower on the south side of the house. New stone hedges had been added to the pastures. And he was adding a pair of larger windows to the master suite.

He cupped his glass in his hand. It was May already. In a few weeks, summer would descend. The spring had passed far too slowly even if he had worked long, endless days, toiling alongside his men like any common laborer. He was ready for the summer. He was going to leave this damnable place. He had never felt more isolated and he was coming to hate Land's End in spite of all the renovations. He always spent a few weeks in Ireland, but usually in July or August. He'd go direct from London this time.

And maybe, this time, he would never come back and say to hell with his estate.

He stared at Lizzie's letter. She was a pretty woman with curves and she had pretty, curvaceous script. Why in hell would she write him now?

He was almost certain that he knew the answer to his question. Tyrell had written him eight weeks ago and there had been no other letters from his family since. Rex had not been able to open it. To this day, he didn't know if the letter contained congratulations or condolences. He had burned it.

Grief rose up. He pulled Stephen's portrait forward, staring at the small, somber dark boy. He missed him terribly. He had spent every day and every night of these past weeks stricken with an acute sense of loss for his son. He could not fathom why such grief would arise now, and not years ago, and with it the terrible yearning to rectify a situation gone awry. Every day he told himself he would write Mowbray and tell him he was intending to meet his child, but he never did. Supper would begin, and with it, there was always a good bottle of red wine, followed by his after-dinner brandy. And then, finally, he would think not of Stephen, but of Blanche, whom he hated and loved—and missed—all in the same terrible breath.

In the darkest hours of the night, he allowed himself an emotional rampage. In those dark hours, he thought of her and wanted to hate her with every fiber of his being. His only solace was his brandy. He recalled their every moment together, when they had been in love—or when she had appeared to be as fond of him as he was of her. Grief, rage, hatred and love became one.

He wasn't going to think about Blanche now, at noon. And Lizzie wouldn't dare meddle, would she? His sister was the nosy one. But Eleanor probably hadn't arrived in town yet, so he had a reprieve. However, for the first time in his life, he did not look forward to the family reunion.

He pushed his thoughts aside. Today he would write Tom. He could not go on this way. He needed to meet his biological son face-to-face. He needed to see him smile and hear his voice. He had so many questions! He would never jeopardize Stephen's future; he wanted Stephen to have the kind of power and privilege his brothers had, but surely there was a way for him to somehow participate in his life. He would become a long-lost family acquaintance of some sort. After all, he and Tom had been in the war together.

He smiled and it was twisted.

Rex drained the glass, not feeling any alcoholic affects. Then he stared at Lizzie's curvy script. He was close to burning her letter, too. But maybe she wanted to tell him of a change in plans. He would be relieved if the anniversary celebration was moved to Adare, in more ways than he cared to think about. He could put off the choice he must make regarding a change in his relationship with Stephen, and he would not be at risk of accidentally running into Blanche. He knew he would not be a gentleman if they happened upon one another at some social event.

He picked up the ivory-handled letter opener and slit the envelope, emboldened now.

Dear Rex,

How are you, my dearest brother-in-law? The earl arrived in town last week, as did Sean and Eleanor and their boys. Virginia, Devlin and their children are due any day. Ned and Michael are once again fast friends and chafing incessantly, as they wish for their ringleader, Alexi, to join them, but Cliff and Amanda will not arrive for another week or so. Rogan is now three and he reminds me of his mother—he is a bold terror, and to make matters worse, running after my Chaz, thinking him the perfect ringleader! Chaos reigns, but it is wonderful, and we miss you! I am writing you to invite you to come to town a bit earlier than planned. Is there any chance you would do so? And do not tell me that you are still preoccupied with renovating your estate!

Rex had to smile, but moisture had gathered in his eyes. Harmon House was indeed brimming with chaos when just half of the family was present, but he agreed with Lizzie, it was a wonderful chaos, caused by so many happy, rambunctious and personable children. He adored each and every one of his nieces and nephews, and usually, he looked forward to the times he spent with them. It was always bittersweet. He was the only bachelor present, surrounded by so much affection and love, and sometimes he would wonder what it was like, to have a loving, loyal wife. He would also think of Stephen, who was growing up without his cousins, aunts, uncles and grandparents. Now, that comprehension hurt vastly. And he was determined to bring Stephen to Harmon House for a visit, even if he couldn't disclose his identity.

He continued to read, and instantly stiffened.

The real reason I am writing you is because I have a grave concern for Blanche Harrington. Tyrell and I remain utterly confused after receiving that first letter of yours, and then no other. We called on Blanche the day after she returned to town, hoping she would regale us with your news, but alas, she did not. So apparently the engagement you wrote of is off. I will not pry, for I know how private you are. However, I also know you must have had some affection for her and this is why I am writing you. I thought that if you still have some care for her, you should know that her condition seems very delicate. If you remain a friend, you might wish to call on her when you come to town; perhaps you can offer her some consolation, or even support. She does not open her house frequently anymore, which has caused great gossip. In spite of that, she does remain deluged with suitors and the rumor is she will soon choose a husband.

Please forgive me my boldness, but my concern for Blanche outweighs my desire to be polite with my own dear brother. And if the two of you had a falling-out, if there is any chance it could be repaired, I so encourage you to step forward and do so. Blanche remains the kindest woman I know.

Sincerely,

Lizzie

Rex stared at the page, stunned. And then panic arose, consuming him.

Blanche was in a delicate condition? He swung to his crutch. By God, did Lizzie mean that she was carrying a child—his child? But it had only been eight weeks! It was impossible to know this soon—wasn't it?

He began to tremble wildly. He could hardly think straight. Panic blinded him. He had lost one child, forsaking it to Clarewood; he could not lose another child, not ever again!

He tried to stay calm. He tried to reason. No woman could know that she was pregnant within eight weeks. He was almost certain—unless some new medical advance had been made. Had there been a recent medical discovery?

Blanche was in a delicate condition. What could that mean, if not what he had first assumed? And no matter what had happened, wouldn't she tell him her news?

And a fist seemed to sink into his chest, cutting off all air. Julia hadn't told him of her condition; she had run off with Mowbray instead.

The tower room spun. He panicked when he wanted to think. He had accused Blanche of being as treacherous as her society friends, as treacherous and disloyal as Julia, but he had never really believed it. She had left him rudely, faithlessly, treacherously, but in his heart, he refused to see her as a black-hearted bitch. A part of him, ridiculously, still thought of her as an angel.

She would tell him if she was with child, wouldn't she?

He didn't know what to think.

Except, no woman could know that she was pregnant with any certainty in a mere two months!

And instantly, he recalled her running from the old church in Lanhadron and collapsing in a dead faint outside.

He leaped to his crutch. His alarm barely receded. Was Blanche suffering from more headaches? Had she fainted again? She had fainted twice while his houseguest. Was she ill? Had she seen a proper physician? Damn it, why hadn't Lizzie been more explicit!

He swung over to the window and stared outside. There was no denying his overwhelming concern—when he did not want to be concerned for her. He had trusted her and she had proven that all women were the same. They were all faithless, selfish creatures, and her facade of kind caring and deep affection was only that. But even as he told himself she was treacherous, his heart protested vehemently, refusing to believe it.

He had made the mistake of trusting his heart twice in his life, and look at where it had gotten him. He would never listen to his heart again. At all costs, he must ignore its shrieking alarm and concern now.

Maybe he would never properly despise Blanche Harrington, but if she was ill, it was not his affair, damn it.

He went back to his desk and poured another drink, but only stared grimly at it. Calmer now, he thought that only one

of two conclusions was possible—either she was ill or she was
with child. When he thought of the last possibility, he knew
gnawing fear, but he was sensible now. Blanche not only
couldn't know such a thing, even if she did, she would not
share her condition with Lizzie de Warenne.

And that meant Blanche was ill. It was *not* his affair. She
was a grown woman, without family but with friends, and
someone else could look out for her. Her new fiancé could
look out for her. But he sat down at his desk, terribly disturbed,
refusing to think about what he must do. Instantly he placed
a sheet of parchment before him, and dipping his quill, he
quickly wrote his sister-in-law.

Dear Lizzie,

   I am pleased to hear from you and I am looking forward
to arriving at Harmon House and being inundated by the
family. I cannot wait to see how the children have grown
and I am more than eager to chaperone Ned, Michael and
Alexi. The boys do need a firm hand! However, I doubt I
will come sooner than the date I have scheduled as I am
busy with my renovations here at Land's End.

   I am sorry that Blanche Harrington continues to feel
poorly. I continue to consider her a family friend and
therefore am advising you that she was in a delicate condition while here in Cornwall. Please encourage her to
seek the diagnosis of the best physicians in town.

He hesitated, well aware that everyone in his family would
want to know what had happened. It was not anyone's affair,
but that wouldn't stop his brothers, stepbrothers or his
busybody sister, Eleanor. He sighed and wrote,

   I am aware of the excitement which my hasty letter
must have engendered. Blanche and I have been friends

for a very long time. We briefly fancied ourselves a suitable match, then as quickly realized we do not suit at all, for obvious reasons. I apologize for the confusion.

Until the end of the month, with Best Regards,

Your devoted brother, Rex

No one was kinder than Lizzie. She had a huge heart, made of solid gold. He felt almost certain she would encourage Blanche to seek the proper medical care.

He dried the letter, and when he was certain it would not smear, he folded it and slid it into an envelope, which he sealed with wax and his crest. And a flicker of fear began.

Blanche was obviously ill. But what if she was also with child?

They had spent an entire night making love. As they had been engaged, and as they both wished for children, he had not used any precautions. In fact, that night he had wanted to get her with his child.

He did not want to remember holding her or making love to her. He didn't want to recall being the first to do so, or the first to give her rapture. His temples throbbed and he stood unsteadily. Ever since Stephen had been born, he had been excessively cautious with his mistresses. He could not imagine anything worse than siring another child he could not claim and raise.

The panic rose. She was about to choose a husband.

And then the panic dulled, replaced by sheer will. He would never allow another man to raise his child. It was simply unacceptable.

BLANCHE SMILED FIRMLY as Jem opened the front door, admitting two dozen suitors. Bess and Felicia stood with her to greet her guests, both women wearing the same facade as Blanche. She had been in town eight weeks now, and once a week she allowed callers. Blanche was well aware of the gossip that raged. Too many gentlemen had seen her in a fit, and there was vast speculation that she was mad, and not suffering from migraines. But there hadn't been another incident, not in public. There had been many fits in private, however.

She remained on a dangerous precipice. Blanche knew her sanity was slowly but surely seeping away. Sometimes she awoke at night in the midst of a nightmare about the riot, and then her night became a living hell, as her bedroom became the London street, the room's flickering shadows the enraged mob.

Sometimes a single thought led to such a terrible pang of heartache that the headache would instantly begin—and she was thrown back into the past instantaneously. Blanche knew many of her servants had seen her crouched on the floor, weeping and screaming, because they walked past her the way she walked past the deranged on the common streets—avoiding eye contact and trying to put as much distance as possible between them.

Bess had summoned up the entire staff to explain that Blanche was afflicted with migraines. She had made a short, firm speech, one in which she had said that any servant caught spreading gossip would be let go instantly. Four servants—a doorman, two housemaids and a kitchen maid—had already been dismissed.

Blanche had refused to see any of the physicians Bess insisted upon. She was afraid of the diagnosis.

Instead, she tried to keep a grasp on her feelings, avoided going out, only entertained once a week, and had become adept at quietly leaving the room the moment she felt the beginnings of a headache. Now, she was extremely calm. She had drunk an excessive amount of herbal tea to prepare for her callers, but her tea had been laced with a spoonful of brandy.

Blanche smiled at the various gentlemen parading into her

salon. The front door remained open to admit them, and just as she was greeting one rather notorious rogue—Harry Dashwood—she saw someone standing outside, someone vaguely familiar.

Blanche felt an odd tension. The man was a commoner, dressed in a shabby jacket, wool breeches and boots, and a tweed cap. He was very tall; he turned to look into her house and his stare was pale and direct.

Blanche froze, recognizing Paul Carter.

He smiled and doffed his cap at her and walked away, out of her line of sight. Her heart exploded. What was he doing back in town? She had paid him off handsomely eight weeks ago, and their agreement had been that he was never to set foot at Harrington Hall again.

"Lady Harrington." Dashwood bowed. "Who is that?"

Blanche tried to control her fear, somehow smiling at Dashwood. "I beg your pardon?"

"That yeoman—the one who gave you such a fright." His dark eyes were benign.

She swallowed, her heart racing and worse, a dull ache beginning in her temples. "I have no idea," she said brightly. "Is it not a beautiful day, Lord Dashwood?"

He grinned. "It is very beautiful, when I am confronted with your beauty."

She knew she had never looked worse. The strain and lack of sleep coupled with an extreme loss of appetite had turned her into someone gaunt and haggard. Dashwood was always showering her with insincere flattery. She didn't mind—it was better than the searching stare of James Montrose, who never failed to call on the single day a week she was receiving.

Dashwood might do. He was thirty, and so vain and egocentric, he would never cease his promiscuous ways—meaning he would quickly leave her be—and he would never have any genuine interest in her. He was handsome, but she wasn't even remotely interested in him. While he was utterly shallow, he happened to have several profitable investments—he was a good businessman. With the help of clever agents, he could probably manage her fortune. He was also the son of a baron.

Of course, she had no intention of marrying anyone unless she was with child. While it was too soon to tell, Blanche knew with all of her being that a life was growing inside of her. She was thrilled—and she was dismayed. How could she mother a child when her grasp on her sanity was so fragile?

"May I dare be bold?" Dashwood continued, dimpling.

"I should never expect anything less," Blanche said automatically, pretending to flirt.

"I would like to stroll with you. May I?" He extended his arm.

Blanche saw Bess watching. She knew Bess approved of Dashwood—but only because of his business acumen. Bess nodded. Blanche turned to Dashwood. "You know I have a salon to entertain," she said lightly. "But I can take a short stroll with you."

They looped arms and went out the front door. Instantly Blanche glanced around, but was relieved when she did not see Paul Carter. As they strolled around the house into the gardens, she felt a sense of relief. She could not manage being confronted by Paul Carter now.

Dashwood started to chat about the opera. Blanche knew he would invite her to accompany him and she listened politely, formulating an excuse to deny him. And then she saw Carter whispering to her head gardener. She stumbled.

Dashwood caught her.

Blanche held on to him, entirely unaware of him, staring at Carter. He turned and stared back at her.

Dread began. What was he saying to her head gardener? What did he want? Why had he come back?

Her temples now throbbed with pain.

It was happening. She was about to have a fit. Her grasp on Dashwood tightened. She wanted to tell him she was ill and about to have a migraine, but no words came out.

He turned white. "Lady Harrington?"

Her mother's screams exploded and the gardens vanished, turning into cobbled streets. The mob raged all around her while she crawled to Mama, the monster shouting furiously at her and just missing seizing her ankle. "Mama!"

Mama's screams intensified.

Someone tripped over her. Blanche froze as she was seized and that was when Mama stopped screaming—and that was when she saw her lying in a pool of blood in the street.

She knew it was Mama's blood.

The stones spun and tilted. She fought for air even though she wished for darkness. And then it came....

CHAPTER EIGHTEEN

TWO WEEKS LATER, Rex nodded at the doorman as he walked into the spacious entry hall of Harmon House. He could hear the wicked laughter of young boys and the high-pitched protest of one of his nieces. He smiled and for the first time in months, was aware of being almost happy.

He limped through the front hall and into the family room, a green-and-gold salon that opened to the back gardens. Ned and Alexi were giggling and waving a beautiful china doll high in the air while Elysse seemed distraught and near tears. Ariella scowled, hands on her hips. Cliff's blond daughter saw him first. "Uncle Rex," she cried. "That doll was a gift from Paris! They are going to break it."

"I hope not," he said mildly to her, marveling at her exotic looks. In spite of her fair hair, she had swarthy skin and strikingly blue eyes. He turned to the boys, who regarded him in surprise. "Cliff will not think twice about keelhauling you both."

The two dark boys shrieked in unison and came running, flinging the doll onto the sofa. He ruffled Ned's dark hair and then Alexi's. "Why do you have to torture your cousins?" he asked Tyrell's oldest. "You are your father's heir. One day you will be patriarch of this family. One day, if Elysse is in trouble, she will turn to you. It will be your responsibility to advance her interests."

Ned flushed. "It's only a doll and she is such a mouse." He looked at her. "Meow."

Rex clasped his shoulder. "Your father might want to know you are running amok with Alexi."

Alexi said boldly, "Uncle Ty said we could fish in the river."

"You aren't fishing," Rex pointed out. "You are acting like a pirate and we both know you know the difference between a pirate and a privateer. That doll is not yours."

Ariella said, "We arrived yesterday, Uncle Rex, because we were becalmed for three days. And Alexi and Ned have been teasing Elysse cruelly ever since."

Elysse nodded, sniffling. "They are picking on me."

"That is because you are the beautiful one, and boys love to tease beautiful girls," Rex said truthfully. Elysse had her father's golden hair but her mother's delicate beauty, and she was as ethereal as a fairy princess. He looked at Alexi. "Is this the first time you have met your cousin?" he asked with sudden suspicion.

Alexi blushed and glanced away from Elysse. "It was Ned's idea to take the doll and hide it. We can't go fishing because Uncle Ty said we had to wait for low tide, even though we are both good swimmers," he added, boasting and glancing at Elysse.

She gave him a haughty look and picked up her doll. "Of course you're a good swimmer. Pirates have to swim, because they are made to walk the plank. And you are more pirate than privateer. Just like your father," she added.

Rex rolled his eyes, but before he could chastise Elysse, he heard footsteps in the hall. He turned and saw both of his brothers and he smiled. He had forgotten how much he needed these family interludes.

Tyrell looked every bit the heir apparent, even in his shirtsleeves and breeches. Cliff looked every bit the pirate he was not, and although clad in a suit, a gold earring graced one ear and huge roweled spurs, studded with rubies, were on his boots, which he wore instead of shoes. "Finally," Cliff exclaimed, grinning. He clasped Rex hard enough to shake his balance momentarily.

"Are they taunting the girls again?" Ty asked with disapproval.

"They tried to steal my doll," Elysse said, tears coming to her eyes. "She is from *Paris*. Papa bought her for me himself." She hugged the doll breathlessly to her chest, awaiting her uncle's reaction.

Ty patted her head and then turned a dire look upon his son and nephew. "No fishing—for the week. Upstairs—I know you have an essay to complete, Ned. I'll read it before supper. Alexi, you may do the same assignment."

Ned hung his head, his expression grim, but Alexi cried out, turning to Cliff. "I'd rather be keelhauled."

"Unfortunately, I have never resorted to the practice. However, I have an odd feeling that you may be my first experiment," Cliff told his son. "Control yourself," he warned. "Or I will leave you at Windsong the next time we come to town."

"Yes, sir," Alexi said.

Both boys left.

Elysse sent a smile of satisfaction at Ariella. Rex thought, she will be trouble, soon. "Thank you, Uncle Ty," she said sweetly, smiling like an angel. She kissed him and turned. "Do you want to play with my doll?"

Ariella hesitated. "I am actually reading a history of India."

Elysse looked at her as if she had spoken Chinese.

Cliff said softly, "Why don't you read later and play awhile with your cousin? You can read anytime and we are not in town with Devlin's family very often."

Ariella was clearly resigned, but she forced a smile. "Of course, Papa."

The moment the two girls were gone, Cliff swung around and shut both salon doors. "What is going on?" he exclaimed.

Rex truly hoped to head off the conversation before it began. "What do you mean?" he asked casually. "I have been toiling like a laborer for well over a year now and my estate is coming along nicely."

Cliff shook his head, staring, while Tyrell gave him a long look. Then Tyrell went to the floor-to-ceiling sideboard and began uncorking a bottle of wine. Cliff clasped his shoulder. "I heard that you wrote Ty and told him you were engaged to Blanche Harrington. What the hell happened?"

He tensed. "I believe I wrote Lizzie and offered an explanation." He pulled away from his younger brother. "We are vastly opposite. Although we are friends, in the end, we would never make a successful go of a marriage."

Cliff stared, speculation written all over his face. "You and Blanche Harrington," he said softly. "I would have never thought, not in a hundred years. Are you in love with her?"

Rex tensed all over again. He had had these exact kinds of conversations with his brothers and stepbrothers countless times while they were struggling with their love lives, but he had never expected to be on the receiving end. "No, I am not."

"Really?" Cliff's tawny brows lifted. "A de Warenne man only marries for love—it is family tradition."

"It is family mythology," Rex growled. "And we are not married."

"No, but you were about to marry."

Tyrell walked over, handing them both a glass of wine. "She is engaged to a notorious rake, Harry Dashwood. Or at least, that is the rumor."

Rex felt his heart turn over hard and sickeningly. After it had slammed back into place, it sped wildly. Dashwood? He knew him. He'd seen him from time to time at White's. They'd never done more than greet one another, but he'd seen him gaming, and the man played cautiously and well, usually winning a small stake and then quitting while ahead. He'd seen him enough times to know that the man was very self-involved. He knew of him, too. He had been involved with most of the wealthiest married ladies in town, and he always seemed to wind up a bit richer after his affairs.

He felt ill. Was Blanche engaged? Was she in love? "What do you know of Dashwood?" he asked casually.

Tyrell said as casually, "Not much. He has had his share of affairs. He has a few profitable investments. He is shallow." He shrugged, but his stare was penetrating.

"And that is your reaction?" Cliff asked. "I was green with jealousy every time a suitor looked at Amanda—when I was the one trying to find her a husband!" he exclaimed.

"Yes, you were a royal arse," Eleanor said, stepping into the room. "What have I missed?" She hurried to Rex and hugged him. "Why aren't you engaged to Blanche? What do you mean, the two of you don't suit? I think she would be wonderful for you!" she cried in a single breath.

"Hello, Eleanor. I am pleased to see you, too, I think." But he had to smile at his tall, unsinkable sister.

"Lizzie wants to call on her tomorrow," Tyrell said, as casually as before. And in that moment, Rex sensed a conspiracy. "Do you wish to join us? I am sure she will be glad to see you—after all, you remain family friends."

Rex felt his damned heart lurch again, and then rush with eagerness. "I have a call to make tomorrow," he said firmly.

"What call?" Eleanor demanded instantly.

"A very private call."

Eleanor's eyes widened. "You are seeing another woman?" she exclaimed.

Rex sighed. "I did not say that."

"Then where are you going and can I join you?" She smiled challengingly at him.

"No, you cannot join me." He was firm.

"Are you avoiding Blanche?" Eleanor demanded.

He sighed and limped to the sofa and sat. "No." But the moment he spoke, he knew everyone in the room realized he was doing just that. He quickly smiled. "I hope she cares for Dashwood. She deserves happiness."

Eleanor simply shook her head, bewildered, and sat beside him. She took his hand. "I was so excited when Ty said you were engaged. I was so happy for you. I want you to have what I have—what Ty has—what Cliff has."

"I am not looking for love, Eleanor," he said quietly.

"Why not? We have all married for love and we are all so happy. And what about children?"

Rex stiffened, assailed with Stephen's image. He knew that if he ever told his brothers and sister about their nephew, all hell would break loose. Eleanor would encourage him to break the agreement with Mowbray, but he thought his brothers would be more practical. His agreement now felt tenuous at best. He firmed his lips and then said, "I don't think children are in store for me."

"That's crap," Cliff said swiftly. "They are if you wish for them to be."

Rex stared at him, thinking about the fact that Cliff was raising his two bastards. Ariella's mother was dead, murdered in a harem, and Alexi's mother, a Russian countess, was married with other, legitimate children. Her husband hadn't wanted Alexi and apparently, neither had his mother.

Eleanor took his hand again. He turned, instantly aware that she was saddened for him. Her eyes mirrored that sorrow. But she smiled. "I can be a pit bull, can't I?"

He was relieved. "Yes, you can. But you are forgiven."

She hesitated.

Cliff took a sip of wine, then said abruptly, "If you won't tell him, I will."

Eleanor grimaced. "I am trying to stand down."

Rex shrugged off her hand and stared at Cliff and then Ty. "Tell me what," he asked, aware of a new tension in the room. Apparently his siblings knew something he did not. "Is it Dashwood?"

"The engagement isn't even official," Tyrell said. He gestured at Cliff.

"There is a terrible rumor going around," Cliff said. "And you should know about it."

Rex swung to his crutch, standing. "Blanche is ill," he said, dread unfurling.

"No," Cliff said. "But the gossip is that she has lost her mind."

Rex blinked.

Eleanor rose to her feet. "That is a terrible rumor," she whispered, "but the truth is, I have seen her myself. And even I have wondered if she is mad."

REX WALKED INTO WHITE'S later that afternoon with his stepbrothers, Devlin and Sean. Although it was just five, the first floor salon was crowded with gentlemen sipping port and smoking cigars. Sean espied a pair of open chairs and an unoccupied love seat. As they crossed the room, Rex felt heads turning.

He hadn't been in society since the previous Season, as they had spent the past holidays at Adare. Still, he had been gone so long, with nothing of consequence happening, that he assumed one of his stepbrothers was the cause for stares. It took him a moment to realize that conversation died when *he* passed, not Sean or Devlin. And he heard a man murmuring, "Broke it off, do you think?"

He paused in midstep.

"I would, wouldn't you?" A blond gent snickered.

He stared at the blond gentleman and his older, gray-haired crony. Both men looked away instantly. What the hell was that about? he wondered. And then he saw Tom Mowbray.

Tension assailed him.

Clarewood sat alone in a thronelike chair, a port on the round tea table beside him, browsing a newspaper. Except, his blue eyes were on Rex, not the printed page. And the moment their gazes met, he jerked his eyes down.

Rex just stood there, his heart slamming, his mind blank—except for the image of his son. He'd written Mowbray a short letter, explaining that he wished to call on him and discuss some private matters, but there had been no response. Mowbray would have immediately known that Rex wished to discuss Stephen.

Devlin strolled up to him. He was a tall man with leonine hair and the casual grace that came with confidence and power. "What's wrong?"

Rex breathed. He smiled at Devlin. "I'll be a moment. I don't know if you are acquainted with Clarewood, but there is a matter I wish to discuss with him."

Devlin's eyes changed. They went from bland to brilliant, then he turned his gaze upon the duke. "What are you drinking?"

"Cabernet," Rex said. When Devlin left he limped over to Clarewood. Tom slowly lowered his news journal. "Mowbray."

Tom Mowbray stared. "Rex."

Rex did not care for his tone or the familiar address. He realized he had not spoken to the man in nine years. He hadn't even glimpsed him in half that time. Mowbray appeared different, somehow, and not just because he was older and leaner. "May I assume you received my letter?"

Mowbray stood. He remained handsome, but his face was gaunt and hard, when in youth it had been soft and full. Even his eyes seemed hard. "I vaguely recall some such missive."

Rex's temper ignited, but he only smiled. "I wish a word with you…Tom."

Mowbray jerked. "You do comprehend that it is Clarewood, Rex. It is Clarewood or Your Grace."

So this was how it would now be, Rex thought, surprised and disturbed. "It wasn't 'my lord' when we stood side by side in Spain, killing Frenchmen and watching our comrades die."

"Those days are long gone," Mowbray said with disdain. "And I do not have a moment. I am running late." He tossed the journal onto the tea table, preparing to leave.

Rex wanted to seize him—and he actually wished to strike him. Instead he said, very low, so no one might overhear, "I am calling on Stephen."

Mowbray whirled to face him. "I think not," he exclaimed.

"Unless you take him from town, I have decided that the status quo is no longer satisfactory."

Mowbray's eyes widened—and chilled.

"I do not mean I wish to make any shocking announcements," Rex said grimly. "But I wish to meet him. I wish to visit. I can no longer wait."

Mowbray stepped closer and said in a harsh whisper, "I will not have any changes to our arrangement."

"I don't want to make substantial changes. In every way except the natural one, Stephen is your son. However, I have some rights. And originally we did agree upon some visitation."

"You gave up any rights long ago—as you should have done—to further Stephen's future! I will not become a laughingstock now," Mowbray said, his voice low and harsh.

Rex did not care for his attitude. "I am surprised you did not state that you had no wish to jeopardize Stephen's future, too."

"I have raised him as my son. I have given him every privilege. I will not have old rumors resurrected now."

"That is not my intention," Rex said grimly, shaken. Did Mowbray care for Stephen as a son? Until that moment, he had always assumed so, for otherwise, Mowbray could so easily declare the truth. Now, he was stunned, uneasy and uncertain. "I merely wish to visit. We are old friends. I saved your life in the war—it is public knowledge. One day, Stephen will learn of it. I have every reason to visit Clarewood and that is what you may tell Stephen." He hesitated, his pulse pounding. When Mowbray stared, appearing repulsed, he added, "You owe me."

"Like hell I do," Clarewood said. "It's been ten years—my debt is paid." He seemed furious. "Call then, if you wish. But do not think to make a habit of it." He stalked away.

Rex stood there, aware that now he was perspiring. What had happened to Clarewood to change him from a carefree boy into a hard, cold man? He only cared for his son's sake, for Mowbray was barely recognizable.

Still, he had taken the man by complete surprise. However, had Tom bothered to begin a discourse by mail, that wouldn't have been necessary.

Clasping his crutch far too tightly, Rex turned back to his stepbrothers. As he sat, Sean skewered him with his pale gray eyes. "What is between you and Clarewood?"

"We are old friends," Rex said, avoiding eye contact. "I haven't seen him in years, not since we served together in the war."

"That was a *very* friendly reunion," Sean said drily.

Rex smiled at him. "Were you eavesdropping?"

"Hardly—my chair is facing that way."

Rex realized that was true. "I thought to renew an old acquaintance, but Clarewood has changed drastically."

"He's a cold, hard man," Devlin said. "I have had dealings with him. He seems quite embittered. Didn't you save his life in Spain?"

Rex stiffened, but smiled. "I carried him from the field when he could not walk. So yes, I suppose you could say that I did."

Devlin sipped a whiskey, his eyes impossible to read. And

Rex realized his stepbrothers, both very astute men, were suspicious of him now. He changed the subject. "Will you spend any time at Adare this summer, Sean? I intend to go up for a bit after I leave town."

Sean smiled, as if he knew evasion when presented with it. "We haven't made our plans for the summer yet." Then, his gaze directed somewhere behind Rex, his eyes widened. "Your friend Dashwood has just come in."

It was very hard for Rex to sit still. Blanche's image now filled his mind, bringing a tension he did not want. He regretted sitting with his back to the room, and slowly, he turned.

Dashwood stood not far from where he sat, surrounded by two young friends, the men laughing and boisterous. Rex had forgotten that the man dressed impeccably and was rather attractive and athletically built. He took in every detail of his appearance, the crisp white shirt, the custom suit, the polished shoes, and he was filled with loathing—and even jealousy. For the first time since hearing that Blanche was engaged, it crossed his mind that she was probably already sharing Dashwood's bed.

He could not stand the notion. He saw red.

"So you're the fortunate sonuvabitch," his friend chuckled, pounding his back.

"No, he's the unfortunate sonuvabitch," the dark gentleman laughed.

"I am fortunate, not unfortunate, Will." Dashwood laughed, too. "And we have just begun to draw up the contracts."

Rex now turned fully, staring. So it was about to be official, he thought grimly.

"Maybe you are as mad as she is," the first rogue said loudly. "Fortune or not, I would never condescend to marry such a woman."

Rex froze. He was disbelieving. Were these morons discussing Blanche? Were they loudly declaring her *mad?*

"I am not condescending," Dashwood said with a grin.

"Oh, so she's not bonkers?" Will asked slyly.

"Oh, she's as mad as a loon. I saw her in a fit, firsthand." Dashwood lowered his voice. "And that suits me well, boys. That suits me well, as a madwoman has no right to such a fortune, if you comprehend my meaning."

He saw red again, but this time, it was blinding.

Sean seized his arm. "Don't."

Rex took his crutch and tapped Dashwood on the back—not pleasantly. And he stood up.

Dashwood turned, his eyes wide. He saw Rex and his gaze narrowed. "De Warenne," he said coolly. "May I assume you wish to offer me congratulations?"

Rex smiled—then took his crutch and slashed the other man behind the knees. Dashwood went down on his back, head thudding on the floor, while Rex grasped the back of his chair to avoid crashing over himself. From his prone position, Dashwood looked at him, stunned. Then he growled, "You bastard."

"Lady Harrington—your future wife—is not mad," Rex said coldly. "And I suggest you reconsider your engagement if you are so disrespectful of her."

Dashwood crouched and leaped up. Rex tried to move out of the way, but too late. Dashwood caught him by the arm and the two of them went down on the floor, grappling like schoolboys. Dashwood wound up on top.

Rex tried to turn aside to avoid the blow and Dashwood smashed his fist into his mouth. Rex wedged his crutch between them and jammed it upward. Dashwood howled as his genitals were struck. And then numerous hands were tearing the two men apart.

Rex stood with the help of his stepbrothers, touching his bloody lip. Dashwood crouched on his knees, holding his groin. Panting, Rex said, "Lady Harrington is a dear friend of this family. I suggest you reconsider all of your plans. We will not allow her to be abused by you, sir."

"Let's go," Sean said in his ear.

"You will pay for this," Dashwood panted. "And she will be my wife—we are signing the contracts tomorrow!"

Rex froze, the urge to turn back and pummel Dashwood consuming. Sean jerked on his arm. Devlin knelt beside Dashwood. "I'd reconsider if I were you, my lad." He smiled and stood. "Let's go."

Rex left White's, Sean and Devlin on either side of him.

REX STOOD BY THE WINDOW in the family room, a brandy in hand, not having taken a sip. He stared out at the star-studded sky, the incident with Dashwood replaying in his mind.

Behind him, his two brothers and two stepbrothers lounged, quietly conversing and having nightcaps. Could Blanche love Dashwood, or was she marrying for convenience and economy? Were they sharing a bed already? And was Dashwood scheming to deprive her of her fortune by declaring her insane after they were wed?

Someone came to stand beside him; Rex tensed. He turned and saw Cliff, who smiled slightly at him. "A night for lovers," he said. "And I am about to go upstairs and join my wife."

Rex couldn't summon up a smile. "Amanda has never been lovelier or happier, I think."

Cliff inclined his head in agreement, and said, "And you have never been as miserable, I think."

Rex tensed. Cliff was but a year his junior, and in some ways, they were very close. On the other hand, they were complete opposites in character. Cliff had been a notorious rogue for most of his life while plying the globe as both a merchant and a privateer, making a vast fortune and a vast reputation for himself; Rex was a war hero, a patriot, ever dutiful as a brother and son, and he worked the land on his modest manor. While he rarely slept alone, he did not change women the way his brother had until he'd fallen for his wife.

"I heard what happened at White's. Clearly you remain fond of Blanche Harrington. I do not understand why you don't do what you wish to do."

Rex made a harsh sound. He would never reveal that she had rejected him. "Dashwood is openly declaring her mad."

"I heard that, too. Someone must stop him." Cliff smiled.

"I believe he thinks to marry her and then legally commit her—and take sole control of her fortune."

"That could be his plan, but that is beyond foul. Are you certain you are not jumping to vastly wrong conclusions?"

"I heard him. I heard him say he witnessed her madness and that a madwoman has no right to a fortune." Rex breathed hard. "You are right. Someone has to stop him."

"So what will you do?"

He stared at his brother. "I am the mad one—for I intend to meddle. I am going to tell Blanche what I heard. But she won't believe that anyone could be so malicious—or so evil. Somehow I must convince her to jilt Dashwood."

Cliff smiled. "I have the oddest notion that might not be too difficult to accomplish."

"Blanche will not appreciate my interference…I am almost certain." Rex turned away. He could barely imagine what their next meeting would be like. Yet in the end, he was a gentleman, for he could not allow Dashwood to go forward with such a despicable scheme.

Cliff clasped his shoulder. "Good luck," he said.

NO ONE CALLED IN MIDMORNING, unless close family. Rex stepped down from the de Warenne coach in the pebbled circular drive before Harrington House. Another carriage was present, but it was too handsome and luxurious to belong to Dashwood. He wondered if Blanche owned it and planned to .

go out at such an hour. He wondered when Dashwood would arrive to sign their marriage contracts. If he was successful, Blanche would not welcome him into her home.

He had been up all night, brooding. Now, a terrible tension filled him as he swung up the front steps to the imposing ebony front door of the house. Two liveried doormen stood there, as still as statues. He knocked loudly. His heart was pounding, for so much was at stake—Blanche's future was at stake, as was her happiness. He was not deluded. He doubted Blanche would be pleased to see him, not that she would ever allow him to see any displeasure. And as well as he knew her, he could not imagine her reaction when he told her about Dashwood's scheme. He thought she might be disbelieving. She would probably politely thank him for his kindness in calling and send him on his way.

His heart lurched wildly, an indication that far more feelings than he wished to have for her remained. Another doorman answered and he was escorted into the reception room. Gilded chairs lined walls adorned with numerous oil paintings, and a pedestal table with a floral arrangement sat alone in the center of the room.

He heard soft, feminine footsteps. He stiffened, his heart exploding, and apprehension consumed him. Then he was surprised, for Lady Waverly entered the room, her face tight and unsmiling.

Dismay began. He bowed. "Lady Waverly."

"Sir Rex, what a surprise," she said, sounding sarcastic.

He stared at her. She was angry? And if so, why? What could Blanche have said about him? "I realize it is early, but there is an urgent matter I must discuss with Lady Harrington."

"It is ten in the morning," Lady Waverly said coolly.

Rex realized a confrontation was unavoidable. "I am aware of the time. Again, I have a very important matter to discuss with Lady Blanche."

Bess stared at him, her face a mask of anger. "She is not receiving today, Sir Rex. She receives on Thursdays. You will have to come back then."

His temper rose. He swallowed a rude response. "Please tell her that I am here. We are friends and she will entertain me."

Lady Waverly placed her fists on her hips. "Actually, she doesn't want to see you. She made that clear two months ago."

Her words had to be a lie; still, they stabbed through him like a knife. "When she left Land's End, we were on good terms. I would be shocked if that had changed." Actually, only Blanche had behaved properly, he thought.

Lady Waverly trembled with her passion, shocking him. "It has changed! Everything has changed! Now good day, sir!"

He did not move. "I realize she is signing marriage contracts today," he finally said, fighting his anger. "It is urgent that we speak before she does."

And Lady Waverly exploded. "I won't let you see her! She doesn't need you here, now! You will only cause grave problems! Good day, Sir Rex," she cried.

He was stunned by her outburst.

"Leave Blanche alone." With that, Lady Waverly turned and strode away, disappearing into another set of rooms.

Sir Rex remained shocked. What the hell was going on? he wondered grimly. And he had no intention of leaving. He glanced across the reception room. The door he had entered from remained open and he could see the front door beyond it, where the doorman was pretending not to have heard a word, just as he pretended not to know Rex stood there.

Rex grasped his crutch and followed in Lady Waverly's wake. He passed through two pleasant salons, hearing nothing but the sound of his own footfalls. He did not know the house, but if Lady Waverly was present, Blanche was undoubtedly with her.

He was traversing a corridor now. Ahead, a door opened. Rex halted, not attempting to hide, hoping to glimpse Blanche. But a man dressed in the rough garb of a country laborer stepped out. As he did, Rex had a clear view of his profile before he turned away from Rex, disappearing outside through a pair of French doors.

Rex stared after Paul Carter, Anne's fiancé, surprised. What was the farrier doing in town—at Harrington Hall? And in that instant, he thought of Anne's malice toward Blanche. A terrible suspicion began. No good could have come from his visit.

And he thudded rapidly to the door Carter had left ajar. He pushed it open and saw a large library, painted pale green, with an abundance of seating. And he saw Blanche, seated in a corner at a small desk, sitting with her hands clasped in front of her, staring at them, like a small, repentant schoolgirl.

His heart lurched and slammed. He forgot that she had cruelly toyed with his heart and treacherously broken their engagement. He forgot that he must despise her, or at least, have no genuine care for her. An angel sat at that desk; a fragile angel in need of his help and protection.

And he didn't move, aware of the fact that he still loved her—that he always had and always would. He drank in the elegant sight of her, aware he might not have such a private opportunity again. The length of the entire room separated them, but she suddenly looked up.

Blanche gasped.

He closed the door and limped slowly forward, his heart roaring so loudly he was certain she could hear it, too.

She sat staring, unsmiling, her tension obvious.

A terrible sorrow began. Why did it have to be this way?

"I had hoped we could remain friends," he said softly. But he hadn't wanted friendship. Until yesterday, he had wanted amnesia as far as she was concerned. In that moment, he wanted to renew their friendship, if at all possible. He could settle for that small crumb.

She swallowed. "How did you get in?"

And now he stared, becoming stunned at her pallor and worse, the haggard look on her face. She had lost weight and she was clearly not sleeping; dark circles ringed her eyes. She looked very fragile…she looked ill. And every protective instinct he had surged forth. "Your doorman." He smiled, showering her with all the charm he had. "Your friend turned me away but I decided to take matters into my own hands. If you are dismayed—which I see you are—I hope you will forgive me." He held her gaze. "You have forgiven me far graver crimes."

She inhaled. "I can't do this, Sir Rex."

He started. Something was so terribly wrong. "You cannot speak with me—as a dear family friend?"

She pursed her lips. He saw her tremble. "It is too hard," she whispered.

"Blanche, I cannot understand. Or did I somehow offend you at Land's End, so heinously, that your affection has turned to disgust and loathing?"

Her eyes widened. "Of course you did no such thing!" She stood, swaying like a young sapling in a strong breeze. "I do not loathe you." Tears came. "I admire you…we will always be friends."

He closed his eyes, fighting the insane urge to stride forward and sweep her into his arms—and make love to her, if she would let him. Then he opened them and smiled encouragingly at her. "Then we are in agreement, as I will always admire you…and I will always be your friend," he said lightly.

She breathed harshly and he heard the intake of breath.

"Why are you crying?" he asked quietly. "And why is Paul Carter here?"

She jerked, lifting her tearful gaze to his. "Haven't you heard the rumors? Or did you just get to town?"

"I arrived yesterday. And I did hear you are about to become engaged."

She flushed and looked away. In a low voice she said, "I meant the other rumors."

He stared until she looked up at him. He understood but pretended not to. "No, I have not."

She smiled grimly. "I am mad."

He tensed, aghast at her firm, unyielding tone. "You are not mad! You are the most sensible woman I know. Do not buy into such claptrap. Is this Dashwood's doing?"

She shook her head, a tear falling. "Of course not."

"I must speak with you about him."

She rubbed her temples. "I can't. I can't discuss him with you. Sir Rex, this is too hard," she cried passionately.

He covered the short distance between him and her desk. She did not stand up and he said, "Blanche, are you having headaches? I do not want to be rude, but you do not look well and I find myself very concerned."

She shook her head. "You need to go." She reached for a teacup with trembling hands.

He started when he saw a bottle of brandy on the desk, a spoon beside it. "What's that."

"The brandy helps," she cried, sipping her tea. And when she set the cup down, the saucer rattled wildly.

He gave in and seized her small, cool hand. "Blanche, I came here to discuss Dashwood, but I am too worried about your health. You must promise me you will not sign any contracts today. Have you seen a physician?"

She stared at their clasped hands. He saw her color rise.

"Blanche?"

She shook her head, touching her temple and whispering, "Let me go."

He hesitated, afraid to do so, but he finally complied. "What is wrong?"

She jumped to her feet, clasping her ears. Her expression contorted, becoming panic-stricken.

"Blanche!"

She screamed, turning away from him and knocking over the chair. He thudded after her but she fell to her knees, holding her ears, sobbing. "What's wrong?" he cried, going down on one knee and the stump of his leg beside her. He put his arm around her and the moment he saw her face, he knew she was not aware of him. She screamed again, fighting his grasp, her face convulsed with fear.

Shocked, he let her go.

She curled up over her knees. And then she was silent.

Horror began. But he was afraid to speak just as he was afraid to touch her now.

Lady Waverly ran into the room. "What have you done?" she screamed at him, kneeling beside Blanche and taking her into her arms. "Get out!"

"No," Blanche whispered, still curled up into herself.

"Get out!" Lady Waverly screamed at him.

Blanche started rocking, muttering so softly he could not decipher her words. But she was saying something over and over again.

Rex found his crutch. He had broken the custom one, so he had to use the desk to haul himself upward to stand. He was very still now. "Her secret is safe with me," he said quietly.

Bess Waverly glared at him. She was crying.

He said, "I wish to have a word with you, Lady Waverly. I will be outside." He hesitated. "Blanche, if you can hear me, nothing has changed. I will do whatever I can to help you."

She kept chanting inaudibly and he was certain she hadn't heard him.

He turned away, finally allowing the tears to fill his eyes. And he limped out, beyond dread.

CHAPTER NINETEEN

BESS STROKED BLANCHE'S BACK, trying to control her own terribly frantic emotions so she could comfort her friend. She feared for Blanche, desperately. Blanche was becoming worse; there was no doubt. She had these violent, shocking episodes daily if not more. Was she slowly slipping away into a world from which she would never return? Bess's greatest fear was that one day, Blanche would have a fit of madness that did not end.

That possibility was horrifying and Bess hated considering it. But she had to, because it was becoming very likely that Blanche was with child. It had been two and a half months since her visit to Land's End with no sign of her monthly time. If Blanche did not get past whatever was afflicting her, how would she be a mother to that child? Bess had been urging Blanche to marry swiftly. Blanche's child was going to need a father far more than Blanche needed a husband.

Bess was relieved when Blanche finally straightened into a sitting position. She wiped her face carefully, not looking at Bess. Bess understood. Blanche was embarrassed—and so was she.

"Let me get you some of that tea," Bess said softly, somehow smiling.

"It's over," Blanche said as quietly.

Bess stood up. Carefully, she asked, "Did you recall something new?"

Blanche finally looked up at her, before rising to her feet.

"No. I have managed to remain at one point in time in that riot." She shuddered. Bess knew she was determined not to recall another detail of that day and her mother's murder, if she could. Then her gaze moved to the closed library door.

Bess thought about Sir Rex, too. Her instinct was to blame him for this latest fit, but how could she? Blanche had fits without his being present. They had become so frequent that Blanche had begun to seclude herself in her suite of rooms. Bess did not blame her, but it didn't matter, because the entire staff knew the truth.

I will do whatever I can to help you.

Bess tensed. Sir Rex had been horrified—she had seen his stricken expression perfectly. But he had been kind, and he was concerned. She had seen that, too.

And he was the child's father.

Blanche hugged her arms to her chest, rubbing them as if cold. "Is he still here?"

Bess poured a fresh cup of tea. "I believe so. But it might be best if you don't see him again, not now, anyway."

Blanche made a harsh sound. "It hurt so much, to see him again."

Bess handed her the cup of tea, staring. "Do you still love him?"

Blanche looked aside. "How could I stop loving such a man?" She cradled the cup and saucer, staring at the closed door as if she wished to look through it at Sir Rex.

"Do you wish to reconsider the engagement to Dash-wood?" Bess was beginning to wonder if that match was appropriate after all.

Blanche faced her. "You agree he is clever enough to manage my fortune."

"I do." Bess didn't add, but so is Sir Rex.

"I can't have this child without a husband," she added. "I am half a pariah already."

"No, you can't." Bess stared grimly.

"I am confused," Blanche said softly. "Bess, I need to retire. My head is hurting all over again."

Bess thought that the wisest course of action. "I'll send Meg." But they both knew it wasn't necessary. Meg remained very much like a soldier on active duty, awaiting her mistress's every need. Bess had come to realize that the young maid truly cared about her employer. She was priceless.

Bess walked Blanche from the room. As they passed the Gold Room, she saw Sir Rex standing inside, leaning on his crutch, watching them closely. Blanche colored and quickly looked away, hurrying up the wide sweeping staircase. Bess turned thoughtfully and went inside the salon.

Sir Rex came swiftly forward. "How is she?"

He was very concerned, she noted. *Your secret is safe with me.* "She is better. She is going upstairs to rest."

"How long has this been going on?"

Bess became wary. She wasn't sure how much she should reveal. "Blanche has severe migraines," she began.

"That wasn't a migraine," he snapped, flushing. "Do not treat me like a fool."

Bess hesitated. "I appreciate your concern. But I am not sure there is anything you can do to help."

"She is not insane," he said, his face pinched with determination.

And Bess saw fear in his eyes. Was he in love with Blanche? Could it be remotely possible? But hadn't she always felt that Sir Rex was the kind of man to stand beside his woman, no matter the circumstance—or illness? "It is not my place to discuss Blanche's privy affairs, Sir Rex."

His gaze shot to hers. "I have never liked you, Lady Waverly. But today, my feelings have changed. You are a loyal friend. I apologize for my past judgments."

Bess shook her head. "I have always sensed that you didn't

think me good enough for Blanche. And I'm not. Blanche is kind and generous. I am frivolous and selfish." She shrugged. "But I love her. I always have and I always will." She smiled grimly. "Blanche returned from Land's End like this. Something happened there to distress her so greatly that she became too emotional for her own good. Do you care to tell me what could have possibly happened?"

His gaze was piercing. "I have the feeling you know. But I also refuse to discuss Blanche's privy affairs, even with you."

Bess had not expected such a noble stand. But this man was honorable, never mind his reclusive nature. And did it even matter what had caused Blanche to spiral to the brink of insanity?

She stared at him. Sir Rex preferred the country. He was reclusive, and he was very concerned for Blanche. Blanche needed that solitude now.

She smiled. "Blanche did not think it wise to see you again, Sir Rex. I supported that choice, which is why I asked you to leave today. However, I am glad you defied me. I think you should know that her migraines are occurring on a regular basis. Daily, if you must know."

Dismay covered his face. "Daily," he echoed. Then his gaze narrowed. "Do not tell me that she thought me responsible, somehow, for these 'migraines'?"

Bess hesitated. "I believe she left Land's End in the belief that these migraines would cease."

He was wide-eyed, his dark brows lifted. "She has blamed me?" he exclaimed.

"I certainly did not say that. I do not even think that. But so much happened at Land's End, did it not? It all *began* at your home, Sir Rex."

Sir Rex squared his broad shoulders. "A great deal did happen, yes. On the other hand, Blanche has been under undue strain since her father became ill and suddenly passed."

That was true, Bess thought. "She secludes herself now. She has no life—except on Thursdays, when she receives. How can she go on this way—hiding from everyone—with the entire ton thrilled to witness her demise when she does step out? The gossip about Blanche is the rage! Everywhere I go, they are laughing about her."

"I don't give a damn about the gossips. I care about her," he said fiercely. "As you do. Has she seen a physician?"

"She won't."

"Why not?" he demanded.

"I believe she fears the diagnosis."

He stared, absorbing that.

"You came here today to discuss her marriage, did you not?" Bess asked bluntly. And her heart raced as if it was her future they discussed.

He stiffened. "She cannot marry Dashwood."

Bess met his gaze. "He is her choice."

"He is the worst of the gossips."

Bess was stunned. "He is also spreading gossip about her?"

Sir Rex leaned close. "I heard him telling his friends a madwoman does not have any right to a fortune. I believe he will legally bar her from any control of the Harrington fortune once they are wed."

Bess turned away, shaken and aghast. Then she faced him. "If he is truly planning something so despicable, then you are right, such a marriage must be prevented at all costs."

"I am glad we see eye to eye, for once," he said grimly. Then he shifted and stared out of the room, toward the staircase. "I wish to speak with Blanche again when she is feeling better."

Bess didn't tell him there would never be a safe time to do so. "I'll tell her." She hesitated, wondering what Sir Rex would do if he knew Blanche thought herself with child. Then she almost pinched herself. He would rally, come forward and insist on marriage.

Hadn't she thought him the right match from the start, before Blanche's descent into madness? But Blanche had broken it off, even though she loved him. Would Sir Rex make her worse? And did it matter? For how much worse could it get? And if it did get worse, at least Sir Rex could be counted on to take care of both mother and child.

"You are staring," he said sharply.

She smiled at him. "I am sorry. I was thinking about what you have said. I will make sure the contracts are lost for a while, until we can sort things out."

His gaze darkened. He had heard her use of the plural pronoun, as she had meant for him to.

"Good day, Sir Rex," she added softly.

SIR REX DID NOT LEAVE Harrington Hall. Instead, he went around the back, through the gardens, his intention to send for Blanche's maid, Meg.

He was sick. He was afraid for Blanche as she was clearly so ill. He understood now why Blanche had broken off their engagement, although not the logic that had led to her decision. Whatever was happening to her, he knew he was not the cause. And he hated himself for having disparaged her these past months. He hated himself for jumping to the conclusion that she was a treacherous bitch like Julia Mowbray. Blanche was an angel. It had taken one glimpse of her a moment ago to instantly recall that—never mind that his heart had never doubted it for an instant. But she was desperately ill. She needed him and she needed his protection from rakes like Dashwood. And she needed a cure—she could not be mad.

But he didn't believe that she had such migraines that sent her screaming to the floor. He had never heard of such a malady. He could not begin to imagine what illness could be the cause for the frightening behavior he had witnessed. She *had* seemed mad. He cringed, thinking about her behavior. He wanted to rule out insanity. No one became insane overnight.

But he also knew that insanity could run in family lines. Harrington had been as sane as a man could be, but Rex knew nothing about Blanche's mother. He was so afraid for her. He reminded himself that Blanche was the sanest, most sensible woman he had ever met.

Rex slowly approached the kitchens, filled with despair. At least Bess seemed to agree that Dashwood should be cut from Blanche's life. The sooner the better, he thought. But then what? The gossips needed to be controlled and Blanche needed a doctor.

And then he saw the Lanhadron farrier, flirting with a young maid, in the kitchen's open doorway.

The farrier was up to no good and he knew it. Blanche did not need to be harassed in any way, nor did she need to face any kind of threat now. He stalked forward, his crutch digging so deeply into the sod that it left holes, spewing dirt. Rage began. Carter jerked upon glimpsing him, his face expressing genuine surprise.

Then his pale gaze narrowed. He quickly removed his cap, inclining his head. "My lord."

"Walk with me," Rex ordered sharply. What was Carter up to? Whatever it was, it was now over. And he did not care for the fact that the man had avoided his gaze.

Carter continued to glance away and still clutching his cap, he left the kitchens with Rex, wandering back into the gardens. Sir Rex halted, facing him. "What business brings you to Harrington Hall, Carter?"

Carter slowly lifted his cool gaze. "My lord, Annie so admires her ladyship and she asked me to bring her a small token of her appreciation. I brought her a tortoise clip. Annie picked it out."

Rex could not control his anger—and he did not want to.

"Like hell. Anne felt nothing but envy and malice for Lady Harrington. That became clear when I was engaged to her. You are up to no good. Have you harassed her? Threatened her?"

Carter looked at him with a sneer. "I do not serve you…my lord."

Rex was not surprised by the lack of respect. He said, "If you ever appear here again, you will never find a day of work in the parish. Nor will Anne. Am I clear?"

Carter flushed with anger. "You high and mighty lords are all the same! You think you're God, don't you? And you don't give a damn for the rest of us poor sots!"

"I am not interested in your worldview. Get off Lady Harrington's property."

"I guess you're still tupping her ladyship, my lord?" He snickered. "I bet her new fiancé will love to hear about that!"

Rex could not believe the man's audacity—and stupidity. But he quickly decided to play along. "I must remind you to mind your own affairs."

Carter sneered. "I am happy to do so—for a price."

And Rex realized that Carter had blackmailed Blanche. It was hard to breathe—hard to see. He fought for control and steadied himself somehow. "Get off these grounds and make certain you never reappear here. I suggest you leave the parish, as well. You have made yourself an enemy and if you do not obey, you will regret it."

Carter hissed, "I'll leave the parish. But my price is two hundred pounds."

Rex smiled coldly. "How much have you taken Lady Harrington for?"

Carter smiled. "Why don't you ask her? She's paid me enough that I can live high and mighty for a year or two!"

In that moment, Rex was blinded. He seized Carter's jacket, pulling him close, his crutch so deep in the ground he did not stagger or fall. *How much have you taken her for?*

Carter hesitated, and Rex saw fear flicker in his eyes. "Plenty—five hundred pounds!"

Rex released him, aghast that Blanche had suffered such abuse from this man. "You are done here."

Carter tugged his jacket down. "I'll tell your fancy friends about your mistress, my lord."

"Go ahead." Rex turned, espied a pair of hulking gardeners, and signaled them over. "Escort this man off the property," he said.

Carter gasped in outrage as each lad grabbed an arm. Carter was tall, but very lean and no match for the men. Rex watched him being half dragged across the gardens, briefly and savagely satisfied. He had just removed another malignant sore from Blanche's life.

Then he felt her.

He stiffened, turning slowly to look at the house. His gaze swept the terrace, the ground floor windows, and then lifted.

She stood in an upper story window framed by a pair of ivory draperies. Their gazes met.

The draperies moved and she vanished.

BLANCHE MOVED SLOWLY toward the hearth in her bedroom. Sir Rex had clearly chased that horrid farrier from her grounds. She had been paying him weekly for his silence and it was one small relief in the vast and terrifying chasm of chaos that was now her life.

Blanche trembled breathlessly. She had never felt so much sorrow and so much yearning. She loved Sir Rex with all of her heart and she missed him terribly. It had taken but a glimpse of him to recall their every moment together, his wonderful friendship, his honesty, his caring and his kindness. But her feelings were for naught, because they were tainted. She had never felt so much shame.

She was mortified. She covered her face with her hands,

sinking down onto the chaise before the fireplace. Sir Rex had seen her in a fit of madness. Sir Rex knew the terrible truth.

And it was the truth. There was no more denying it. Every day, she became worse. She had lied to Bess. Every episode brought another vivid and horrific detail to light. Every episode was more terrifying and more violent than the one before. Every fit seemed to last longer. Each time she went into the past and became a child lost in that riot, her grasp on the present seemed more tenuous and fragile. The part of her mind that always knew she was an adult woman at Harrington Hall was becoming fainter and weaker; the child stronger. Blanche wondered if, one day, the adult would finally vanish, leaving a terrified, sobbing child in her stead, one who's hands and clothes were covered with her mother's blood.

I am a madwoman, she thought desperately. A madwoman carrying Sir Rex's child.

Her admission, she realized, was long overdue.

For it did not seem likely that her life would ever return to any semblance of normalcy. If that was the case, then how could she mother this unborn child when it came into the world? What if she had a fit while the babe was in her arms? Blanche shuddered, for she might inadvertently kill her own baby in such an instance. What if, years later, her toddler saw her mother frothing, shrieking and weeping in a moment of insanity? Worse, what if, one day, she went into the past and never came back to the future? Who would care for the babe then? Dashwood?

Blanche laughed hysterically and then began to cry. She cried freely, grieving for her son or daughter now. Her child deserved so much more than a mad mother like herself. And Dashwood would be a terrible father—what had she been thinking?

Once, she had hoped that by leaving Sir Rex, she could live the kind of life that would not invite such incidences to occur again. But she hadn't been strong enough to hold the insanity at bay. She had tried to live calmly, without feeling, but she had failed. There was no calm and there was no peace. There was interminable strain, incessant fear and moments of madness. Her life had become unbearable. Worse, realizing the truth about herself, there was no more hope.

She was mad. The world knew it; Sir Rex knew it now, too.

Blanche wiped her eyes and stared up at the ceiling. She stared without any more feeling, for her life had now forever changed. And finally, the comprehension was almost a relief. She was never going to be able to recapture the life she had led for most of her years, before falling in love with Sir Rex. She was never going to be that gracious, elegant, genteel lady again, the woman the ton thought a perfect lady. That was evident now. As evident was the fact that she could not be a proper mother to her child, but she was still a mother.

The child was hers, and she must protect him or her, from herself, and she must also make certain that child had a secure future in every possible way.

Determination began. She could not salvage her own life, and she no longer cared to try. But she had a child to consider now.

Sir Rex was the child's father. Sir Rex would be able to raise their child—he would be a wonderful father, Blanche had no doubt. It seemed irrelevant now that he was reclusive or that he imbibed heavily at times. He was honest, moral and dependable. He was strong and kind. He would love their son or daughter, raising him or her in the best manner possible, and their child would have a wonderful and extended family, with cousins, aunts, uncles and grandparents. He was the kind of father every child deserved and should have.

He had every right to know that she was pregnant. Blanche knew she had to tell him, and soon. She wasn't sure why it had taken her so long to arrive at the only possible conclusion.

But she dreaded seeing him again. She dreaded the way he would look at her. He would avoid eye contact, avoid a mistaken touch. They all did.

She hugged herself. Once, he had looked deeply into her eyes before kissing her, while moving inside her—while making love to her. Once, he had admired her—he had told her so. She had been a fool, not to appreciate what she'd had, even so briefly. Now he pitied her. He might even be repulsed.

Bess had been pushing marriage, but only because of the unborn child, and Blanche now knew that she had been going through the motions with her suitors and Dashwood. No man wanted an insane wife. Dashwood wanted her fortune, not that she had cared. She had chosen him because he wouldn't bother her or the child very much. Now, she knew she could never go through with that union. In fact, there was no point in marriage at all.

Sir Rex would never turn his back on their child. The solution was so clear.

She would retreat to her country home to have the babe, and then turn him over to Sir Rex.

Blanche cried again.

CHAPTER TWENTY

IT WAS AS IF ONE FEAR led to another. Rex stood in the domed entry hall of Clarewood, Blanche's image engraved on his mind, his fear for her welfare now caught up in his need to see his son and somehow, find reassurance that he had done what was best for him. Two arched entryways were on the far side of the marbled room, one leading to a larger reception room, the other, to a wide corridor, from which various salons could be glimpsed. Rex limped toward the reception room. The size of a luxurious salon, it, too, had gold-streaked marble floors. Beyond it, he saw a sweeping marble staircase, carpeted in crimson. His gaze instantly went to the portrait that hung on the wall above the stairs.

Julia and Stephen stood beside one another, a pair of springer spaniels with them, a lush tree behind them. Julia was blond, elegant and lovely. Stephen was severely dressed in suit and tie and although no more than six or seven, his expression was so serious he seemed more a little man than a boy.

Rex's heart broke apart in his chest. The small miniature Julia had sent him was so similar in expression. Did that mean Stephen rarely laughed? Was his character so entirely serious already? Was he grim in nature? Or had he posed for the portraits, obeying instructions to appear grave and even aloof?

The light footsteps of a woman wearing heeled shoes sounded. Rex tensed as Julia appeared from the corridor beyond the stairs. Her eyes were wide in her still nearly flawless face. Although he felt no attraction to her, he saw that she had aged well. He was surprised to realize he felt no hostility, either. He had despised her for so long—for an entire decade—that he was briefly astonished by his indifference to her.

But he had so much more to think about than despising the woman who had, once and long ago, betrayed him.

She, however, was not indifferent, he saw. "Sir Rex," she said, her tone a pitch higher than he recalled. "I wasn't aware that you were in town." Her smile was strained.

He bowed. "Lady Clarewood. You are looking very well," he said with a smile.

Surprise flickered in her gray eyes again. Cautiously, she said, unsmiling, "So are you." She stared at him, making no move to walk into another room where they might converse.

She was defensive, he thought. And he was consumed with anxiety now. "I saw Tom at White's. Did he not mention I intended to call on Stephen?"

She inhaled. "No, he did not!"

He realized she was afraid of him. "Why don't we retire to another room so we might chat?" He smiled again, hoping to reassure her.

It was a moment before she nodded. She glanced toward the butler, who remained behind her in the shadows, but Rex forestalled her. "I do not need refreshments."

She led the way briskly through the reception room and into a library which looked out onto magnificent gardens, replete with water fountains, man-made lakes and ponds and an incredible maze. There, she closed both doors behind him. She turned abruptly. "How can you do this?"

"I see you are distressed." He glanced around the gilded salon. It might have been a room in Buckingham Palace. "That is not my intention. However, may I remind you that I have been distressed over the loss of my child for almost a decade?"

She stiffened, her back to the door. "And suddenly you decide to call—and do what?"

"I want to see my son in the flesh. I want to speak with him. I want to hear his voice and see him smile. Is that too much to ask?" He spoke quietly.

"And for such selfish needs, you will ruin his future?" she cried.

"I have no intention of telling Stephen who I am. I am not reneging on our agreement. But I do intend to see my son from time to time. Nothing and no one will dissuade me," he warned.

Julia stared at him, her eyes filled with tears.

And it was not theatrics. "I would never think to take him from you, his mother," he added softly. "Such a notion is appalling."

She finally nodded. "You startled me. I have always wondered when you would appear in our lives to take him away—or at least, tell him the truth."

"You do not know me well."

"No, I do not, because I made a terrible choice ten years ago and I have been paying for it dearly." She walked away from the door, past him, so he could only stare at her rigid back. What did that mean? Did she regret her treachery—and her marriage to one of Britain's premier noblemen?

He was bewildered. "What do you mean?"

She shrugged and faced him. "I want you to know that I intend for Stephen to be the next duke of Clarewood, and I will do *anything* to make certain he comes into his inheritance."

He became uneasy, but not alarmed. "You love him greatly."

"Of course I do. He is my son—my only child—and he is entitled to all of this." She gestured at the grand room.

"I want him to have the power and wealth that you and Tom

can give him, Julia," he said quietly. "But I cannot go on apart from him this way. You may introduce me as a family friend."

Julia hugged herself, a gesture of anxiety he had never before seen. "Maybe it is best that you become a part of his life."

His suspicion arose. "What is wrong?"

"Nothing is wrong—except that I am married to a difficult man. He is a difficult husband—and a difficult father. I cannot please Tom. No matter how I try, nothing is ever enough."

Alarm began. "And Stephen?"

"Stephen is a constant reminder that Tom is lacking in manhood."

Rex thudded over. "What the hell does that mean?"

"It means," she said, holding his gaze, "that Stephen excels at every endeavor and it is never enough for his father."

Rex felt his heart slamming with painful force. "So Tom has become exactly like his father."

"Yes."

"Is Stephen unhappy?"

She hesitated. "He is not unhappy, Rex. He has a serious and responsible nature. He wishes to apply himself and succeed. He seems driven to take up task after task. He already speaks three languages fluently and has advanced from simple mathematics to algebra. He is studying anatomy now, and by that, I mean he has excelled at biology already. His tutors say he is brilliant."

"He is nine years old!" Rex exclaimed, unsure of whether to be thrilled or frightened, proud or dismayed.

"I am so proud of him and you should be proud of him, too," Julia said, plucking his sleeve. "But he seems to have missed out on his childhood entirely." Then her eyes widened. "There he is."

Rex whirled and saw Mowbray and his son approaching the house from outside, both dressed in formal riding attire.

His heart turned over hard and he felt faint—he couldn't quite breathe. Mowbray wasn't speaking and neither was Stephen. He instantly noticed that the small boy carried himself like a prince—his posture stiff, proud and terribly correct.

He limped to the terrace doors and through them. When he stood at the white plaster railing, Mowbray saw him and displeasure crossed his features. He glanced down and said something to Stephen.

Stephen glanced across the lawn and for the first time in his life, Rex met his son's gaze. A distance separated them, but he saw what he thought was cool disdain.

He is as haughty as Mowbray, he thought with a touch of despair. But with the power he would one day have, he could be as haughty as the Prince of Wales or a visiting King.

Man and child climbed the terrace steps. Rex now saw that Stephen was regarding him with aloofness, but curiosity flickered in his eyes, too.

"Darling," Julia cried, stepping in front of him. "We have a caller. It has been a few years since you have seen Sir Rex!" Her enthusiastic tone matched her smile. She took Stephen's hand. "Did you enjoy hacking with your father?"

"Yes, I did, Mother. I showed Father how well Odysseus takes the stone hedge wall."

Julia faced Rex. "He rides the way you did when you were in the cavalry, Sir Rex. He is quite the horseman already."

Rex was very aware of how nervous Julia was. But he was afflicted with nerves, too. He could barely believe he stood an arm's length from his son. He didn't want to take his eyes off Stephen, and he wasn't sure he could. He nodded at Mowbray. "Hello, Your Grace. It is good to see you again."

Mowbray's face was pinched. "Sir Rex. How pleasant of you to call. I am sorry you did not send word first. I have appointments in town and I will not be able to linger, I'm afraid."

Rex somehow smiled and then glanced at Stephen, who

was staring closely at him, as if assessing every nuance in his every word and his every gesture. "Hello," he said as casually as possible, a terrible feat.

"Stephen, please greet Sir Rex de Warenne. He is an old family friend. His father is Adare."

Stephen bowed, but barely, clearly aware of his superior rank. "Good day," he said solemnly. "I believe I have met your father during a hack in the park."

Rex did not even attempt to breathe normally. "I hadn't realized. I am glad." He realized what he had said and added, "How high is that stone hedge?"

Stephen seemed to want to smile. "Almost a meter."

Rex was impressed. "That's a high jump for a young boy."

"I can jump higher," Stephen returned very factually.

"My son excels at everything he attempts," Mowbray said, his tone oddly mocking. "There is nothing he cannot do. If he decided to fly to the moon, I am sure he would."

Stephen flushed. And Rex wanted to slam Mowbray to the ground, for cutting his son cruelly and without cause.

"Do not rush your call." Mowbray smiled coolly. "I am sure my wife is thrilled to see you after so many years." He nodded and strode across the terrace, disappearing into the house.

Rex instantly turned to Stephen, who had clearly recovered his composure. "I am sure your father is very proud of you," he said softly. "I know your mother is."

Stephen's gaze narrowed. "How do you know that my mother is proud of me if you haven't called in years?"

Rex realized Stephen would not miss a trick. "I have seen her once or twice at various affairs and she has praised you highly." He smiled, wanting to touch his son but knowing he must not dare.

Stephen nodded. "My mother is easy to please. I have decided most women are." He left unsaid what was now obvious, that his father was not. "I don't think my father likes you."

"That's not true!" Julia gasped.

Rex said simply, "I have known your father since the war. War changes men, Stephen, and it has changed both of us."

Stephen stared, keenly interested now. "I have read a great deal about the war. Father served in Spain. He was in the cavalry, too," Stephen said with pride. "He was in the 11th Light Dragoons."

"I know. He was under my command," Rex said simply.

Stephen stared into his eyes, his gaze sharp and searching. Then, "I didn't know."

Julia came forward. "You should know that Sir Rex is a decorated war hero. He has received the medal of valor for his heroism. He rescued your father, Stephen, when he was so injured in battle he could not leave the field. He probably saved Clarewood's life."

Stephen squared his shoulders, although his eyes were wide. "Then this family owes you a vast debt, Sir Rex," he said gravely. "One day I will repay it, even if my father has already done so."

Rex was undone. His son was already a man of honor. How could he ask for more? "You need repay nothing. I would rescue any man in my command in a similar circumstance."

"Then medal or not, you are truly a hero," Stephen said. "Is that how you lost your leg?"

Rex knew he must control the moisture gathering in his eyes. But he was so proud, so moved, and so adoring of this child, his son. "I lost my leg while carrying your father to safety," he said softly.

Stephen stared at him, eyes wide.

"It is the past."

Stephen turned and looked at his mother. "Why haven't I met Sir Rex before?" he demanded.

Julia hesitated. "He spends a great deal of time on his estate in Cornwall. You are too young to attend the affairs of the ton." She shrugged. "But I am glad this day has finally come." And she sent Rex a smile.

Stephen turned back to Rex. "Clarewood has estates everywhere, but not a single one in Cornwall. I have never been to the south. What is it like?"

Rex inhaled. This was an opportunity and he meant to seize it. "Stark, desolate—and very majestic."

Stephen's eyes widened. "I am going to read about Cornwall," he said flatly.

Rex didn't hesitate. "The most beautiful time of the year is July when the heather and gorse bloom. Your mother can bring you for a visit, if you wish. We can hack the moors. There are many hedges for jumping."

Stephen suddenly smiled, and a small boy's enthusiasm flickered on his face and in his blue eyes. "You ride astride?"

"Yes," Rex said softly.

Stephen turned to Julia. Rex knew he was trying to be calm, but he heard the tremor of excitement in his tone. "Mother? I would like to go. I have been to France and Holland, Germany, Portugal and Spain, Scotland and even Ireland, but I have not been to Cornwall!"

Julia briefly glanced at Rex. "I am sure it can be arranged."

"SIR REX IS IN the family room, Lady Harrington," the de Warenne butler said.

Blanche trembled. She had to somehow face Sir Rex, but after what he had seen, she was ready to turn tail and flee. Her cheeks burned with embarrassment already, yet she lifted her chin. Breathing shallowly, dreading the look in his eyes when he saw her, she followed the servant through the foyer and into the hall.

She heard small children giggling and speaking in childish tones. The door to the green salon was open, and as the butler paused there, Blanche could see inside. Her heart slammed.

Sir Rex sat on the couch, two small boys by his leg, one fair, one dark, playing with toy soldiers and horses on the floor. A pretty honey-haired girl of eight or nine sat by him, so absorbed in the thick book she was reading, she did not look up. Another boy, a year or so younger, sat on Sir Rex's other side, and he was the golden image of his father, Devlin O'Neill. He was saying something to Sir Rex and his uncle was listening so carefully that it made Blanche's heart break. He was going to be a wonderful father. She saw from his expression that he adored being among his nieces and nephews.

"Is it true?" The golden boy was asking eagerly.

"Yes." Sir Rex said to the younger boys on the floor, "Rogan and Chaz! If you fight over the toys, I am taking them away from you. They are to be shared. You are cousins, not rivals."

The blond boy thumped his fists on the floor, irate. The dark boy grinned triumphantly at him. Blanche decided the first boy was Eleanor's son, Rogan, the dark one, Chaz, Tyrell's. The golden boy sitting next to Sir Rex said, "Then can't you stay with us this time, at Askeaton?"

Sir Rex tousled the boy's shoulder-length hair. "I will make a point of it, Jack. You are right. I haven't spent enough time at your father's."

Jack beamed, delighted. He so clearly adored his uncle.

Blanche trembled, now noticing two women sitting by the fire. Amanda and Lizzie were rising to their feet, obviously surprised by her presence but smiling warmly, too. Cliff's wife had matured into a very elegant young lady, Blanche realized with a pang. Recalling their love story made her want to weep for what she would never have.

The terrace doors opened and Cliff de Warenne strode inside, spurs jangling, holding two boys, each by the elbow. He was flushed with annoyance, while the boys were flushed from their mischievous behavior and trying to appear chagrined. "They have been targeting our neighbors with their slingshots," Cliff announced. "Alexi actually struck Lady Barrow in an unmentionable place. That is, they were also trespassing on Barrow's grounds. Ned was about to fire a shot at her daughter."

"It was an accident," Alexi began.

"It was Alexi's idea," Ned said grimly.

Such beautiful children, Blanche thought, and only half the cousins were present. Cliff faltered, espying Blanche in the doorway. She continued to stand hesitantly behind the butler, trying to find some composure. His son fell silent, as did his cousin, both boys aware they were now off the hook due to the presence of a guest.

Blanche somehow smiled at Captain de Warenne, Lizzie and Amanda. Then, trembling, she turned her gaze on Sir Rex. He was standing and staring at her as if she were a ghost.

"Sir Rex, Lady Harrington has called," the servant said.

"Thank you," Sir Rex said, his gaze unwavering upon her.

Blanche tried to breathe. She couldn't look away from his dark, searching gaze, her cheeks burning as her sense of shame and humiliation escalated. Surely he thought her a loon now, too. But to her surprise, she saw only kindness and concern in his eyes. Where was the scorn she had been so certain she would receive?

The salon felt off-kilter, the floor seemed to tilt, and she was so afraid everything would spin and she would be whirled away into the past in front of everyone in the room.

Sir Rex hurried to her, taking her arm as if to steady her— as if he knew her balance was precious and fragile, at best. "Lady Harrington," he said softly, their gazes locking. "This is a pleasant surprise. Come inside and sit down."

Blanche could not understand why he wasn't looking at her as if she had the plague. She could not imagine why he touched her without recoiling. She managed to smile as the women hurried over. "Amanda, I am so pleased to see you again," Blanche said, meaning it in spite of her distraction.

The slender blond woman hugged her hard and earnestly. "I had hoped we would see one another," she exclaimed. She glanced at her husband, sending him a message Blanche did not even wish to try to decipher. "Cliff, why don't you take Alexi and Ned upstairs? Maybe a few hours spent separately in their rooms will make them realize they cannot terrorize the poor Barrows. I will help Lizzie with the rest of the children as it is time for the boys' naps, and Ariella, it is time for your French lesson."

Ariella slid to her feet, holding her book, looking bemused. "I already had my French lesson," she said.

"You are having another one," Cliff said swiftly, "and Jack is joining you."

The golden-haired boy who had been seated with Sir Rex looked shocked. He began to protest. Blanche felt as if she were in a whirlwind, for as Lizzie hugged her and whispered, "Thank God you have come," the salon emptied, every adult and child vanishing, until she was impossibly alone with Sir Rex.

Blanche somehow looked up into his hazel eyes again. He still held her arm and his gaze was so direct and searching she had the urge to move into his arms and weep against his chest for everything and everyone, her father, her mother, their love, her broken heart, their child and herself.

"Come sit down," he said softly, guiding her to the sofa.

"Thank you," Blanche whispered, sitting. She watched him rapidly cross to the door and close it, turning back to her. Her heart flipped over hard. He was so handsome; she had forgotten just how attractive he was. But it was more than that. She was adrift in the Cornish sea, and he was a towering rock, that solid place she could cling to, an anchor to keep her safe.

He limped over to her and sat down. "How are you today?"

Blanche flushed and looked away. "Well enough."

He shocked her by touching her under the chin and lifting her face so she had to meet his gaze. And his touch did the un-thinkable—her heart raced and her skin hummed with pleasure, reminding her of the passion they had shared. His gaze flickered and he dropped his hand. "Do not dissemble with me."

She tensed, avoiding his gaze again. Did he wish for some kind of intimate confession of madness? "I am fine…today, Sir Rex."

"You seem distressed."

She stared at her lap. "I want to thank you for your kindness yesterday."

"Don't."

She jerked, her gaze flying helplessly to his.

"Kindness had nothing to do with anything. You are ill. I care," he said bluntly.

She cringed. "I wish you had never seen that!"

He took both of her hands, stunning her. "I want to help you, Blanche."

She inhaled in disbelief. "How can you think to help me when I jilted you?"

"Because it is what I wish to do. Besides, I understand more, now."

She tore her hands free, flaming. He understood that she was a madwoman. But at least he would not condescend to revulsion and scorn.

"Can you tell me what is happening?" he asked quietly, after a pause.

Blanche closed her eyes. She was close to confiding everything, she thought, because she so desperately needed his strength. Instead, she looked up. "I have come here today for a reason."

His brow furrowed. "I cannot fathom what that reason might be."

She couldn't smile. "I believe I am with child."

He stiffened, surprise crossing his face, but he was not shocked.

Blanche wet her lips but couldn't speak now. When she left Harmon House, it would be the beginning of the end for her as a mother. It hurt more than everything else she had previously experienced.

"I had wondered. I must ask." His tone was harsh. "Do you know if the child is mine?"

She started. And then she realized he thought she had had an affair, or affairs, with other men. "There has been no one else."

He breathed harshly, his gaze fierce, and he nodded. "I am glad."

She could not begin to understand what he meant. And then he took her hands again. "We have a great deal to discuss. And you must see a doctor, Blanche."

She fought for courage and found it. "I am going to my estate in Kent. I will have the babe there. And then—" she swallowed and felt tears sliding down her face "—I should like you to take our child and raise her or him."

His eyes widened. He was stunned.

Blanche could not look away. "Obviously," she whispered desperately, "I cannot mother this child. But you will be a wonderful father. Our child needs you, Sir Rex."

His stare remained huge. "No."

"What?"

"I am not forsaking you, the mother of my child. I would never do such a thing. I will take care of you and our child. There is no other choice, no other decision to make," he exclaimed passionately.

Blanche was stunned. Didn't he comprehend the truth? "You saw," she said, her voice low, "what happened the other day. You know…what I am. I can't burden you…it isn't right.

But I thank you. Just promise me, you will give our child every benefit you can."

His chest rose and fell. "We will find a cure for what ails you. I will marry you, and our child will have both a mother and a father," he said forcefully.

Blanche was in shock. She could not speak.

"And please, do not try to argue with me!"

She began to comprehend what he had said, what he meant, what he intended. "You want to marry *me?*" she asked in disbelief.

"Yes, I do, immediately. In fact, considering your condition, we should elope within the week." His gaze was hard and fierce, holding hers.

Blanche reeled, but not because she was on the verge of a fit. "I am mad. How can you seek a mad wife, and worse, a mad mother for your child?"

He grasped her shoulders. "You are not insane. I will never believe that. I will help you through this period of illness. Blanche, that is my oath to you."

She shook her head. "And if this period never ends? You will rue the day you insisted on marriage—you will rue this day!"

"I cannot forsake you. I will not forsake you. No matter what," he said grimly. His grasp on her shoulders eased fractionally. "What kind of man forsakes the mother of his child?"

And relief began. She should not be relieved; she should protest. Sir Rex deserved more! But Blanche could not restrain herself. Relief overwhelmed her, for she had been so terribly alone for so long. She moved closer to Sir Rex, and he cupped the back of her head, pressing her face to his chest. Blanche sobbed softly against the hard wall of his body, and as his arms closed around her, she wondered if there might be some hope for just a little happiness now.

He stroked her head, her hair. "I wish to discuss your illness."

She shook her head.

"Please."

Blanche had stopped crying. She remained in Sir Rex's embrace, her cheek to his fine cotton shirt, aware of the slow but strong beat of his heart. She wished such a moment might last forever. She slowly sat up and met his unflinching, concerned gaze.

He was a tower of strength. She needed him, now. And if she dared to agree to become his wife, then he needed to know the entire truth, as painful as a revelation would be.

And he clearly sensed her capitulation, because he smiled a little at her and laid his finger against her cheek, stroking it there. The caress caused a flurry of excitement to fill her, when she had no right to such feelings, not now. "I want to marry you, ill or not," he said softly. "Have you not heard the phrase, through sickness and in health?"

"Of course I have." She smiled and was stunned by the feeling a genuine smile engendered. And she did begin to thrill. "You are the most honorable man I have ever met."

He shrugged. "Tell me."

"I have been recalling the day of the riot."

He started.

She wet her lips. "If I talk about it, I may have a fit."

He cupped her cheek. "And I will be here to hold you."

Blanche had never felt so much trust for anyone. "It is more than memories. I have been reliving the past, so much so that I feel I am in the past, in that riot. And when that happens, I have no connection to the present."

His gaze widened. "Go on."

"The mob was violent. They carried knives, pikes and pitchforks." She tensed, recalling the men as they swarmed the Harrington coach, recalling her fear and her mother's pinched, white face. Her temples throbbed; she feared a spiraling descent into the past now. She whispered, "They accosted our carriage, cut the horse loose, beat it to death. They dragged Mama out—and then me." Sir Rex grasped her hand. "Mama screamed and screamed, but I couldn't see her—they murdered her." The aching intensified, but not in her temples, in her chest. She looked into Sir Rex's steady gaze. He was anguished, but he did not move away. Blanche realized she was clinging to his hand as if it were a lifeline. It felt as if it had become one.

"Her screams were screams of terror—and pain. They stabbed her to death, Sir Rex. With knives and pitchforks."

"My God."

"And the screams stopped." Blanche stared at their locked hands through blurred vision. Knives were going through her heart now. "I escaped the monster that held me and crawled through the mob to her. I will never forget how she looked." She had been a bloody mangled mess. Blanche looked up, waiting for the room to tilt and spin.

Instead, she found herself in Sir Rex's powerful embrace. He whispered, "I understand," which confused her, because he couldn't possibly understand. She closed her eyes, breathing in his scent, relishing his muscular strength, fighting the dizziness, the bloody images. A knife stabbed through her temples and Blanche felt the room spinning at last. She tensed, awaiting her mother's screams.

"Don't leave me."

Blanche jerked, eyes opening, looking up. Sir Rex's dark gaze held hers and he smiled grimly at her. "I have to tell you something."

The knives slid out of her skull. The memory of Mama's mangled body receded, but it did not vanish. What could he possibly say? she wondered.

He smiled again, caressing her face. "When I came back from the war, I would awake in the middle of the night—or the day—and I would be clawing bloody dirt, lying on a hard plain in the burning Spanish sun. Men were screaming in pain, sabers were ringing and cannons boomed. I could smell the gunpowder, charred flesh, blood, death."

Blanche sat up straighter. "What?"

"And then suddenly I'd realize I was in my bed, or on the sofa. I was in Harmon House—or Bodenick—not Spain."

Blanche was astonished.

"It was so real," he said thickly. "A few times, I would be having a conversation, with my brothers, or with a servant— and everyone would vanish. I'd be back on that battlefield, lying there wounded, my leg blasted apart, hearing the men, the battle, smelling it, feverish and thirsty. And then I'd be standing in a salon again, realizing I wasn't still in the war and that I was having a terrible memory, but one as real as a dream."

Blanche began to tremble wildly. "What happened? Do you still have these dreamlike memories?"

"No. They lasted six months, maybe a year. Day by day, they occurred less frequently, until it was once a week, once a month, and then not at all."

Blanche cried out. "What are you trying to say?"

"Blanche, I am not the only one. Many soldiers have suffered with 'fits,' if you will, after the war. I have friends who had the same fits I had. I know other soldiers who never were afflicted, but we all know some of us suffered so badly in the war, we brought those memories home with us. The war was violent and traumatic. That riot was as violent and as traumatic as any battle. I now believe your illness is the same condition I suffered and that other soldiers have suffered, as well."

Blanche whispered, still stunned, "But my fits are worse— and more frequent."

Rex stared at her. "The first time this happened to me, I was shocked and afraid. And these 'fits' started occurring frequently. But then, as my life returned back to normal, they tapered off. Bess said this all began at Land's End. That is very recently, considering the riot was over twenty years ago." He touched her face again reassuringly.

Blanche seized his hand. "It does sound like I am having the same ailment," she whispered.

"There is one doctor in London who has made it his life to care for these afflicted soldiers. He has even named this ailment, but I cannot recall what he calls it. In any case, you must see him. We will go together."

Blanche realized they were holding hands so tightly that their knuckles were white. She stared at Sir Rex and he stared back.

She might not be mad after all.

There was hope.

"Thank you," she gasped.

He pulled her close.

CHAPTER TWENTY-ONE

REX FOUND CLIFF UPSTAIRS in the suite of rooms he shared with his wife and two children. Alexi was seated at the secretaire, industriously penning an apology to Lady Barrow, his father standing over him, arms sternly folded. Ariella was curled up on a chaise before the fireplace, reading, as usual, but when he paused in the open doorway, she looked up at him, smiling. Amanda stepped out of the bedroom, also smiling. Her green eyes sparkled with delight. "How is Blanche?" she asked.

He hesitated. He had insisted Blanche retire to a guest room, for she was clearly under a terrible strain and exhaustion was mirrored in her expression and her eyes. And the fact that she had agreed, collapsing in bed when he escorted her there, had been proof that he was right. But now he knew she wasn't insane. Time would cure her illness. And she was carrying his child—she was to be his wife.

He was so worried about her, so much so that he couldn't really consider the future they would share—and the child they would have. His immediate concern was that she rest. His second concern was that she recover from the trauma of the riot—and he wished he could speed that recovery along, but he was fairly certain he could not. However, because of the child, they must marry as soon as humanly possible. And that was where his brother, Cliff, came into play.

"She hasn't been feeling well for some time now, and she

is resting in one of the guest suites," he said. "I was hoping to steal your husband away for a moment."

Amanda looked closely at him and he saw that she was trying to control her curiosity. "As long as you return him," she said lightly. Then, "Will Blanche join the family for supper?"

"No." He did not want her to endure any additional strain. He knew she feared an episode and he also knew she was ashamed to be thought mad by the ton, much less his family.

He could not wait to take her far away from London, he thought. He could not wait to have the right and the privilege to hold her in his arms and comfort her, care for her, provide for her and protect her, from everything and everyone.

He could not wait to tell her about Stephen.

Cliff strolled over, his blue eyes sharp with interest. Rex gestured at the hallway and they stepped into the corridor, Cliff closing the suite door behind them. Rex said bluntly, "I need a favor." For once, he was glad his brother was so unconventional and eccentric.

"And you shall have it."

Rex had not expected to be denied. "Before I make my request, you must swear to me that what happens next is between us and only us—no one must know—not even your wife."

Cliff's eyes widened. "I am intrigued. But I do not like keeping secrets from my wife. In fact, I have never done so and I do not wish to start now."

"The secret will be a temporary one—and only because Blanche is ill."

Cliff became grim. He touched Rex's arm. "What can I do to help you, Rex—and to help her? And of course, you have my vow of silence."

"I wish for you to marry us," Rex said.

Cliff seemed dazed. Comprehension began. "So the two of you will wed after all—but you wish to elope?"

"Can you keep your voice down?"

Cliff became incredulous. "And you want me to marry you on my ship?"

"Cliff, Blanche is ill. She cannot withstand the strain of a formal wedding and a reception. We are eloping, one way or another. It will be easier on Blanche if we can do so right here in the harbor. I was hoping to be wed within the week." He stared.

Cliff stared back. "How ill is she?"

Rex hesitated. "She has yet to see a physician, but she is not mad, Cliff. She is suffering from the same illness that I was afflicted with after the war and that many soldiers bear. I am certain you do not know, but her mother was violently murdered when she was a child, and she witnessed the event. She is only recalling that murder now, very much the way I relived my last days of battle when I first came home from the Peninsula. Time will heal her, I am certain, as it healed almost everyone I know."

"I had no idea and I am sorry," Cliff said seriously. Then, "Is there a reason for such haste, Rex?"

"It appears so." The brothers shared a knowing look.

Cliff smiled and clasped his shoulder. "I am very happy for you—for you both. Of course I will marry you. However, you do realize how disappointed the women in this family will be when they learn you have eloped?"

"I do, but Blanche's welfare comes first."

"Spoken like a man in love." Cliff grinned. "In the end, everyone, even Mother, will be thrilled, except for Eleanor. She may never forgive you," he warned.

"I will worry about our determined sister another time." Rex finally relaxed. He hadn't expected an argument, but now he began to feel a terrible relief. In a few days, perhaps a week, he and Blanche would be wed. And then he would take her away to Land's End—or Ireland. As long as it was the country, where there was peace and quiet so she could rest, he did not care where they went.

Soon after they were married, they would be on their honeymoon. He tensed. Newly wedded bliss would have to wait. He doubted desire was on Blanche's mind. It wasn't really on his mind now, either. He wanted her well.

"Let me know when you wish to do the deed," Cliff said. He clasped his brother's shoulder again.

"Thank you," Rex said.

BLANCHE AWOKE SLOWLY, in stages, as if she had been severely dosed with laudanum. She floated as if on soft, fluffy down clouds, aware of a huge sense of relief and even, oddly, of peace. After the past months, it was blissful to have such feelings. She realized she was smiling as she opened her eyes…and she found herself in a strange bedroom.

She stared at the ivory, mauve and pink starburst molded on the ceiling above the four-poster bed and instantly recalled that she was at Harmon House—and she and Sir Rex were to be married. Dusk had fallen and the room was filled with shadow, but a fire blazed in the sculpted plaster hearth. Her gaze moved to the pale chaise facing it and met Sir Rex's direct stare. He sat up.

She slowly sat up, as well. He had escorted her to the bedroom, and she vaguely recalled leaning heavily on him as they came inside. She had been sleeping on top of the covers, but beneath an ivory wool throw. She realized she had collapsed on the bed and fallen instantly asleep. Sir Rex had obviously covered her with the blanket; she was pleased he had cared enough to do so.

She smiled, her heart skipping with an excitement and delight she could not deny. "How long have you been sitting there?"

He limped over. "Two hours, I think."

He had been watching over her while she slept. Blanche

had never felt so safe—and she felt cared for and cherished, too. "You didn't have to stay," she said softly.

He hesitated. "May I?"

She understood and nodded; he sat down on the edge of the bed, by her hip. "I wanted to sit with you while you slept," he said quietly. "I am concerned for you, but that is not why. I have missed you."

Blanche thrilled entirely and impulsively reached for his hand. "I have missed you, too—so much."

His gaze darkened.

Blanche hesitated. She thought he wanted to embrace her and perhaps even kiss her—and she had never wanted anything more. But he only smiled at her. Then Blanche decided she was a fool. She was gaunt and thin, he had seen her behaving like a mad woman, never mind the explanation, and Sir Rex might want to marry her and take care of her, but he couldn't possibly find her desirable now. The woman he desired had been dignified, graceful and elegant—a perfect lady—not an imperfect bride.

"Cliff has agreed to marry us," he said softly.

Blanche started. It took her a moment to realize what he meant. "He is a ship's captain—he can marry us on his ship!"

"Yes." He smiled. "I felt certain you would not wish for a formal ceremony, not even a small one with my rather large family. We only need two witnesses."

Blanche nodded breathlessly. "Bess and Meg. I must have them both present."

"As you wish." He hesitated. "I do not want to press you," he began, then stopped.

Blanche shook her head. "I would marry you tonight if you wished me to."

His eyes widened.

Blanche realized she wanted to marry him as soon as possible. She felt herself blush. "I know this is an odd situation and I do not mean to push," she whispered, glancing aside.

He seized both of her hands. "Blanche, you cannot push. There is a reason for haste. Besides, I would like nothing more than to be wed tonight, if you are serious."

Blanche stared. "Do you think we dare try?" And a profound excitement began.

"I'll speak to Cliff," he said, standing. He smiled, pleased. "But I see no reason why we can't elope after supper."

ALL SAILS TIGHTLY FURLED, masts and rigging touching the star-studded sky, the frigate drifted at anchor against the gleaming ebony water. The moon was incandescent and full. Blanche paused on the dock beside Sir Rex, a soft breeze caressing her cheeks, incredulous. She had gone to Sir Rex that afternoon to tell him about her child and make the ultimate sacrifice possible for a woman. Instead, they were getting married.

Blanche noticed a few ghostly figures on the main deck. She turned to Sir Rex. "If I pinch myself, I wonder if I will wake up?" she whispered.

He smiled. "I have been thinking the very same thing. Come. Everyone is already here."

Blanche nodded, trembling, and they started up the walkway. She recognized Cliff de Warenne as they crossed the gangplank, as he made a formidable figure, and even in a dark suit, no one could mistake him for anything but the ship's master. The other men were clearly sailors, lighting the great ship's lanterns. Blanche prayed she was not in the midst of a wonderful dream.

Bess waved at her, urging her to hurry, and beside her was Meg, who even from a distance, was clearly a bundle of excitement. Blanche now realized that the third woman was Eleanor de Warenne. A huge smile wreathed her face.

Rex said softly, "I needed rings. It was an excuse to bring my indomitable sister into the loop."

"I have always liked Eleanor and I am glad she is here,"

Blanche said as softly, her heart racing so wildly it was impossible to breathe. Rex helped her step onto the ship's main deck. His grasp was sure and strong and steady, just like the man. *I am so fortunate,* Blanche thought, very close to becoming overcome by the moment.

Instantly, Bess was upon her, her eyes wide and incredulous. "When I received your note that I must meet you at Captain de Warenne's ship, I thought, Blanche is truly out of her mind tonight! And then Meg arrived and told me you are really marrying Sir Rex!" Bess was already embracing her. "And then Eleanor showed me the rings and Captain de Warenne confirmed it. I am so pleased!"

Blanche laughed and hugged her back. "I am pleased you are pleased," she teased.

Bess started.

Blanche realized she hadn't laughed in months—nor had she had the inkling to be playful, either. She sobered. "Wish us good fortune," she said, her voice low.

"Of course I wish you the *best* fortune," Bess cried, her gaze searching.

Blanche glanced around and saw Sir Rex and Cliff quietly conversing. "Sir Rex knows *everything,*" she whispered. "He is the kindest man you or I will ever meet and more importantly, he is familiar with my illness, as it is common among war veterans. I am hardly mad, Bess."

Bess gasped. "Is there a cure?"

"Time seems to heal everyone from this brutal affliction." Blanche smiled at her and turned to hug Meg. "I am so glad you are here."

"My lady, this is a great day—evening!" the redhead cried. "I am so happy for you. I knew you loved him and I knew he loved you, too!"

Blanche heard herself laugh again. She wasn't sure love had been a factor in Sir Rex's decision, but it didn't matter.

He was her anchor and she was happy—and she couldn't recall when she had been as happy, not since leaving Land's End.

Eleanor strode forward. "I have been waiting for this moment," she grinned. "You and my brother are perfect together. I knew the two of you would find your way back to one another!"

Blanche blushed. She wanted to deny it, but in that moment, she believed Eleanor de Warenne. Sir Rex was so perfect for her. She couldn't recall why there had ever been any doubt. She wanted to be perfect for him, and maybe, once cured, she could become the perfect wife. She turned her gaze upon him and found him watching her, almost protectively, but he was smiling, too. She smiled back instantly. He seemed happy.

He thudded forward. "Shall we commence? Cliff is ready if you are."

Her heart thundered. "I am so very ready."

Cliff indicated that they should stand before him, side by side. "You do know the *Fair Lady* seems destined to bring lovers together," he said to her. "Amanda and I were married on this ship."

"I had heard. All of town heard that she stole your ship and you didn't just chase her down, you married her, as well." Blanche smiled. "I dismissed the tale as gossip. Was it true?"

"It was very true," he said with a smile, his gold earring glinting in the lanterns' light. Then he looked at Eleanor. "Do you have the rings?"

"Of course I do," Eleanor exclaimed.

"Then we shall proceed." He looked at the assembled company. "We gather here tonight in the grace of God to bring this couple together in matrimony." He smiled at his brother. "Do you, Sir Rex de Warenne, take this woman, Lady Blanche Harrington, to love and to cherish, in sickness and in health, until death do you part?"

Blanche stared at Sir Rex's beautiful, strong and so classic profile. He turned to her. "I do," he said softly, his eyes shining.

Blanche smiled at him.

"Do you, Lady Blanche Harrington, take this man, Sir Rex de Warenne, to love and to cherish, in sickness and in health, until death do you part?"

Blanche wanted nothing more. "I do."

"Eleanor, the rings, please," Cliff said.

Eleanor produced the rings; one a plain gold band, the other a pearl set in diamonds, and Sir Rex took the latter and slipped it onto Blanche's finger. The ring was lovely and Blanche knew it had belonged to Eleanor. She smiled at her gratefully, taking the gold band and slipping it onto Sir Rex's blunt finger. She looked up and their eyes met.

Blanche trembled at the warm but very possessive look in his eyes. She loved him so much and she decided she would find the courage to tell him how much he meant to her. He smiled at her, as if he was feeling all that she was—as if he knew her innermost thoughts.

"You may kiss the bride," Cliff added wryly.

Rex leaned close and Blanche closed her eyes. His mouth feathered hers and her heart raced with happiness, joy and excitement.

"By the power vested in me as captain of this ship," Cliff said softly, smiling, "I hereby pronounce you man and wife."

BLANCHE SMILED AT JEM as they stepped into the foyer. The carriage ride from the docks had been a half an hour at most and she was still holding Sir Rex's hand. She felt like a blushing bride, all nerves and smiles. She was almost dizzy from the madcap wedding. It remained unbelievable—like a fairy tale. Blanche wondered what to do now.

They hadn't spoken during the carriage ride, but Sir Rex had stepped into her coach as if it was his right—which it was.

Would he stay with her now? And what would they do about sleeping arrangements? She was fairly certain he had no intention of consummating their marriage that night or any time soon. But shamelessly, she wished for just such a union. She knew her cheeks were hot. "Jem, I am Lady de Warenne now. Sir Rex and I have just wed."

Jem's eyes widened briefly and then he bowed, but he was smiling and trying to hide it. "Welcome to Harrington Hall, my lord. And congratulations, my lady, sir."

Blanche bit her lip, glancing at Sir Rex. He seemed terribly at ease. If he was concerned or anxious about what would happen next, she could not tell.

"Thank you," Sir Rex said. "Tomorrow at eight precisely, I will meet the entire staff."

Jem inclined his head.

Sir Rex turned to Blanche. "Shall we have a celebratory glass of champagne? Or are you too tired to do so? I realize this has been a long and surprising day."

Her heart skipped. She was too overcome to give in to her fatigue, and too giddy with bridal excitement. She wanted to linger with Sir Rex—her husband.

They were man and wife.

She had to be the most fortunate woman in town.

"Of course I will take champagne with you."

He sent her a warm smile, one so warm she believed, in that moment, that he desired her still, in spite of everything. He turned. "Jem, if you please, a bottle of your finest."

"Shall I serve caviar, sir? Lord Harrington has quite the stock from the Caspian Sea."

"If Lady Harrington desires it," Sir Rex said, smiling at her.

Blanche somehow nodded. Sir Rex was stepping into his role as master of Harrington Hall as if born to it. But then, he was Adare's son and he had been born to enjoy power, privilege and wealth. It was his right.

But Meg hovered uncertainly behind them as Jem left. "My lady?" she whispered, as if she did not want Sir Rex to overhear.

Blanche faced her nervously. She knew what Meg wished to know and she hesitated, daring a glance at her husband. He was industriously studying the marble floors.

Blanche asked softly, "Sir Rex? What shall we do about tonight's sleeping arrangements? I realize we have married in a flash, and there has been no time to prepare a master suite, and your family is certainly expecting your return—"

He took her hand. "I wish only to please you," he said, lifting her hand to his mouth. "And my family, by now, knows every detail of our wedding. No one is expecting me and I prefer to stay here."

She wanted him to stay. She could not get the words out. She could not remind him that it would take a few hours at least to prepare a honeymoon suite for fear of a rejection. It would take longer to prepare a new master suite if they ever decided to share one.

"I will take any guest chamber," he said softly.

Blanche smiled but jerked her gaze away, dismayed by his preference. "Prepare the Emerald Suite, Meg."

Meg nodded and rushed off.

"It won't take long. Guests often stay there and it is always ready," she said swiftly, smiling very brightly.

He clasped her hand. "What is wrong?"

She tensed, her gaze rushing to his. "How can anything be wrong when you have just rescued me from a terrible fate?"

He dimpled. "With Dashwood?"

"I do not know what I was thinking!"

"I know what I was thinking," he said, his voice low and swift.

She looked into his bold stare. Such a masculine look made her knees weaken.

"Are you ready to collapse?" he asked softly, taking her elbow.

"I don't know how I feel," she said truthfully. "I am a jumble of giddy emotions! Except I am relieved, of course, I am so relieved. It has been a nightmare...but that nightmare seems to be ending."

"That nightmare is over," he said firmly. Then, "I want you to be happy."

"I am," she managed. "I am so very happy, but I realize you are merely doing your duty."

His gaze briefly widened. "Let's sit down."

Blanche nodded and when they were seated in the Blue Room, he said, "Blanche, I do have a duty to you and our child, but I have not been forthright if you believe I have only done my *duty* in marrying you."

Blanche couldn't smile. "Even if I recover, I am not the same woman who enjoyed your hospitality at Land's End."

He stiffened. "I beg to differ! You are the same woman— a woman I am terribly fond of—and there is no 'if.' You will recover. I thought we had cleared that up."

"At Land's End, I was the perfect bride."

"You are the perfect bride now," he said firmly.

"Are you ever unkind?" she gasped.

"It is not my nature," he said, somewhat perplexed.

Suddenly Blanche realized she hadn't thought about the riot and her mother's murder since her conversation early that afternoon with Sir Rex. There had not been one single memory, but now, perversely, the bloody images loomed. She saw the dead horse and her mangled mother. The mob hovered. She tensed.

"Blanche?"

She stiffened with dread, wishing she hadn't thought about that terrible day, waiting for that knife to pierce her temples. It did not.

Sir Rex clasped her face. "Stay with me," he said softly.

Still, she expected to hear her mother's screams; she expected to be thrust into the midst of that riot, all of six years old again.

"It is such a beautiful night," Sir Rex commented. At first, Blanche did not quite hear him. "Can you hear the crickets?" he asked.

She met his gaze, suddenly aware of the chirping in the gardens outside, the images vanishing as she looked into his brown-and-gold eyes. She trembled with uncertainty. "They were only memories, I think." Dear God, she hadn't been jerked into the past.

He smiled as if they were discussing a picnic or the races. "Did you enjoy the ceremony—as brief as it was?"

She smiled back. "It was lovely."

He laughed. "I don't think my brother had a clue as to what he was doing, my dear."

Blanche became still. His laughter washed through her like a warm, sensual wave and her heart sped while her skin heated, everywhere. And he had called her "dear." She wanted to be in Sir Rex's arms. She wanted far more than a feathery kiss. And she wanted him to call her "my dear" again.

His eyes darkened. His hand drifted across her cheek. "I do not know if I can be a proper gentleman when you look at me with such invitation," he said softly.

Her heart thudded. "We are married," she whispered. "I know I am hardly attractive now, but you need not be gentlemanly, not at all."

His eyes widened fractionally. And his regard turned to smoke. "Blanche, you appear as fragile as the newest bud on a rose. I don't want to hurt you, discomfit you or distress you in any way. You have been through enough."

She was so surprised, but she should have known Sir Rex would think of her welfare before anything else. "I won't break, Sir Rex," she said tremulously. "I am certain of that." But she wasn't certain, because the last time they had made love, she had broken mentally and emotionally and maybe in spirit, as well. This time, though, she would take the risk.

He hesitated and then he clasped her shoulders. "I have never desired anyone more. Blanche, I will *always* desire you." His gaze was searching. "I will always love you."

She went still on the outside while her heart exploded in joy on the inside. Then she breathed, throwing all caution to the wind, "Please."

His eyes turned to black flames. He bent over her as his lips claimed hers. And suddenly she was crushed in his arms, weeping silently with joy and need, as he kissed her deeply, again and again.

Blanche felt every inch of her body flame. Wet heat gathered. She wanted to explode and she wanted his touch and his invasion so urgently that she trembled in his arms, moaning. His kisses changed, veering down the soft column of her throat.

Blanche heard the door close.

She tensed, as did Sir Rex, glancing at the door, which was now solidly closed. They had left it open. Sir Rex turned to her, his gaze brilliant, and Blanche cupped his cheek, relieved to realize he still wanted her as he had at Land's End. "Don't stop. Take me upstairs, please," she cried.

He pulled her close. "Are you certain I will not hurt you? Blanche, we are husband and wife now. We have our entire lives ahead."

"I am certain. I need you so."

IT WAS HARD to exercise control. But he had meant his every word, and no matter how he had missed her and how urgently he wished to move inside her now, he did not want to hurt her or cause more strain. Rex unbuttoned the back of Blanche's pale gray silk gown, aware that his fingers were clumsy and his hands were shaking and inept.

She was breathing in a rapid, shallow manner. As her gown parted, revealing her chemise and corset, he could not resist. Inhaling, he bent and kissed her skin on the ridge of her spine, between her shoulder blades. Instantly her skin prickled with goose bumps.

Blanche gasped in pleasure.

He was already painfully aroused and he fought it; he turned her as the dress fell in a pool at their feet. Blanche's eyes became blue-green smoke. She was so beautiful and so feminine, he thought. He cupped her face and kissed her, long and deep, rising up high and hard against her hip. She moaned.

He became frantic; all he wanted to do was bring her pleasure now.

And he crushed her against his chest, his torso, his hips and loins. She gasped again and he pulled her up even more tightly against the firm ridge of his manhood, briefly resting his mouth against her cheek when he wanted to invade her body and plunder, sweetly and savagely, now. "Are you certain?"

"Yes," she cried, clinging to his shoulders.

A flurry followed—the rest of her clothes and all of his vanished. They crashed onto the bed and he moved over her, kneeing her pale thighs apart. Rex knew he had no control left. But he somehow paused. "I am so pleased to be your husband," he murmured.

Her gaze widened.

And he smiled, slowly easing his swollen length into her, watching her expression tighten, her eyes glaze.

She cried out, feeling the same hot, exquisite friction, cheeks turning pink, eyes losing all focus, and he could not stand it. He gave in, his sanity finally vanishing, and there was only the savage need to hear her climax and to find his own explosive release. Slick sensation and intense pleasure became a passionate frenzy. She gasped, eyes flying wide-open and he felt a terrible sense of triumph.

He was blinded by the sight of her climax. He drove deep into her wet heat and gave over to his manhood. The ecstasy was white-hot and consuming. He gasped again and again. *"Blanche."*

A long time passed and he held her, breathing harshly. When he had recovered somewhat, he moved to her side because she had become as small as a young girl and he truly feared hurting her accidentally. Cradling her in his arms, he kissed her temples and hair, still breathless. *My wife,* he thought. *My perfect, beautiful wife.*

"I think I am the most fortunate man on this earth," he murmured.

Her lashes lifted and she looked at him, the dazed expression on her face slowly receding. She smiled and he thrilled; she laid her small palm on his broad chest and pressed it there.

Unable to control himself, he reached for her hand and lifted it to his mouth. He was bursting with love. He had meant his every word. Dear God, they were wed now, and Blanche Harrington was his. "Are you all right?" he asked softly.

"I am wonderful," she said as softly. And then she shocked him, taking his hand and pressing her mouth to it. A beautiful and delicate flush covered her face.

He leaned up on one elbow. Finally breathing naturally, he had to admire her face and her figure. Although thin, he found her slender body impossibly attractive. "You are so beautiful, Blanche." He slid his hand over one small breast.

Her eyes widened. "You must be the mad one," she began, and when she realized what she had said, she tensed.

But he smiled. "And you are so modest!" He moved his hand down to her narrow waist.

Blanche hesitated, studying him. "I am glad you think me pretty."

"I think you beautiful—and next time, do not attempt a refutation," he said gently. Now he caressed the small mound of her belly where their child grew. He thrilled and smiled. And he could not help it; her pale curls drew his gaze.

A lovely smile began. "Only if I can be as bold."

He grinned, tearing his eyes to her face. "How bold?"

"You are so handsome!" she cried, running her hand over his hard chest. "And talented," she added, biting her lip.

Rex laughed, terribly pleased.

Blanche became still, her smile fading. She looked past him, as if expecting an intruder. In that instant, he knew. She was thinking about the riot. His concern knew no bounds. "Darling, you do not know the difference yet, but such speedy lovemaking is not desirable. However, I am glad you think me talented and I assure you, once some time has passed, you will be very pleased. I intend a long and enjoyable honeymoon."

Her gaze moved back to his; she smiled. "But I wished for speedy lovemaking."

He became still and entirely hard. "I'm glad," he said roughly.

"You always know when I need you," she said softly.

He bent over her and kissed her, comprehending exactly what she meant. "Do you wish to talk about it now?"

She hesitated, her gaze moving past him again. "No," she breathed.

He stared closely and felt certain she was not in danger of slipping away. Although he could so easily shift his weight and do what he wished to do, he said, "I know you are exhausted now—"

She slid her hand down his belly. "Not really."

And she gave him the most seductive look he had ever received.

CHAPTER TWENTY-TWO

BLANCHE AWOKE with her cheek on Sir Rex's naked chest, her body entirely pressed against his, one of her legs between his thighs. Sun was streaming into the bedroom, as no one had dared come in to pull the draperies. Her ivory-and-pink quilt was pulled to their waists but no higher. Joy swelled.

I love my husband so, she thought, smiling. She inhaled his scent, relishing it, cherished the feel of his skin, muscles and even his hair, and she thought about the miraculous fact that they were man and wife. Last night he had made love to her twice. She had been exhausted, because she recalled his love-making, but not the aftermath—she must have dozed off immediately. Sir Rex was a wonderful lover as well as a wonderful man.

She loved him so much her heart ached in a delirium of emotion.

Her gaze moved past him, to the windows on the other side of the bedroom. Images began to form, images she hated, dreaded and wished would go forever away. At Land's End, after he had made love to her, she had been assailed with her memories—and she had been flung back into the horrible past.

She had been in love with Sir Rex then, too. She had realized that joy and passion also brought recollection and pain. Blanche tensed.

Her temples throbbed but not with knifelike intensity. The

images were vivid—she would never forget the sight of that beaten horse, the monster-man, or her murdered mother. She waited for her mother's screams to sound, driving her from the bed and into another world.

"Blanche?"

Her mother's face was white and pinched with fear—an expression Blanche would never forget as the monster demanded she get out of the carriage. She knew the words by heart. *Get out of the carriage, lady.*

Blanche was assailed with dread, even though she felt as if she were rehearsing the memory, not reliving it. The bed dipped. She glanced up and saw that Sir Rex was sitting up.

Her mother's face had become frozen with fear. The monster-man was waiting and Blanche waited to feel her mother's grip, hurting her own hand. She waited for her mother to be seized and dragged from the coach; she waited for fear to consume her.

A light caress drifted from her shoulder to her arm. Blanche jerked, looking up at Sir Rex.

"We're at Harrington Hall," he said quietly. "We are man and wife."

She sat up, now remarking his splendid torso, delineated with so much muscle, tendon and ligament that her body flushed with the stirrings of desire once again. It had been so long since she had been able to admire him in broad daylight. "I know," she said as quietly.

The image of her mother's masklike face remained, as did the pale, manic eyes of the monster-man. The images whirled and changed into the dead horse and her equally dead and brutalized mother. Pain stabbed through Blanche, very much like a knife, but it was in her chest, not her head, and she recognized the pain as grief.

"Tell me what is happening, Blanche."

She flinched. "I am remembering how my mother looked after they stabbed her to death."

Sir Rex nodded, and he paled. "Can you stay with me?" he asked, moving a mass of her light hair back over her shoulder.

Blanche realized how naked she was and she dragged a cover up to her chin. "I am waiting for my mother's screams to erupt in my head," she said. "I am waiting to become six years old again, but instead, there are these images, as clear as ghastly portraits, and there is so much grief."

He clasped her shoulder. "You never had a chance to mourn your mother, as you forgot the riot and her murder, instead. Maybe it is time for you to grieve."

Blanche was horrified when she realized she wished to weep over her mother's loss—and then, over her father's death, as well.

He amazed her by saying, "And you never grieved for Harrington. Do what you must, Blanche. Everyone must grieve for the loss of loved ones."

She looked at him, her vision blurring. "I loved her so. She was the sweetest, kindest mother a child could have. I recall all of that now."

"That is a good memory to have."

"Why did they have to kill her? Why?"

He slid his arm around her. "When a crowd becomes a mob, it is like a pet dog becoming rabid. There is no rhyme, no reason. The mob becomes a savage, uncontrollable beast. There will never be an explanation for what happened that day, Blanche."

She wiped her eyes, silently mourning her mother now. And Father, how well she recalled his grief, twenty-two years ago. "Father never recovered from that day. He loved my mother—I remember now, how grim and pale he was, how red his eyes were. I recall being confused."

Sir Rex merely stroked her shoulder.

Blanche wiped her eyes. "I wasn't able to cry when Father died, but I told you that. It was like a dream. I knew he was gone, but I just couldn't feel." She suddenly turned to Sir Rex. "It hurts so much now."

"I know it does. But there is no avoiding this, Blanche. You are human and you must mourn your parents, sooner or later."

"I think it is sooner," she whispered, because the tears were streaming, and so was the grief. She hadn't realized how much she missed her father—and how much she had loved her mother.

Sir Rex pulled her into his arms.

BLANCHE LEANED OUT of the carriage window as the Harrington coach entered the short shell drive leading to Bodenick Castle. She started, for she saw the ruined tower had been restored, changing the castle's silhouette as it jutted into the cloudless, brilliantly blue sky. The moors beyond were awash in purple and gold and she saw a band of mares racing with their young foals. Ahead, past the far tower, she saw the ocean frothing below against the sheer black cliffs leading to the beach head. Three days ago Sir Rex had suddenly suggested they leave town and retire to the country for the summer. Blanche had been eager to agree.

But there had been apprehension as well as anticipation. She could not forget that her memory had started to return at Land's End, and subsequently, those fits hurling her backward in time had begun there, as well. In the past three days since becoming husband and wife, there had been many memories, but she had not been jettisoned into the past. Her husband, Blanche thought, had been a huge part of that. He had been doting on her the way a parent did an ill child. When she became consumed with her memories, he had a knack for distracting her. Blanche knew his concern for her was absolute. She didn't mind. He had become such an anchor, helping her though this difficult time.

Yet Sir Rex had also known when to vanish and leave her

to her newfound grief. The grief would arise so suddenly it would surprise her, but it was far better than being swept back to the day of the riot. Before leaving town, Blanche had gone to visit both of her parents' graves. She had chosen to go alone.

Blanche sobered now. She was thrilled to have returned to Land's End but she wasn't sure what to expect. She turned and said softly, "I do love it here. The air is so clean and I can smell the ocean."

He smiled, his eyes holding a very familiar gleam. "I am glad."

Blanche warmed, a now familiar moisture gathering. She had never expected a honeymoon when she had agreed to marry Sir Rex, but Sir Rex was far more than her husband; he was her lover. He shared her bed every night since their wedding and she had encouraged his lovemaking. She anticipated the darkness with shameful intentions. And she was becoming somewhat familiar with him. From the intent, almost indolent gleam in his dark eyes, she had the feeling she might not have to wait for the coming evening to enjoy his passion.

He reached out and stroked his long fingers over her gloved hand. Blanche had never expected such affection, either. She thrilled as the coach halted. Her postillions leaped to open the doors and a moment later, Blanche let Sir Rex help her down.

She glanced around, pleased to see the new stable finished, then turned back to admire the now-renovated tower. "Have you decorated the new tower rooms?"

He dimpled. "They shall be your rooms and you may do so."

Blanche couldn't wait. She was also eager to expand the gardens and add flowers to every nook and cranny of the courtyard. Sir Rex limped over to her. "This is a rare moment, for I am regretting the loss of my leg," he said softly.

She was entirely surprised.

"But only because I wish to carry my bride over the threshold."

She touched his face. "Why don't you kiss your bride on the threshold, instead?" she murmured, but she wasn't thinking about his kisses. She was thinking about the night to come.

Sir Rex took her hand and once on the threshold, he pulled her close and kissed her, uncaring of their audience. Blanche forgot that the coachman and postillions were standing in the courtyard and she kissed him back. When she was breathless—when he was so clearly aroused—she whispered, "Maybe you can help me unpack my bags?"

He laughed at her. "I can unpack anything you wish, darling."

Blanche felt her heart turn over with a joy she would never take for granted, when a shadow fell. She turned and all joy vanished.

Anne curtsied. "My lord, my lady," she said.

Blanche stared at the buxom maid who had once been Sir Rex's mistress and instantly, she saw them entwined on the sofa in the tower room. She then thought of Paul Carter, who had taken her for a handsome sum, obviously put up to blackmail by his lover, and she was enraged.

"I am sorry." Sir Rex said quietly. "There was no time to send word."

Blanche didn't care. She walked over to Anne, who stiffened, a sly look coming to her eyes. Her head high, she said, "Get off of these grounds now."

Anne jerked. Then she turned to look at Sir Rex. He simply stared.

"I am speaking to you," Blanche said tightly.

Anne turned her gaze back. "I can hear you perfectly, my lady." Her tone was insolent.

"Good, then hear this. You and your lover have profited handsomely from blackmailing me, therefore, you are dismissed without any references whatsoever. Do not bother to gather your things. I will send them along."

Anne stared coldly. Hatred flickered in her eyes. "You can't dismiss me. But don't worry. I am leaving, because I know his lordship will dismiss me if I don't."

Sir Rex started to speak but Blanche turned furiously to him, indicating that he must not interfere. He said nothing. She faced Anne. "You had every right to your affair with Sir Rex. I do not blame you for lusting after his lordship."

Anne's eyes widened.

"I only blame you for your malicious intent to bring *me* down after I had left Bodenick. That was despicable and speaks of your true nature, which is base indeed. It is the nature of a woman who wants what her betters have—as if it is owed. I owe you *nothing*. You owe me *respect*. Get off *my* property now," Blanche said furiously. "Before I have my coachman bodily remove you."

"So you went and married him," Anne spat at Blanche's feet. Then she shrugged and stared defiantly at her.

Blanche trembled, close to striking the maid. But she had never abused another human being in such a manner and she never would. "Good day, Anne."

Anne stalked off.

Blanche trembled as Sir Rex approached. Then she whirled on him. "Were you bedding her these past two and a half months?" she cried. And she was aghast with herself the moment she spoke.

"No, I was not. I was too busy renovating the estate by day and drowning my sorrows by night." He was terse.

"I am sorry," she cried, seizing his hand. "I shouldn't have spoken to you in such an accusatory manner." And she was terrified Sir Rex would hate her now.

But he smiled at her. "You had every right to be suspicious of me, Blanche. But I am not a liar and I will never lie to you. Anne remained here because I needed a housekeeper. My heart was too broken for me to even think of bedding her or any other woman."

She was so relieved. "I *am* sorry."

"Don't be." Then, "I applaud your management of her."

Blanche continued to hold his hand. "Aren't you angry with me now?"

"Even if I was—which I am not—that isn't going to change my feelings for you—or the vows we made."

She stared at him, thinking about her friends, who were in love with their husbands one moment and taking lovers another, and then she thought about his exceptional family, where trust and loyalty defied all convention. She had not a doubt that his brothers and stepbrothers—and his father— remained faithful to their wives. In fact, she couldn't imagine any of the de Warenne or O'Neill men even thinking about straying.

"We will have arguments from time to time, it is human nature. There may be rousing arguments, if the passion I just witnessed was any indication. But that doesn't change the commitment which we have made to one another, and it will never change what is in my heart."

Blanche threw her arms around him. "Sometimes I don't recognize myself," she whispered honestly. She had never been as enraged as she had just been with Anne. She had never been so happy, either. And at night, in Sir Rex's arms, she was as passionate as a courtesan.

"Then it is fortunate I always recognize you," he murmured.

Blanche looked into his darkening eyes. She touched his jaw, loving the stubble. "Maybe Meg should take some dinner while we unpack our things."

"Yes, maybe she should."

A WEEK LATER, Blanche sat beside Sir Rex as he halted a one-horse gig on Lanhadron's main street. He had taken her to town for some shopping and a small lunch at the inn. They were on their way home, as it was late afternoon, but he turned to her. "Do you mind waiting a moment while I run into Bennet's to see if my cigars have arrived?"

Blanche smiled at him. "Of course I don't mind," she said. "When you have patiently let me purchase a dozen flowerpots and vases."

He set the brake on the gig and stepped down to the street. "I like the changes you are making at Bodenick," he said. "It now looks like a home."

Blanche had spent the week planning the decor for the new tower rooms and the expansion of the gardens behind the original tower. Sir Rex had already hired additional gardeners, who were busy planting shrubs and flower beds, and her next efforts would be for the courtyard. "It is a home. It is our home," she said warmly.

He smiled at her. She watched him cross the nearly empty street, filled with contentment. Who would have ever thought married life to be so pleasing and so fulfilling? And she did not miss town at all.

Her mother's pale image came to mind, tense with fear. Blanche wasn't as afraid of her memories now, because she'd had several headaches, but they had not been accompanied by fits. Her memories appeared as suddenly and as frequently as her grief. Now, she thought about her mother, filled only with sadness.

She thought she heard musical pipes of some kind.

She knew it was her imagination, but she turned, and she heard a violin very clearly. Blanche stared down the street, suddenly seeing several oddly colored wagons approaching, in shades of red, blue and yellow, surrounded by a crowd of people. In that instant, as the jaunty tunes became clearer, Blanche realized a band of gypsies was entering the town.

She forgot about her mother, staring at the approaching crowd. She had never seen genuine gypsies, just the occasional fortune teller at a fair or market.

Men, women and children were walking down the street alongside their bright wagons, colorfully dressed. Villagers came out of their shops and homes to line the street and watch the parade. The women, clad in rainbow-hued skirts and blouses, threw flowers at the men. A tall dark man in their forefront paused to speak with the ladies and children. She saw him sweep two very pretty young ladies a courtly bow. They giggled, blushing.

Blanche hugged herself, glancing toward the store across the street where Sir Rex had gone. She reminded herself that he was a moment away but she couldn't help it, she hated public crowds and being a married woman now wasn't going to change that. Tension stiffened her as the first gypsies approached, led by the swaggering dark man.

He was tall and handsome, clad in high boots, breeches and a white lawn shirt, and he wore a brilliant crimson sash. He saw her and smiled, his manner friendly enough. Blanche didn't smile back. She glanced across the first wagon as it passed by, toward Bennet's. Sir Rex was nowhere in sight.

Her heart was racing with some anxiety, and she told herself, very firmly, that they were harmless enough, by day, anyway, and except for their low station in life, they had little in common with the mob that had murdered her mother. But she was an intelligent woman and she didn't need a gypsy's crystal ball to know that this kind of event might throw her back into the day of the riot. She waited for her head to pound.

The dark gypsy veered in her direction, the second wagon now passing her gig, along with some skipping children. "My lady, you don't seem in a festive mood. Can I possibly change that?" His smile was engaging, as were his blue eyes. He had a cleft chin, deep dimples, bright teeth and curly hair. He was the kind of man most women would swoon over.

Blanche almost smiled back, as his smile was very infectious. "I will be in a festive mood when my husband returns," she said softly.

He paused, his gaze moving slowly over her face, and a broader grin appeared. "A woman in love is a beautiful sight, indeed. A woman in love with her husband, more so. You must be newlywed."

"You are very impertinent," Blanche said, but she smiled. "Yes, I am newly wed."

"Then congratulations are in order," he said, and he swept her a dashing bow. "Now, when you are less wed, you might think of me sometime. I shouldn't mind."

Blanche felt herself relax entirely. "I will never be less wed," she said softly. "You must flirt elsewhere."

He laughed, clasping his chest over his heart. "I am distraught, fair lady."

"Blanche!"

Blanche whirled at the sound of Sir Rex's voice. He was across the street and she instantly knew he was frightened for her. Although some small apprehension remained, she felt a niggling relief, and she waved, to let him know that she was fine.

The dark gypsy turned to follow her gaze. "A strong handsome fellow—undoubtedly possessing both a title and wealth. Clearly a gypsy prince cannot compete." He swept her another bow and strode off.

Blanche turned to stare after him, amused as he had wished for her to be, and then she glanced at the passing gypsies and their wagons. Through the band, she saw Sir Rex standing, seeming distressed but unable as yet to cross the street. Blanche breathed deeply, allowing her racing heart to subside.

The last wagon passed and Sir Rex swung rapidly across the street. He seized the gig door, opening it. "Are you all right?" he asked, pulling himself up to sit beside her.

"Yes, surprisingly, I am," she said, moving closer to him.

His gaze was searching. Then, "Were you afraid?"

"A little." She thought about it. "But the fear was softer. I didn't have to fight memories. I thought about the gypsies in comparison to the mob, but that was all." She finally smiled as a profound realization began. "I was never in danger of slipping away."

"Good." He took her hand and kissed it. "You are getting better, Blanche. I can see it in the color in your cheeks, and I can see it in your eyes."

BLANCHE STARED AT HERSELF in the mirror. Sir Rex was right, she thought, regarding her reflection very critically. Her appetite had returned and she had gained a touch of weight, enough so that her face did not have such a gaunt appearance anymore. And a soft pink color tinged her cheeks, while her eyes were no longer clouded with fear and despair. In fact, her eyes were shining and bright.

Blanche touched her face. *I am pretty again,* she thought, and she smiled.

She was healing. If a parade of gypsies could not undo her, what would?

Her smile faded as she thought about her husband. She had fallen in love with him months ago as his guest here at Land's End, but she had never thought to adore him to the extent that she did—or to want him so urgently, so often. And he was healing, too.

When she woke up in the middle of the night, he lay soundly asleep beside her, his arm flung over some part of her body. He had not isolated himself from her once to sit and brood with a bottle of brandy. In fact, he no longer took an after-dinner drink at all. But that was undoubtedly because he had repaired his relationship with his son. Yet she also thought it was because of her love and their love for each other.

Blanche smiled, trembling, and somewhat faint. It had become an unspoken agreement, but after supper he gave her a quarter of an hour or so and then he would appear at their chamber door and sweep her into his arms and their bed.

He was outside now, speaking with the head groom. Blanche recalled his grim, fearful expression in the village when he had assumed the worst. She thought about the way he looked at her and watched her while they made love, until his own passion erupted.

It was the high afternoon, and her body had become tight and feverish, yearning for his. Blanche turned and walked over to the window overlooking the courtyard and beyond, to the stables and pastures. Sir Rex stood almost directly below with the head groom, Ted, holding a prancing young stallion. Both men were engrossed in a conversation and ignoring the young horse's restlessness.

Her mouth became dry. She was deeply in love with her husband. He had become everything to her—friend, lover, spouse and that anchor she could always reach for. She had survived a brush with insanity, thanks to him, and finally she was on the mend. She was feeling almost normal, except the old Blanche Harrington was gone. Instead, a woman of substance remained—a woman capable of great joy and great sorrow, of great passion and love. And her husband was also in love with her.

Staring down at him, her heart swelling with emotion, Blanche reached up to pull a pin from her hair, at first unthinkingly. Then she pulled another one, realizing she was undressing. She wasn't ashamed—she was intent. She pulled a third and a fourth and her hair began to spill from its coiffure. Silently, she waited. Suddenly Sir Rex looked up.

She stared down at him and their gazes locked. In that moment, she felt his sudden interest. Blanche began removing the last of the pins slowly, one by one, as he stared up at her. She reached up and used her fingers to comb her pale hair into soft, errant, shoulder-length waves. She never took her gaze from the man she had wed.

He finally faced the groom, who led the horse away. Below, Sir Rex moved toward the front door, vanishing from her sight.

Blanche trembled as her flesh swelled with anticipation and need. She undid the top buttons on the back of her dress, and was struggling to reach another one when the bedroom door opened.

Sir Rex paused there, his gaze filled with heat, a very rigid line in his breeches. His gaze moved over her face, her hair, and then to the collapsing bodice of her dress and to her bare shoulders. He closed the door and thudded forward. "I have been helping the gardeners plant that huge tree you insisted upon," he said softly as she turned her back to him.

Blanche closed her eyes as his hands skimmed her bare shoulders before moving to the remaining buttons on her dress.

"I am hot and I have been perspiring," he said, as he opened the last buttons, his blunt fingertips deftly skimming her skin as he slid the gown to her waist. He held it there.

Blanche shifted her weight against him and felt a shocking sense of pleasure and even triumph as her buttocks pressed into his hard manhood. In response, his hands closed on her waist. "I don't care," she said.

Throbbing against her now, he slid the dress and petticoat down her hips and let them pool between them on the floor.

Clad only in a frilly corset, silk chemise and lace drawers, Blanche remained still for one more moment, allowing his huge hardness to continue to swell between them, against her.

Then, slowly, she turned and slid her hands into the open neckline of his shirt. His skin was wet and hot. His eyes blazed.

Blanche ran her palms over his hard chest, across his tightening nipples, aware of Sir Rex becoming impossibly tense and still. She pulled the shirt apart, not quite meaning to rip it, and she pressed her mouth to his sweaty skin. He gasped.

Blanche tried to move closer, and as she began kissing his chest, she brushed herself against his manhood. Then she slid her tongue across his skin. It was salty.

"Blanche," he said harshly, a protest.

Blanche smiled against his flesh. "You have tasted every inch of me," she whispered, and then she sent her tongue across his nipple.

Sir Rex gasped again, this time closing his hands on her hips and pulling her hard against his arousal.

Blanche scraped her teeth across him and he groaned. She slid her hands lower and seized the waistband of his breeches. Sir Rex became absolutely still, except for his heavy breathing.

She unbuttoned them, whispering, "Come with me to bed."

"You don't have to do this," he said thickly.

She smiled as he sprang up against her hand. "I want to love you the way you love me."

He choked, sitting on the bed. Blanche bent over him and finally tasted his hot, slick flesh. Sir Rex seized a hank of her hair, grunting, and passion blinded her. With her tongue, she scraped and laved his length while she hollowed so greatly, only he could soon fill the empty space.

He cried out and suddenly she was beneath him, in his arms, as he pulled her drawers away. He held her face, kissing her deeply, with the same frenzy she was feeling. Instantly Blanche shifted to welcome him. He slid deep; he slid home.

"DID THAT GYPSY SAY something to you to turn you into a shameless hussy?"

Blanche laughed, snuggling in Sir Rex's arms. "I am afraid someone has turned me into a shameless hussy, but it was not a vagrant gypsy."

He pulled her impossibly closer and kissed her gently on the temple. "I love hearing you laugh," he said softly. "I love seeing your eyes shine with laughter—and happiness."

"I am so happy I can hardly breathe," Blanche said as softly. She stroked his arm. "My only fear is that I cannot make you quite as happy." And it was true. She gazed expectantly at him.

His eyes widened. "I have never dared to dream of such happiness. I had expected to spend my entire life alone. And here we are, Blanche." He dimpled. "When I saw you standing at the window, and realized what you wanted, I thought, this must be a dream." His grin widened. "Lady de Warenne!" he chided. "To think of making love to your husband in the middle of the day!"

Blanche laughed and kissed his chest. "Was it terribly improper of me to signal you to come to me at such an hour? Please be honest, Sir Rex."

"You may request my services anytime, my dear. Never feel reluctant." He touched her cheek. "Will you ever call me Rex?"

"No."

He started.

Blanche smiled at him. "You will always be Sir Rex, my darling, but do you really mind?" She ran her hand over his chest again, simply because she loved touching him, and now, she also loved being able to express herself with him, without any reservation.

"Can you not try to call me Rex in private?" he asked, but he was smiling, too.

Blanche ran her fingers across his ribs. "I prefer Sir Rex."

She kissed the hollow spot between his rib cage. Then she laid her cheek there and looked up. "Darling."

His eyes turned dark. His smile vanished. He ran his hand over her hair. "I can accept that. Blanche, call me 'darling' again."

She sat. "Darling—you are more than my love, you are my life." She was very serious now.

As seriously, he also sat and pulled her close. "Thank you. I feel exactly the same way."

Blanche hesitated, because she had so much to say. "You saved my life."

His gaze held hers. "I wish it were true, but I am certain, time healed you, Blanche, not I."

She shook her head. "You awoke my bruised and battered heart, Sir Rex. You showed me joy and passion…and love. And those terrible memories came. Three months ago, I thought the price too painful, but I was wrong." She took his hand and clasped it to her bare breasts. "The fear seems to be gone. I can manage the memories and the sorrow. Every day it becomes easier. More importantly, I don't want to forget. My mother deserves to be remembered."

"Yes, she does," he said solemnly. He reached out and clasped her shoulder. "You have come a long way in a very short time. I am so happy for you, for our child, for us."

Blanche smiled. "I cannot wait to have our child—and I cannot wait to meet Stephen when he comes to visit this summer."

Rex smiled. "There is so much to look forward to," he said softly.

Blanche met his gaze. There had been a time when she marveled at his ability to know her thoughts. Now, she looked into his dark gaze and knew exactly what he was thinking. She completed his thoughts. "With so much to anticipate, it is hard to know where to start."

His gaze softened. Then, slowly, he slid his hand down her

bare back. "Maybe it is best to remain focused…and in the present."

Blanche thrilled. She watched his eyes lower to her breasts, which had finally become full, lingering on her quite taut nipples. She watched a flush mar his achingly high cheekbones and she felt his hand slip to her waist. He slowly lifted his gaze, and the intensity there sent a terrific jolt through her. But the sheet that covered his hips was as terrifically tented, not that she needed any evidence to know that her passion was shared.

But he surprised her. He said, "You also saved my life, Blanche."

Tears came as she thought about the solitude and isolation that had been the hallmark of his existence. "You will never be alone again."

"I know." His gaze changed, smoldering.

Blanche felt her body hum and she wet her lips. "Why don't we have supper in our room, my darling?" she asked softly.

Sir Rex smiled, but he was leaning over her and nuzzling her breasts. "Did that gypsy teach you to read minds, too?" he asked, not looking up.

Blanche laughed, but then her laughter died, for Sir Rex's mouth was on her skin, causing so much delicious sensation, and she let him pull her down.

Joyfully.

And she didn't need a crystal ball to know what their future held.

Dear Readers,

I hope you have enjoyed Rex's and Blanche's journey of healing and love. When I began thinking about Rex's story, I never intended to pair him with Blanche. Readers began posting on my message boards, asking me to do just that and my editor made the same request. I was certain Rex's fate was someone far different from Blanche—until I awoke in the middle of the night, with their entire story dancing through my head. In that moment, I knew Rex had secretly admired and subconsciously loved Blanche for years. In that moment, I knew Rex was going to show her passion and be her lifeline—I knew he was her destiny!

I have never done a heroine as complicated or as wounded as Blanche. Blanche was a difficult character for me to identify with and her journey was a painful one. But as you know, Rex had some healing of his own to do, and for that, he needed Blanche just as much as she needed him.

For those of you who have not met the de Warenne Dynasty until now, *The Perfect Bride* is the seventh novel about this family. The order of the novels is:

The Conqueror, (Norman Conquest); *Promise of The Rose* (early medieval); *The Prize* (Devlin O'Neill); *The Masquerade* (Tyrell de Warenne); *The Stolen Bride* (Sean O'Neill and Eleanor de Warenne); *A Lady At Last* (Cliff de Warenne); *The Perfect Bride* (Rex de Warenne).

Ariella de Warenne's story is next in *A Dangerous Love*. She is as eccentric an adult as a child, proud of being an independent thinker and she is a great heiress. He is the viscount St Xavier, half English and half gypsy, a dark man accustomed to being scorned and feared. They come from different worlds and they should never meet, and Emilian is acutely aware of it. But when he begins to question his very identity, he turns to the Roma camping at Rose Hill and they do meet—in an explosion of passion that implodes their worlds. For more information on the de Warennes and *A Dangerous Love*, please visit my website, thedewarennedynasty.com.

And now, let me introduce you to the most powerful, sexiest heroes in the world—to quote Claire Camden. Let me introduce you to the Masters of Time...

If you have loved my historical heroes, you will love the Masters of Time—medieval Highland warriors sworn to protect Innocence through the ages. These are the most arrogant Alpha heroes you will ever meet. As they have sworn to protect Innocence no matter the century, they have the ability to time travel. Courageous, smart, witty and sexy contemporary heroines suddenly find themselves in a dark dangerous world where the shadows should be feared—besides these bold Highland warriors who have more than "protection" on their minds. Falling in love with a medieval Highland warrior with extraordinary powers is not an easy fate!

Of course, there is an upside to being the object of desire by the hunk of all ages....

I hope you will check out both *Dark Seduction* (May, 2007) and *Dark Rival* (October, 2007). These books are sexy and romantic, as well as dark and thrilling; the Masters are heroes a woman can die for...literally. For more news and excerpts on the Masters of Time, and to view videos for both *Dark Seduction* and *Dark Rival,* check out *mastersoftimebooks.com*.

Black Royce and I hope to see you at Carrick Castle—in 1430 and 2007!

Brenda Joyce
Destiny is the last weapon

REQUEST YOUR FREE BOOKS!

2 FREE NOVELS
FROM THE ROMANCE/SUSPENSE
COLLECTION PLUS 2 FREE GIFTS!

YES! Please send me 2 FREE novels from the Romance/Suspense Collection and my 2 FREE gifts. After receiving them, if I don't wish to receive any more books, I can return the shipping statement marked "cancel." If I don't cancel, I will receive 4 brand-new novels every month and be billed just $5.49 per book in the U.S., or $5.99 per book in Canada, plus 25¢ shipping and handling per book plus applicable taxes, if any*. That's a savings of at least 20% off the cover price! I understand that accepting the 2 free books and gifts places me under no obligation to buy anything. I can always return a shipment and cancel at any time. Even if I never buy another book from the Reader Service, the two free books and gifts are mine to keep forever.

185 MDN EF5Y   385 MDN EF6C

Name _____ (PLEASE PRINT) _____

Address _____ Apt. # _____

City _____ State/Prov. _____ Zip/Postal Code _____

Signature (if under 18, a parent or guardian must sign)

Mail to The Reader Service:
IN U.S.A.: P.O. Box 1867, Buffalo, NY 14240-1867
IN CANADA: P.O. Box 609, Fort Erie, Ontario L2A 5X3

Not valid to current subscribers to the Romance Collection,
the Suspense Collection or the Romance/Suspense Collection.

Want to try two free books from another line?
Call 1-800-873-8635 or visit www.morefreebooks.com.

* Terms and prices subject to change without notice. NY residents add applicable sales tax. Canadian residents will be charged applicable provincial taxes and GST. This offer is limited to one order per household. All orders subject to approval. Credit or debit balances in a customer's account(s) may be offset by any other outstanding balance owed by or to the customer. Please allow 4 to 6 weeks for delivery.

Your Privacy: Harlequin is committed to protecting your privacy. Our Privacy Policy is available online at www.eHarlequin.com or upon request from the Reader Service. From time to time we make our lists of customers available to reputable firms who may have a product or service of interest to you. If you would prefer we not share your name and address, please check here. ☐

BOB07